La Vegas
Scandals

NINA BRUHNS
LORETH ANNE WHITE
CARLA CASSIDY

MILLS &
BOON

Published in Great Britain 2014
by Mills & Boon, an imprint of Harlequin (UK) Limited,
Eton House, 18-24 Paradise Road, Richmond, Surrey, TW9 1SR

LAS VEGAS: SCANDALS © 2014 Harlequin Books S.A.

Prince Charming for 1 Night, Her 24-Hour Protector and *5 Minutes to Marriage* were first published in Great Britain by Harlequin (UK) Limited.

Prince Charming for 1 Night © 2009 Harlequin Books S.A.
Her 24-Hour Protector © 2009 Harlequin Books S.A.
5 Minutes to Marriage © 2009 Harlequin Books S.A.

Special thanks and acknowledgement are given to Nina Bruhns, Loreth Anne White and Carla Cassidy for their contributions to the LOVE IN 60 SECONDS series.

ISBN: 978 0 263 91185 5
eBook ISBN: 978 1 472 04480 8

05-0514

Harlequin (UK) Limited's policy is to use papers that are natural, renewable and recyclable products and made from wood grown in sustainable forests. The logging and manufacturing processes conform to the legal environmental regulations of the country of origin.

Printed and bound in Spain
by Blackprint CPI, Barcelona

PRINCE CHARMING
FOR 1 NIGHT

BY
NINA BRUHNS

Nina Bruhns credits her Gypsy great-grandfather for her great love of adventure. She has lived and travelled all over the world, including a six-year stint in Sweden. She has been on scientific expeditions from California to Spain to Egypt and Sudan and has two graduate degrees in archaeology (with a speciality in Egyptology). She speaks four languages and writes a mean hieroglyphics!

But Nina's first love has always been writing. For her, writing is the ultimate adventure. Drawing on her many experiences gives her stories a colourful dimension and allows her to create settings and characters out of the ordinary.

A native of Canada, Nina grew up in California and currently resides in Charleston, South Carolina, with her husband and three children. She loves to hear from her readers and can be reached at PO Box 2216, Summerville, SC, 29484-2216, USA or by e-mail via her website at www.NinaBruhns.com.

To Dorothy McFalls, Judy Watts
and Vicki Sweatman: wonderful friends,
insightful critiquers, amazing writers
and rockin' concert buddies!

Chapter 1

"Hey, Vera, whatcha think?"

Vera Mancuso—or as the patrons of the Diamond Lounge gentlemen's club knew her, Vera LaRue—glanced over at her friend Tawnisha and nearly dropped her makeup brush.

"My God, Tawni! Kinky Cat Woman?"

When she looked closer, she *did* drop her jaw—all the way to the floor beneath her own four-inch crystal-clear heels. Why she continued to be surprised by her friend's outrageous outfits she'd never know. Vera had worked at the club for nearly four years now and Tawni's daring outfits still managed to shock her. Tawni always teased her for being too naive for an exotic dancer. Maybe she was right.

"Too much?" her friend asked.

Vera choked on a laugh. "Uh. Maybe too *little?*" Yikes. "Aren't there parts missing?" The black latex Cat Woman costume—complete with whip—was minus several stra-

tegic bits. The outfit left pretty much nothing to the imag-
ination.

But then again, Vera reminded herself, that was the whole
idea here, wasn't it?

Tawni grinned. "Only the important parts."

"Too hot to handle, girl!"

"Just the reaction I'm going for." Tawni wiggled her hips
in imitation of what she'd be doing onstage in a few minutes.
"Rumor is there's a real hottie out there tonight."

Vera grinned. "Loaded, too, I hope? Because I could seriously use a few good tips tonight."

"You and me both." Tawni crooked her fingers playfully.
"Come to mama, baby. Let's see you boys flash those twenty-
dollar bills."

"Twenties? Damn. That outfit's gonna bring out the *fifties*."

"What I like to hear, girlfriend," Tawni said. "Those poor
slobs don't stand a chance." She gave the mirror a final check,
winked and strutted out of the dressing room.

Ho-kay, then. Great news for Tawni. Bad news for Vera. If
the punters tossed all their cash at the Kinky Cat Woman
during the first set, there'd be nothing left for Vera's Naughty
Bride half an hour later. No, not good. Joe's retirement home
payment was due in a few days, and after her vintage Camry
finally broke down last week she was still three hundred bucks
short, let alone her own expenses for the month.

Unbidden, her eyes suddenly swam at the thought of her
once-burly stepfather lying in his antiseptic white room. He'd
been so full of life, had so many friends, before. Now…she
was his only visitor, and he hadn't even recognized her two
nights ago.

She blew out a breath, fanning her misty eyes. *Don't go
all weepy on me, Mancuso. Spoil your makeup and forget
about those big tips. Buck up, girl!*

Besides, tears wouldn't help—they never did.

And if she got really desperate, she could always borrow the money from Darla, her sister. Well, half sister. Except Darla had taken off, and who knew when she'd be back. Maybe Tawni could help out if worse came to worst. *If* her friend hadn't already spent all her money on some outrageous new costume by that time. The woman went through expensive stage outfits like Vera went through romance novels.

Not that Vera should be complaining about the costumes. In fact, she was very grateful for them. Tawni was one of the big reasons the punters kept coming back night after night— and telling their friends back home in Des Moines about the great club they'd found in Vegas on their last business trip. *Diamond Lounge: Women in the rough, perfect and polished.* Yeah, that's what it actually said on the playbill out front. Seriously. With a sigh, Vera rolled her eyes. Lecherous Lou's idea, of course. Who else? Now *there* was a loser. Why couldn't *he* get Alzheimer's and forget all about Vera and his relentless campaign to get her to sleep with him?

Anyway, Tawni was one of the rough girls. Supposedly, according to Lecherous Lou. And Vera was polished. She snorted. Ha. Tawnisha Adams had graduated from UCLA magna cum laude and was one of the smoothest operators she knew. *Vera* was the only trailer trash around here, living the life her mother had lived before her. Mentally kicking and silently screaming.

Ah, well. It was what it was.

She leaned forward toward the big lighted mirror that covered an entire wall of the dressing room and critically examined her already generous eye makeup. Maybe a bit more mascara.

There was a fine line between virgin and whore. In her act, she was supposed to be a blushing, innocent bride who revealed her inner bad girl on her wedding night. Right. Like a *real* virgin would ever know those moves she did onstage. Hell, *she* barely did. But whatever. The punters loved it. Which kept Lecherous Lou from firing her even though she steadfastly refused to "do the dirty" with him, as he disgustingly referred to it. That's all that really mattered. Keeping her job.

At least until her Prince Charming came to sweep her away from all of this. Maybe tonight would be the night.

Uh-huh.

She sighed. More mascara it was.

"Vera!"

Her sister burst through the dressing-room door and skidded to a halt against the vanity counter, scattering bottles of nail polish and hair products willy-nilly.

Darla's expression was wild. "Thank God you're here!"

"Whoa!" Vera jumped up and steadied her. "Sis, what's wrong? Where have you *been* all week? You have to stop disappearing like that. Tell me what's going on!"

"Trust me, you don't want to know," Darla said, yanking open her purse.

Darla'd done one of her runners two weeks ago. Which in itself wasn't unusual. Her ditzy sister took off for parts unknown all the time, at the drop of a hat. But she always came back happier and even more relaxed than she normally was, never looking like hell warmed over. Or agitated.

Like this.

"Darla, you look something the cat dragged in," Vera said, genuine worry starting to hum through her. "Seriously, are you all right?" She'd never seen her chronically anesthetized and laid-back half sister so upset. Well, not since their poor excuse for a father had tried to throw Vera out of Darla's penthouse apartment for being a, quote, "money-grubbing gold-digging daughter of a streetwalker." But that was a whole different story.

"Yes. *No!* Oh, I don't know," Darla wailed. "Where the hell *is* it?" Stuff spilled all over the dressing table as she clawed desperately through her designer purse. A new Kate Spade, Vera noted. The real deal. Not like the knockoff Vera was carrying today, sitting on the counter next to Darla's purse. What a difference.

She caught a lipstick that went flying. "Sis, you're talking crazy. Where's *what?*"

"I gotta get out of town for a while, Vera. And I need you to do something for me— Yes! Here it is!"

Triumphantly, her sister held up a ring. A big sparkly one. Jeez Louise, was that a *diamond?* Nah, had to be fake. Even rich-as-Ivanka-Trump Darla St. Giles wouldn't have a rock that huge.

Darla thrust the ring at her. "Can you hide this for me back at our place somewhere?"

Despite their father's objections, Vera shared Darla's penthouse apartment, for which—at Darla's insistence—she paid a ridiculously small amount of rent. Amazingly generous, and a true godsend. Without it Vera'd be living in some low-rent dive in the burbs, an hour from work. Or on a sidewalk grate.

Half sisters, Vera was a product of their playboy father Maximillian St. Giles's legendary philandering. It pleased Darla— whom he basically ignored in favor of her older brother— Henry—to no end to throw their father's many faults and mistakes in his face. Sharing a penthouse with his by-blow ranked right up there. Why should Vera feel guilty about that? The man had treated them both like crap. And it was fun having a sister, even if Darla was a bit out of control at times. Okay, most of the time. They even looked alike. Superficially, at least. Darla meant a lot to her. She'd do anything for her sister.

She looked at the diamond ring in her hand. "Omigod, it's

gorgeous! Where'd you get it? Why do you want me to hide it?" Vera asked, instantly drawn in by the astoundingly beautiful sparkling jewel.

Darla scooped her stuff back into her Kate Spade. "Just as a favor. Lord, you're a lifesaver. I—" Her sister turned and for the first time noticed what Vera was wearing. Her eyes widened and a fleeting grin passed over her lips. "Dang, sis. *Great* corset. Man, that'll have 'em whackin' off in the aisles."

Darla always did have a way with words.

"Thanks, I think," Vera said wryly. Another thing about Darla: she might be an unholy mess, but she was an honest and genuine unholy mess—and never, ever judged Vera. About *anything.* "It is pretty spectacular, isn't it? I had it made to match my bride costume. What do you think? I designed it myself."

Seeing the fake wedding dress hanging from the mirror, a lightbulb went off behind eyes that looked so much like Vera's own. "Oh, it's fabulous," Darla exclaimed. "Hey! The ring'll blend right in! Go ahead, put it on," she urged.

She didn't have to ask twice. Vera slid the flashy ring onto her finger. "Wow. A perfect fit. It is so incredibly beautiful." And Darla was right. It went great with the bride outfit.

Again Vera's eyes were dazzled by the kaleidoscope of colors swirling in its center—green and blue and violet. Like one of those pinwheel whirly things used to hypnotize people in bad movies.

She shook her head to clear it of the weird feeling. "Seriously, what's the deal with the ring?"

A noise sounded out in the hall. Her sister darted a panicked glance at the door, then gave her a smile she knew darn well was forced. "No deal," Darla said. "Just hide it for me, okay?"

"Okay, but—"

"And whatever you do, do *not* talk to Thomas."

As in Thomas Smythe? Darla's ex-boyfriend? Before Vera could ask anything more, Darla pulled her into a quick, hard hug, then grabbed her Kate Spade and vanished out the door as quickly as she'd arrived.

Okay, *that* couldn't be good. Something was up.

Darla was *never* like that—all twitchy and in a rush. Darla never rushed anywhere. Or panicked over anything. Possibly because of the drugs she used far more than she should, but no doubt also because she had learned long ago that money could solve anything and everything. Even a messed-up life.

Tell her about it. Vera only wished *she'd* had the chance to learn that particular lesson.

Speaking of which, she'd better get her butt moving. If she missed her cue to go onstage, Lecherous Lou would pitch a fit. And have one more excuse to hit on her and expect capitulation. Gak. As if.

Luckily, because of her close association with the wealthy St. Giles family, Lecherous Lou—along with everyone else at the Diamond Lounge—was under the mistaken impression that Vera was loaded, too, and didn't need this job. That she just played at exotic dancing as a lark, to piss off conservative parents or whatever. Thank God for small favors. She knew other girls at the club didn't have that kind of leverage against Lecherous Lou to resist his overtures. Or other, shadier propositions. She'd heard about the "private gentlemen's parties" he ran off the books. It was really good money, and she'd been sorely tempted a time or two, but in the end, the thought of what else she'd be expected to do—according to those who did—made her just plain queasy. She shuddered with revulsion.

She might really, *really* need this job…and she might not have had sex in so long she'd probably forgotten how to do it…but she would never, ever, *ever*—

No. Way.

Hell, she wouldn't even do lap dances.

Brushing off the sordid feeling, she carefully shook out the satin skirt of her faux wedding dress and wrapped it around her waist, fastening it over the sexy white, beribboned corset she was wearing. Then she slid on the matching satin bolero-style jacket that made her look oh, so prim and proper, just like a blushing bride. Gathering the yards and yards of see-through veil—the punters particularly liked when she teased them with that—she attached the gossamer cloud to a glittering rhinestone tiara that held it in place on her head.

There.

She checked herself in the mirror. Not bad. The dress was actually gorgeous. In it, she felt like Cinderella stepping from the pumpkin coach. Every man's fantasy bride come to life.

For a split second, a wave of wistfulness sifted through her at the sight of her own reflection. Too bad it was all just an illusion.

She sighed. Oh, well. Maybe someday it would happen for real.

Sure. Like right after Las Vegas got three feet of snow in July.

Face it, Prince Charming was never going to sweep her off her feet and marry her. Who was she kidding? She knew when she got into this gig that no man she'd ever want to marry would look twice at her in that way again. Not after he found out where she came from, and on top of that, what she did for a living. It didn't matter that she'd graduated high school at the top of her class and could have gotten a full ride to any college—even Stanford. Wouldas and couldas didn't matter to men. Only perceptions. She knew that. Look what had happened to her own mother, a woman as smart and loving as any who'd ever lived, bless her.

She knew it would kill Mama, absolutely eviscerate her, if she were alive to see what Vera was doing.

But what choice did she have?

A mere high school graduate could not find an honest, decent job that paid enough to keep Joe in that pricey retirement home. And she'd be damned if she let the best man she'd ever met waste away his last years parked at some damn trailer park day care because she couldn't afford to pay for a proper assisted-living facility. No sirree. Never. Not as long as Vera had breath in her body. And boobs and an ass that could attract fifty-dollar bills. Heck, even the occasional hundred.

So. Off she went to the stage. And truth be told, she didn't even mind that much. Honestly. She *liked* her body. She'd been born with generous curves, and it did not bother her a bit to use them to her advantage. She'd never been shy. And if looking at her nude body could bring a few moments of pleasure to some lonely businessman jonesing for his far-off wife or girlfriend, well, hallelujah. Maybe she'd saved their marriage. Because men could look all they wanted, but they could not touch. That was a firm and fast rule. Both for the club and her personally.

"Two minutes!" Jerry, the bored UNLV senior and part-time stagehand, called from the hallway.

Pursing her bright red lips, she blew a good-luck kiss to the framed photo of Joe and Mama that sat at her spot on the dressing-room vanity, then hurried out and up the stairs toward the black-curtained wings of the stage. Tawni was just coming off.

"How's the house tonight?" Vera whispered.

Smiling broadly, Tawni shook a thick bundle of green bills in her fist. "Hot, baby, hot. Some real high rollers tonight. And, oh, those rumors were true. There's one singularly fine-lookin' man out there. You go get 'em, girl. Knock their little you-know-whats off."

Vera giggled. "You are *so* bad."

Tawni waggled her eyebrows and snapped her Cat Woman whip so it cracked the air. "And lovin' every minute." She raised a considering brow. "Though, Mr. Handsome didn't pay me no nevermind, so maybe he's ripe for a more frilly feminine type."

"One can only hope." *And* that he was rich as Croesus.

"Ten seconds, Miss LaRue." That came from Jerry.

Tawni gave her a wink, and Vera stepped up to the curtain.

"And now, gentlemen—" Lecherous Lou's smarmy, fake-Scottish accent crooned over the club PA system. Her music cued up with a long note from a church organ. "—you are in for a verra special treat, indeed. This next lass is guaranteed to make all you confirmed bachelors out there want to slip a gold ring on her finger and take her home for your verra own fantasy wedding night."

Stifling a yawn, Jerry stood with his nose buried in a textbook, curtain in hand, timing her entrance to exactly when the applause and male howling peaked. He didn't even look up. She didn't take it personally. Jerry'd just come out of the closet. Besides, he had exams this week.

"The Diamond Lounge is verra proud to present…"

She took a deep breath. The stage went black.

Showtime.

"Miss Vera LaRue!"

Chapter 2

Defense attorney Darius "Conner" Rothchild couldn't believe his luck.

What were the chances he'd go out on a little fishing expedition for the Parker case and end up running into Darla St. Giles, the very woman he'd been trying to track down for two weeks? At a strip joint, of all places…called, of all things, the Diamond Lounge.

The superb irony of the name did not escape him. Nor did the amazing coincidence of running into her there. Normally, Conner didn't believe in coincidences. But this just might be the genuine article.

Peeling a twenty from the roll of various bills he always carried in his pants pocket, he paid for another beer and scanned the dark club again.

Talk about two birds with one stone.

Being a Rothchild, a full partner in the family law firm of

Rothchild, Rothchild and Bennigan, and independently wealthy, all allowed him to take on a number of pro bono cases in between his paying clients. The Suzie Parker case was one of his current charity projects—a sordid affair concerning organized prostitution, unlawful coercion and sexual harassment. Several club managers on the Strip had gotten it into their minds to make their more desperate dancers attend infamous "gentlemen's house parties." Nothing more than sex parties. The girls were made to do disgusting things, often against their will, according to Suzie Parker. Unfortunately, the same reasons that led them into the coercion kept them from talking to Conner. And if he couldn't prove Suzie was telling the truth, she'd go to jail for prostitution, and her abusers would go scot-free.

But Darla St. Giles had nothing to do with the Parker case.

No. *She* was going to tell him what had happened to the missing Rothchild family heirloom, the Tears of the Quetzal, a unique chameleon diamond ring worth millions. She'd tell him, or he'd personally wring her spoiled-little-rich-girl neck. Or better yet, have her tossed into jail where *she* belonged.

He just had to find her first. Where had she disappeared to?

As Conner made a second circuit of the club looking for her, his mind raced over the facts of this case. Going into the Las Vegas Metropolitan Police Department headquarters last week, he'd literally run into Darla, one of two heirs to Maximillian St. Giles's billion-dollar fortune. Though they'd met many times socially because their families ran in the same lofty circles, Darla hadn't given Conner a second glance. She'd been too busy arguing with a cop on the sidewalk across the street from Metro headquarters. The pair of them had sounded like they were furious at each other, lost to the world in the throes of their disagreement. There'd also been something about the cop, Conner remembered thinking, something that didn't quite fit—other than his disgusting cheap cologne—although Conner hadn't been able to put his finger on it.

At the time he'd dismissed the incident as one of Darla's notorious public tantrums and continued on the errand his uncle Harold had sent him on: attempting to retrieve the Tears of the Quetzal diamond from police custody. The priceless ring was being held by LVMPD as material evidence in a high-profile murder trial—the victim being Conner's own cousin Candace Rothchild.

Her murder had hit the whole family hard, especially Conner's uncle. Hard enough to make Harold set aside a lifelong animosity and deliberate distancing of himself from all things connected with his rival brother—including his two nephews—in order to beg Conner for a favor. Get back the ring, or Harold was absolutely convinced terrible things would befall *everyone* in the family, due to some ancient curse connected with the ring. His daughter Candace had apparently been killed when she, against her father's strict orders, had "borrowed" the ring and worn it to a star-studded charity function at one of the big new casinos. She was just the first to die, Harold had warned. The man seemed genuinely terrified, convinced the so-called curse was real. He had become obsessed over retrieving the ring…especially after the near-fatal accident that befell his other daughter, Conner's cousin Silver, a few weeks back. An accident her new fiancé, AD, now suspected was a murder attempt.

Conner didn't believe in curses, but he did believe in family. He had a good relationship with his own parents and brother, but relations with Harold and his various offspring, Conner's cousins, had been more than strained for as long as he could remember.

Growing up, the deceased Candace and her coven of siblings and half siblings—Natalie, Candace's twin, who was now a Metro detective; Silver, the former pop star who'd recently made a stunning comeback; Jenna, the Vegas event planner; and the newest addition, Ricky, the devil child—every one of them used to bait him mercilessly about being born into the "wrong" side of the Rothchild family. Conner's highly respected attorney father, Michael Rothchild, was worth millions, but not billions like casino magnate Uncle Harold. Of course, that side of the family didn't even get along with each other, especially tabloid-diva Candace. Things had only gotten worse when she'd married and divorced a drunken loser drummer in a would-be rock band, leaving two beautiful but very neglected children in the constant care of nannies.

Wasn't family wonderful.

But to everyone's credit, things had changed dramatically after Candace's murder. Olive branches had been extended. Although, to be honest, he'd been reconciled with his cousins Natalie and Silver for a while now. They'd actually become good friends over the past few years…much to the chagrin of Uncle Harold. But he had changed now. And this was Conner's big chance to help bring the whole Rothchild family—imperfect as it was—back together. He did not intend to blow it.

Which was why he'd agreed to try to retrieve the ring from the police. Technically, the Tears of the Quetzal belonged to the entire family, having been unearthed in the Rothchild's Mexican diamond mine by his grandfather over five decades ago. But Uncle Harold had always been the ring's caretaker. And now with the ring's disappearance, he was obsessively worried it would bring danger to the family.

Although Conner still dismissed the ridiculous notion of curses, he did agree the diamond was not secure, even surrounded by hundreds of cops. As a lawyer, Conner knew firsthand that evidence disappeared from police custody all the time. Lost. Tampered with. Deliberately "misplaced."

And wouldn't you know it. Two weeks ago when he'd gotten to the evidence room, minutes after running into Darla St. Giles, he'd discovered, to his frustration, the unique and unmistakable chameleon diamond ring had vanished. Switched. Replaced with a paste copy that had gone missing from Harold's current wife's jewelry box. At Metro police headquarters, the theft had been pulled off by a cop who had apparently simply walked in and checked the real ring out of the evidence room on the pretense of having it examined for DNA, and left the clever fake in its place when he returned it an hour later.

Conner had gone ballistic. What was *wrong* with these people? Didn't they check ID? His cousin Natalie, the LVMPD detective, had led the search.

Then he'd remembered Darla arguing outside with that not-quite-right cop only ten minutes before he'd discovered the theft. And *that's* when he'd figured out what was wrong with the guy. His boots. They'd been brown and scuffed up. Regulation was black and spit-polished.

Conner was absolutely convinced that phony cop and Darla St. Giles were responsible for the theft of the ring from police headquarters. Damned unexpected, but not outside the realm of possibility. According to the tabloids, Darla had been scraping the proverbial bottom of the barrel of late, friend-wise and behavior-wise. Dating fake cops, stealing jewelry and hanging out at strip clubs would be right up her alley.

The question was, was the pair also involved in his cousin Candace's murder? He couldn't believe it of Darla. She was a wild party girl and definitely sliding down a slippery slope. A thief, yes. But a murderer? He could be wrong, but he didn't buy it. Still, he owed it to the family to find out for sure.

Naturally, after Conner raised the alarm, by the time Natalie had launched a search, Darla and the man had been

long gone. Just in case, Conner had spent hours on the
computer with Natalie by his side, looking at photos of every
single police officer in Las Vegas. The man he'd seen was not
among them. Therefore his instincts had been right—the
culprit was not a real cop.

On that same day Darla had dropped out of sight completely, confirming his suspicions of her guilt. Despite Natalie
assigning an officer to stake out her penthouse apartment
24/7, other than a single roommate, no one had seen hide nor
hair of her there, or anywhere else, since.

Until now.

At least, ten minutes ago… But he'd lost her.

With mounting frustration, Conner had searched the
Diamond Lounge from top to bottom for the illusive Darla.
Twice. And come up empty.

Where the hell was she?

"Can I get you something, doll?" one of the waitresses asked
him with a sultry smile. She was pretty. Blond. And topless.

Hello.

He glanced around, catapulted back to the present by the
sight of so much skin. Whoa. Where had his famous powers
of observation vanished to?

The Diamond Lounge was an Old Las Vegas landmark, a
throwback to the times when total nudity was permitted along
with serving alcohol. Naturally, he'd vaguely noticed the
naked woman dancing on the stage. But how could he have
been so angry and distracted that he hadn't noticed the all but
naked women prancing around him carrying trays of drinks?

"You looking for someone special?" she asked, her smile
growing even more suggestive.

Oy. He slashed a hand through his hair, composing himself.
One always learned more playing nice than coming off like a
demanding nutcase. And, hell, she was hot. No hardship there.

He smiled back. "Yeah. I thought I saw a friend of mine. Darla St. Giles. You know her by any chance?"

"Oh, sure," the waitress said, interest perking. He could practically see dollar signs flashing in her baby blues. As one of the rich and reckless, Darla's male friends were sure to be rich and reckless, too. Emphasis on the rich part. "She's in here all the time."

Popular landmark or not, that surprised him. "She is?"

"Uh-huh. To visit her sister. She works here."

He-llo. A St. Giles? Working at the Diamond Lounge as a topless waitress? Hell's bells. Ol' Maximillian St. Giles must be spitting disco balls over that one. Except now that Conner thought about it, he had never heard of a second St. Giles sister. There was a brother, Henry, but not… Unless… He tipped his head. "Are you *sure* they're sisters?"

"*Half* sisters, if you know what I mean. Although that's all hush-hush." The waitress waggled her eyebrows and leaned against the bar, folding her arms under her bare breasts so they pushed up toward him. Oh. Subtle. "Guess she likes walkin' on the wild side, or somethin'."

Or something. Whoa. All Conner's stress just oozed out of him. A deep, dark St. Giles secret, eh? A secret so hidden that Darla felt safe coming here tonight, even when she hadn't been to her apartment in two weeks and hadn't called her own family. Hell, all he had to do was put a watch on the secret sister and sooner or later Darla'd turn up here.

The Tears of the Quetzal was as good as found. And Natalie could bring her in for questioning about Candace's murder as well.

Damn, he was good.

"How 'bout you, doll?" the waitress asked, interrupting his thoughts again.

"Me, what?" he asked.

"You like walkin' on the wild side?"

He smiled at her. "Maybe." Then took a second look at what the blond waitress was offering up. He was used to women throwing themselves at him, one of the perks of his looks and his famous last name. Normally he was just too damn busy to take advantage. But what the hell, it had been a long time; maybe the Parker case could wait another night. But first… "Darla's sister, she around?" Just so he'd know who to look for. Tomorrow.

"Sure, she's coming on right now. That's her." The waitress pointed toward the stage.

The stage? He tore his eyes from her and turned. "You mean she's a—"

He froze, literally, instantly oblivious to everything else around him.

The sister… At first Conner thought it was Darla; they looked so much alike. But then she stepped into the spotlight, and all resemblance vanished. The woman was the most amazingly, lusciously gorgeous thing he'd ever seen in his life. She glided out on the horseshoe-shaped stage to the tune of Mendelssohn's *Wedding March*. Eyes cast demurely down, she was dressed in a frothy, whipped-cream wedding dress, complete with a long poofy veil covering her face and spilling over her shoulders and back clear to the floor like some kind of gossamer waterfall.

Wow.

Normally, the merest glimpse of a wedding dress made him break out in hives and sprint hell-bent-for-leather in the opposite direction. Not this one.

"Her?" he asked the waitress, totally forgetting that just seconds ago he'd been contemplating—

Never mind. What waitress?

Was he actually hyperventilating?

"Yeah. How about we—"

"What's her name?" he asked, his eyes completely glued to the perfect vision onstage.

The waitress was not pleased. He could tell by the way she huffed and turned her back on him. Working on autopilot, he dug out his ubiquitous roll, peeled off a bill and held it over his shoulder for her. "Her name?"

She gave a harrumph and snatched it. "It's Vera. Vera LaRue."

Vera… Wait. Wasn't that the name Natalie had said belonged to Darla's roommate? The *sister* was the roommate?

The churchy organ music morphed into a slow, grinding striptease number. Conner watched, beguiled, as Vera LaRue slowly started to move her body in a sinuous dance. And, damn, could the woman ever move her body. Her eyes were still cast innocently at the floor doing her vestal virgin bit, but there wasn't a man in the place watching her face.

Conner pushed off the bar and signaled a passing waitress, peeling off another few bills. Without saying a word, he was shown to a table, front and center. He sat down, and a glass of champagne appeared in his hand. Vera paused just above him on the stage. Oh. Man. She was close enough to touch. He was more than tempted to try.

She raised her lashes and looked down at him.

He looked up at her.

Their eyes met.

And sweet holy God. He was struck by lightning.

Or maybe just blinded by the flash of seven carats of chameleon diamond on her finger as she slowly unbuttoned the top of her gown. He almost fell off his chair. That was *his* seven carats of chameleon diamond! She was wearing the Tears of the Quetzal!

Well, hot damn. If this was Harold's so-called danger, bring it on.

The top of the white gown slid provocatively off Vera

LaRue's pale, pretty shoulders. Conner watched her slowly tug the sleeves down her arms, inch by tantalizing inch. For several moments his brain ceased to function.

Until he gave himself a firm mental kick. What was *wrong* with him?

She couldn't be nearly as innocent as she appeared, clutching the top of that dazzling white gown to her breasts like a blushing virgin. Hell, she *must* be involved with Darla in the theft of the ring. The evidence was right on her finger!

Logic told him she had to be innocent of involvement in Candace's murder. Only a complete, brainless idiot would kill someone, or even be remotely connected to a murder, and then flash the evidence in front of a room full of people. Obviously, she couldn't know of the link between Candace's murder and the ring she was wearing.

Come to think of it, maybe she didn't even know the ring was stolen. Now, *that* would make more sense. It could easily be she was just being used. Or set up.

In which case, he had to give Darla props. Hiding the unique ring in plain sight, as part of her sister's stage costume, was brilliant.

Too bad he was even more brilliant.

Brilliant and ruthless.

And did he mention intrigued as hell? Who *was* this Vera LaRue, Darla St. Giles's gorgeous, secret, illegitimate half sister?

And who'd have ever thought Conner Rothchild would be so captivated by a stripper? His snooty family would have a cow, every last one of them. Especially his dad, who'd always held Uncle Harold in contempt for his questionable taste in multiple women.

But thoughts of family vanished as Vera LaRue stopped in front of him and slanted him another shy glance. She held his gaze with a sexy look as she pulled at the waist of her wedding gown and the whole thing slid down around her trim ankles in a pool of liquid silk.

For a second he couldn't breathe. Sweet merciful heaven. All that was left was the most erotic, alluring bit of lace he had ever seen grace a woman's body. Parts of it, anyway. And a veil. Straight out of Salome.

Please don't let me be drooling.

Then, with a sultry lowering of her eyelashes, she scooped up the dress and let it fall provocatively right into his lap. Her eyebrow lifted almost imperceptibly.

Okay, seriously wow. A challenge? Clearly, she did not know him. Conner didn't lose. And if there was one thing he never lost, it was a dare.

Oh. Yeah.

He looked up at her and conjured his most seductive smile.

Still moving to the music, she knelt down on the stage. Right before him. With those melting eyes and amazing mile-long legs…encased in white thigh-high stockings and impossibly sexy crystal-clear high-heeled shoes. She dropped to her hands and knees. Just for him.

His brain pretty much disintegrated. The rest of his body was set to explode. He was hard and thick as one of those columns at the Forum. The *real* one in Rome.

The Rothchild heirloom flashed on her finger. His family's ring. A smile curved his lips.

She wanted his family jewel? Well, then. He just might have to be a gentleman and give it to her.

Oh, yes. This curse could prove to be very, very interesting, indeed.

Chapter 3

The applause for Vera LaRue was deafening. Conner watched mesmerized as she took her final bow and swished off the stage.

He let out a long, long breath. Lord, have *mercy*.

By the time she'd finished her incredible dance of temptation, she'd made her way all around the stage, weaving her erotic spell over the dozens of men who were pressed up to the edge like pathetic dogs panting for a treat. But Conner was the only one who'd rated personal attention from her. It was like she'd danced for him alone, even when she was all the way across the stage. Of course, probably every guy there thought exactly the same thing. That's what a good stripper did to a guy. Or maybe she singled him out because he was the only one who hadn't attempted to put his hands on her. Hadn't tipped her. Hadn't done anything but hold her sultry eyes with his and silently promise her anything she wanted. Anything at all.

On his terms.

She'd ended up gloriously, unabashedly naked. Or, as good as. Down to a G-string, stockings and those take-me heels…and the Quetzal diamond. Oh, yeah, and a thick layer of fluttering greenbacks stuck into her G-string, making it look like a Polynesian skirt gone triple X.

Her bridal veil was around Conner's neck. He was still sweating over the way she'd put it there.

Da-*amn*. The woman was Salome incarnate. But Conner fully intended to have her dancing to *his* tune before the night was over. Singing like a lark about how she'd ended up with his ring on her finger…without even benefit of dinner and a movie. Not to mention if she knew anything about Candace's death.

Conner was a damn good lawyer, skilled at making witnesses trust him enough to spill their guts. It was all about the approach. So…how to best approach this one…?

He looked around the room. And almost laughed out loud. The answer was beckoning from the back of the club. Aw, gee. He'd just have to sacrifice himself.

Throwing back the last of his champagne—not that he needed the Dutch courage—he signaled his waitress.

"I'd like Miss LaRue to join me," he told her as the fickle crowd roared for the new cutie who'd just come out onstage.

The waitress took the dress and veil from him. "Sure, hon. I'll have her come to your table."

He pulled off another bill. "No, somewhere private."

"Oh, sorry. I'm afraid Ms. LaRue doesn't do that."

"Do what?"

"Private parties. She's strictly a stage dancer."

"Really."

Now, *that* was interesting. Apparently being a St. Giles let her pick and choose her jobs. Normally the private VIP rooms upstairs were where the big money was made by these women.

And the big thrills. Personally, he'd never gotten into the whole lap dance thing. A nice sensual session in the privacy of your own home with a woman you knew and liked, sure. But an anonymous grind for cash? A bit sleazy if you asked him.

"Well," he told the waitress, "then it's good I only want to talk to her."

She rolled her eyes. "Sure you do, hon."

He could understand her skepticism. Hell, *he* was skeptical, and he knew he only wanted to talk to her. Honest.

He peeled off a few more bills and pressed them into her palm. "Tell Miss LaRue I have information about her sister. And that I'll match whatever she just made onstage."

Where she'd practically seduced him, by the way. But the woman didn't do lap dances. Something didn't add up about *that* picture.

The waitress shrugged. "You're wasting your time. Don't say I didn't warn you." She beckoned him with a crooked finger.

He strolled along behind her to the back of the club and followed her up the red-carpeted stairs to the second floor, where the inevitable small, "private entertainment" VIP rooms were located. Though gentlemen's clubs weren't Conner's favorite hangouts, one couldn't be a defense attorney in Vegas without doing a certain amount of business in them. Especially since his frequent pro bono work tended to involve hookers and runaways. So he was fairly familiar with the standard club setup.

Because of its enduring fame, Old Vegas reputation and pricey cover charge—and thanks to a complete renovation in the nineties—the Diamond Lounge wasn't too bad, compared to most. Clean. Sophisticated decor. Unobtrusive bouncers. Nice-looking, classy ladies. He supposed if you had to work in a place like this, the Diamond Lounge was definitely top drawer.

But once again he wondered why über-conservative Maximillian St. Giles let his daughter work at all, let alone take off her clothes for money. Even if she was illegitimate, and as far as he knew, unacknowledged, a negative reflection was still cast on the family.

Not that Conner was objecting to her taking off her clothes. Hell, no. The woman had an incredible body.

She also had his family's ring.

He wanted it back. That was his primary objective here. And nailing down Darla's involvement in his cousin's murder. Not nailing Vera LaRue. But if in the course of things, he ended up close and personal with her, well, who was he to protest? Especially considering the unmistakable signals she'd given him from up onstage. She had to be expecting this.

Handing the waitress his credit card, he did a quick survey of the tiny, soundproof room, then sprawled onto the heavy, red leather divan that took up most of one wall. Soft music played in the background. Scented candles littered the surfaces of two low tables at either end of the divan, as well as on the heavy wood mantel of the fireplace across from it. The tasteful cornice lighting was recessed and rose-colored, lending a pastel glow to Oriental rugs over cream-colored carpet and gauzy curtains that looked more like mosquito nets draped all around the walls of the room. It was like being cocooned in some exotic Caribbean bordello.

Oddly arousing.

The curtains over the door parted, and Vera LaRue suddenly stood there, holding a sweating champagne bottle and two crystal flutes. She'd put the wedding dress back on.

Hey, now.

"Hello," she said, her voice throaty and rich like a tenor sax. "I understand you wanted to speak with me about my sister."

Suddenly, talk wasn't at all what he wanted.

Wait. Yes, it was.

"Why don't you come in and open up that bottle," he suggested, indicating the champagne in her hand. The hand with the Tears of the Quetzal diamond on it. *Focus, Conner.*

"I, um…" She suddenly looked uncomfortable. "I'm sorry, sir. I really don't think so. Truth is, I don't do this."

He hiked a brow. "Drink champagne?"

She blinked. Flicked her gaze down to the bottle then back to him, even more flustered. "No. I mean yes, I drink champagne. Of course I drink champagne. Everyone does. But I *don't* do lap dances. I only came because you mentioned my sister. Now, what was it—"

"I understand," he cut in agreeably. Not having to endure her gyrating on his lap without being able to touch her was probably a good thing. If maybe a little disappointing. Fine, a lot disappointing. "Let's have some bubbly and then we can talk."

She gave him a look. What? She didn't believe him, either? "Sir, I'm serious. It's nothing to do with you. You seem like a nice guy. I just really don't—"

"Please. Call me Conner. If you don't want to dance for me, Ms. LaRue, that's fine. As appealing as that might be, it's not why I'm here." He held out his hand with a smile. "Here. I'll open it."

When she still balked, he stood up. That made her jump. But she recovered quickly. She gave him the bottle and pulled back her hand a little too fast. As though she were…afraid to touch him?

Impossible. The woman who'd practically had sex with him with her eyes from the stage could not possibly be nervous about physical contact, regardless of what he might or might not have had in mind for this tête à tête.

Which was *just* to talk.

Honest to God.

Or…did she perhaps realize who he was? *That* hadn't occurred to him. Had Darla warned Vera someone might come looking for the ring? Maybe asking questions about a murder? Was this modesty thing all a big ploy to throw him off?

Nah. If so, she would have run away, not flirted mercilessly and then locked herself and the ring in a tiny room with him.

The cork flew, startling her into raising the flutes to catch the golden liquid. Her satiny gown rustled against his legs as he stepped closer to fill the glasses. The scent of her perfume clung to the air around her—sweet and spicy. Very nice.

Suddenly, the most insanely irrational thought struck him. What if she really *were* his beautiful bride, that this really was their wedding night and he really *was* about to peel that bridal gown off her and—

Whoa, there, buddy. Hold on.

Where the hell had *that* come from?

Totally inappropriate temporary insanity, that was where. Obviously he'd gone without sex for *far* too long, and it was somehow damaging his brain's ability to function in the presence of a beautiful woman.

He eased a flute from her stiff fingers and clicked it with hers. Back to business.

But instead of a trust-inducing get-to-know-you question, what came out of his mouth was, "You do have some amazing moves, Ms. LaRue."

To make matters worse, his rebellious gaze inched boldly down her delectable body, all of its own volition.

Help.

"Um, thanks, Conner. I appreciate your…um, appreciation. But now you really need to tell me whatever information you have about my sister, or I'll be leaving."

Damn, she looked good. And so sweetly uncomfortable, he pulled out his roll, thumbed off two C-notes, held them up, and confessed, "Okay, you were right. I *would* like to see you dance up close."

Okay, way to go, you total moron. What was *wrong* with him? This was *not* the way he conducted business.

"I knew it." She shook her head, taking a step backward, away from him. "Look, I'm really sorry, but this is not happening. I'll just go find someone else—"

An incredible thought flew through his mind as she chattered on about getting him another girl. Could this befuddling change in his self-control be the mysterious power of the ancient Mayan legend-slash-curse Uncle Harold was always talking about? The part he was obsessed with portended terrible things would befall anyone who possessed the ring with evil intentions. But the *other* part said the spirit of the Quetzal would bring any truly worthy person within its range of influence true, abiding love.

For a second he just stood there, stunned.

He-*llo?*

Had he gone completely *insane?*

Mystical powers? True love? With an exotic dancer?

He gave himself a firm mental thwack.

And smiled at her. "No, it's you I want, and the room is already paid for." By the quarter-hour, no less. He held up his money roll. "Tell me, what did you make in tips onstage? I promised to match it." *To talk,* he tried to compel his mouth to say. But the words just wouldn't come out.

She didn't even blink. "That's very nice of you, but no. Thank you. As I said—" She launched into her spiel yet again.

But he wasn't listening. It was like he was standing next to himself watching as he was being taken over by pod people. He should be taking it slow. From arm's length. Gaining her trust. Not trying to jump her bones. Certainly not until after he'd gotten his answers. And his family's ring back. He *knew* that. But she was simply too delicious to resist.

Ah, what the hell.

He surrendered to it. Changed tactics. *Her* first. Answers later. Then the ring.

Yeah, that worked.

Determined, he thumbed out several more bills, bringing her chatter to a stuttering halt. He didn't doubt for a second she'd eventually capitulate. One thing his ruthless family had taught him—*everyone* capitulated. It was all just a matter of negotiation. "Four-hundred? Five?"

She swallowed. "Really. I don't think you under—"

He started peeling and didn't stop till he reached ten. "Let's say an even thousand, shall we?"

That really shut her up. She stared at the money, then shifted her gaze to stare at him for an endless moment. "Why?" she finally asked.

Good freaking question.

Vera LaRue was so different from the type of woman he was usually attracted to…this was completely unknown territory. Sure, he frequently worked with hookers, dancers and runaways in his legal practice. *Worked.* But he was definitely not attracted to them. Never slept with them. Ever.

So what was different about this woman? What made him want *her?* And no—hell, no!—it had *nothing* to do with mystical powers or curses.

A matter of pride maybe? Conner Rothchild wasn't used to being denied. The only time he took *that* without protest was in court.

Okay, bull.

Not pride. Not some stupid Mayan curse.

But chemistry. *Sexual* chemistry. Plain and simple. He wanted her in his bed, naked and moving on top of him. She was the sexiest woman he'd met in decades. Was this rocket science?

He wanted her. A lap dance seemed like a damned good way to convince her she wanted him, too. It was a start, anyway.

"Why?" he echoed. And gave her his best winning jury smile. "Let's just say you intrigue me."

She regarded him for another endless moment, her eyes narrowing and filling with suspicion. "Who are you, anyway?"

Uh-oh.

But as luck would have it, he never got the chance to answer. Because just then the door whooshed open and the mosquito net curtains blew aside as though from a strong wind. Two men in suits strode through and halted right inside, looking so much like federal agents that just on reflex Conner was about to warn Vera to not to say a word.

One of the men stepped forward. "Miss St. Giles?"

With a frown, Vera turned to the newcomers in confusion. "What?"

Conner frowned, too, when Forward Guy spotted the Tears of the Quetzal diamond on her finger, looked grimly smug, then officiously snapped up an ID wallet. "Special Agent Lex Duncan, FBI."

Oh, come on. Seriously?

But it was Special Agent Duncan's next words that really seemed to confuse the hell out of Vera. And him, too.

"Darla St. Giles, I am hereby placing you under arrest."

Chapter 4

"**Y**ou can't do that!" Vera exclaimed as an honest-to-goodness FBI agent spun her around, grabbed her wrists and snapped handcuffs onto them. "Hey! Watch the dress!" she cried. "What the heck—"

"Ms. St. Giles, you have the right to remain silent—"

"*What?* Are you kidding? I am *not*—"

"Vera," Conner, her would-be john, cut her off over the drone of the FBI agent—what was his name? Lexicon?—reciting her rights, "don't say anything. I'll take care of this."

Not only was the man annoying but he was a real buttinsky, too. "You don't understand. I'm not—"

"I know you're not," Conner cut her off again. "But obviously *they* think you are."

"Move away from the suspect, sir," her second would-be arrestor admonished her would-be lawyer briskly, with just a touch of disdain in his voice, as Agent Lexicon continued his recitation. Great. Already with the attitude.

All at once his words registered. "Suspect?" she echoed, horrified. "*Me?* I'm *not* a suspect!" she insisted, growing more frustrated by the second. And more worried. She could see a crowd gathering outside the door. If Lecherous Lou got wind of this, her butt would be fired for sure.

One thing a club in this city did not need was bad publicity of any kind. Kept the tourists away. And her boss had just been waiting for a good excuse to fire her. Mainly because she refused his disgusting advances, but also because she wouldn't get involved in that shady business he was running on the side with a few other club managers, providing high-class dancers for private parties.

"That's right. You're no mere suspect," Agent Attitude agreed. "You've been caught red-handed, sweetheart, guilty as hell. Do not pass go, do not collect two-hundred dollars." He snickered at his own lame joke.

"What do you mean, guilty? I haven't done anything!"

"Vera," Conner headed off her impending tirade, "do *not* say another word." She snapped her mouth shut in irritation as he turned to Lex Luthor. "I'm Conner Rothchild, the lady's legal counsel. She is invoking her right to silence and to an attorney."

Wait. Oh, no. Conner *what?* Did he just say his name was—

"And by the way," Conner continued, "this woman is not Darla St. Giles. So if you would kindly take off the handcuffs and let her go?"

Rothchild! As in—

Agent Lucifer whipped around and peered closer at her. "Then who is she?" he demanded.

Rothchild! Oh, no. No way, Jose. She knew the reputation that went along with the name Conner Rothchild. She'd heard plenty of horror stories from his own cousins, tabloid-diva

Candace and pop star Silver, who used to be two of Darla's best friends. Not only was Conner a sleaze-bag shark of a defense attorney according to Candace, but according to Silver he was also possibly the biggest skirt-chaser in the state.

"She's—"

Hell, no. "I'm terribly sorry, but this man is *not* my attorney," she jumped in indignantly. "And I can answer for myself, thank you very much. My name is Vera Mancuso, and Darla St. Giles is my—"

"Stop!" Conner-freaking-playboy-of-the-year-Rothchild cut her off again with an exasperated glare. "I *said* not another word! I *am* her attorney, but since she is not the person you are looking for—"

"Oh, she's the right person, all right," the Devil's agent said resolutely. He pointed an accusing finger at her left hand. "Whoever she is, she's in possession of material evidence stolen from police custody. Therefore, Vera Mancuso, is it? I am placing *you* under arrest—"

"What?" The rest of his words faded out as Agent Attitude pried the ring from her finger and dropped it into a small Ziploc bag. "Oh. My. God. I cannot believe this." Her incredulity continued to pour out of her mouth all on its own as desperate thoughts bombarded her mind even faster.

Stolen? From the police? *Oh, Darla! What have you gotten yourself into this time?* Wait a second. Darla, nothing. Heck, what had her sister gotten *her* into this time? Now Darla's request to hide the ring made perfect sense. Stolen! She could go to jail!

Despair swept over her as the FBI agents pushed her out into the main part of the club, where every single person stood and gaped in avid interest as she was led through the room in handcuffs, tripping over the bridal gown because with the restraints she couldn't hold it up to walk. Even the new girl onstage stopped gyrating and stared wide-eyed. And, damn it, there was Lecherous Lou, looking murderous as he watched her being taken away.

Great. So much for *that* job.

What would she do for money now? How would she pay for Joe's retirement home from prison? Too bad she hadn't accepted gazillionaire Conner's proposition earlier…and gotten paid up front. That thousand bucks would at least have bought her a week or two respite. Then, oh, darn, got arrested, can't do the lap dance. Sorry, no refunds.

Yeah. Like her conscience would have let her do that, even if a thousand bucks to this man was merely a night's meaningless amusement. Honesty was such a bitch.

"You have a change of clothes in your dressing room?" Mr. Persistent Attorney asked as she was herded through the club's front door. She glanced back at him. And wondered what his real agenda was. He couldn't possibly care what happened to her.

Yeah, like she couldn't guess.

Conner Rothchild was a blue-blooded playboy who made the gossip columns nearly as often as Darla and Silver and their jet-setting, hard-clubbing cronies. Always with a different woman on his arm. He probably thought slumming it with Darla St. Giles's exotic-dancer sister would be a hoot. For about five minutes. Meanwhile, she'd be outed to the world at large, and good ol' Maximillian would be furious.

"I'll grab your purse and follow you," Conner said when she deliberately didn't answer. "Don't say anything until I get there. Nothing. I mean it."

"Look," she made one last stab at reasoning with him as she was being stuffed into the back of an unmarked SUV. The white frothy wedding dress filled the entire seat, and she had to punch it down. "Please don't bother following me. You can't be my attorney. I have no money to pay your fee, and even if I did, I—"

"Don't worry about the fee," he responded with a dismissive gesture.

Uh-huh. A girl didn't need a telescope to see exactly where this was going. "And I don't pay in kind!" she yelled just before the door slammed.

He grinned at her through the window. And had the audacity to wink.

She groaned, closed her eyes and sank down in the seat. Swell. Just freaking swell. Broke. Fired. Arrested by the FBI. And pimped out to the city's most charming keg of sexual dynamite.

What the hell else could go wrong today?

Special Agent Lex Duncan was being a real pismire.

Conner folded his hands in front of himself to keep from decking the jerk. They were standing in the observation room attached to interrogation out at the FBI's main Las Vegas field station. Vera was sitting at a table on the other side of the one-way mirror, looking tired, vulnerable and all but defeated. She hadn't started crying yet, but Conner felt instinctively she was close. Very close. Duncan had been interrogating her hard for over two hours, asking the same questions again and again. He hadn't even let her change out of that sexy break-away bridal gown into the jeans and T-shirt Conner'd brought for her along with her purse from the dressing room. Pure intimidation. The bastard.

"Listen to me. She's not involved," he told Duncan for the dozenth time. He wasn't sure when he'd started being a true believer, but he was now firmly in the Vera-isn't-involved-in-the-ring-heist-*or*-Candace's-murder camp. In fact, he was pretty convinced she wasn't guilty of a damn thing, other than a crapload of bad luck.

"And you know this how?" Duncan asked, brow raised.

"It's *my* family's damn ring, and my own murdered cousin we're talking about. Not to mention possibly the same person nearly bringing down a theater scaffold on my other cousin Silver. Don't you think I want the guilty party or parties caught and fried?" he asked heatedly.

He and Candace might not have gotten along all that well, but she was still family. He'd see the killer hanged by his balls, no doubt about it. "But I want the *right* person caught and punished. Vera Mancuso is a victim of her half sister's bad judgment. Nothing more."

Duncan pushed out a breath. "Okay. Just for sake of argument, say I agree with you. My problem is, the stolen evidence was right on her finger."

"And she explained how it got there. About fifty times. I, for one, believe her story."

"So, what, I'm supposed to release her just because *you* have a damn hunch? Or more likely, have the hots for her and want to impress her with your prowess…as her attorney?"

Conner clamped his teeth. Okay, he might have the hots for Vera, but that would have ended abruptly if he'd still had the least doubt she was part of either the ring's theft or his cousin's murder. And, yeah, maybe he didn't have any real solid reason to believe that, but there you go. A man had to trust his gut instincts. Especially if he was a lawyer.

"Yeah," he said evenly. "Just release her."

Duncan started to shake his head. "No can do."

"I have an idea," Conner said, thinking fast. "We can use her. To get her sister. That's who you really want to question about the ring."

Duncan exhaled. "I'm listening."

"Darla trusts her. She gave Vera the Tears of the Quetzal for safekeeping. Believe me, she'll be back for it."

"And?"

"And when she shows up, I'll call you and you can come arrest her. You can get to the real truth. The *real* perps."

Duncan briefly considered. "Even if I went along with this, what makes you think Ms. Mancuso will let you stick around that long?"

Conner shrugged modestly. "I'm not without my charms."

The FBI agent's eyes rolled. "And yet, she keeps telling me you're *not* her lawyer. Besides, wouldn't your representing her be a conflict of interest?"

"Not if she's innocent."

And, damn, she really did look innocent sitting there in that bleak, gray interrogation room, holding back her tears by a thread. Innocent, and incredibly brave. While Duncan questioned her, Conner'd had his legal assistant do a quick workup on Vera Mancuso. Her background had been far from easy. He'd been all wrong about her relationship with her biological father, Maximillian St. Giles. The man didn't want to know her, was openly hostile to his illegitimate daughter and kept her existence deep in the closet. The scumbag.

Duncan raked a hand through his hair. "I don't know if you're aware of this, but the FBI is not in charge of your cousin's murder case. That's strictly Metro at this point."

Conner glanced at him in surprise. "Then why didn't *they* arrest Vera?"

"Because of that ring. My current investigation is a series of high-end interstate jewelry robberies for which Darla St. Giles is a prime suspect, along with a couple of her friends. Possibly even a family member," he added pointedly. "I got a tip from an informant that Darla was seen entering the Diamond Lounge, so we closed in. I thought she might be fencing some of her stolen goods. The manager there's had some illegal dealings in the past."

"So when you saw Vera wearing the Quetzal…"

"I recognized it right away. And she looks enough like Ms. St. Giles to have fooled me for a minute. I have good reason to believe Darla's gang had targeted the Rothchild diamond on the night your cousin was killed. You seeing her with that phony cop at the police station, and the ring showing up in her half sister's possession are both pretty strong evidence to connect her to the theft."

"But what about the phony cop I saw her with?" Conner said. "And didn't you say Luke Montgomery's new wife was there at the casino the night of Candace's murder, and was later stalked by someone wanting the ring?"

Duncan crossed his arms. "All true. But even if I agree with you in theory, my hands are tied. Until Darla is in custody and corroborates Ms. Mancuso's story, and Vera's alibi is checked out, I'd be insane to let the only suspect I have go free."

Conner stuck his hands in his pockets. "Okay, I see your point. Still, keeping Vera in custody is probably the best way to drive Darla so far into hiding you'll never find her. She certainly has the means to disappear for a good long time if she feels threatened."

"So what do you propose I do?"

"Let Vera out on bail. I'll pay it. Then we use her as bait, like I suggested."

Both of them turned to contemplate Vera through the mirrored window. She'd put her head down on the Formica table and buried her face in her arms. Had she finally broken down? Conner's heart squeezed in sympathy.

"If I agree to this crazy scheme," Duncan finally said, "I'd want something in return."

"Like what?" Conner asked.

"I'd want your help figuring out exactly who is part of the jewel theft ring I'm investigating. You move in the same social circles as Darla St. Giles. You go to the same parties and charity events, know the same people. I'd want you to nose around, ask questions. Narrow down my list of suspects." He turned to look Conner in the eye. "Help LVMPD figure out if your cousin's death was a jewel robbery gone bad, or something else entirely."

Conner raised his brows. "Kind of a tall order, isn't it?"

"That's the deal. Take it or leave it."

"Fine." Obviously, Vera wasn't going to get a better offer. Nor was he. "I'll take it."

Chapter 5

They were letting her go.

Vera couldn't quite believe it. But she wasn't about to question her good luck.

Right up until the devil's Agent Lex Luthor—whose name actually turned out to be Duncan—said to her as he handed over her bag of belongings, "Your attorney, Mr. Rothchild, has posted your bail and personally vouched for your where-abouts until the arraignment. As a condition of your release, you must agree to check in with him at least three times a day."

She stopped dead. "You can't be serious."

"Bear in mind you are a potential murder suspect, Ms. Mancuso," the agent said sternly. "Personally, I'm opposed to releasing you at all, but the Rothchild name wields a lot of influence—"

She handed him back her bag. "Forget it. If that's a require-ment, I'll stay arrested, thanks."

The FBI guy's jaw dropped. "Excuse me?"

"No one ever listens to me. I've told you over and over, he's *not* my—"

"Actually, he is." Duncan held up a paper. "Court appointed. I have the order here if you need proof."

She blinked. Oh, for crying out loud. The man was totally relentless. "Let me see that."

It didn't matter that for some mysterious reason she found the loathsome Conner Rothchild so incredibly, toe-curlingly sexy that every time she looked at him she practically melted into a limp noodle at his feet. Or that the whole time he'd sat in the audience at the Diamond Lounge—*before* she knew who he was—she'd girlishly pretended he was the only man in the whole room, and danced for him alone. When had *that* ever happened before? With any man? Never, that's when.

But even so. She wasn't about to trade sex for lawyering. Or anything, for that matter. She knew what he must have in mind, and she wanted none of it. Well. Not like that, anyway. She probably wouldn't say no under other circumstances or if he were anyone else. But selling herself? No way. Regardless of how mouthwateringly and wrongly tempting he was. And how much she really wanted to find out what it would be like to lie under his ripped, athletic body and—

Oh, no. Banish *that* thought.

She looked over the paper that Duncan had handed her. Sure enough, it was a one-paragraph court order appointing Conner as her legal counsel.

What. Ever.

At least she didn't have to pay him. *Or* owe him in any other way. That was a huge relief.

But did she want to have to check in with Mr. Cutthroat Playboy Attorney three times a day like she was one of his low-life parolees? Heck, no.

"Have you ever been to prison, Ms. Mancuso?" the federal agent asked. Apparently mind reading was part of the FBI arsenal.

"Of course not."

"Trust me, you wouldn't enjoy it." He took back the paper and slid it into her file. "Mr. Rothchild seems like a decent attorney. Let him help you."

She regarded him. "Special Agent Duncan, if I were your little sister, would you be saying the same thing?"

He gazed back steadily. "If you were my little sister, you wouldn't be in this mess, and you sure as hell wouldn't be stripping for a living. You might think about what kind of future you want for yourself before choosing sides, Ms. Mancuso."

With that, he put her bag of belongings back in her hand, took her arm and hauled her down the hall and out into the reception area where Conner Rothchild was waiting.

Why, the arrogant bastard! She'd never been so—

"Everything okay?" Conner asked, eyeing the two of them. Vera was so mad she didn't trust herself to answer. Who knew what would come flying out of her mouth, landing her in even worse trouble?

"Just peachy," Duncan said, and unceremoniously handed her arm over to Conner, like a recalcitrant child turned over to her father for disciplining. "Make sure you know where she is at all times, Rothchild. If I were you, I wouldn't let her out of your sight."

"I'm sure we'll come to an understanding," Conner said, his face registering wary surprise.

"Just don't forget our agreement," Duncan admonished him, then without another word, he turned and stalked off.

"Okay, then," Conner said when he was gone. "What was *that* all about?"

She didn't know why she was so upset. This sort of thing

happened all the time, whenever anyone outside the business found out what she did for a living. She could call herself an exotic dancer all she liked. To everyone else she'd always be a stripper. She should be used to the disdain by now. But it still hurt every darn time.

"He doesn't approve of me," she muttered.

The lawyer frowned. "He said that?"

Some people could be so righteous and judgmental. They had no clue about the vicious cycle of poverty a woman could so easily fall into. She was one of the lucky ones who'd found a way out. Or at least a way to stay above water.

She sighed. *Get over it, girl.* "No. He said I should trust you."

"Well, you should," Conner said, brows furrowing. He glanced after the FBI agent. "Listen, if he said anything inappropriate, I'll go back in there and—"

"No, please—" She reached out to stop him…and got the shock of her life. The second she touched him, a spill of tingling pleasure coursed from her fingers—her *ring* finger to be exact—down her arm and through her torso, straight to her center.

She gasped.

He looked just as stunned.

She jerked her hand back. Too late. A flood of emotions washed through her. Not just physical desire, though God knew that came through strong and clear, but also a disconcerting mix of tenderness and trust. And…a kind of soul-deep recognition. That this man was *her* man. The man she'd been waiting for all her life. Her Prince Charming.

She swallowed heavily. Okay, so yikes. It was official. She'd totally lost her mind.

If only he'd stop staring at her like that. Like she had two heads or something.

"I'll take you home," he said abruptly.

"No," she said. "I can take a cab."

"Don't be ridiculous."

He put a hand to the small of her back and ushered her out the front entrance and into the night nearly as quickly as Duncan had dragged her through the field office's brightly lit inner corridors. Conner must have changed his mind about her, too. That was quick. Maybe that jolt knocked some sense into him. Too bad it hadn't for her. More like the opposite. He kept getting more and more attractive every minute that went by.

The shimmering heat of the Las Vegas nighttime enveloped her as she stepped into it, calming as always. It tamed the shivering in her chest and limbs. Filled her lungs with sage-scented comfort, like on long-ago evenings spent in her mama's lap in an old secondhand rocker in a tiny patch of garden behind their mobile home.

"Please," she said when they hit the parking lot. "Slow down. These shoes aren't really meant for walking in." Or maybe her knees still needed to recover from that Prince Charming nonsense.

He halted, glancing down at her four-inch-heeled glass slippers, which sparkled back at him in the reflected streetlamps.

Ah, jeez. The symbolism was just too damn perfect. She felt herself going beet red in embarrassment.

"Really, th-thanks for your assistance," she stammered, "but I'd prefer to take a cab home."

She turned toward the fenced perimeter and the street beyond and realized with a sinking feeling that taxis would be few and far between in this neighborhood, even during daylight hours. And it must be three in the morning by now. She'd have to go back inside and have them call—

Suddenly she found herself swept up in Conner's arms, her wrist looped around his neck.

"Hey! What are you doing?"

"Kick them off."

"Huh?"

"The shoes. Lose them. They're ludicrous."

"And expensive! No way!"

He made a face. "Lord, you're stubborn."

She mirrored it right back. "God, you're obnoxious."

They glared at each other for a moment.

"Fine," Conner said. "Keep the damn shoes."

"Thank you, I will. Now if you'll please put me down."

He actually snorted at her. "Can't you just accept my help gracefully?"

Before she had a chance to respond, he was carrying her toward a midnight-blue convertible sports car sitting in the first slot of the parking lot. It was the most dazzling car she'd ever seen in her life. And totally intimidating. Low, sleek, catlike in grace and Transformer-like in technology. It had to have cost more than she earned in a year. Or two. His hand moved and a couple of beeps sounded. The two car doors rose up like the wings of a giant bird.

"Holy moly. What is this, the Batmobile?"

"No, a Mercedes-Benz SLR McLaren Roadster." He lowered her into the passenger seat. She sank down into the buttery leather and it hugged her backside like a lover spooning her body. Softly firm and enveloping. "You don't like it?"

"It's, um…" Luxurious. Flashy and unreasonably sexy, like its owner. Totally out of her league. Like its owner. "Nice."

"Nice, huh?" He gave her a lopsided grin as he dropped down to sit on his heels next to her car door. He pulled the seat belt over her lap, leaned over and fought with the airy poofs of her faux wedding dress for a moment finding the socket to snap it into.

She heard the click. But his arms stayed lost in the volu-

minous folds of the gossamer fabric. Almost like he was
looking for something else. His fingers suddenly touched her
legs. A shiver of unwilling excitement shimmered through her
body. Under the white silk skirt she was still only wearing her
thigh-high stockings and a G-string. If he wanted, he could
slip his hands up under and touch her. For one crazy second
she almost opened her legs to let him.

Good grief, what was *wrong* with her?

Instead, his hands glided down her calves. Slowly. Deliberately. As though he were memorizing every inch of the
descent. Her heart pounded. When he reached her ankles he
paused, then wrapped his fingers around her crystalline shoes
and tugged them off.

With a flick of his wrist they sailed into the narrow space
behind the driver's seat. "There. That's better."

She couldn't decide if she felt more outraged, or breathlessly aroused. "Do you manhandle all your clients like this,
Mr. Rothchild?"

"Only the ones who need handling," he said with a completely unrepentant smile. He came around and slid behind
the wheel. "And it's Conner."

"Not if you're my lawyer, it isn't."

"What, because I'm your attorney we can't be friends?"

She searched his eyes. Which were the exact color of the
morning desert, she noticed for the first time. A morning
desert in the springtime, when the landscape was at its most
beautiful. Falcon brown with flecks of rich green. Surrounded
by long, dark lashes, and a sensual tilt to arched brows that
matched his movie-star-perfect brown hair.

He was dazzling.

And so colossally out of her universe it made her stomach
do crazy somersaults.

His smile widened. "I'll take that as a yes, we can."

Huh?

The engine revved and they took off, were waved through the FBI guard post and drove out onto the street. As they gained speed, the billowing skirt of the wedding dress fluttered up around her shoulders, filling the open convertible.

The night was dark and desert-warm, the winking lights of the Strip just ahead. Rusty mountains ringed the city, sometimes a cozy cocoon that circled the city in its own private haven, sometimes menacing omnipresent watchers of the multitude of sins that went down there in Vegas.

But for now, the bright lights reigned supreme, shiny and colorful, lending the city its famous carnival atmosphere.

As soon as they reached downtown, it started—the honking horns and the shouts and thumbs-up. Tourists waved and whistled. Obviously everyone thought she and Conner were newlyweds, coming straight from some outlandish Las Vegas wedding chapel with a preacher dressed as Elvis or some other zany impersonator.

She wanted to sink right through the soft leather seat and disappear forever. "Damn. I should have changed clothes," she said, chagrined. "Sorry."

Conner waved back to a blue-haired old lady walking with an equally old guy in a pair of screamingly loud plaid shorts. "Don't be. Haven't had this much fun since I drove the UNLV homecoming queen around the football field at halftime."

Figured he did that.

Probably dated her, too.

Probably last year.

Damn.

"How old are you, anyway?" she asked, suddenly irrationally, absurdly and completely inappropriately jealous.

The flashing neon lights of the Strip glinted back at her from his eyes as he smiled. "Thirty-three. You?"

"Twenty-four." Her mouth turned down. "Obviously a little too old for you."

He chuckled. "More like a little too young. I generally prefer my women older, more experienced. Fewer misunderstandings that way."

Red alert, girl. Well. At least he was honest about it. "I'm sure."

"That's a bad thing?"

She sank farther into the seat and scowled. "Not at all. Very considerate of you not to break all those young, impressionable hearts flinging themselves at you. I suspect you could do some genuine damage."

"Hmm. Sounds like you've had yours broken by some insensitive older guy."

The lawyer was too perceptive by half. She shrugged as casually as she could manage. Her heart was none of his damned business.

"I apologize on behalf of all older men," he said. "The jerk must have been a real idiot."

"Which one?" she muttered.

"Ouch." Somehow his hand found hers in the folds of her dress and squeezed it. "Every last one of them."

Their eyes met, and again that weird feeling sifted through her. Part longing, part relief, part visceral hope.

Totally insane.

She pulled her hand away. As seductions went, his technique was pretty low-key. But pretty darn effective. And very dangerous. Already she was wondering what it would feel like to be curled up in his arms, warm and replete after making love to him. To have those amazing feelings of tender belonging she'd gotten just a glimpse of, as they lay skin-to-skin and…

And heaven help her.

He stopped at the red light at Flamingo Road, just up the block from the faux Eiffel Tower. A clutch of tipsy tourists tumbled across the street in front of them. Naturally, the whole group noticed her white dress and started to cheer and clap.

"Kiss the bride!" one of them shouted. Soon they were all whistling and yelling, "Kiss her! Kiss her!"

He turned to grin at her.

Oh. No.

"Don't you dare even *think* ab—"

But his lips were already on hers. Warm. Firm. Tasting of sin and forever. She sucked in a breath of shock as his tongue touched hers, and he took the opening in bold invitation. His hand slid behind her neck and tugged her closer. His other arm banded around her, pulling her upper body tight against him. His tongue invaded her mouth, his fingers held her fast for a deep, lingering kiss the likes of which she'd never, ever experienced.

Oh. No.

The cheers of the onlookers faded as the world around them spun away. Wow. The man could *really* kiss. She was light-headed, dizzy with the taste of him and the feel of his body so close to hers. She couldn't help but want more. She wanted to crawl up into his lap and hold him tight and never let him go.

All too soon his lips lifted and the blaring of car horns and wolf whistles all around invaded her consciousness. She moaned. Unsure if it was the loss of his nearness or the reality of her immense stupidity that made the desperate sound escape her throat.

Oh, what had she done?

And, damn it, now he had that look on his face again. Like she was some kind of apparition or two-headed monster he couldn't quite believe he'd just kissed.

Nope, she sighed, as a slash of hurt ripped her heart once

again. Nothing quite so dramatic. Just an ordinary exotic dancer…make that *stripper*…from the wrong side of the tracks.

Way to go, Mancuso.

He revved the engine, and the car leaped forward. It took about three excruciating minutes to reach her gated apartment complex, where he zoomed into the underground garage and squealed into her parking spot. She was still too flustered and mortified to wonder how he'd known her address—or which slot was hers. He'd only opened his mouth again to confirm that she still lived with Darla. He shut off the engine and the headlights. The dim overhead garage fluorescents flickered and hummed.

She struggled to get the seat belt unfastened but naturally her fingers refused to work. Mentally she scrambled to prepare her Don't-Worry-I've-Already-Forgotten-It-Happened speech when he came around, reached in and unsnapped the belt. Then once again she was swept up in his arms.

"Conner!" she squeaked, clutching her bag of belongings to her chest uncertainly. "I can walk by myself!"

"Not with those ridiculous shoes, you can't. Pure instruments of torture." He looked down at her, an inscrutable look on his face. "Believe it or not, I *am* a gentleman."

His tempting, downturned mouth was dangerously close.

No.

No.

No.

The man had horrified himself by kissing her. Clearly, he didn't want her. She was *so* not going to embarrass herself even further.

He saved her the decision by looking away. And strode through the dark garage toward the lighted elevator without giving her a chance to protest. Her dress billowed. Her heart thundered. He didn't look like he wanted to seduce her. He looked like he wanted to devour her alive. And not in a good way.

The elevator whooshed open, and he carried her into it. He pressed the correct button for her floor—the penthouse, of course. Nothing but the best for Darla.

Darla, who wouldn't be home to run interference for her tonight. Was that why he'd asked?

Oh, great.

She was all on her own. To fend off this overpowering attraction for the most inappropriate man alive. Or…to let him in to break her heart.

She had to get a grip. Fast.

She was just under some weird, arrest-induced erotic spell. This wasn't like her. Not at all. She didn't do flings, or men she'd just met. She didn't even do men she knew well. How could she consider making such a fool of herself over this one who obviously didn't—

"Key," he broke into her chaotic thoughts before they reached the top floor. You couldn't get off at the penthouse without a special key. Naturally, he'd know that.

She juggled her purse out from the bag. Except—

"This isn't my purse. It's Darla's." Her sister must have grabbed the wrong one in her haste to get out of the club.

"Does she have a key?" he asked, his voice deep and dark. Something in his tone sent a shiver tripping down her spine.

She looked up at him. His eyes were smoldering. She faltered and dropped the belongings bag, but managed to hang on to the purse. What was going on here?

"Yes," she stammered, fumbling through its contents. "I—I th-think so."

"Let me have it."

Her pulse jumped a mile. "Conner," she managed, digging out the key and handing it to him. "You're not planning to come in, are you?"

"What do you think?"

He really didn't want to know what she was thinking…

"Please. This is really not a good idea."

"No damn kidding," he shot back. But then his mouth was on hers and she couldn't turn him away if her life depended on it. She moaned in surprise, opening herself to him, and wound her arms around his neck. This was *so* not a good idea. He swung her down so she was sitting on his forearm, and her legs instinctively wrapped around his waist.

The elevator doors opened, and they kissed madly, all the way across the square marble foyer to the penthouse entrance. Her back slammed up against it, and a moment later the door swung open and he followed the solid wood around with her, keeping her back pressed up to it as he devoured her mouth.

The sound of Velcro ripping apart was followed by a whoosh of cool air on her legs and bottom. A billow of white floated to the floor. Another rip and her breakaway top joined it. He groaned, pulling away to look at her spilling out of her lace corset, then his hands found her bare flesh.

They kissed and kissed, and he touched her everywhere. They ground their bodies together in a frenzy of desire. His fingers slid between her legs and parted her blossoming folds. She cried out as he found the center of her need and touched her there.

"That's right, give it to me," he whispered into her mouth. His fingers circled, driving a moan from her. "I want it all."

"Conner," she cried. "Please, I— Nhh…"

It was no use. He was too skilled, too perfect, and she was too aroused to stop the tidal wave of pleasure that crashed over her. She arched, her body shuddering over the edge, and surrendered to the sensation.

He drew it out as long as it would go, playing her flesh like a professional gambler caressed his cards.

By the time he let her slide to her feet, she was trembling

so hard she could hardly see straight. So at first she didn't even notice.

But when he demanded huskily, "Where's your bedroom?" and they turned into the living room, both of them halted dead in their tracks.

The place was in a complete shambles.

"Omigod," she whispered, barely catching her breath.

Someone had broken in. And ransacked the apartment.

On the wall, big sloppy letters had been scrawled in bright red paint.

GIVE IT BACK BITCH OR YOU'LL DIE NEXT.

Chapter 6

Conner took one look at the destruction in front of him and instantly visions of Candace's murder scene slammed through his brain. The wreckage. Her pale face lying in a stain of blood.

Oh, no, please not another victim.

He grabbed Vera and whisked her back out the door and pushed her against the foyer wall.

"Don't move," he admonished as he whipped out his cell phone and Lex Duncan's card from his pocket. "Someone may still be in there." Like Darla. Sprawled dead on the floor as Candace had been. Though he hadn't seen any blood or body in the quick visual scan he'd done. Thank God.

Vera looked like a deer caught in the headlights. "Someone like who?" she asked in a strangled croak, grasping his suit jacket sleeve with both hands.

"Whoever did this," he answered, punching buttons on the phone and trying not to think about what he'd just done with those same fingers. What he'd been *about* to do with them. *Damn.*

"Duncan."

"It's Conner Rothchild. Vera and Darla's place has been broken into," he told the FBI agent. "It looks bad."

Duncan swore. "Darla?"

"Not here that I could see."

"Exit the apartment and wait for me outside," he ordered, then hung up.

"I don't understand," Vera said, her voice cracking. Her eyes filled as he pulled her fully into his arms. "Why would anyone write something that horrible on my wall? Give *what* back?"

"I'm not sure," he said. Though he knew damn well. Silver had received a nearly identical message scrawled on her mirror about being the next one to die—just before someone maliciously brought a scaffolding down on her head. That someone must still be after the Tears of the Quetzal. And didn't know it was now in FBI custody. Until the culprit was found, Vera could be in danger.

Conner gathered her up in his arms again, heading for the elevator. "Let's get you away from here."

For a second she looked like she wanted to object. But then she just put her arms around him and clung to him. Not in a sexual way—despite the fact that she was nearly naked and just moments ago had all but given herself to him—but like a frightened woman would hold a man who made her feel safe.

His stomach roiled into a clot of opposing emotions. Anger at whoever had done this. And a strange, completely alien sense of wanting to protect her from all harm.

Okay, that and a gnawing sense of panic.

Something was going on deep inside him, in his heart, that he did not understand. Did not need. Definitely did not want.

The elevator opened and he swept in, pushed the button for the ground floor.

"Vera," he said. "I know you didn't want me as your lawyer, but I'm hoping you trust me as a friend, after—" He stopped, suddenly feeling awkward. Damn. If not for the break-in, they'd be in bed by now, naked, and he'd be deep inside her. Making love. He was still aroused, still aching for relief. Still wanting her like she was the last woman on earth and he hadn't had sex for at least a decade.

He cleared his throat. "In light of…what happened between us, I'll be turning over your case to my assistant in the morning. Meanwhile, I hope you believe I have your interests as my top priority in this incident."

For once she didn't argue. She bit her lip and nodded. It obviously hadn't occurred to her that her sister might be inside hurt—or worse. He didn't intend to enlighten her. But there were also other issues at hand.

"Here's the thing. The FBI is on its way. Vera, think hard. If there's anything, any reason at all, they shouldn't go into your apartment, you need to tell me now. Before they arrive."

She gazed up at him, her green eyes wide and uncomprehending. Man, she was guileless. Did that mean his instincts were right about her?

"You mean…like drugs or something?" she asked.

Again he cleared his throat, not understanding why it was so damn important to him that she be innocent. "For example, yeah."

She continued to worry her lip. "Um. Darla might not want them in her room. There could be…some illegal substances."

He nodded. No shock there. "They'll probably look the other way on that, this time. Anything else?"

"Like…?"

"Did Duncan tell you any of his suspicions about your sister?" he asked carefully.

"Suspicions of what?"

Okay, apparently not. "I'm not really sure how much I should be revealing to you, but since you're still my client, I feel I should be up-front and warn you. That ring you were wearing isn't the only thing Darla is suspected of stealing. There may be more."

"Stolen jewelry?" she asked, her jaw dropping. "That's not possible. Darla is rich! An heiress. Why would she ever…" Vera's words trickled to a stop.

He gazed down at her. "Could it be true? Because if the FBI finds stolen goods in your apartment, it could get really ugly."

"I don't know," she said worriedly. "Really. I wouldn't have thought so, but…Darla is… Well, sometimes she gets these crazy ideas. For thrills, she says. Or to get back at our father. For his neglect. I suppose…" She looked miserable. "I suppose it could be true. I just don't know. But I don't think anything would be kept here. I would know."

"Fair enough." The elevator doors opened and suddenly he remembered what she was wearing…or rather, *not* wearing. He was about to slip off his jacket to give her when he realized the bag of belongings she'd dropped on the ride up was still lying in the corner of the elevator.

He grabbed it and pressed it into her hands. "Here. Better get dressed before someone sees you."

"Oh, jeez," she said, glancing down at herself. "Not exactly street attire."

More's the pity. He admired how she was so totally comfortable in her own bare skin. The women he knew would be dying of embarrassment to be seen like this in public, every last one, convinced their bodies were too fat or too skinny or had some other terrible imagined flaw, making them unduly self-conscious. Women could have such hang-ups about their self-image. It was refreshing to be around one who so obviously liked how she looked.

She quickly pulled on the jeans and T-shirt. He forced himself to concentrate. "You stay down here in the lobby and wait for Duncan. I'll go back to the apartment and take a quick look around. If there's anything that shouldn't be found, I'll deny him permission to search there. Okay?"

Fear leaped into her eyes. "You're leaving me alone? Why can't I go with you?"

"Just in case," he said, and she looked even more panicked. "Don't worry, you'll be fine. Duncan will get here in a few minutes." Unable to help himself, he bent down and kissed her. The taste of her lips swirled on his tongue, and a painful ache of arousal swept through him again. *Too good.* He pulled away.

"Conner, wait," she began. She glanced down at his mouth, and then his body, and something shifted in her expression. Uh-oh, trouble ahead. "I, um, don't—"

He put a finger to her lips. "Shh. We'll talk later, all right? I've got to go up."

She nodded reluctantly. "What if someone's up there with a gun?" she asked nervously.

"Anyone's probably long gone," he assured her, then led her out of the elevator, gave her a last kiss and got back on.

Watching him unhappily, she wrapped her arms around her middle. "Please, be careful."

He smiled, touched by the sincere worry in her eyes. "Count on it."

Once up in the apartment, he was able to give the whole penthouse a cursory search before the FBI showed up. No Darla, thank heaven. Nothing else out of the ordinary was visible in the piles of debris left by the break-in or in any of the bedrooms, either, so granting Duncan and his CSI techs access would not compromise his client.

He took one last look around. If the place hadn't been such a mess, it would have been really nice. If nothing else, Darla had good taste. At least in interior decorating. In friends and lifestyle, maybe not so much.

Of course, an exotic dancer would normally be included in his general condemnation. In the Las Vegas legal community, aside from his take-no-prisoners ruthlessness in the courtroom, Conner was known for a generous pro bono policy toward the homeless, drug addicts and sex workers. But he'd never considered them his equals in any sense of the word. His family would disown him if they even suspected he was considering a serious liaison with a stripper…even if she was the illegitimate daughter of billionaire Maximillian St. Giles.

Hell, *especially* if she was the illegitimate daughter of Maximillian St. Giles. Or any other woman not in his social class or better. The key word there was *illegitimate*. His father had given Uncle Harold a lifetime of grief for marrying beneath him. More than once. Conner had no intention of repeating that mistake and lowering his father's respect for him. Or giving his blue-blood family any reason to question Conner's loyalty to their highbrow ideals, even if he thought they were at times silly and sometimes destructive.

He'd seen firsthand what those kind of elitist notions could do to families. Look at Candace. He was convinced she'd still be alive today if she hadn't been summarily dismissed from the family fold after marrying Jack Cortland, the druggie rock-star boy. Those two poor kids of hers. God only knew what would become of them without the support of family, with only a questionable father to raise them, stuck out on some ranch in the middle of nowhere.

Anyway. Under all the broken glassware and china, disheveled books and shelf items and knife-slit, unstuffed cushions and furniture, Conner recognized a beautiful living space, subtly sophisticated and timelessly chic. He didn't know why that surprised him, but it did. Pleasantly so. *Some* of Darla's wealthy upbringing must have rubbed off on her, after all.

He gave a wry sigh. That probably explained why she'd gone after the Tears of the Quetzal. The ring was the classiest piece of jewelry he'd ever laid eyes on. And now it had passed from Vera's finger straight into FBI custody. Forget about retrieving it any time soon. *That* place was like Fort Knox. Uncle Harold was not going to be pleased.

The sound of the elevator approaching pulled Conner back to the situation at hand. He went out to the foyer and met Special Agent Duncan as he exited the lift, followed by two other men in white jumpsuits carrying CSI cases. Vera popped out like a nervous jack-in-the-box.

"Are you okay?" she asked him before Duncan could open his mouth. "Did you see anyone? Any more messages written on the walls? Talk to me!"

"Whoa, slow down," he admonished gently and put an arm around her shoulder. "No more graffiti. No sign of the intruders," he told Duncan, and gave a surreptitious shake of his head at the agent's silent query about Darla.

Duncan looked relieved, then gave Conner's protective arm a brief, disapproving frown.

"Not that it's any of your business," Conner said to stave off any comments, "but I'm turning over Vera's case to an associate so there's no conflict of interest."

Duncan's frown deepened as he signaled the CSI techs to proceed into the penthouse to get started. "That wasn't part of our deal," he said.

"What deal?" Vera asked.

"Nothing's changed," Conner assured him. "Can we just—"

"What deal?" Vera asked again, more insistently. She turned under his arm to look up at him.

"Never mind—"

Duncan addressed her. "For your release."

"What about it?" she asked, eyes narrowing.

Damn. *So* not good.

"Rothchild agreed to help us bring Darla St. Giles into custody. He promised to call us when she contacts you."

Ah, hell.

Shock went through her expression. She stepped away from him angrily. "Oh, really. What makes you think she'll contact me? And even if she does, what makes you think I'll tell you? How dare you! What would make you agree to such a thing?" Her voice was getting louder and louder.

"Vera, please believe me, it was for your own good."

"My own *good?*" she spat out. "Are you *kidding* me? Betraying my sister?"

"He's right," Duncan interjected stonily. "You were apprehended with the Rothchild's diamond on your finger. Until it can be established exactly how it got there, *you* are our—"

"Wait just a cotton-picking minute!" Her expression went even more furious. She glared at Conner. "The *Rothchild's* diamond? That was *your* ring?"

He was in *such* deep trouble. "My family's, yes. But—"

She looked like he had slapped her across the face. Hard. "And you were going to tell me this little detail *when?*"

"Vera, who the ring belongs to is not what's important here."

"My God, Conner! If *that's* not a conflict of interest, I don't know what is! And you expect me to trust you? What else are you lying to me about?"

It was his turn to be indignant. "That's not fair. I never lied to you."

"I may not be some rich, fancy-schmancy lawyer, but even I know what lying by omission means," she ground out. "And to think I—" Her mouth snapped shut, and she squeezed her eyes closed.

He fisted his hands on his hips, ignoring the all-too-personal dig. "Do you recall in the club when I said I had information about your sister? I was going to tell you then, but was interrupted when…let's see…oh, yeah, you got *arrested!*"

"Speaking of which." Duncan stepped between them. "Why exactly were you at the Diamond Lounge in the first place, Rothchild? Quite a coincidence, wouldn't you say?" The FBI agent's tone was neutral, but his meaning was unmistakable.

Conner tamped down on his quickly rising hackles. Forced himself into composed, professional lawyer mode. "Are you by any chance asking me for an alibi?" he asked coolly. "For this?" He swept a hand toward the mess in the apartment.

Duncan lifted a shoulder. "It occurs to me that a Rothchild would have the strongest motive to search Miss St. Giles's home. Missing family heirloom, and all. And you being convinced she stole it." He looked smug. "It would also explain your presence at the Diamond Lounge. You didn't find the ring when you searched the apartment and Darla had disappeared, so you took a chance her sister might know where she went."

Damn. It all sounded *far* too plausible.

Except it was all bull, and Duncan knew it. They both knew whoever did this was the same person who'd stalked and almost killed Silver. And possibly Candace. But, okay, he played along.

"Just one thing wrong with your theory," Conner said evenly. "I had no idea Darla had a sister. Oh, and the fact that I *do* have an alibi. I was working another case. The Parker case, if you want to call my firm. I spent the whole afternoon asking questions of the dancers up and down the Strip. At least a couple hundred witnesses, plus video surveillance, I'm sure. The Diamond Lounge was my next stop." He held up a hand. "And, yes, I do have a checked-off list to prove it. Thank you. Thank you very much."

At least Duncan cracked a smile. Vera was still glaring at Conner.

"Okay," Duncan said. "I'll get that checked out, but I believe you're telling the truth. Meanwhile, I still have the problem of Ms. Mancuso. Because if *you* didn't do the break-in…"

Conner nodded. "It was most likely the same guy who's been after the ring since it disappeared from Candace's hand the night she died."

Duncan nodded, too. "A thief whom Darla seems to have double-crossed. And since the FBI now has the ring in its custody—"

"He didn't find it in his search. And since Darla has disappeared—"

"He'll be looking for Ms. Mancuso next, thinking she knows where to find her sister, and therefore the ring."

Vera had been watching the back-and-forth like a spectator at a tennis match, but now she finally caught on with a gasp. "Are you saying…I could be in danger?"

"Did you *read* the message he left on the wall?" Conner queried.

"This man has already gone on the attack for the ring," Duncan said. "Don't take any chances with your safety."

"So what am I supposed to do?"

"Ms. Mancuso was released into your recognizance, Rothchild." Duncan turned to remind him. "And the terms of her bail still stand. But if you prefer, I'll take her back into custody. I can't risk losing my only suspect. In any manner."

"What? Hold on!" Vera exclaimed. "His recognizance or police custody? There has to be a door number three here."

"I respect your dilemma, Ms. Mancuso," the agent said. "But the only reason you are not in a cell right now is because of Mr. Rothchild's spotless reputation as an attorney and his formidable social standing in the community. I've already stretched the law as far as I'm willing to go in that regard. He stays with you or you come with me."

There was a pregnant pause, the silence in the marble foyer only broken by the sounds of the CSI techs' cameras clicking inside the apartment.

"Fine," she said at length, but obviously mad as a hornet. "I'll move a futon for him out into the vestibule." She rounded on Conner. "You can set it up in front of the elevator so there's no way I—or anyone else—can slip past—"

His brows shot up. *Excuse me?* He shoved aside the insult. "You *want* to stay in a ransacked apartment?"

"Like I have a choice?" she fired back.

"Sorry," Duncan interrupted. "Not possible. No one's allowed into the apartment until the techs are finished processing for trace and fingerprints. That'll take at least a few hours."

"She'll stay at my place," Conner said through clamped teeth, ready to strangle the woman. A freakin' futon? He didn't *think* so.

She opened her mouth to protest but he nipped it. "I have plenty of room. And can provide an armed guard," he added pointedly.

"Good," Duncan said, passing Conner his notebook. "Write down the address and phone number."

Almost sputtering, she crossed her arms over her ample chest. Sending an untimely reminder through his body that he was still more than half-aroused. But her vehement, "I am *not* going anywhere with you," jerked him right out of his momentary hormonal stupor.

Which probably made him point out more sharply than

strictly necessary, "I happen to know you have no money and nowhere else to go." He ignored her gasp and went on, "And if you think I'm paying for a hotel when I have ten bedrooms sitting empty at my house, you're dead wrong."

She blinked and her eyes shuttered. He realized too late he'd reacted like a defense attorney, trampling her objections like a charging rhino. And he'd hurt her.

Well, too damn bad. She'd hurt him first.

He pushed out a calming breath, chagrined at his childish outburst.

God.

Was he actually whining like a two-year-old?

"I'm sorry," he said gruffly. "That was a thoughtless and unnecessary remark. But the reality is, it's my house or jail."

She looked like a Nile cat chased into a tree by that charging rhino. Angry. Cornered. But undefeated. "In that case," she said with chin held high, "I'll take jail."

Chapter 7

Vera stared up at the stunning mansion in front of her.

Holy mackerel.

The rising sun was just peeking over the desert horizon, spreading a magical spill of golden light over the soft coral-colored adobe walls and arches of the Southwest-inspired manor house and surrounding lush green lawns and gardens.

"You live here?" she asked her jailer. *"Alone?"*

They were the first words she'd spoken to Conner Biggest-Bully-in-the-Universe Rothchild since she'd grudgingly hunched into the passenger seat of his ridiculously ostentatious car to be driven here. To his house. Where he lived.

How she'd let herself get talked into going *anywhere* with the lying jerk, let alone his own home, she'd never know.

Okay, not true. It was the work of the usual catch-22: absence of money, family or personal influence.

Story of her life.

"Alone, yes. But I have a lot of friends who visit," he answered her rhetorical question.

She just bet he did.

Never mind that ninety-eight percent of the women in the state of Nevada would kill to take her place. Or that *Las Vegas Magazine*'s official Most Eligible Bachelor was undoubtedly the sexiest, most attractive man breathing on this earth. Vera knew very well when she was outclassed, outplayed and miles out of her comfort zone. About ten-and-a-half miles to be exact—the distance between the mobile home park where she'd grown up and Conner Rothchild's sprawling, multimillion-dollar neighborhood.

No, Vera Mancuso had no freaking business being in this place, with this man.

"Must be nice," she responded as he drove through the ten-foot-tall iron security gate, which closed automatically behind the car. "And you have a lot of family, too, from what I hear. Quite the Las Vegas dynasty, the Rothchilds."

"Don't believe everything you read in the tabloids," he said, pulling to a stop under the entry's porte cochere.

"I don't," she assured him. "My information comes straight from the horse's mouth."

"Oh?" He gave her a mildly curious hike of an eyebrow as he opened the car door for her and helped her out.

"Darla was good friends with your cousins Candace and Silver. I still have lunch with Silver occasionally."

"Ah."

She stopped suddenly and turned back to his car. Before leaving the apartment, the CSI techs had packed her a small overnight bag, including a pair of flip-flops, but she needed her stage shoes for work tonight. They were still behind the seat where he'd tossed them back at FBI headquarters. "I'd like my shoes back, please. From last night."

"Of course." He leaned over the side of the car to fish them out.

Oh, boy.

His suit pants stretched over his tight backside, revealing every luscious dip and muscle of that tasty bit of anatomy. She had to stuff her hands under her armpits to keep from touching.

He handed her the glasslike shoes with a wry smile. "Don't lose one, Cinderella," he teased.

She made a face and snatched them from his hand. "You know, she talked about you all the time. Your cousin Candace."

"Did she, now." He took her overnight bag and led her up the mansion's sweeping front steps.

"She didn't like you very much."

"Now there's a shock." He did something with his key chain, and the ornately carved entry door swung open.

"She said you're mean, stubborn and ruthless and will do anything to get your clients off."

"Never a good thing in a lawyer," he said dryly. "After you."

She met his amused gaze, so strong and confident. Not to mention devoid of shadiness or deceit. With a sinking feeling she suddenly knew Candace was completely wrong about him.

She shouldn't be surprised. The rivalry between the Rothchild family cousins was legendary in Vegas, where each sought to outdo the other in glamour, media notoriety and wild living. Conner was no exception. He regularly figured in the gossip columns.

But Vera, of all people, was acutely aware that a public image did not always reflect the real person. Although she got along with Candace okay, and Darla adored her, Candace always did have a family ax to grind.

"Touché," Vera acknowledged, thinking just maybe *she'd* been wrong about Conner, too.

Not good. She did *not* want to like this man. Bad enough

she was so hopelessly attracted to him physically. How depressing would it be to have him turn out to be honorable and principled, too?

He ushered her in. "Welcome to my home."

Said the spider to the fly.

"Wow," she murmured, stepping into a stunning showplace of glossy, contemporary elegance. Clutching her shoes in her hand, she walked from the soaring foyer into a grand salon and did a slow three-sixty, totally awestruck. She'd decorated Darla's penthouse because when she'd moved in it had white walls and hotel furniture, and she'd been darn proud of the results. But this…this was utterly gorgeous. "Nice place," she managed.

He chuckled. "Apparently I live for nice."

Just then, an older woman in a fuzzy robe hurried into the room. "Oh, Mr. Conner, sir! I didn't expect you back tonight."

"Sorry to wake you so early, Hildy," he said in warm apology. "This is Vera. She'll be spending a few days with me."

Days?

"Certainly, sir."

The housekeeper didn't even bat an eyelash. Obviously not unusual for her employer to bring home women at the crack of dawn and announce they'd be spending more than one night chez Conner. Vera ground her teeth. Well, what did she expect?

"Will you be needing anything, sir? Coffee, or…?" Hildy asked.

"No, nothing, thanks. Just sleep." He handed her Vera's overnight bag, and the woman turned to go.

"Uh," Vera interjected before it was too late, "by 'with me' what Mr. Rothchild really meant was 'here.' As in 'here,' but in a separate bedroom. And 'here,' but as far away as possible from where he sleeps." She pasted on a smile.

This time Hildy did blink. And glanced at Conner for confirmation.

His mouth quirked. "As the lady says. You can put her in the guest cabana. That should be far enough away."

Hildy's eyes met hers for a split second, and Vera could have sworn the older lady was holding back a smirk. Vera wondered idly if she'd just joined the ranks of Too-Stupid-To-Live, or Girl Folk Hero....

"Oh, well. I need the sleep anyway," he said philosophically when the housekeeper had gone. "You'll like the cabana. It's very private out there. But don't get any bright ideas about escaping. I was serious about the armed guard. I've already called the security company."

She didn't know whether to be insulted or flattered. "Don't worry. I took Agent Duncan's warning to heart."

Before leaving the penthouse, the FBI man had cautioned her against going anywhere alone, or without Conner's permission, for her own safety. After finding out about the connection between the stolen ring and the murder of Candace Rothchild and attack on Silver Rothchild, the whole 'Give it back or you'll die next bitch' thing was plenty to convince Vera not to take any chances.

"I don't know why you didn't just let Duncan put me in jail," she said without thinking.

Then she remembered.

Whoops. Yeah, she did know. Because Conner'd expected to have sex with her, that's why. Which would surely have happened had it not been for the timely interruption of the break-in and the subsequent revelations into his motives for seeking her out in the first place.

She'd so totally lost her mind in that elevator. Thank God she'd found it since.

More or less.

Though being reminded of the delicious things he'd done to her during her temporary insanity wasn't helping.

She looked up and realized he was gazing at her sardonically, his thoughts as transparent as hers apparently were.

"Forget it." She wagged a finger. "No bodyguard necessary. Literally or otherwise. I saw the size of the fence around this place, and the only person I'm in danger from here is you." And possibly herself.

"Only thinking of your safety," he said amenably.

"Sure you are."

Seeking a distraction, she glanced around the glamorous room, filled with the trappings of wealth, and was suddenly struck with a pang of regret. What would it be like to be part of this world, even for a few days…or nights? Would it be such a sacrifice to sleep with him, to find out?

God, no. Not in the least. The man was to die for. And she'd be using him just as much as he was using her. But…

"I'm sorry, casual sex isn't something I do." She felt the need to explain, but it came with a belated inward wince. "Embarrassing evidence to the contrary."

He smiled. "Nothing embarrassing about it. In fact, it was pretty damn hot if you ask me. For, you know, not being casual sex."

She actually felt a flush work its way up her throat to her cheeks. Good grief. When was the last time she'd blushed?

Help.

"You said something about a guest house? I really should get some sleep or I'll be a mess at work tonight." She sighed. "Assuming I still have a job."

He looked surprised. "You're going back there?"

"Hell, yeah. If the boss will let me. I have no choice, Conner. I have bills to pay. Money doesn't grow on trees." She glanced around again. "Well, for some of us anyway."

He ignored the barb and rubbed a hand over his mouth. "Okay. I guess I can do that."

"You? What do you mean?"

"So quickly they forget."

"Oh. Right." They were stuck like glue until Special Agent Duncan decided to arrest her. Which meant Conner'd have to come to the club with her.

A memory washed over her, of him sitting in the front row sipping champagne like a dissolute sultan, watching her take off every stitch of clothing. And—oh, God—how turned on she'd been. By him. By his negligent air of wealth and power. And the hungry look in his eyes as his gaze had caressed her nude body. No wonder she'd gone off like a rocket when he touched her later on.

She swallowed. "I suppose you'll insist on going with me."

"Oh, absolutely. Wouldn't miss it." He winked.

That's what she was afraid of.

That, and the nutcase who might now be after her because of that damn ring. Maybe it wasn't such a bad idea he went with her, after all.

Bad enough she'd invaded his dreams all night like some kind of teasing succubus, but even now, the next morning, sun shining, birds singing, the little witch was still torturing him. Deliberately. With malice aforethought.

Conner frowned, taking in the sight that had nearly made the tray of coffee and croissants he was carrying spill all over the Mexican patio tiles. The French doors to the cabana had been flung open. Sheer curtains billowed out from them in the hot desert breeze. Inside the dim room, the scene was straight out of one of the erotic dreams he'd been haunted by all night.

Vera. Nude. Sprawled on her stomach across her bed... Except in his dreams of course it had been *his* bed. Sheets in a tangle. Her skin moist with a sheen of sweat. Her hair in a mess as though from his fingers… Except his fingers had unfortunately been nowhere near her last night.

Seeing her like that, he'd been shocked enough that his first thought was that she was dead. Lying there brutally murdered, like his cousin Candace. The memory of that crime scene had streaked through his mind, nearly tipping the tray in his hands. Thankfully she'd stirred immediately at the sound of the rattling dishes so he knew she was okay, or he would really have lost it.

As it was, he was now close to losing it for an entirely different reason.

The woman was a sensual vision. Her hot body even sexier than in his dreams.

Easy, boy.

She'd made it clear last night she was no longer interested in sex with him. He'd honored her wishes and hadn't pushed it, although he was pretty sure he could have changed her mind with very little effort. They obviously had chemistry. Potent chemistry. And lots of it.

But this…this was unfair.

Or maybe it was an invitation? Had she gone to bed naked, hoping he would come to her?

What an idiot. He should at least have tried…

"Conner?"

He started at the sound of her throaty, sleep-muzzy voice. The dishes rattled, and he had to catch the tray for the second time to keep from dumping it.

"Yeah. It's me."

She turned over in the bed, and he gripped the tray even harder. *Pure torture.* "What have you got?"

Besides a hard-on? "Breakfast," he croaked. "Interested?"

"Mmm." Her arms rose in a languorous stretch. "Coffee, I hope?"

Lord, help him.

"Yep." He reached a nearby patio table just in time, depositing the tray on the round glass top with a clatter. After righting the cups and returning the croissants to the plate, he turned, ready to abandon all pretense and just go in and devour her, when she strolled by with another stretch, heading for the pool.

"I feel divine! Haven't slept so well in ages," she declared, pushing her mane of chestnut hair back from her face. "I love sleeping with the doors open, with the warm air and the smell of the desert. Haven't been able to do that since I sold the mobile home."

He paused, nonplussed. Okay. Obviously *not* an invitation. He grappled for a thread of conversation that didn't involve the words *condom* or *go down*. "Mobile home?" he asked.

She shot him a look, stopping at the edge of the pool and dipping a toe into it. A toe that was bare, just like the rest of her. "I grew up in the Sunnyvale Mobile Home Park, just outside of town."

He knew that. He was just momentarily brain-dead. "No air-conditioning?" he ventured.

She smiled. "No."

She executed a perfect dive into the water. He let out a long, long breath, and for a few minutes he watched her expertly cut through the water, the joy in her movements contagious. He wanted to join her in the worst way, but in a sense it would have been like some fool painting daisies into a Monet. Perfection spoiled. He forced himself onto a patio chair, peeled off his shirt because he was suddenly far too warm and poured coffee instead.

She bobbed up at the side of the pool, folding her arms along the coping. "Hope you don't mind. I couldn't resist a quick dip. We have a pool in our apartment building, but it's indoors." She wrinkled her nose as though that were a cardinal sin.

"Take all the time you like. I'm enjoying the view."

She tilted her head. "Not misinterpreting, I hope."

"I'll have to admit," he said, taking a sip of strong black coffee to jolt his mind back up where it belonged, "your...lack of inhibition did take me in a certain direction. I now stand corrected."

She smiled and lithely hoisted herself from the water and onto the deck in one fluid movement. Like Venus rising from the sea. She padded to the table with water flowing from her lightly tanned skin like drops of molten gold, and reached for his cup. She put it to her lips with eyes closed and long lashes sparkling with water droplets. He had to grip the arms of his chair to keep from surging to his feet to lick them off. Along with the rivulets trickling down her perfect breasts.

He stifled a groan.

She set the cup down on the table. "Give me a minute," she said. "I'll get dressed." Then she disappeared into the cabana.

He cleared his throat, found his voice and called after her, "Don't bother on my account!"

And he knew then if he hadn't before—which deep down he had, but up until this very moment had chosen total, blind denial. One thing was for damned certain.

He had to have her.

Really *have* her. All to himself. For a few days. A week. Maybe even a month. Long enough to explore that chatterbox mouth with its guileless smile, that amazingly sensual body and the wonderfully sassy woman inside it.

Oh, yeah. He'd have her, all right.

He'd find a way to make her want him.

And the sooner the better.

Or he might just go completely out of his mind.

Chapter 8

"I have a proposition for you."

Vera halted her coffee cup halfway to her mouth and glanced at Conner. "What kind of proposition?" she asked. Like she couldn't guess.

Frankly, she'd been expecting this. She was actually surprised he'd managed to hold out as long as he had. Nearly a whole hour. While they'd talked of her childhood, his crazy relationship with his famous cousins and what it was like to stare up at the night sky out in the vast desert and see a billion gazillion stars up there and wonder if there was any other life in the universe.

Nevertheless, disappointment sifted through her. For some unfathomable reason, she'd thought he might be different from all the other men who tried to get in her pants. She'd *hoped* he was different. He'd been lost in thought for the past few minutes, and she'd really believed he was adjusting his perception of her. Starting to see her as a whole person and not just a nude body onstage or an easy seduction in an elevator.

Oh, well.

"More like an exchange of services," he explained.

"Uh-huh."

Her expression must have betrayed her skepticism, because he rushed to say, "I'd pay you, of course."

She set down her cup very, very carefully. "For what, Conner?"

He exhaled. "You know that deal I made with Duncan for your release? Well, there was more to it than just reporting in on Darla's movements."

Okay, he'd managed to surprise her. Not that this sounded much better than some kind of sexual favor. "Like what?" she asked cautiously.

"I promised I'd help him find out about the jewel theft ring Darla's allegedly part of. Try to narrow down suspects for him."

"I told you I don't know anything about that."

"But I'd like your help investigating."

"Me?"

"I've been thinking about how much you look like Darla. It's obvious you're her sister. You could get people to talk to you. A lot easier than I could."

"But I don't know anyone involved," she said. "Who would I talk to?"

"That's what I need your help figuring out. I'll bet someone from her circle of friends is either in on the jewelry thefts or knows something about the ring of thieves doing them. You've met most of her friends, right?"

"Well. Not really. Only the ones who've been to parties at our apartment or who we've occasionally gone out with together, like to casinos or clubs. But that doesn't happen very often. And very few know I'm her sister. We've mostly passed off our resemblance just as a fun coincidence."

He tilted his head. "Really? And she didn't invite you to other people's parties? Social events? That sort of thing?"

She glanced away. To her credit, Darla *had* invited her to lots of things. Vera had even gone. Once. And stood in a corner the whole time paralyzed with feelings of inadequacy. "I don't really fit into her social stratosphere."

He regarded her for a moment. "Her evaluation or yours?"

"Mine," she admitted with a shrug. "And my father's. He threatened to disown Darla if she spread it around that he'd spawned an illegitimate child. He'd make my life hell if it got out."

"I assume you're talking about Maximillian St. Giles."

"Daddy dearest." She sighed. After twenty-four years, you'd think she'd be used to the hurt. But it still cut like a shard of glass to the heart when she thought about his categorical rejection.

"What could he possibly have against you?" Conner asked, echoing the question she'd asked herself a thousand times. Always with the same answer.

She looked back at Conner. "I take my clothes off for a living. And I suppose I remind him of his vulnerability. Or failings. Or both."

"And whose fault is all that? Not yours." He shook his head. "The man's a dolt. If I had a daughter as smart, gorgeous and determined as you, I'd be showing her off to everyone, not hiding her away like she was something to be ashamed of. I wouldn't care how she came into the world."

Vera blinked, blindsided by the sincere indignation in Conner's voice…on her behalf. No one had ever defended her honor so vehemently. No one.

She swallowed the lump that welled up in her throat. "Thanks. Too bad he's not quite as broad-minded as you are."

"That settles it," Conner said, folding his arms over his chest and surveying her with a resolute smile. "No argument. You're coming with me."

Alarm zinged up her spine. "Where?"

"The Lights of Las Vegas Charity Ball on Friday night."

He had to be kidding. The Lights of Las Vegas Charity Ball was the biggest annual charity fund-raiser in the city; everyone who was anyone went—provided you were a gazillionaire or a famous star of some sort.

"What, *me?* No! *Hell,* no. Are you nuts?"

"All of Darla's friends will be there. It's the perfect opportunity for you to ask questions. Hey!" he exclaimed with growing excitement. "Maybe the thieves are planning to work the event and we can catch them in the act."

"One small problem."

"What's that?"

"Aside from the fact that I'd never in a million years be able to pull it off, I work Friday. It's our biggest night."

He waved a hand in the air dismissively. "I'll pay you better. Name your fee."

"*And* I have nothing to wear that doesn't fasten with Velcro," she added wryly.

"With a clothes allowance."

God, so tempting. He waggled his eyebrows, and for a nanosecond she actually considered it. Then she shook her head. "I can't. Honestly. I'd be lost at one of those fancy society bashes. I wouldn't have the faintest idea what to do or how to conduct myself. People would laugh—"

He took her hand in his over the table and gazed intently at her. "Trust me, no one will laugh. Not after I'm done with you."

Her eyes widened. "What do you mean?"

"Ever see *My Fair Lady?*"

She gave him a withering smile and yanked back her hand.

"Yeah, and look what happened to Eliza Doolittle at the horse race. I rest my case."

He chuckled. "The difference being, you wouldn't need to change a single thing. Just be yourself as you ask around after Darla. Say she's disappeared and as her roommate, you're worried about her."

"I wouldn't be lying. I *am* worried."

"Good. Then you'll do it."

She pushed out a breath, still unconvinced. "What if my father shows up?"

"You leave Maximillian St. Giles to me. C'mon, Vera. Take a chance. Be Cinderella for a night. Hell, you've even got the perfect shoes."

She laughed at his handsome, open face and charmingly amused smile. And felt herself weaken.

She shouldn't.

God knew, she had no business even pretending to belong at a highbrow event like that. Let alone with a man like Conner Rothchild.

"You're wrong about Darla," she said. "If I go to that ball, it's only for one reason. To prove my sister isn't a criminal."

"Fair enough," he said. "It's a deal." He looked at her triumphantly. "So, when can we go shopping?"

Silk. Satin. Lace. Bamboo, for crying out loud. When had they started making clothes out of bamboo, anyway?

Vera had never felt so uncomfortable in her life. Not even the first time she'd gone onstage at that seedy titty bar five years ago and taken off every stitch in front of a pack of drooling men had she felt this vulnerable. At least onstage *she* was in control.

"Utterly stunning," the duchesslike boutique owner said with a satisfied smile at her creation. Meaning the slinky, floor-length evening gown clinging to Vera's every curve. "What do you think, Mr. Rothchild?"

He considered. "I think the neckline could be lower."

"No way," Vera muttered. "Any lower and you'd have to call it a waistline."

"So charming," the duchess cooed. "Your lady friend's modesty becomes her, my dear."

Get me out of here.

"Yes," he deadpanned. "It's one of my favorite things about her."

"I'm standing right here, you know," she said evenly, shooting him a warning glare.

"Well, which gown do you like best? The blue, the red, the gold or the white?" he asked with an unrepentant smile, motioning with a twirled finger for her to spin around one more time in the blue one she was wearing. She grudgingly obliged.

She'd tried on about a thousand different dresses over the past three hours at a dozen or more trendy boutiques before finding a designer Conner approved of, and he had narrowed it down to four choices. Vera hadn't dared voice an opinion other than about the ones she didn't care for, because she had no clue what was expected at the Lights of Las Vegas Charity Ball. Each event on the Vegas social calendar had its own dress code, known only to the city's Chosen Ones. If you violated the Code, people knew and smirked at you behind your back. Or so she'd surmised from the stories of fashion faux pas Darla had come home telling with a superior air of glee.

"They're all exquisite," Vera said. And meant it. "And all far too expensive." And meant that, too. The dresses in this store were so expensive they didn't even have price tags. "You should donate the money to the charity instead."

He signaled the boutique owner to give them a minute alone, then smiled at Vera indulgently. "I've already made out the check, and trust me, this wouldn't even put a dent in it. Besides, I want my assistant to be the most stunning woman there."

Assistant? Oka-ay.

"You wouldn't deny me that satisfaction, would you?" he asked.

She ignored the deliberate hint his slight emphasis on the word *that* carried. "So I take it this isn't a date," she casually said.

"Definitely not. I'm paying you," he said oh-so-reasonably. "I wouldn't want there to be any…misinterpretations."

Ha-ha. The man was hilarious. And transparent as glass.

"Good," she said with a quick smile, not falling for the ploy. "Keeping it business is for the best." Though that did make her stomach sink a little with disappointment. "And since this is on your dime, boss, *you* choose which gown you like best."

"Very well. If you insist."

He studied her again from head to toe, taking so long she was in danger of melting under his scrutiny. The man had a way of undressing her with those dreamy bedroom eyes that made her toes curl and her mouth go dry. Which was a pretty good trick, considering her profession.

"You are so incredibly beautiful," he said at last and looked up with a funny little smile.

Surprise washed through her at the heartfelt compliment. "Thank you," she said, flustered by the admiration lingering in his eyes as he continued to gaze at her. "For everything." She went up on her tiptoes and gave him a soft kiss on the mouth. "You're being so generous, I don't know what to say."

He smiled and kissed her back—a gentle, easy kiss. Then pushed a lock of hair behind her ear. "You've said it. Thank you is plenty."

"I really do feel like Cinderella getting ready for the ball."

His smile went roguish. He brushed his knuckles down her

bare arms, producing a shower of goose bumps. "So, if you're Cinderella, who does that make me?"

He was so fishing. "My fairy godmother?" she suggested impishly.

He made a face. "Not exactly what I was going for."

She grinned, her heart spinning in her chest. "I don't recall reading anywhere that Cinderella was Prince Charming's *assistant*."

"And I don't remember her being such a smart-aleck." He tapped her on the end of the nose. "Get changed and I'll settle up."

"Aren't you going to tell me which dress you chose?"

"Nope. It'll be a surprise."

"No fair."

He winked. "Who said anything about fair?" Then he was gone from the dressing room.

She eased out a long breath to slow her fluttering heart. Who, indeed? Nothing was fair about this whole situation. Not Darla involving her in felony theft. Not having to go to this stupid ball and make a fool of herself. Certainly not the fact that she was falling hard and fast for Conner Rothchild, a man so breathtakingly wrong for her it defied all odds. Talk about a fairy tale! Too bad Cinderella was just a story. The kind that *didn't* happen in real life.

She really had to make herself remember that. Because after Conner was finished with her, no longer needed her help to fulfill his obligations to the FBI, she knew darn well the magical bubble she'd been floating in would morph back into a pumpkin. It would leave her standing alone, right back where she'd always been. And the only glass slippers she'd be trying on would be on a stage along with a fake wedding dress.

But in the meantime, she had no choice. She must go

through with this. Darla would be the one to suffer if she wimped out and didn't help prove her sister's innocence.

No, she was well and truly stuck in this crazy situation. So she may as well try to enjoy the ride as best she could. Prince Charming and all.

She just hoped she could hang on to her heart—and not let Conner Rothchild steal it along the way.

Chapter 9

Traffic was a bitch. Parking was even worse.

"Just drop me off," Vera told Conner after glancing at the dashboard clock for the tenth time in as many minutes.

He knew she was worried about being late for her shift, convinced her boss was looking for an excuse to fire her after she'd been hauled off by the FBI yesterday. To tell the truth, Conner wished she *would* get fired. She was better than that job. Did not belong at the Diamond Lounge—or anywhere else she had to bare her breasts to make a decent living.

Oh, she'd told him all about her lack of education and her stepfather's Alzheimer's and thus the need to keep him in an assisted-living facility. Conner understood her reasons. He did. He was just unconvinced she had no other recourse. She'd simply had no one tell her about other options.

He planned to. As soon as they'd put this FBI mess behind them, he'd show her how she didn't have to continue in the same vicious cycle as her mother'd been stuck in. There were ways out. To that end, this afternoon he'd paid the bill for the retirement home for the next month. Call it a bonus for her help. That would give her a few weeks' breathing room to help him. It was the least he could do.

Actually…it was far more than he *should* be doing. More than he'd ever done for a client before. He'd always prided himself on staying aloof from the all-too-unfair predicaments life had heaped upon many of his clients…hell, most of his clients. He was a defense attorney. People who did crimes had myriad reasons for committing them, but none of those reasons were fair or happy. Like a doctor with his patients, a good attorney needed to distance himself from the world of hurt he dealt with every day. Treat everyone as a case number, even as he helped them.

But Vera was different. She affected him like no one ever had. As a representative of the law—and as a man. She was incredibly smart, grounded and determined. Not to mention the hottest woman he'd ever met.

He was in deep trouble here.

"Seriously," she said, "I can walk to the club. It's just a couple of blocks. It'll be faster than this mess."

No doubt correct. Sundown on the Strip was a giant traffic jam. "All right," he said, though he didn't like the notion of her being on her own for even a minute. Whoever was stalking the Tears of the Quetzal was still out there. Conner had checked in with Lex Duncan, but no new leads had turned up. "Promise me you'll go in through the front of the club, not from the alley."

"You know I have to use the stage door," she said as she ducked under the car's gull-wing door as it rose to let her out. "Lecherous Lou will have a fit if I—"

"Tell him you have a new sugar daddy who's coming to

spend lots of money in his club—but only if you walk in through the front entrance."

She rolled her eyes and pulled her garment bag from the backseat. "Sugar daddy?"

He shrugged with a grin. "Sounds better than fairy god-mother."

She laughed. "You're crazy, you know that?"

Yeah, about her. "More so every minute."

He watched her walk away on the tourist-crowded side-walk in a simple pencil skirt and blouse, and a pair of sexy, do-me shoes that should be illegal, her hips swaying entic-ingly. Leaving a trail of turning male heads in her wake.

He wanted to jump out of the car and strangle every one of them for looking at her that way.

Damn, he was in *such* deep trouble.

Traffic barely inched along, so he fell farther and farther behind her. For a moment he lost sight of her in the moving throng. His pulse jacked up. He didn't like this. He shouldn't have let her get out of the car. To his relief, she got stuck at a Do Not Walk sign at the next corner and actually obeyed it. Meanwhile his lane jerked forward half a block so he almost caught up with her. She didn't know it, though, and he smiled at her impatient foot tapping as she waited.

Suddenly, he noticed someone else watching her. Closely. From the sidewalk just behind her. A man. Tall, muscular, with an olive complexion, thick black hair and a furtive look about him. A *familiar* furtive look. The guy stepped closer to Vera's back. *Too* close. As the man surreptitiously checked the crowd to both sides, Conner saw high cheekbones that gave him an exotic Hispanic or maybe Native American look.

And then it struck him. It was the man who'd been arguing with Darla! In front of police headquarters!

Alarm zinged through Conner's insides. Just as Vera's

stance went straight and rigid. Slowly, she put her hands out to her sides.

Holy hell! The bastard had a gun to her back!

Conner leaped from the car and barreled down the street to her aid, knocking people aside, apologizing as he ran. It took him about seven seconds flat to reach her. They were the longest seconds of his life.

"Hey!" he yelled just before flinging himself onto the douchebag's back. "Get away from her!" A mistake. The man was quick. He spun, saw Conner and took off, just missing being tackled. Conner managed to avoid mowing down Vera, but when he veered, he slammed into the streetlight post. Stars burst in his head.

"Conner!" Her voice echoed like he was in a tunnel. "Oh, my God! Conner! Are you okay?"

He gave his head a shake to clear it as well as his hearing. "Did someone catch that guy?" he demanded, scanning the area around them. Concerned tourists looked back at him blankly.

Damn.

"That was him, wasn't it?" Vera said, obviously totally freaked out. "The guy who broke into my apartment. He had a gun, Conner! He was going to shoot me!"

The circle of tourists glanced nervously in the direction the man had run, and started to back away. Out on the street, car horns started honking.

"Damn. I left the car running down the block." He grasped her elbow firmly. "Come on. We're going back home."

She dug in her heels. "No, Conner," she protested. "I have to go to work!"

He towed her along unwillingly. "You were nearly mugged, woman! Or worse. How can you even consider—"

"I told you. I don't have a choice. I *need* my job. Please,

Conner. Let me go. He just wants the ring, and I don't have it. I'll be fine."

Silver had thought she was safe, too. Right before a thousand tons of pipe and wood had crashed down on her. She was still emotionally traumatized by the attack.

Damn it, he didn't want Vera in danger, too. But that determined look was back in her eyes. He knew he'd lose this argument. "All right. But I don't care how long it takes. You're not walking. Get in the car."

Thankfully she didn't argue but slid back into the car, if reluctantly.

"Did you get a close look at his face?" Conner asked her once he'd calmed down enough to think rationally. "Would you recognize him again?"

She shook her head. "No. I didn't dare turn around when he had his gun in my back. I didn't see his face at all. Did you?"

"Just from a distance, and I only caught a glimpse of it. But I think I've seen him before. I'll have Duncan pull video from the traffic cam." He pointed to the unobtrusive camera pointed at the intersection. "With luck, it got a good shot of him, and we can identify the bastard once and for all. At least see if he's the same guy I suspect of taking the Quetzal from police headquarters."

And hurting Silver.

And possibly murdering Candace.

"Damn it! I don't want you going to work tonight," Conner said, slamming his fist on the steering wheel. "I'll pay your salary—whatever you would have made."

She stared at him for a moment, then smiled weakly. "I know you just want to help, but…I can't do that."

"I'm not trying to buy you, Vera."

"I know that. But, no, thanks."

It took them ten minutes to drive the block and a half to

the Diamond Lounge parking lot. By the time they got out of the car and he escorted her to the stage door, she'd composed herself completely. He didn't know how she could be so calm. Or so stubborn about accepting his help. A man had just tried to kill her!

Since Conner wasn't an employee of the club, the guard wouldn't let him in the side entrance.

"Be careful," he admonished Vera, giving her a worried kiss. "I'll be in the audience all night. If you need me just yell."

She smiled and touched his cheek. "My hero."

He knew it was just teasing, but her endearment made him feel warm all over. Or maybe it was just the hot Las Vegas night wind. People had given him a lot bigger compliments, accompanied by far more substantial rewards than a smile. So why did every little thing this woman do affect him so deeply?

He made his way around to the front, directly to the head of the line of schlubs waiting to get into the exclusive club. As an Old Las Vegas landmark, the Diamond Lounge was extremely popular with tourists and locals alike. But it didn't surprise him that the bouncer immediately recognized him, either from the society pages, or because he'd been part of the stir last night.

"Evening, Mr. Rothchild. Welcome back," the brawny man said, ushering him past the velvet rope.

After paying his exorbitant cover, he was immediately shown to the same table as last night, right in front of the stage. He suppressed a chuckle of amusement. Had Vera really told them he was her sugar daddy? He wouldn't put it past her. She had a wicked sense of humor, that woman.

This time a whole bottle of champagne appeared on his table, served by a pretty petite brunette who displayed her nearly nude body invitingly for him as she poured.

He was so not interested.

A beautiful redhead came out onstage in a sexy French maid's outfit and for the next fifteen minutes did a very energetic number with the center pole. The men perched on the bar stools arranged against the edge of the stage cheered and groaned in approval.

Conner drained a glass of champagne and was actually bored. He was only interested in seeing one certain, particular woman take off her clothes. And the thought of her doing it in front of all these clowns was making him want to swallow the whole damned bottle.

He checked his watch. Eight-thirteen.

Vera didn't come on until eleven.

Hell. It was going to be a really, really long night.

He was out there.

Conner.

Why did the thought of that one man being in the audience put butterflies in Vera's stomach and impossible feelings in her heart? Feelings of warmth and affection, and sadness and regret, all balled up in one giant knot?

She was falling in love with the man. That's why.

Despair filled Vera as she prepared to go out onstage. For the first time ever, she didn't want to do this. Wished she'd chosen a more conventional means of making a living. Hadn't let a thousand men see her wearing nothing more than a G-string.

Stop it! she told herself.

There was nothing wrong with what she did. And it wasn't as though she'd had a lot of choice.

As Jerry the stagehand pulled back the curtain for her, she thought about all the times she'd strutted out onstage and enjoyed the heck out of it. She'd loved the power of her female body over the punters. Loved the effect she'd had on them, reducing strong, intelligent men to blithering bundles of testosterone willing to give her everything they had for just one more peek. Loved that she was giving a thrill to those who had no one, and to those with someone waiting for them a reason to go home and give that woman a thrill of her own.

And then she thought of Conner, out there, waiting for her to come out and perform. How terrifying was that? Because suddenly she realized there was nothing she wanted more than to have him take her home and give *her* a thrill.

She was nothing if not realistic. She knew a man like him would never love her back. But that didn't mean she couldn't enjoy him while he still wanted her. And he did want her. Anyone with eyes could see that.

So why was she wasting time? The man was out there, waiting, needing to be seduced. Quickly. Before Agent Duncan found Darla and the Quetzal-crazed maniac, and Vera had to go back to her old life.

This life.

Without Conner.

The long chords of her organ music started. Her cue.

She fluffed the skirt of her faux wedding gown and gave her breasts an extra push up.

Okay. This was it.

The man didn't stand a chance. When she was done with this performance, he'd be putty in her hands.

At least for a little while. Longer if she was lucky. Until life intervened and he came to his senses.

But in the meantime he'd be hers. All hers.

Her very own Prince Charming.

For one magical night.

Chapter 10

Conner sat back in his seat, exhaled a long, long, *long* breath and willed the goose bumps running up and down his arms to go away.

His body was painfully aroused, throbbing hard and craving satisfaction.

The woman was a witch, pure and simple. She'd bewitched him. Again. Totally. Thoroughly. Unabashedly. She'd danced her dance of the seven veils with that gossamer white wedding costume, and he'd been as lost as King Herod, ready to throw whatever she wished at her feet. Money. Fame. His heart on a platter.

Damn. How pathetically cliché was this? Rich man falling for a much younger stripper, willing to alienate his family, his friends, his entire social circle, to be with her.

How could he even consider it?

He'd be on the front page of every tabloid, laughed at

behind his back. His career would suffer. His family would be embarrassed. Probably end up being disowned by his overly socially conscious father.

All because he suddenly couldn't imagine his life without Vera Mancuso in it.

And yet, there it was.

He wanted her anyway.

He wanted her.

But he just couldn't. Couldn't do that to his family. Couldn't toss aside everything he'd worked so hard to achieve.

There had to be another way.

A way to have her, all to himself, but not expose either of them to the severe downsides of a relationship like theirs.

Relationship.

He shuddered, and even more goose bumps broke out on his flesh. What was he *thinking?* There must be a—

"Mr. Rothchild?"

With a start, he came back to the present. Vera had left the stage ages ago, and another girl had replaced her. Ever since, he'd just been staring into space, his mind whirling in a chaos of growing panic.

He turned to see a middle-aged man with an obviously expensive but still oddly ill-fitting suit standing by his table. "Yes?"

The man extended his hand. "I'm Lou Majors, the manager, Mr. Rothchild. Welcome to the Diamond Lounge."

Ah. If it wasn't Lecherous Lou himself. Conner projected his voice over the bass-heavy stripper music blaring from the loudspeakers, "Thank you. Won't you join me?" It never hurt to schmooze the enemy.

"Don't mind if I do." The manager snapped his fingers at a hostess, who hurried over with another bottle of champagne. This time it was Cristal. Nice.

Also pretty nervy, because Conner was the one who'd end

up paying for it. Not that he cared. Beat the hell out of the cheap stuff he'd been drinking.

"Enjoying the floor show?" Lou asked politely, leaning in so he could be heard.

"Absolutely. Some parts more than others." Conner sent him a knowing, male-bonding-type smile.

Lou smiled back amiably. "Couldn't help but notice. You're acquainted with Miss LaRue, I take it?"

LaRue? Oh, right. Vera's stage name. "Yes. Met her here, actually. Yesterday."

At the reminder of the disruption, a shadow of annoyance passed through the manager's eyes but was quickly gone. "Her lawyer, I take it."

Conner winked lasciviously and leaned in closer. "Who could resist?" May as well go for broke. If the scumbucket thought she had a wealthy protector, he'd never dare fire her. "But I'm no longer her lawyer. I passed her case to a colleague." He lowered his voice, confidential-like. "Conflict of interest, if you get my drift."

He did. Lou couldn't have looked more pleased if Conner'd just handed him a stack of hundred-dollar bills. Which no doubt was exactly what the old roué had in mind. "I see." Several seconds went by as the manager regarded Conner. Finally he said, "Mr. Rothchild, I have a very special offer to make you."

"Yeah? What's that?"

Lou beckoned, rose and led him through the club to the sweeping red-carpeted staircase that led upstairs. On the way up, he refilled his champagne flute and handed it back. "I think you'll be very interested in this unique opportunity."

They ducked into the same VIP room as yesterday. Conner raised a brow questioningly. "What's this all about?"

Lou cleared his throat. "Are you the kind of man who likes…private parties, Mr. Rothchild?"

His brows rose higher. "That depends on who's invited."

"Men such as yourself. Wealthy. Discriminating. Discreet."

Suddenly, it hit him. *Good Lord.* If this was going where he thought it was going, the Parker case just got a huge break. "Go on."

"The ladies are of the highest caliber, of course. Only the best, most beautiful women are in attendance. Women who will cater to your every whim."

Lou looked at him expectantly, the man's crude excitement coming through loud and clear. Whether it was excitement over the prospect of the power he wielded over helpless beautiful women, or the prospect of all the money Conner would have to spend to attend that shindig, he couldn't guess. Suzie Parker had told him the attendees paid five thousand dollars each for an invitation to these exclusive gentlemen's house parties.

But Conner was a very, very rich man. He could get any woman he wanted for no more than the cost of a drink. His reputation was well-known.

He shrugged, playing it cool. "There's only one woman I'm interested in catering to me," he said, feigning indifference to the whole thing. "And I've been told in no uncertain terms she doesn't do private parties. Of any kind."

Lou's eyes narrowed, his lip curling. After a brief pause, he said, "What if I could change her mind?"

Whoops. Not the direction Conner'd meant to go. He scrambled for a reason to refuse, but Lou beat him to the draw.

"I'll make you a deal. If she'll do a party here in the VIP room with you, you'll give my other invitation a try." Because he was so sure after one visit, Conner'd be sucked into the decadence.

Hell, that's what a man got for cultivating his reputation as a player and a heartbreaker all over town. Which, ironically enough, he'd done in order to *avoid* breaking hearts. He'd never been interested in hanging with one woman for more than a few days.

Before now.

Temptation loomed large. On both counts.

This was an unprecedented opportunity to help Suzie Parker by witnessing firsthand what she'd been forced to do. To gather hard evidence against the culprits running these parties and shut them down for good. So other innocent girls weren't caught in the trap, lured by the money into selling themselves short.

Not to mention being able to have Vera all to himself in the VIP room, driving him crazy with her delectable body, dancing up close and personal.

Except she'd be madder than a coyote if Lou made her do it. She'd probably never speak to Conner again.

Which could, of course, solve that other problem. The one where he was about to throw away his whole life to have her. No sense doing that if she wasn't even speaking to him.

He hesitated. Just long enough for Lou to pull out his cell phone and make a three-word call. "Send her up."

Oh, crap.

Vera was sitting at the dressing-room mirror touching up her makeup and listening to Tawni prattle on about some man she'd just met. Some computer IT guy from New Orleans.

"Always wanted to visit the Big Easy," Tawni said. "Do you think I should go?"

"Is he married?" Vera asked.

Tawni flung out a hand. "Who cares? We're not talking about having the guy's kid, here, just a little fling!"

"Which can lead to all sorts of heartache for everyone involved, especially if he's married," Vera pointed out. "I'd ask before I even considered it."

Tawni sighed. "I suppose you're right. Wouldn't want to have my eyes scratched out by some dumb punter's irate wife."

"Very sensible."

"What about your guy?"

"I have no guy."

Tawni snorted. "Yeah? Then who was Mr. Tall, Rich and Handsome in the front row drooling into his champagne? For the second night in a row, I might add. The one whose ten-million-dollar mansion you happen to be staying at?"

Vera swiveled on her stool to face her friend. "We haven't slept together." Well. Not technically. It didn't count when only one of the parties got off and there was no bed involved. Right?

Tawni's eyes bugged out. "Are you *insane?* What are you waiting for?"

Vera sighed dreamily. "Nothing, anymore. I decided to seduce him tonight."

"Good plan," Tawni said in exasperation. "Jeez, girl, the man is worth megabucks. You've got to hurry up and soak him for all he's worth!"

She shook her head, feeling a loopy smile spread on her face. "No. I couldn't. It's not like that. He likes me. Respects me."

Tawni slapped her hands to the sides of her face. "Are you out of your mind? *Respects* you? Look at yourself in the mirror, Vera May Mancuso. Does that look like the sort of woman a man has any kind of honorable thoughts about? Mark my words, he's after something you've got, but it ain't R-E-S-P-E-C-T."

"Maybe. Maybe not. It doesn't matter. I've decided to give it to him anyway."

Something in her voice must have given her away. Tawni gasped. "Oh, sweet heaven. You're *in love* with the man! My God, girl, you just met him yesterday!"

"I know. Totally insane, isn't it? I took one look at him, and it was like…like I'd been zapped by a magic wand or something. Bells rang. Stars exploded." Or maybe that part was just the stage lights reflecting off the incredible ring she'd been wearing. The Tears of the Quetzal. She'd been blinded by its hypnotic brilliance. No wonder some lunatic had become obsessed by it.

Tawni was still staring at her incredulously.

Vera held up a hand. "I know. I'm certifiable. Believe me, I wasn't going to touch him—" much "—but oh, God, Tawni, I want him. I want to feel what it's like to be with him. Just once. Don't worry, I'm not fool enough to think it'll last."

Sympathy filled Tawni's gaze. "Oh, sweetie, you do have it bad. Come here, girl." She stretched out her arms, and Vera went into them, grateful for a hug, grateful for a friend who knew exactly what she was going through. No matter how jaded they pretended to be, their hearts still broke like everyone else's.

"You're right, sweetie," Tawni murmured. "Don't you worry about the future. You go for it. Get all the loving you can out of him. Just hang on to that precious heart of yours. Don't you give that to any man, you hear?"

Vera nodded. "I won't."

But it was too late, and they both knew it.

Still, she told herself, at least she'd have some amazing memories.

She pulled back from Tawni's hug, filling with a jittery kind of excitement. She really *was* going to go for it.

Jerry poked his head in the door just then. "Miss LaRue?"

She looked up, surprised. She wasn't on again for another two hours. "Yeah, Jerry?"

"Lecherous Lou wants to see you. Upstairs. Room seven."

Now what? Lou knew she was absolutely adamant— Okay, wait. Maybe… "Do you know if there's anyone with him?" she asked Jerry.

"That rich dude's been panting after your bod."

Excellent. "Tell him I'll be there in a minute." Jerry left. She met Tawni's I-told-you-so gaze in the mirror. "Don't say a word. Not a blessed word."

"Did I say anything? Here, look, this is me not saying a single damn thing." Tawni made a zipping motion over her lips as Vera gathered her skirts and headed out the door. "You go get 'im, girl," she called after her. "Make the boy wish he'd never been born with that thing between his legs."

That was the whole idea. For now. But later, after they went home, she'd make him glad again. Oh, so very, very glad.

And her, too.

"There you are, my dear," Lecherous Lou said when she swept into the VIP room.

Conner was standing next to him, looking too handsome for his own good. Damn, the man was fine, as Tawni would say. Broad shoulders; square jaw; long, hard, muscular legs; strong hands. And those eyes. She'd never known eyes so bone-quiveringly sexy as those hot-as-the-desert hazel ones gazing at her from under his perfectly shaped masculine brows. "Vera," he said in greeting.

"Hello, Mr. Rothchild," she said with demure formality. "Lou. What can I do for you gentlemen?"

"I think you know what Mr. Rothchild would like, Vera," Lou said. Subtlety had never been his strong suit.

She allowed herself a coy smile at her would-be lover. "I'm pretty sure that would be illegal. Wouldn't want to get any of us into trouble with the law, would we?"

Those perfect brows flicked. She'd caught him by surprise. He'd been expecting her to flatly refuse, as she had yesterday.

"Of course not!" Lou blustered. "Nothing illegal. Just a standard lap dance, that's all. The VS1 Special."

Which was code for total nudity.

She swallowed.

She'd avoided this for so long that the words almost stuck in her throat. "All right," she said.

Omigod, what was she doing?

What they both wanted. That's what.

Lou almost fell over. He'd been expecting a total refusal, too, and to have to threaten her with her job. "Get lost," she told him. "Before I change my mind."

He was out the soundproof door, and the gauzy curtains were drawn closed faster than she could blink.

"Surprised?" she asked Conner when they were alone.

The lingering shock and the slight parting of his lips belied his causal stance. "I could have sworn you don't do lap dances."

"This isn't a lap dance."

"Strange. I'm pretty sure that's what you just agreed to."

She smiled. And took a step toward him. "Then, it'll be our little secret—" and another step "—what we really do."

That's when he started to get nervous. And in spite of himself, excited. She could see his body reacting to the fantasies in his mind. The ones she'd planted there. "Vera? What's going on?"

"I hope you're prepared, Mr. Rothchild," she said, lowering her voice to a throaty purr, and with one finger pushed him backward onto the divan. "To be seduced."

Chapter 11

Vera seduced him slowly, minute by minute, inch by inch, the way she'd done onstage earlier. If Conner had any notion of resisting her, the man could just forget it.

She was an expert at very few things, but this was one of them. She knew how to make a man want her.

Not that he needed any help in that department. He'd made no secret of his desire to sleep with her. He hadn't pressed her on it, but only because she'd told him no. The man was a true gentleman, just as he'd said.

And now he would get his reward.

Well. Sort of. She knew he'd do his damnedest to follow club rules and not touch her. It would be pure torture on him. Heck, for both of them. But it would make the coming night all the sweeter, once they got back to his place.

She adjusted the music to a low, bluesy song she loved, and took her place in the middle of the small room. He sat sprawled on the divan, looking like a tiger who couldn't quite believe a kitten had wandered into his cage.

"You don't have to do this," he said.

Making her fall for him all the more.

"I want to," she assured him. "Just relax and enjoy the show."

"I already did. You were incredible onstage. It felt like I was the only man in the room and you were dancing just for me."

"You were." She smiled and started to sway her hips to the music. "And I was."

His eyes darkened, his smile going sexy. "What brought on the change of heart?"

"You," she said simply. And let her body take over.

She knew all the moves, but suddenly they had a whole new meaning for her. She wanted to seduce this man, body and soul. Wanted to entice him. Enthrall him. Make him pant. Make him sweat. Make him never, ever forget this dance of temptation…

Or her.

Slowly, she peeled off her wedding gown. Taking her time. Moving her body to the music. Teasing him. Provoking him. Making the anticipation last and last. Until she was left wearing only the lace corset, stockings and shoes. The G-string of tiny seed pearls she'd selected for tonight hardly counted as attire.

His gaze devoured her, lingering on the special wax job her line of work demanded.

"Like what you see?"

"I'd like it a whole lot better closer up."

She smiled. "Yeah?"

He looked relaxed, arms lying along the back cushions of the sofa, his legs spread wide. But she knew it was a hard-won facade. There was a film of sweat on his forehead that had nothing to do with the outside night heat, and the pulse on the side of his throat throbbed wildly. Not to mention that solid ridge in the front of his pants. "Oh, yeah."

She moved closer. He swallowed.

He couldn't touch, but there were no such restrictions on her. She put a knee to each side of his, kneeling on the red leather divan with her hands on his shoulders, and straddled his lower thighs. Keeping distance between them.

"This better?" she asked.

"Not nearly close enough," he murmured darkly.

The fabric of his suit was smooth and luxurious, cool to the touch. But the man in it was sizzling. She ran her fingers down his shirtfront. "Mmm. You're hot," she observed.

"Burning up," he agreed.

She peeled off his jacket and tossed it aside. Loosened his tie.

"Take it off," he ordered huskily.

"Why, Mr. Rothchild…"

"The tie."

She obliged, using the length of silk like a sex toy. Drawing it off slowly, teasing him with the end, glancing at his wrist debating whether to tie him up to the iron ring attached to the wall above his head.

"Don't even think about it," he warned.

She smiled, setting it aside. "Later, then."

"We'll see about that."

One by one, she teased his shirt buttons open. Touched his broad chest. Reveled in the feel of his skin under her fingers. In the soft scratch of the curls of masculine hair. He shifted under her, and she could feel the slight trembling of his thighs.

She wet her lips and brushed them over his. He groaned softly. "You're killing me here, you know that."

She put her hands to his chest, rubbed her thumbs over his tight nipples. "Hope you have nine lives."

He sucked in a breath, lifted his knees and tipped her into his chest. "Not fair," he gasped.

She tilted her head up, taking her time pulling her body away from his. "Who said anything about fair?"

He gave a strangled laugh. "Witch."

"Candy-ass."

"You are so getting a spanking when we get home."

She winked. "Promises, promises."

His eyes cut down to hers, darkened to the color of a forest in a storm. "You are a naughty girl."

"Want to see how naughty?" she whispered in his ear.

"I'm your lawyer. I need to know these things."

Her corset was held together in front by a row of bows. She reached down, found the end of one of the ribbons, and tugged it almost open. Then she put the ribbon to his lips. With a jerk of his head, he finished the job. Her breasts spilled out of the garment…just enough to be a tease.

She lifted up on her knees a little. Like lightning he grasped the end of the next ribbon with his teeth and tugged that one open, too. Her breasts tumbled out, brushing his face. He groaned, trying to catch a nipple with his tongue and teeth.

"Uh-uh," she scolded, wagging a finger. Feeling the intimate contact like a wave of shivers.

"Let me," he pleaded.

"Finish undoing the bows. Then we'll see."

His hot breath puffed over her skin, his wet tongue grazed her flesh as he bent to his task. Her nipples spiraled harder. Achy coils of desire tightened around her center.

He made quick work of the bows. Clever man. The corset slid to the floor. On impulse, she unclasped her G-string and let it slither off, too. She wanted to be completely naked for him.

His expression was pure sin as his gaze caressed her.

"You are so damn beautiful," he whispered.

Still up on her knees, she bent forward, offering him her breasts. She wanted to feel his mouth on her. He latched on like a hungry babe, suckling one then the other, until she was panting with need.

With a groan, she pulled herself away. "Any more and I'll come," she murmured.

"Do it," he urged. "I want to see you come apart for me again."

"Not here." She eased out a shuddering breath.

He blinked and glanced around, as though he'd completely forgotten where they were. He'd dug his fingers deep into the divan back, holding on to the cushions with a death grip, but now he eased them off and flexed them. "God. You're right. What was I thinking?" He nuzzled his lips against her throat. "Let's get out of here."

"I still have another show."

"Forget it. You're coming home with me." He stood up, sweeping her into his arms. *"Now."*

She didn't protest, other than to insist on picking up her discarded costume and his jacket and tie. He and Lecherous Lou seemed to have some kind of understanding. Hopefully she wouldn't lose her job over this.

Not that it would change her mind if she did. She was ready to be his. In every way. More than ready.

Conner drove like a madman, making the trip to his house in less than twelve minutes. He didn't want to waste a single second. He wanted to be inside her, now, finding release for this volcano of desire roiling inside his body.

Before leaving the club, he'd allowed her to slip back into her pencil skirt, peasant blouse and do-me shoes, but nothing else. He could see her tawny nipples through the almost-sheer fabric of the blouse. He was dying. He needed her under him.

As soon as they got inside the door of his mansion, he had her up against the wall, his mouth to her breast. She moaned, clasping his head in her hands, pulling him closer.

"Conner," she pleaded, her voice strangled, writhing against the wall as he ground the silk blouse onto her nipple with his wet tongue.

"I'm here, baby." He threw aside his jacket and practically ripped the buttons from his shirt, ridding himself of it. She lifted her shirt up over her ample breasts, baring them for him. They were breasts a man could lose himself in. Soft, round, full. Perfect.

He could smell the feminine scent of her desire, lightly musky and spicy, an alluring aphrodisiac that made him twitch in an agony of want.

With a growl, he banded his arms around her and carried her into the living room, swept the things off a low coffee table, and lowered her onto her back on it. Wrenching her legs apart, he tasted her, covering her with his mouth and tongue.

She gasped, arched and splintered apart. So fast he didn't have time to enjoy it. So he did it again.

When he finally climbed up on the table and lowered himself on top of her, she was totally wrung out and he was ready to detonate. He grasped under her knees and spread them.

"Protection?" she managed to murmur.

"Taken care of," he told her. Thank God he'd tucked a few condoms in his trouser pocket. Just in case.

"Mmm."

He thrust into her. The feel of her hot flesh surrounding him burst through his consciousness like a kaleidoscope of erotic sensation. He froze. If he moved a muscle he'd be lost. She held him tight, her chest expanding and contracting against him. It wasn't helping. He groaned.

"Conner?"

"Yeah, babe?"

"Is anything wrong?"

"Other than me being about to shame myself and totally ruin my macho reputation?"

She let out a surprised laugh. Her muscles contracted around him.

Jeez-uz.

"Baby, have mercy," he begged.

Her eyes softened, joy suffusing her whole face. She was so lovely his breath caught in his lungs. Was it really possible *he* had done that to her? Made her so happy she glowed with it?

"Kiss me," she whispered.

So he did. Long and wet and thorough as a spring downpour in the Mojave. She wrapped her legs around his waist and held him tight and used her heels on his backside to push him deep, deep, deep into her. So deep he found he couldn't hold back.

"It's okay. Let yourself go," she whispered into his mouth, her voice low and thready with emotion.

He shuddered, fighting it. Not wanting it to be over so quickly. "Too soon," he gritted out.

"We have all night," she refuted breathily.

Which was a good thing, because he had no more strength to resist.

An overwhelming surge of pleasure crashed over him. And he surrendered. Surrendered to the carnal bliss. Surrendered to the emotional rightness. Surrendered to the deep inner knowledge that after this night, he would never be the same man again.

This was just the beginning.

Chapter 12

"No, Dad. Because I don't—" Speaking on the phone, Conner did not look like a happy camper. In fact, he looked downright angry. "What about Mike? Why can't he—"

Vera wrapped the silk robe Conner'd lent her a bit tighter around her body and sank a bit deeper into the leather recliner she was curled into, trying to make herself invisible. They were in his study while he'd put out a fire or two at work. This didn't sound like work, though.

"Yes, Dad. Of course I am. But—"

They'd made love all night. And all morning. And half the afternoon. They'd shared passions and done things together she'd never done with another human being. He'd claimed her body; she'd given him her heart and her soul.

But she still felt like a trespasser in his world.

"Fine, Dad. Yes, I understand." He slammed the phone down with a curse, a scowl etched on his face.

She didn't dare ask him what was wrong. Not her place.

"Too early for a drink?" she ventured. It was just past four. Hell, it was five o'clock just down the road in Denver. At least she thought it was. Of course, one never knew with Mountain Time.

He looked up, apparently surprised to see her sitting there. *Oops.* Should have kept her mouth shut.

"Come here," he ordered.

She untangled her legs and did as he bid. Normally she wasn't such a "yes" girl, but last night she'd quickly realized the considerable benefits of doing as he asked.

He patted the desk blotter in front of him, and she duly climbed up and sat.

"Open your robe."

She smiled. The man was truly insatiable. Okay, this she could do. Her body already quickening, she unbelted the robe and held it open in anticipation of whatever he had in mind to make himself forget the conversation he'd just had with his father.

He didn't touch her. Just looked. And looked.

"You have the body of a goddess," he finally said. "You could have any man you want at the charity ball tonight."

"Why would I want anyone else when I have you?" she asked, reaching out for his hand and raising it to her cheek. She kissed his palm. He frowned.

She knew it was the wrong thing to do. Men didn't like it when a woman got all clingy after sex. But she just couldn't help herself.

Heart on her sleeve? Look it up. Her picture would be right there under the definition.

Did she care?

Ask her tomorrow.

She brought his hand to her breast. He cupped her,

running his thumb gently over the nipple. Shivers of pleasure went up her spine.

"And you make love like a god," she murmured.

Abruptly, he rolled his chair forward and leaned her backward onto his arm, bracing her as he took her other nipple in his mouth. Using his tongue, he imitated what his thumb was doing to the first one.

She sucked in a sharp breath, already rushing toward climax. Her body had gotten so tuned to him, physically, all it took was a touch or a kiss and she was practically there.

He withdrew, kissing her on the mouth instead. A sweet, tender kiss.

Her stomach sank.

A goodbye kiss.

Momentarily stunned, her heart squeezed painfully. Wow. That had happened more quickly than she'd thought.

But okay. She was a big girl. She could handle it.

She steadied herself, physically and mentally, for the inevitable.

"Are you ready for the ball?" he asked. "You still okay with what you have to do?"

The question caught her off guard.

In between their lovemaking and occasional foraging trips from the bedroom to the kitchen, they'd talked about what she would do tonight, how she'd go about getting the information about Darla that they needed. How to lure Darla's accomplices in the jewelry theft ring out into the open. *Alleged* accomplices.

Vera was still convinced Darla was innocent. But she'd sworn to do her best for Conner and she would. She'd rather know the truth about her sister, either way.

"Of course," she answered. She was nervous as hell about it but ready as ever. She thought about that phone call. "Why? Has something happened?"

His gaze dropped to her breasts again, and he stroked his hands over them possessively. "No," he said. "Nothing that affects anything important."

Now, there was a nonanswer if ever she'd heard one.

"What was that argument with your father all about, Conner?" she asked, a sick foreboding knotting in her stomach. "What did he want?"

Her lover leaned over and pressed his lips to her abdomen, trailing down to her belly button. He flicked his tongue into it. "Nothing important," he repeated.

Which probably meant it was. So important he didn't want to tell her. Which probably meant she wouldn't like it, whatever it was.

His tongue trailed lower still. "Spread your legs."

"Conner—"

"Open them."

He was definitely trying to distract her.

It was working.

She moaned as his tongue slipped between her folds, still swollen from hours of lovemaking. It felt warm and silky on her tender flesh. *So good.*

Ah, well. She'd find out soon enough what the problem was. No sense borrowing trouble.

Meanwhile, she planned to enjoy every minute she had left with him. And this was a very, very good start.

He had to tell her.

Consumed with guilt—and fury at his meddling father—Conner helped Vera into the white stretch limo he'd ordered to take them to the Lights of Las Vegas Charity Ball.

She looked like a princess in the strapless sapphire-blue satin gown he'd selected for her tonight. Worldly, sophisticated, stunning. He wanted her to be on his arm. All evening.

So there'd be no possibility of other men charming her, dancing with her, tempting her away.

Unfortunately, that was not to be. Dear old Dad had unknowingly made certain of it.

The old bugger'd be even more delighted if he actually knew what he'd done. Conner's father was a stand-up guy, but completely unreasonable when it concerned the family's reputation. Dad had tolerated Conner's rakish behavior—barely—up until now only because he was young, single and male. But he couldn't imagine Michael Rothchild ever in a million years condoning his son taking a stripper to a high-profile social event like this one. Much less dating one. No matter how amazing a person she was. Or how incredibly gorgeous.

Conner took his place beside her in the limo and tucked her under his arm. She nestled against him, resting her hand on his thigh.

"Nervous?" he asked.

She nodded. "Terrified."

"Don't be. You'll do fine. And you look exquisite."

She smiled up at him as she had so often today. Happy. Trusting. "Thank you." Her long lashes swept shyly downward, making his heart squeeze.

"You take my breath away, Vera Mancuso," he said and gave her a lingering kiss.

"The feeling's mutual, Conner Rothchild," she whispered.

He reached into his pocket for the velvet pouch he'd had his secretary deliver to the house that afternoon. From it he pulled a solid gold Byzantine rope necklace that had been his grandmother's. "I thought this would go nicely with your dress."

"Oh, Conner, it's beautiful!" she exclaimed, fingering it reverently after he'd fastened it around her neck. "But—"

"There's more."

When he pulled out the ring, her eyes went wide as saucers. "My God! Where did you get that? I thought the Tears of the Quetzal was stolen!"

He slipped it on her finger.

"It's a copy. Paste. The thief left it in place of the original when he stole that from police evidence. Not sure how he got hold of this one. It was supposedly in my aunt's jewelry box in her bedroom. My grandfather had it made decades ago for family members to wear out in public. Before he decided the ring was cursed and locked it away for good in a vault somewhere. Anyway, LVMPD turned over the paste ring to the FBI, too, and Duncan said we could borrow it tonight, thinking its appearance might help lure the thieves."

Conner had debated long and hard with himself about this. Having Vera wear the fake Quetzal could potentially put her in danger from the psycho thief. But as long as she only wore it at the ball, where security would be ultratight, and went home with him afterward, she should be safe. It also reassured him knowing that Duncan would have his men watching his property all night, too.

As an extra precaution, Conner had hired a bodyguard to discreetly follow her around at the ball, because Conner wouldn't be able to watch over her personally.

She held her fingers up to the limo's overhead light. Even in the dim wattage, the faux chameleon diamond shot off a shower of purple and green sparks, almost like the genuine article. "Wow. If I hadn't had the real thing on my own finger, I'd sure be fooled. It's nearly identical."

"Not many could tell the difference," he agreed.

Just then, the limo made a turn into a circular driveway. Damn. His time was up.

Vera peered out the tinted windows at the private mansion they'd pulled up in front of. "Where are we?" she asked.

"My brother's house," Conner said, steeling himself to meet her eyes. "We're picking him up, along with his date. And mine."

She did her best to hide her visceral reaction, but he clearly saw the flash of shock and devastation in her eyes before she managed to mask them. Her lips parted, then closed. "Your…date?"

Damn his father. "The daughter of an important client. She flew in from Paris yesterday and—"

Vera held up her hand. "No, it's okay," she said, though she couldn't quite squelch the strain in her voice. "You don't have to explain. We agreed I'd be coming as your assistant, not date. It's more believable this way."

So much for happy and trusting.

"Vera—" He reached for her, but she scooted away, all the way to the other side of the limo. He moved to go after her.

"Don't," she said, just as the door opened.

He halted, torn. She was his lover. He should never have let his father bully him into this farce. And yet…there was a microscopic part of him that was secretly relieved not to have to reveal their relationship just yet—and bear the brunt of social and familial disapproval.

He was such a damn coward.

"Howdy, bro," his brother, Mike, stuck his head in the door that had been opened by the chauffeur and greeted him. "Hey, now, what have we here?" Mike's confusion was obvious when he spotted Vera sitting in the corner. Then he really looked at her, and his face lit up. "A threesome? You dirty old man, you."

Mike, or Michael Rothchild Jr., was the older brother, but acted like a kid sometimes. He had no emotional radar.

"Just get in the damn car," Conner said evenly.

Mike stepped aside and his striking blond fiancée, Audra, slid into the seat opposite Conner. She leaned over and air-kissed him on the cheek. "Hi, Conner. Good to see y—" She also spotted Vera and halted in mid-word. "Hello," she said, glancing between her and Conner. "This is, um, interesting."

"My assistant, Vera Mancuso." Conner cut off her blatant rampant speculation. She was as bad as his brother. The perfect pair. "Vera's helping me with a case tonight."

Audra's brows rose delicately. But she refrained from comment, because Conner's date had just glided onto the seat next to him. She was model-thin with shiny black hair and long legs exposed by a slit running up the side of her gown. *Way* up. Aristocratic features, olive skin, a long neck and slim arms dripping with jewelry. The woman oozed class and sophistication.

His father knew him well. She was just his type.

Up until two days ago.

She raised her hand, European style. "Annabella Pruitt," she said in a cultured voice. *"Enchanté."*

He knew he was expected to kiss her hand, but he couldn't make himself do it. He shook it awkwardly instead, introducing himself, trying to subtly ease his body closer to Vera, who sat primly on the other side of him, maintaining a perfectly blank face.

"Did I hear you say assistant?" Mike queried after he'd climbed in and gotten settled next to Audra. He smiled at Vera when Conner introduced her to him and Annabella. "Just like my little brother to be working a case on a night like this," he said with good-humored disapproval.

"That's why he brought me," Vera said smoothly, the first peep she'd uttered. "So he wouldn't have to work. Now he can devote all his time to his lovely date." She smiled genially at the other woman, but Conner knew better than to think he'd been forgiven.

"Now *that's* a waste of a beautiful woman," Mike

remarked disgustedly, and Audra smacked him in the arm—but there was no heat in it. "So what kind of case does one work at a fancy ball?" he asked, patently intrigued by the whole situation.

"The confidential kind," Conner interrupted before Vera could answer. He sat back and folded his arms over his chest irritatedly. This was *so* not the night he'd envisioned.

Audra hadn't taken her curious eyes off Vera. "I didn't know Conner had hired an assistant," she ventured. "You're very young. Are you a junior associate in the firm? Paralegal maybe?"

"Confidential informant." Conner cut off whatever Vera'd opened her mouth to say. "She knows people."

"You do look familiar," Mike said with a curious tilt of his head. "Have we met somewhere? At another charity event perhaps?"

Vera's glued-on smile didn't waver. "You probably know my sister, Darla St. Giles."

Mike's brows shot into his scalp. "Good God. Darla has a sister? How did I not know that?"

"Vera isn't into Darla's social whirl," Conner supplied.

"I prefer to stay out of the tabloids." She folded her hands in her lap.

And that's when Mike noticed the fake ring on her finger. His eyes bugged out, and his shocked gaze snapped to Conner.

Annabella apparently noticed it, too. "What an unusual ring you have," she said. "May I see it?"

"Of course," Vera said, and held out her hand. Annabella let it rest on her fingers as she examined it. Over his lap. His brother peered at him over their fingers. Conner peered back, grinding his jaw.

"Extraordinary. Where on earth did you get it?" Annabella asked.

"Why," Vera said innocently. So innocently he knew he was

in trouble the second the word left her mouth. "From your date." Her lips smiled up at him, but her eyes were shooting daggers. "Conner gave it to me earlier tonight."

Chapter 13

She pretended she was onstage.

That was the only way she could get through this. Being onstage gave her permission to be someone else: a brave, confident woman whose power came from deep within her. Not the terrified, heartbroken, barely hanging on woman she really was.

She could do this.

She *had* to do this.

The thought of everyone's shock in the limo when she'd announced Conner had given her the Tears of the Quetzal gave her the boost she needed to pull this off. They'd naturally all jumped to the same wrong conclusion. Oddly enough, Conner hadn't corrected it. He'd actually glanced at her just as surprised as the others, but she could have sworn she'd seen him hide an amused smirk. Anyway, she'd set them straight herself, five seconds later, by adding, "For the investigation, of course!" in an innocent exclamation. But those five seconds had been glorious.

What. Ever. Now she was on her own, Conner having wandered off with his glamorous date, leaving Vera standing alone in the middle of a huge ballroom full of high-society mucky-mucks. And the uneasy feeling that someone was watching her. Conner had warned her to be on the lookout for the man who'd attacked her on the street. Thank you *so* much for that.

Damn, she needed a drink.

"Darla?" A surprised male voice assaulted her. "Is that you, babe?"

This one, at least, didn't sound dangerous.

She turned. Nor did he look like the Hispanic guy from the fuzzy traffic cam photo—but that was fairly useless. He was a raffish man about her own age, all decked out in the latest trendy Eurotrash style, blond hair going every which way.

"No," she said, taking a breath of relief and putting on her brightest smile. "I'm Vera, her roommate. Have you seen her by any chance?"

"Wow. You sure look like her. I'm Gabe. No, I haven't…"

And so it started. If she thought she'd be left alone, she'd totally misjudged Darla's friends. They might be wild and crazy, but they circled wagons for one of their own. She'd met some of them at the apartment already, so she wasn't totally out to sea. They took her under their wing, pulling her along with the flow as they made the social rounds, laughing, dancing and speculating madly with her over where Darla could have disappeared to this time. No one was worried about Darla. While everyone remarked on her ring, and a few had even read the newspaper reports that linked the ring to Candace Rothchild's murder, no one seemed overly interested in it other than as a ghoulish souvenir of that tragedy.

Unique, expensive jewels with a history were a way of life for these people. And everyone had on their most unique and expensive pieces for tonight's ball. Hers was just one more fabulous diamond to admire, gossip about, then forget.

And speaking of forgetting…she didn't think about Conner more than once, all night.

Okay, once a minute, all night.

But she was proud of the fact that she didn't track him all over the ballroom, keeping tabs on his movements, how many drinks he had, how many times he danced with that bitc—er, date, or if he ever looked across the room, searching for Vera.

She *so* didn't care.

At least, that's what she kept telling herself.

Once a minute, all night.

"Ms. Mancuso?"

She almost choked on her drink. Despite the uneventful evening so far, she'd still had the creepy feeling someone had been watching her the whole time. But probably not this guy.

A tall, elegantly dressed man with salt-and-pepper hair, who looked so much like Conner he could only be his father, or uncle, gazed down at her pleasantly.

"Y-yes," she stammered, all her hard-won poise and confidence vanishing in a fell swoop.

He extended his hand. "I'm Michael Rothchild. I understand you came with my son tonight."

Oh, God. More than once, she thought with half-hysterical irreverence. And last night, too.

She blinked, frozen by the howlingly inappropriate thought, with her hand in his. The one with the ring on it. *His* ring. "Um. Yes. But, uh, not as— I mean, I'm just working—"

He glanced at the fake Quetzal, then up again. "I just wanted to thank you." At her deer-in-the-headlights look, he added, "for helping with—" he glanced around "—well, you know." She did. She was just surprised *he* did. "Your discretion is appreciated."

"My, um—" She was about to say "pleasure," but it wasn't really, was it? So she just let the inane half comment hang there.

"*Greatly* appreciated." Michael Rothchild was still holding her hand. So firmly she couldn't politely extract it. He kept looking at her, taking in her whole person, expensive outfit and all, and it was like he saw straight through her charade. "I don't approve of your sister," he said. "but I respect family loyalty. I hope you find what you're looking for."

He released her hand, gave a little bow and walked away to join a petite ashen-haired woman who must be Conner's mother. The woman smiled at her uncertainly, then they both turned and vanished into the crowd.

Okay. That was very weird. Talk about cryptic.

"Who was that old geezer?" Gabe asked.

"Michael Rothchild."

"Dude! You know them, too? Man, Vera, for someone who doesn't get out much, you sure get around."

He had no idea.

She turned to Gabe. It was getting late, and she was ready to call it a night. She'd been dancing around the topic of Darla and her craziness with everyone all night and gotten nowhere. So she decided to just come out and ask. "Gabe, have you ever heard of Darla being involved in anything illegal?"

He regarded her skeptically. "Like what?"

"Like stealing jewelry."

"Whoa, dude." He shook his head. "No, nothing like that."

Vera nodded. "Good. I'd heard a rumor. But I just couldn't believe it myself." She met his eyes. "If you ever hear of her being involved in—"

"What the *hell* are *you* doing here?" The furious words were growled from behind. A firm male hand clamped around her arm and yanked her away from the group, then pushed her off toward a large potted palm that was part of the decor. She could hardly keep up and nearly tripped several times. Alarm zoomed through her. He wouldn't let her turn to look at him. But he didn't have the right color hair. It was thick and silver. Like—

She gasped. *Please, anything but this.*

They were attracting stares, so he slowed down until they reached the palm, then spun her to face him.

God help her. It *was* him.

Maximillian St. Giles.

Her father.

Vera's heart thundered so hard she was afraid it would pound out of her chest. She opened her mouth, but didn't know what to say. "Hello, Daddy," somehow didn't seem appropriate. So she firmly shut it again.

"You little gold-digging whore," he snarled, his piercing green eyes identical to her own glaring at her in hatred. "What do you think you're doing here?"

The *bastard.*

She resisted the urge to slap him across his sanctimonious face. For the insult. For all the insults she'd endured over the past twenty-four years. For snubbing her her entire life. For abandoning her mother, leaving the poor woman pregnant and alone with only a token cash settlement as compensation for a ruined life. But mostly for being a selfish, womanizing, egotistical prick.

She resisted, but her control was hard-won. She started to shake with bitter fury. And a stinging hurt that refused to be ignored.

"Why I'm here is none of your business," she snapped, glaring at his hand on her arm. She'd dealt with plenty of men like him. Bullies covering up their insecurities with threats of violence. "Let me go, or I'll call security."

He finally let her go. And leaned his anger-reddened face right into hers. "It *is* my business if you've come here to make trouble for me and my family."

"Trust me, you are not worth the bother," she spit out, keeping her chin up, shoulders straight. She *wouldn't* let him intimidate her.

"You've been asking questions about my daughter," he accused. "My *real* daughter."

More pain sliced through her chest. How could he *say* that? She fought to keep tears from filling her eyes. She wouldn't give him the satisfaction. "Darla's disappeared. I'm worried about her."

He snorted. "More like upset she's not there for you to leech off."

She curled her hand into a fist to keep from smacking him. But maybe she should give in to her first impulse. A fist in that hypocritical, self-righteous face sounded really good about now.

"Get out of here," her father sneered. "Go back to that strip club where you belong. And if I catch you asking questions about my daughter again, I'll hit you with legal action so hard you'll be living on a grate for the rest of your life."

With that, he turned on a heel and stormed off.

She stood watching his wake disappear into the crowd, fighting to control the trembling in her limbs.

Okay, then.

Another sentimental family reunion. Always a fun time.

"Are you all right?"

She looked up to see Conner. Her tongue tied in knots and she couldn't speak. Because suddenly, she had a blinding insight.

Conner Rothchild was just like her father.

Oh, not abusive, or overtly insulting. Nothing like that. But he was the same kind of man. With the same kind of lifestyle. And the same kind of prejudices. Against people like her.

Conner was *ashamed* of her.

That was why he'd insisted she come to the event as his assistant. Why he'd accepted a date with Ms. *Paris Vogue*. Why he hadn't told his brother, or anyone, the true nature of his relationship with Vera. If you could call two days of monkey sex a relationship.

"N-no," she stammered. Shook her head. "I mean yes. I'm fine. Really. Go back to your date."

"I don't want to—"

"Conner, please. I'm tired. There's nothing more to learn here. I'm going home now."

He frowned, managing to look concerned. Maybe he really did care. Yeah, that she'd blow their cover and reveal herself to his blue-blood family. She'd seen him with his famous hotel magnate uncle, Harold Rothchild, and his young trophy wife. Wouldn't they get a kick out of—

No, stop it. Conner wasn't like that.

Except he was. And now finally both of them knew it.

"I'll call the limo for you," he said.

"No. I'll take a cab."

"Don't be ridiculous." He pulled his cell phone from his tuxedo pocket.

"All right, fine." She didn't want to argue. She just wanted to be gone from this nightmare of a night.

"The driver has the pass code for the gate."

For a second she didn't know what he meant. Then it hit her. He expected her to go back to *his* home.

Can you say no way in hell? But she decided not to tell *him* that. "Yes, I remember."

"Good. I'll tell Hildy to be expecting you."

It occurred to her that this must be a huge relief for him. Now he wouldn't have to come up with lame excuses as to why he needed to drop his assistant off *after* he dropped off his date. She'd just be waiting for him at home. Preferably in bed. Preferably nude.

No wonder he hadn't protested.

She went to take off the ring. "You should take this."

"No, keep it for now," he said.

She couldn't argue or he'd know she had no intention of going to his place. She'd just have to send it back to him tomorrow.

"All right. Go." She made a shooing motion. "Your friends will be wondering where you are."

He hesitated, his brow furrowed. "Are you sure you're okay? You look…"

"I'm fine," she lied. "Go find your lady."

"She's not—"

But Vera was already walking away, not listening. *Back straight, head up,* she told herself as she threaded through the throng. How many of these strangers had witnessed Maximillian's tirade against her? It didn't matter. She just had to make it to the door without being stopped. *Pretend you're on the catwalk. You're not naked,* they *are.*

"Vera?"

Oh, God, now what?

She resolutely ignored the unfamiliar male voice and went right on walking.

Long fingers grasped her shoulder. "Vera, wait."

She suddenly remembered the thief. She opened her mouth to scream. But then she recognized who it was. From pictures. In her living room.

"I'm Henry St. Giles," he said, removing his hand. "Darla's brother."

Fortyish with thinning hair, he was still good-looking in a boring businessman sort of way. Darla was always telling stories about his out-of-control, crazy youth, but somehow he'd ended up selling out to their father and going to work for him after he was cut off for a year. Which explained why they'd never met.

"I know who you are," she said curtly, bracing herself for round two. "What do you want?"

He looked abashed. "I'm sorry, Vera. I just wanted to apologize for what happened back there. With my father."

"Why?" she asked suspiciously.

"We don't all think the way he does."

She arched a brow but didn't comment.

"I know you have no reason to believe me," he continued, "but I honestly regret not getting to know you like Darla did. You're my little sister. I should have made the effort, not cowed under to my father's…stupidity."

Wow. She hadn't known what to expect from Henry St. Giles when he stopped her, but this definitely wasn't even on the list.

"That's, um, very nice of you to say." Not that she particularly believed him.

"You look like her," he said, with a little smile.

"Yeah. So we've been told."

The man actually looked bashful. Either he was a hell of an actor or he was sincere. You could have knocked her over with a feather.

He held out a business card to her. "This is me. I've written my private line on the back. Call me. I'd love to get together for lunch or dinner. Get to know you. If you like."

She decided to be flattered. "Thanks. Maybe I will." Could she actually be getting a brother? She reached for the card. The second he spotted the ring on her finger, Henry's eyes popped. "What the—" They shot to hers in shock, even wider. "Vera, is that what I think it is? The ring from Candace Rothchild's murder?"

She smiled at his bewilderment and shook her head. "No. It's paste. Pretty good copy, though, don't you think?"

"Where on earth did you get it?" he asked, still awestruck by the jewel.

"Long story," she said with a laugh.

"I thought it was stolen?"

"No, the original was stolen. Well, actually both. But now they're back—"

"Miss Mancuso?" the doorman interrupted. "Your limo is here, miss."

"Thanks, I'll be right there." She tucked Henry's card in her beaded bag and held out her hand to him. "It was nice to finally meet you, Henry. And I will call. I look forward to lunch."

He nodded and waited just inside the entrance, watching as she walked to the white stretch limo and got in. He waved as the chauffeur closed the door.

Vera let out a long sigh of relief, bending down to pull off her shoes and wiggle her toes on the plush limo carpet. Thank God the night was over. Just one more thing to do. She picked up the phone to the driver.

"Yes, Miss Mancuso?"

She gave him her home address.

"But Mr. Rothchild said—"

"Change of plans," she said. "Just take me to the address I gave you."

"Very well, Miss Mancuso."

She didn't want to think about Conner right now. Didn't want to let herself be depressed about their doomed affair. Or her bastard of a father. Or even about not making any headway on the investigation of Darla and the theft ring.

She did smile when she thought of Henry. Well, at least the night hadn't been a total disaster.

Her brother. Who'd have thought he'd want to get to know her after all this time?

It was so amazing, it almost made up for losing Conner.

Almost.

Chapter 14

"Babe? Where are you?" Conner jetted out an impatient breath. "Vera, pick up the damn phone!"

Her answering machine clicked on. Conner slammed down his receiver and paced back and forth in frustration. "Damn it!" Where *was* she? She must be there. Ignoring him.

He *knew* he'd be in trouble over that freaking date.

He ripped off his bow tie and threw it onto his bed. The bed Vera should be tucked into, waiting for him.

Not that he blamed her, if he were honest. He wouldn't have been nearly as civilized about it as she was if *she'd* turned up with a date for the evening. He would have ripped the guy's throat out.

Or at least kicked him out of the limo onto his damn ass.

He picked up the phone again and dialed the number of the bodyguard he'd hired to follow her tonight.

"Barton."

"Where is she?" he demanded, not bothering with the niceties.

Barton rattled off the address of her apartment. "Limo dropped her off just over an hour ago. She's still up there."

"You sure? She's not answering her phone."

Barton was wise enough not to comment. "I'm camped out in the lobby, and I paid the security guy to keep an eye on her, too. I'll know if she budges."

"Good. Anything else I should know about tonight?"

"Some guy spoke to her as she was leaving the event." Conner heard the sound of notebook pages being flipped. "Name of Henry St. Giles. Gave her a business card."

Darla's brother? Hell, *Vera's* brother. What did *he* want? "Was it amicable?"

"Seemed to be."

As opposed to her confrontation with Maximillian. Her own father. "You'll be there all night?"

"That's the plan."

"Good. I'll expect your full report in the morning."

"Will do, sir."

Thoughtfully, Conner put the phone back in its stand. Should he go check on her? Or just let her cool off... He wasn't too worried about her safety, not with Barton there standing guard all night. And Conner'd hired a cleaning crew to tidy up the apartment after the FBI was done with their evidence collecting, so she didn't have to deal with that.

But, damn it, he *missed* her.

He'd been bored stiff all night, stuck at that stuffy ball with his stuffy family and the stultifyingly sophisticated Annabella Pruitt, slowly drinking himself numb. Or trying to. Unfortunately, he'd remained distressingly sober the entire time, despite the copious amounts of alcohol that had passed through his system.

Guilt?

Possibly.

Probably.

He wasn't proud of the way he'd treated Vera. In fact, he was downright ashamed. What was wrong with him? Was he such a damn wuss that he couldn't just tell his socially paralyzed father to take a flying leap if he didn't like Conner's choice of women?

Not to mention the whole Maximillian St. Giles thing. Conner should have pounded him into the dance floor like a wooden peg. Or at least shamed him into apologizing to his daughter, admitting he was being an ass.

So, why hadn't he?

Because Conner was an even bigger ass, that's why.

Setting his lips in a thin line, he strode into the hall. "Hildy!" he yelled. "Get the limo back here! I'm going out again."

Naturally, Vera refused to answer the intercom. So Conner had to talk the security guard into letting him into the penthouse.

Luckily, he'd been introduced as Vera's lawyer the other day after the break-in, so he didn't have too much trouble convincing the man he was worried about his client and wanted to check on her well-being. The C-note deposited discreetly in his uniform pocket didn't hurt either.

Conner found her in the bathtub. Up to her neck in bubbles, the mirrors steamed up and a dozen scented candles lit. The room smelled like a hothouse filled with damask roses. A bottle of red wine was propped on the edge of the tub. Half-empty. No glass.

The fake Quetzal was sitting on the tub's front rim, winking in the candlelight like a multicolored disco ball.

"Go away," she mumbled, not opening her eyes.

"How do you know who it is?" he asked, chagrined that she wasn't worried and didn't even check. He could be the thief returning, for all she knew!

"I can smell you," she said thickly. "The demonic scent of wealth and temptation."

Had he just been insulted? He made a mental note to change his cologne.

He stepped into the room and closed the door. "Sweetheart—"

"Don't!" Her hand shot up from the water, fanning out a cascade of droplets. "Don't you 'sweetheart' me, you…"

His eyes widened as she called him a *very* bad name.

Ho-*kay,* then. Looked like he wasn't the only one drinking himself into oblivion. "Been watching reruns of Deadwood?" he muttered. Walking over, he plucked the wine bottle from the tub and deposited it on the marble vanity counter.

"Hey!"

"Any more of that stuff and you'll drown yourself," he said.

"Drown *you,* you mean," she muttered. Then called him that word again.

Okay, so maybe he deserved the moniker. But he couldn't help smiling. She was even more beautiful when she was calling him bad names.

"Vera, I'm sorry."

"Tell it to someone who cares."

"Look, honey, I know you're mad, but—"

"Mad? Me?" She cracked an eyelid, gave him a gimlet eye and made a really rude noise.

"I can see you're not going to make this easy on me."

"Sure, I am. What part of 'go away' don't you get? I'll be happy to e'splain it to you." She hiccupped.

He desperately wanted to chuckle. But he figured it would be the last thing he ever did. So he did the second best thing. Toed off his shoes and socks and climbed into the tub with her. They'd have to cut his tuxedo pants off him, but what the hell, he didn't like this suit anyway.

"What the—" she sputtered, wheeling her arms to get away from him. But he just grabbed onto her and held tight as he slid down behind her into the water, leaning his back against the end of the oversize spa tub. "You are such a freaking Neanderthal," she gritted out.

"So sue me. But I warn you, I'll win."

Damn, it felt weird taking a bath in his clothes. But she really would have screamed bloody murder if he'd gotten undressed.

Besides, he didn't want to give her the wrong idea, either. He wasn't here for sex. He was here for forgiveness. For her.

At least she wasn't fighting him anymore. With a huff, she let herself fall back against his chest, closed her eyes again and refused to look at him.

Progress.

She sighed. "Conner, what are you doing here?" she asked him, sounding suspiciously uninebriated.

"Apologizing."

"That's not what it feels like," she said dryly.

He realized his hand had unconsciously found its way to her breast and was gently fondling it. Since she hadn't clawed his eyes out, he didn't stop.

He kissed the top of her head. "I'm sorry, Vera. I acted like a jackass. You have every reason to be angry with me, and I wouldn't blame you if you never spoke to me again."

"Good, because I don't plan to."

"Which would be a damn shame, because I'd really miss you ordering me around when we're in bed."

Instead of snorting and telling him *he* was the one who did all of the ordering around, as he'd hoped she would, she just sighed again.

"Conner, you and I, we're not going to work," she said quietly. "I don't fit into your world. I'd never be accepted by your family. What's the point?"

He hugged her closer, leaning his cheek on her head. "Because I don't want to give you up."

"You did a pretty damn good imitation of it tonight."

Guilt assailed him anew. "I know. And I couldn't be sorrier. I was wrong. It'll never happen again. I swear."

"You're positive?" she asked bleakly. "Because if it came down to a choice between me or Rothchild, Rothchild and Bennigan, I have a feeling I know which way it would go."

"I'm not so sure." He fell silent, and for the first time he seriously thought about what would happen to him if he left the family law firm. Or was asked to leave.

Would he be sad? Sure, he would. Would it take a while to regroup and start over? Undoubtedly. But he had more than enough money in the bank never to have to work another day in his life. So would his world fall apart? Definitely not.

The only question was, if it came down to a choice between Vera and his *family,* which way would *that* go?

"You're jousting at windmills," she murmured.

She sounded tired. And he was totally beat himself.

"Let's get out of this water," he said. "And go to bed. We can talk about all this in the morning."

"Conner…"

He kissed her on the temple. "We don't have to make love if you don't want to. Just let me hold you while you sleep."

She hesitated, then let out a resigned breath. "You're a real bastard, you know that?"

He'd been upgraded. A good sign. "I'll take it," he said, kissing her ear. "As long as I can be with you tonight."

The next morning Vera got breakfast in bed. It was Saturday, and Conner didn't have to work.

The sun was streaming through the floor-to-ceiling bedroom windows looking out over the city below and the mountains beyond. The sky was so blue it hurt. A lone hawk rode the thermals that rose off the desert floor, scouting for its morning meal…or maybe just windsurfing for the sheer joy of it.

She had no right to be so happy. She knew the bliss wouldn't last. Conner was fooling himself if he thought they had a prayer.

But it was enough that he wanted to try.

Or said he did.

That was a miracle in itself.

He'd made no declarations of love, given her no vows of forever. She could live with that. For now. Just having him here with her was more than she'd ever expected.

"Coffee?"

"Mmm." It smelled delicious. "Who made the French toast?"

"I did," he said proudly.

She was impressed. "A man of many talents."

He leaned over and gave her a slow, thorough kiss. "And a woman of rare appetite," he said in a low rumble.

They'd made love. Of course they had. Like she could take him to her bed and not touch him. Not have him touch her. Impossible.

He'd been so tender it nearly broke her heart. It almost felt like… No, she wasn't going there.

They'd just nestled together into the propped-up pillows to eat the savory breakfast, when his cell phone rang. He checked the screen.

"It's the office. Guess I'd better get it." They rarely called him on weekends, so when they did it was usually important.

"Conner here."

"It's your father."

Hell. "Hi, Dad. What's up?"

"You got an e-mail about a surveillance from someone named Barton."

Conner glanced at Vera and smiled. "Yeah?" How the hell had his father gotten hold of that?

"It came in on the general e-mail account," his dad said, answering the unspoken question. "You're surveilling Vera Mancuso? What's that all about?"

Double hell. "Hang on, Dad." He climbed out of bed, giving Vera a kiss. "Reception's bad in here. I'm gonna take this outside." He grabbed a towel to wrap around his waist and trotted out the double sliders to the huge tiled patio that circled the penthouse, closing them firmly behind him.

"I told you about the case she's helping me on. The whole Quetzal thing. She could be in danger, so I'm making sure she's safe."

"From between her sheets? Mike says—"

Anger shot through Conner. He tamped it down. "That's none of Mike's business, Dad. Or yours."

"It is if I think you're getting personally involved with this woman."

"Why would that matter?"

"You have the family name to think of."

"Oh. You mean like Uncle Harold? Or Candace, or Silver?" All stars of the local gossip columns due to their endless "inappropriate" love affairs. Although Silver seemed to have settled down now that she was a newlywed and expecting a baby.

"That's not our side of the family. *Our* side—"

"I know, I know. We're the respectable ones. We only defend murderers and rapists. But we marry decent women."

His father made a choking noise. "If you have a problem being a defense attorney—"

"I don't. But if I want to date a stripper, I'll date a stripper. Besides, it's not serious." Yet. "I just met the woman. No doubt I'll get tired of her soon, just like I get tired of all the women I date."

It was disturbing how easily the half-lie slipped out. Half, because he *did* go through women like popcorn at the movies. But he didn't want to deal with his father now. He *had* just met Vera, and although his feelings about her were totally different than for any other woman he'd ever dated, how could he be so sure she was The One? That this affair was forever? Why alienate his dad until he was a hundred percent certain?

That wasn't being a coward. That was being prudent.

"Did you at least get the paste Quetzal back from her? That's an extremely valuable piece of jewelry."

"Yes, Dad. I got it back," he said exasperatedly. And made a mental note to retrieve it from the tub.

"All right. Good. Anyway, just be careful, son. Women like her—"

"I will, Dad. Don't worry. Just forward the e-mail to my private account, okay?"

"Your mother is asking if you'll come to dinner tonight. Ms. Pruitt and her father will be here."

Saints preserve him. "Sorry, can't make it. I've got a good lead on the Parker case and will be working it tonight until all hours."

"The Parker case?"

"One of my pro bonos."

"I see. Conner, I really wish—"

"I know, Dad. Give Mom a kiss for me."

He punched the end button on the cell phone with an annoyed curse. He knew his dad meant well. But he was all grown up now—thirty-three years old. He could run his own life.

And if he wanted Vera in it, that was *his* decision to make, no one else's.

Chapter 15

It's not serious… No doubt I'll get tired of her soon…

Vera hadn't meant to eavesdrop. She really hadn't. She'd just gone into the bathroom and noticed it was still humid from last night's bath and opened a window. Could she help it if Conner was talking on the phone practically right under it?

And now his casual pronouncement was seared into her brain.

Nothing she hadn't already known. Nothing she hadn't been telling herself over and over for the past three days.

But hearing it spoken out loud like that, from her lover's own mouth in such a matter-of-fact manner, well, that really brought it home with a sick thud in her heart.

Everything he'd said last night was a lie. She really was just a temporary plaything for him.

As her mother had been for her father.

For the first time ever, she finally understood why her mother had done what she had. Thrown away her life for a man who didn't care about her for more than a few nights of pleasure. She'd been in love with wealthy, powerful Maximillian St. Giles, just as Vera was in love with wealthy, powerful Conner Rothchild. And love made women do foolish, foolish things.

Taking a deep cleansing breath, Vera quickly finished up and slid back into bed before he knew she'd overheard his conversation.

For now it didn't change anything. Outwardly. But she was so glad she'd found out his true feelings. Or she might have believed his pretty lies and allowed herself to dream of the impossible. Heartbreaking as it was, better to know the truth.

Putting on her best smile, she greeted Conner with a kiss when he came back to bed.

"Mmm," he hummed approvingly. "You taste sweet."

"You'll never guess what I found on the breakfast tray."

He grinned against her mouth. "Yeah? What's that?"

She held up a can of whipped cream. "Funny, I don't remember this being in the kitchen yesterday."

"I found it in the limo fridge. Those chauffeurs do think of everything, don't they?"

She squirted a dollop on her finger and slid it into her mouth suggestively. "Gee, and I thought you didn't come here for sex last night."

His grin widened. "A man can always hope, can't he? I did apologize. Abjectly and sincerely. *And* I ruined my tuxedo getting back into your good graces."

"Or pants, as the case may be."

"As I recall, there were no pants involved."

"Hmm." She flipped back the covers, revealing his magnificent naked body. His magnificent and *aroused* naked body. "It appears you're right."

His eyes went half-lidded. "I was talking about you."

"And I," she said, giving the can a shake, and then a well-aimed squirt, "was talking about you."

He moaned as she bent to lick the sweet cream from his shaft, melting back onto the pillows in willing surrender to her tongue.

He may well give her up in the end, but when he did, he'd be giving up the best damn lover he'd ever had. She'd make sure he remembered her for the rest of his life, seeing her face in the face of every future lover, feeling her touch in every brush of their fingertips.

He might give her up. But he'd always regret letting her go.

Almost as much as she did.

Conner was totally wrung out.

Ho. Lee. Batman.

The woman was amazing. Agile. Clever. Mind-blowing. Among other things.

Last night they'd done tender and loving. The night before had been hot and ravenous. This morning had been…well, every one of his fantasies come true.

Yeow.

She'd left him sprawled limply in bed, waving at him from the door with her fingers and a wicked smile, and gone to visit her stepfather, Joe. It was Saturday, her usual day to have lunch with him at the assisted-care facility.

Conner had a feeling she wouldn't be all that hungry. She'd eaten a ton of whipped cream at breakfast.

Oy.

The woman would be the death of him yet.

But what a way to go.

He *really* did not want to do this.

But he had no choice. It was the only way to get the

evidence he needed to exonerate Suzie Parker and put the scumbags who'd abused her away for good.

Conner reluctantly hit the "Pay Now" button on the PayPal invoice he'd received from Lecherous Lou for tonight's private gentlemen's party. He'd much rather be watching Vera dance at the club. And he was still worried about her safety. So much so he'd put Barton back on her tail after letting him get a few hours of sleep. He'd just called in after catching up with her at the assisted care. The guy was good. And thorough. The report he'd e-mailed this morning was detailed as hell, including background sketches on all the people she'd spent more than five minutes with last night at the charity ball. Apparently, Barton liked to while away his hours on stakeout doing research on the Internet from his BlackBerry.

From his notes, Darla's friends seemed to be mostly aging spoiled rich kids who seemed harmless enough, with no huge red flags among the bunch of them. Her brother, Henry, on the other hand… The guy was a real piece of work. His record up until his early thirties read like a Primer for Troubled Young Men. Everything from joyriding without permission, to a dismissed assault charge for beating up a love rival, to a variety of drunk-driving charges. All dismissed as well. His daddy had very deep pockets.

Conner shot off a note to his secretary to give Barton a raise, then reached for the phone to call Vera's cell.

"Where are you?" he asked when she picked up.

"Are you stalking me, by any chance?" She sounded more amused than irritated.

He sat back in his chair and grinned. "Hell, no. Well. Maybe. But in a good way."

"Good," she said. "Then I know I've got you hooked."

"Hook, line and sinker, baby."

She chuckled softly, but he detected a sadness lurking in the tone.

"Something wrong?" he asked. "Your stepdad okay?"

The question elicited a sigh. "No, not really. He's getting worse. It's so depressing to watch."

"I'm so sorry, sweetheart. I know he means a lot to you."

"Yeah." There was a pause. "So what's up? Where are *you?*"

"At the office catching up. And I'd like to point out, you never actually answered where you are."

She laughed gently. "On the way home. I have *got* to get some sleep before work tonight."

"I've got a few hours free," he said suggestively. "I could come over and—"

"Forget it, Batman. I can barely walk as it is. God knows how I'm going to perform tonight."

He gave a bark of laughter. "That bad?"

She made a throaty moan. "That good."

He sat there beaming. You could pull down the blinds and the room would still be fully lit. "Yeah," he said. "For me, too." He made a frustrated noise. "I sure wish you were here so I could kiss you."

"Me, too. Maybe later?"

"Absolutely." Suddenly, he remembered why he'd called. "Listen, about later. I'm going to have to work until pretty late. There's a lead I need to follow on another case, but it'll only happen tonight."

"Oh. I understand," she said, trying to hide her disappointment but failing. God, she made him feel good.

"I've assigned you a bodyguard," he continued. "His name is Barton, and he'll stay with you at the club until I can get there."

"Really? You think that's necessary?"

"I hope it's not, but I won't take any chances."

She hesitated, then, "Okay."

He breathed a sigh of relief. "Thank you for not arguing."

"I can still feel that gun sticking into my back. Something I'd just as soon not experience again."

"Beautiful *and* smart," he said. "Just do what Barton says, okay?"

"Everything?" she teased.

"Ha-ha. Only if you want me in prison for homicide."

"Sweet-talker."

"You have no idea."

He heard a soft puff of breath. "I'll be waiting for you."

"Your place or mine?"

Her voice went low and throaty. "Where would you like me?"

A loaded question, if ever he'd heard one. He matched her tone. "Where haven't I had you yet?"

"You are so bad."

"That's why you love me."

Suddenly there was an awkward pause.

Ah, hell. Why had he said *that?* He covered quickly. "If I don't get to the club before your shift ends, go to my place, okay? I'll be there as soon as I can. Barton will keep me informed with what's up."

"Right," she said. "I'm home now. Gotta run. Bye."

"Be careful, honey."

But she'd already hung up.

He took a deep breath.

Way to go, idiot. Talk about almost stepping in it. He knew she was deliberately keeping her distance from him emotionally. Which was a *good* thing. Because he was, too. This affair between them was too new, too potentially disastrous, for either of them to take it lightly. Dropping the L-bomb like that…already…not good timing on anyone's clock.

Maybe she hadn't noticed.

Uh-huh.

Which was why she'd been in such an all-fired hurry to hang up.

Damn.

Vera lay in bed staring at the ceiling for two solid hours, trying to take a nap.

It was no use.

Thoughts whirled in her head, around and around at the speed of light, keeping her wide awake. Because when Conner had made that joke about her loving him, she'd almost blurted out and told him the truth. That she really did.

Love him.

Thank God she'd had the presence of mind to stop herself. What a joke. Yeah, on her.

She finally gave up and got ready for work instead. May as well go in and pick up an extra set. At least she'd be using her insomnia productively. She needed all the money she could make.

Joe was worse. A lot worse. He'd picked up an infection in his lungs, and if it didn't get better, it could easily turn into pneumonia. His nurse said a lot of Alzheimer's patients died of pneumonia. So he needed a lot of extra medications. Which cost a lot of extra money.

When she got down to the lobby, a man rose to his feet.

"Are you Burton?" she asked. When he nodded and showed her his ID, she suggested they carpool. "Seems silly to take two vehicles when we're going to the same place."

"Good idea. I'll drive," he said, and made a notation on a small spiral pad.

When they arrived at the Diamond Lounge, Lecherous Lou called her into his office right away. Barton insisted on following her and standing guard outside the door.

Seemed a bit obsessive. But it did make her feel safe.

"So," Lecherous Lou said as soon as the door was closed, "you on for tonight?"

She frowned in confusion. "Well, yeah. That's why I came in early."

He smiled, all teeth. "Great! I knew you'd come around eventually." He leered at her. "Nothing like a big spender to open a woman's eyes—and her legs—I always say."

Wait. "What are you talking about?" Obviously not the same thing she was.

"The private party tonight. You are coming, right?"

Disgust straightened her spine. "No. I've told you a million times—"

"That was before your sugar daddy signed up," he said smugly. He lifted a shoulder. "Naturally, I assumed you'd want to reap the full benefit of his generosity, and not let some other girl in on the action. After all, it's only because of your performance in the VIP room he decided to take me up on my offer."

Conner?

Shock hit her square in the gut. "You're talking about Conner Rothchild? He's going to one of your parties?"

Lou dangled a PayPal receipt in her face. "Want to change your mind? I'm telling you, the man's got a thing for you, babe. Play your cards right and your take-home pay for the night will be in the thousands. Guaranteed."

But her mind was still reeling over the fact that Conner was attending a private stripper party. *Her* Conner!

Okay, so apparently not as hers as she'd thought.

He'd lied to her! He'd said he was working tonight!

What else had he lied about?

No doubt I'll get tired of her soon...

Obviously, not about that part.

She'd been right. He *was* just like her father.

"So, you in?"

Fuming, she gave herself a severe reality check. The jerk wanted a private party? Fine. She'd give him a damn private party.

And then she'd give him a big fat piece of her mind. Right before she left him and his lying self high and dry.

For good.

"Sure," she declared, already planning her exit strategy. "Count me in."

Chapter 16

Conner was wearing a wire. Well, technically, not a wire but a tiny video camera and wireless transmitter, a handy gizmo he'd had a techie friend build into an old Rolex watch a few years back. The device beamed sound and video images to a small laptop, which he'd set up back in his room to record everything. The laptop was being monitored by a Metro vice officer recommended to him by his cousin Natalie.

Lou's party was being held in a luxurious multibedroom suite in one of the most exclusive hotels in Vegas. Unbeknownst to upper management, Conner assumed. He'd registered for a room of his own on the floor directly below, where he'd gotten ready, made sure the vice officer was comfortable and well-stocked for the night, then ridden the elevator up to the party suite.

Imagine his surprise when he found Barton standing guard outside the door.

What the—

He scowled. Heading him off, Barton jammed a thumb in the direction of the door. "Sorry, sir. She took my BlackBerry. I didn't want to leave my post to find a phone."

Conner ground his teeth. What the freaking hell? "It's okay. You did the right thing."

He rang the buzzer and waited for a long minute until the door was answered. When it finally opened, his worst fears were realized.

Vera. Wearing red silk lingerie and red satin high heels.

She looked ready to work. Hell, she looked ready to sin.

"Hello, Mr. Rothchild," she said smoothly. "Welcome."

The unforeseen development threw him for a total loop. Hadn't she said she refused to dance at these parties? "What the *hell* are you doing here?" he demanded under his breath.

"I could ask the same," she said pleasantly, crooking her arm around his elbow and drawing him inside. Except her arm was stiff and her smile glued on.

Which was his first clue that she was furious. *Really* furious.

Oh.

Hell.

Lou must have bragged to her that he was coming tonight. And invited her to join the fun. Damn. He should have anticipated that and told her himself.

"I can explain," he said.

"I'm sure you can," she said, piercing him with a look that would wither flowers. "Although I could have sworn you told me you'd be working on a lead tonight. You know, lawyer stuff."

He glanced around the large, opulent room populated with a dozen well-dressed wealthy men and maybe twenty mostly undressed girls—a couple of whom were not looking happy to be here—making sure they weren't being overheard. Behind them, the buzzer sounded and another man was ushered in by a different lady.

"I *am* working on a lead," he whispered, starting to get ticked, himself. After what they'd shared together, she should have a *little* faith.

She stared at him in abject disbelief.

Conner raised his wrist, pretending to check his Rolex. "Smile for the camera," he gritted out under his breath, and pointed the face at her. "Click."

At least she had the grace to look taken aback. "But…I thought—"

"You thought what?" he quietly demanded, leading her to the side of the room. "That I'd go off looking for a good time somewhere else? That I'd betray you like that? That I can't be *trusted?*"

Her suddenly remorseful face said it all. No. She *hadn't* trusted him.

"Great." He raked his fingers through his hair, not knowing whether to be more hurt or angry. "Thanks for the overwhelming vote of confidence."

"I'm sorry," she whispered contritely. "I didn't know. Lou said—"

"And naturally you believed him, not me. Because *he's* so trustworthy."

Definitely hurt.

Her lips turned down unhappily. "I'm sorry, Conner. The men in my life haven't had the best history for being icons of trust."

His heart zinged. Right. How could he forget? Especially after the scene last night with her own father.

With a monumental effort, he pushed back his anger. Given her background, she had every right to be wary, and he had no right to chastise her for it. With a sigh, he put his arms around her and pulled her into an embrace. "No, *I'm* sorry, honey. This is my fault. I should have told you the whole truth. I just thought—"

"You couldn't trust me?"

He gave her a sardonic smile. "No, I thought maybe you'd get jealous and want to be here for me, regardless of personal consequences. You know, so I wouldn't go with another woman."

She stared at him, chagrin clouding over her pretty green eyes. "Touché." Then her gaze darted to the door, where another pair of men had arrived, and back to him. "What lead *are* you following?"

He sent her a warning look. "Whatever it is, I can't do it with you here," he said in a low voice. "You need to leave."

"But I could help."

He set his jaw. "I don't want you involved."

"But—"

"You should go. Now. Unless you want to wind up arrested, or faced with testifying in open court."

She shook her head, eyes wide. "No."

"I didn't think so." He brushed his fingertips down her cheek. "Go home. Wait for me there." He tilted her chin up and gave her a kiss.

"Okay, I—"

"Well, well, well." They looked up at the nasty tone of an all-too-familiar figure standing next to them. "If it isn't the little gold-digging stripper again."

Conner's back went right up.

Maximillian St. Giles. He should have known a reprobate like St. Giles would show up at one of these things.

Vera's father continued his harangue of her, barely taking a breath. "What's the matter? Didn't find a big enough sucker to leech onto at the ball last night?" He puffed up and tried to look down his nose at Conner but was several inches shorter. He only succeeded in showing off his nose hairs. "Rothchild, isn't it? Michael's oldest. I see you've met my bastard daughter. Careful, she'll—"

Conner couldn't take another word. "The only bastard around here is *you,* St. Giles," he growled, easing Vera protectively behind his body. His hands were literally itching to flatten the jackass. "Tell me, if you're so high and mighty, why are *you* here?"

Maximillian glared. "I have every—"

Conner knew he shouldn't draw attention to himself, but he just couldn't stop from saying, "Not getting it at home? Is that it? The wife finally had enough and cut you off?"

"Why you—"

For every syllable Conner uttered, he was getting angrier and angrier. "Maybe you should try being a little less hypocritical, eh? And clean up that mouth of yours around a lady."

"How dare you! She's no lady."

"Vera is your *daughter,*" Conner spat out. "Your own flesh and blood! You should be loving her, taking care of her. Not heaping her with your scorn and two-faced disdain. Forcing her into this lifestyle because you refuse to take responsibility for your own actions. You are one damned poor excuse for a man, St. Giles. You're not fit to clean this woman's shoes."

He turned to find Vera covering her mouth with both hands, tears brimming over her eyelashes. She looked up at him with such an expression of misery, Conner's heart broke right in two. "Ah, sweetheart. Forget him. He's not worth your anguish." He pulled her close, turned her away from the jerk.

Another man hurried up to them anxiously. "Mr. St. Giles, are you having a problem with this girl?" The pimp du jour, no doubt. Without waiting for an answer, the pimp discreetly took her arm and urged her toward one of the bedrooms, presumably to get her things. "We can't have any disruptions. I'm afraid I'm going to have to ask you to leave immediately, Ms. LaRue."

"I understand." She glanced back at Conner, tears glistening on her cheeks. "Thank you," she said, her voice cracking, her heart in her eyes.

"Go on and get your things. I'll take you home," Conner said.

"Oh, but—" She shook her head, wiping her tears, and straightened her shoulders. "No. I'll be fine. You stay, Mr. Rothchild. I know you were looking forward to a night of pleasure." She pretended to toss it off and smile carelessly. "Please don't let this spoil your evening."

"Vera, I really—"

"Here." To his shock, she reached out and unclasped his Rolex, then took Pimp Man's wrist and put the watch on him. She gave Conner a meaningful look. "Mr. Black here is in charge of all the night's entertainment. He'll see to it you have everything you could ever wish for, Mr. Rothchild. Isn't that right, Mr. Black?"

The pimp's eyes were glued greedily to the expensive Rolex. Thank God it actually still functioned. "Everything and more," he assured Conner, glancing at a group of girls who were nervously looking on.

Conner knew what Vera was doing. The vice officer downstairs was probably having an orgasm about now. With the audio-video transmitter on the very man who set the price for every criminal act being committed here tonight, they'd have ample ammunition to make the man testify against the club managers who ran the show, and all the evidence needed to shut down these parties for good.

But Conner had never been so torn in his life. He *had* to stay. Make sure nothing went wrong. Set Black up to get the best evidence possible and protect the girls who didn't want to do the things they were being coerced into doing. But if he stayed, Vera would go home alone and crushed. Again. He'd seen how hard she'd taken her father's rejection yesterday. He didn't want to think about the tears she would surely shed tonight if he wasn't there to help her through the emotional turmoil.

"Vera—"

"It's okay, Mr. Rothchild. We'll hook up next time." She went up on her toes and gave him a long, sensual kiss filled with warmth and promise. "And I'll be sure to thank you properly."

He kissed her back, barely able to keep the love and concern spinning around inside him from bursting out of his chest. He whispered, "Promise you'll go to my place."

She nodded and gave him one last hug, then was whisked away by Mr. Black.

A few moments later, head held high, dressed and carrying her purse, she was escorted out of the suite.

He turned to see Maximillian St. Giles watching her with a look of guarded unease on his face.

The bastard.

Conner couldn't help himself. He clamped his jaw, pulled back his fist and punched the man as hard as he could.

Miraculously, Conner's not-so-little outburst did not cost him the Parker case. For some reason, St. Giles didn't press charges. In fact, he was strangely docile about the whole thing. He got up, brushed himself off, excused himself with as few words and as much dignity as he could muster and left the hotel.

After things settled down, for the next several hours Conner walked a tightrope between pretending to be a conscienceless lecher who was interested in the dozen or so women thrust at him by Mr. Black and pretending to drink copious amounts of the champagne they kept filling his glass with. He sure hoped the potted geraniums survived. All the while convincing everyone he really didn't give a damn about Vera other than her body. That Sensitive New-Age Guy performance earlier? Just him trying to get laid.

It would have stretched the thespian skills of a seasoned actor, let alone a lawyer whose skills in that direction came solely from the drama of the courtroom.

Somehow he managed to pull it off, though, and by around three in the morning the officer downstairs had gotten enough evidence to send the Metro vice squad bursting into the suite to take down the whole operation. Everyone got arrested except Conner. But he nevertheless spent the rest of the night arranging bail and deals for the handful of dancers who'd been coerced into working the private party. They'd be good witnesses, and their testimony would corroborate the story of his original client, Suzie Parker, and her prostitution charges would be dismissed.

All in all, a very good night's work, but by the time he got out of there, it was almost noon.

He should be proud, and heading home to a well-deserved night's…well, midday's…sleep. Instead, he was breaking all speed limits to get back home to Vera. He was worried about her and couldn't wait to pull her into his arms and sink down into his bed and just let out a long sigh of relief that she was okay. Maybe get a little sleep before showing her how hard he was falling for her.

Maybe even telling her.

Wow. How terrifying was *that?*

He was just passing the Luxor when his cell phone rang. It was Barton.

"Hey, what's up? Is Vera okay?"

"She's fine, Mr. Rothchild. As I texted you, I drove her to your place last night, and your Miss Hildy took good care of her. Put her to bed, and I sat outside her door the whole night. No suspicious activity at all."

"Excellent."

Barton continued, "But this morning she got a call from

Mr. Henry St. Giles and apparently made plans to go out to lunch with him in a few minutes. I'm sorry, sir, I didn't find out until just now. Do you want me to follow them?"

Hell's bells, Barton must be dead on his feet. Conner definitely was, and he'd actually been able to catch a long catnap in an empty LVMPD conference room while everyone was being processed into the system.

He pushed out a breath. "Where are they going, do you know?" Barton named a small restaurant just off the Strip. "Okay, can you make sure she gets there safely? Then you're done for the day. I'll meet you and take over from there."

"Sure thing, Mr. Rothchild."

He thanked the man for his diligence and made a quick right, heading for the restaurant.

He got to the parking lot before Vera and didn't see Henry waiting. Which gave Conner time to figure out how to handle this. It would be stupid for him just to sit in his car and stake out the place. Aside from which, he might easily fall asleep. Or something could happen to her inside the restaurant.

Because to be honest, Conner was a bit concerned about Henry's motives in courting Vera's favor. His sudden appearance in her life out of nowhere was more than a little suspicious.

Conner was not forgetting his assignment for Special Agent Lex Duncan, to narrow down possible suspects in the interstate jewelry theft ring the FBI was trying to crack—the same ring Duncan highly suspected Henry's sister, Darla, of being part of.

Vera was hoping Darla was innocent, but Conner wasn't so sure she was. What would be more natural than a brother-sister team of high-end thieves?

And if either of them was involved in his cousin Candace's murder, Vera could be in genuine danger meeting with Henry. Conner'd already seen Darla arguing with the man he was convinced stole the Quetzal from the police—likely the same man who later attacked Silver and then Vera, searching for the illusive diamond after he'd failed to hang on to it while he had it. Duncan was waiting for more concrete evidence, but Conner was convinced that man was the link between the ring and Candace's murder.

Would it be such a stretch if Henry somehow had his fingers deep in this mess, too? Even if he didn't, he was Maximillian St. Giles's son and heir. What did he want with Vera after all these years? Nothing good, Conner figured.

Conner decided to let Vera and Henry go into the restaurant after they arrived and got seated; then he'd casually walk in and spot them like his being there was a pure coincidence. Vera would probably twig, but after her quick uptake and play-along last night, he wasn't worried she'd give him away.

That way he could simply join them for lunch. Vera would be safe. And he could subtly pump Henry for information while they ate.

Problem solved.

Except, unfortunately, that's not how things worked out.

Henry arrived first, not unexpectedly. He should have realized something was up when the other man didn't let the valet park his car. But Conner was distracted by Barton cruising past the McLaren and giving Conner a thumbs-up, indicating Vera was right behind him.

Henry, leaning against the door of his Lexus, waved to Vera when she drove into the lot and let the valet whisk her Camry away. Conner raised a brow at the touching hug they exchanged, Henry smiling broadly as he then teasingly touched her earlobe. *Oh, please. Don't fall for it, sweetheart.* The guy had serious bloodsucking scum written all over him. How could Vera possibly miss that transparently fake smarm?

Because she was looking for something else in the man. Like acceptance. Affection. Warmth.

Family.

But still, Conner was not prepared when Henry went around and opened the passenger door for her and she climbed into the Lexus. With a spin of the wheels, Henry peeled out of the parking lot.

Whoa! What had just happened? Had they decided to go to a different restaurant? Or was something else going on?

Conner jackknifed up, gunned the engine and took off after them.

When Henry made a sharp turn onto an all-too-conveniently-situated freeway ramp onto the I-15 south, the major route heading out of the city, Conner really started to worry. So much so that he pulled out his phone and speed-dialed Duncan and then his cousin Natalie.

He wanted backup. Just in case.

Because suddenly, he had a really, really bad feeling about this whole thing.

Chapter 17

"Where are we going, again?" Vera glanced around at the downtown area fast disappearing behind them and bit her lip. "I thought you were taking me to lunch."

"I am!" Henry grinned over at her. "There is this amazing little bistro up in the mountains above Henderson I want you to try. Very chichi. The food there is so incredible, and the view is spectacular. You can see all the way to Lake Mead."

"Okay…" Vera knew Henderson was a growing tourist destination all on its own, but she'd never heard about a fantastic restaurant in the mountains *above* the Vegas suburb. But Henry—she couldn't believe she was finally getting to know her brother!—was presumably a lot more dialed into the hideaways of the rich and famous.

"You're not in a hurry, are you?" he asked politely, even though he was driving like a speed demon.

"No, of course not," she rushed to say. She didn't want to

annoy him the first time they did anything together. Either about his choice of restaurants or his driving habits. She smiled over at him. "I can't wait."

But still… When he bypassed the main exit to Henderson but took a long back road in, she started getting concerned. Not nervous, exactly. More like…uneasy. But he was happily chatting about the Lights of Vegas Charity Ball and how he wished he'd known earlier she was there, and how terribly embarrassed he'd been about his father's—*their* father's, he quickly corrected himself—behavior that night, and how he'd heard so many good things about her from Darla. He seemed so kind and attentive that Vera just couldn't interrogate him about their destination.

Nevertheless, she wished she'd called Conner to tell him where she was going.

Lord, she'd been so upset last night when he never came home. She'd stared at the ceiling until the sun was streaming through the windows and still he hadn't gotten home. In her mind she knew why. She understood what he was doing. That he was not cheating on her. That he hadn't gotten tired of her already and was out having fun with another woman. He was working. He'd probably gotten caught up in…well, God knew what. But whatever it was, she was sure he had a good reason why he couldn't be there for her.

But she'd needed him so badly. She'd been devastated by her father's renewed attack on her and had desperately wanted Conner's warm, comforting presence to soothe the razor-sharp pain in her heart. And in that same hurting heart, she'd felt the slightest bit betrayed.

Even though she knew it was wrong to blame him, that he had an important job to do, she'd been mad enough to arrange this lunch with her brother and take off without paying any heed to Barton's warnings that she shouldn't leave Conner's house. She saw now she'd been acting like a selfish baby.

Surreptitiously, she glanced in the side mirror to see if she could catch a glimpse of Barton following her. But she hadn't seen him since before leaving the restaurant where she'd met Henry. At least she didn't think so. She thought there might have been someone following far behind them, but it wasn't the same color car as Barton had been driving and had since disappeared. Probably wishful thinking on her part. Last night she'd tried to get him to lie down on the sofa, but he'd insisted on sitting up the whole night on a chair outside her door punching buttons on his ubiquitous BlackBerry. No doubt Barton had figured she was safe having lunch with her own brother and had gone home to get some sleep.

So she was on her own here.

Her heartbeat kicked up as Henry turned the car onto an old macadam road heading up into the craggy desert bluffs. "Doesn't this go up to where all those old quarries are located?" she asked.

He glanced at her in surprise. "You know about those?"

"Doesn't everyone?" She gripped the car seat with her fingers. "Are you *sure* this is the way to the bistro?"

"Actually, we're making a quick stop first."

Okay, now she was officially nervous. "Where?" She hadn't been able to stop her voice from squeaking.

He glanced over at her, an enigmatic look on his face. "To see Darla."

"What!?" Confusion coursed through her. Along with a tingling of fear. Why wouldn't he have said that in the first place? *Oh, God.* Had she made a horrible mistake trusting him?

Her pulse doubled. She should bail. Even though the car was climbing up a steep incline and on her side a sheer cliff dropped a hundred feet practically straight down, she should jump out right now. Take her chances on foot—if she survived the fall—while they still weren't too far from civilization and she had a shot at making it back alive.

A shot…

Cold fear surged through her veins. What if he had a gun?

"I had to hide her where no one could find her," he said all-too calmly. "You'll understand when you see her."

Yeah, because she was probably *dead*. The man was a sociopath!

Blind panic had her grabbing the door handle and yanking hard. It didn't budge. *Ohgodohgodohgod.* He had the child safety locks on.

"What are you doing?" he barked, slashing her a glare. "Are you nuts?"

"No, but *you* are if you think I'm just going to sit here and—"

Suddenly, he swung the car behind a huge boulder and pulled to a halt amid a cloud of dust that nearly obscured the silhouette of an ancient mining hut.

"Don't be stupid, Vera," he said, unlocking the doors.

She jerked it open and lunged out, taking off at a run. And immediately tripped in the gravelly sand. Hell! She'd wanted to impress Henry so she'd dressed to the nines, including the pair of exorbitantly expensive high heels she'd borrowed from Darla's closet for the ball. The spike heels pierced the sand like tiny jackhammers, and one of them broke off, hurling her forward into a warm body.

She screamed.

"Vera! Oh, thank God you've come!" wailed Darla, grabbing onto her and giving her a death-grip hug, then pulling away to peer frantically into her eyes. "You've got to help me!" Her voice was filled with desperation.

And her face was covered by knuckle-size cuts and livid purple bruises, her wrist wrapped in a discolored bandage.

"Oh, God, Darla! What has that monster done to you?"

"He beat me up," she wailed, "and I didn't know what to do. I'm so sor—"

Behind her, the car door slammed. Vera didn't wait to hear more of Darla's explanation. She kicked off the ruined shoes, and at the same time as she spun to face Henry, she swooped down and grabbed a fist-size rock from the ground, shoving Darla behind her.

"Vera? No! Wait!" Henry rushed toward them, reaching into his pocket. Going for his gun!

She raised her arm, prepared to fling the rock at his head.

"Vera!" Darla grabbed her wrist. "What are you *doing?!*"

Vera hesitated in confusion. Just as a loud gunshot rang out, cracking the air like thunder.

To her shock, Henry cried out and jerked backward, a cloud of red blossoming around his right shoulder as he fell to the ground.

"Henry!" Darla shrieked. "My God, *Henry!*"

He'd been *shot!*

It hadn't happened often, but there had been one or two shootings at the clubs where she'd worked, so Vera knew enough to hit the dirt. She pulled Darla down with her and immediately started tugging her toward Henry and the car.

"What the hell is going on?" she asked, keeping the panic at bay by a thread as they scurried. "Who's shooting at us?" And from where? The hut?

"It's Thomas! Oh, Vera, I'm so sorry I got you into this! He threatened to kill me if we didn't get you up here! You have to believe me, we didn't want to, but he swore he wouldn't hurt any of us if you only came."

Thomas? Darla's ex-boyfriend, Thomas? "*Me?* Why me?"

Another shot erupted and whined off the boulder just above her.

"The ring!" Darla cried in despair. "He wants the diamond ring! You know, the one I told you to hide for me?"

They sprinted the last few feet. "But I don't have it! The police do!"

"What?" Darla looked at her in horror. *"Noooo!* Now we're dead for sure."

But there was no time to explain. They'd reached Henry. "Grab his feet!" she ordered her sister as she put her arms around her brother's chest to drag him to safety behind the vehicle. As she did, a newspaper clipping fluttered from his fingertips. Not a gun.

"Oh, Henry," she murmured distraughtly. He hadn't wanted to kill her. Some maniac was trying to kill *him!*

Three shots in succession punched through the windshield of the Lexus as she and Darla frantically hauled Henry around to the other side between the car and the boulder.

Correction: someone was trying to kill *all three of them.*

Lord. How had she gotten things so wrong?

Darla was sobbing, and if Vera weren't so terrified, she'd be dissolving into tears herself. But her instinct for self-preservation was too strong. It kicked in big time. One advantage of growing up hard and fast, she thought sardonically.

She pulled off her summer jacket and pressed it to Henry's bleeding shoulder. "Here, hold this here," she told Darla, taking her hand and pushing it firmly onto the cloth. "Harder, or he'll bleed to death."

Darla shuddered out a sob but obeyed. "What are you going to do?"

"Get my cell phone."

Vera reached up from the ground and eased open the Lexus door. Immediately a shot took out the driver's window. Lord, how many shots did that gun have? She tried desperately to remember how many Clint Eastwood counted before he asked the bad guy if he felt lucky…

Okay, that *so* didn't matter. *Focus!*

Sucking down a deep breath, she opened the door wide and snaked onto the car's floor on her belly, snagged her purse from the other side and wiggled out again. Success!

She whipped out the phone and frantically hit speed-dial number one. *Conner.*

"Please answer. Please, please, please," she prayed. "I swear, I'll never doubt you again. Or get mad at you. Or do anything to make you—"

"Ver…? Where the…ll are…?" His anxious voice surged across time and space to yell at her. Well, space anyway. Sort of. Static broke up the words, but she got the drift.

She sobbed with relief. "Thank God. Oh, thank God."

"…alk to me, damn it! I…rd *shots*.…where the h…id he take…ou?"

"We're on a little road up in the mountains behind Henderson!" she said, exchanging a desperate look with Darla when Henry moaned in agony. "Nearly up to those old gravel quarries!"

"…reaking know that! *Where?*"

Two more shots blasted through the noon heat, plinking through the car hood and zinging off the engine block right above them.

She and Darla both let out bloodcurdling screams.

"Vera! V…! Are y…ight?" Conner's voice shouted through the phone.

"Yes! Sorry! We're just so scared!"

"Wh…'s wit…ou?"

"Darla and Henry are with me. Henry's been shot! Oh, Conner, he might die if he doesn't get—"

"Vera, list…me! H…the…rn!"

"What?"

"...orn! Hon...e horn!"

"Horn?" What did he— "Oh!" Suddenly hope blasted through her chest. Was he that close by? "Hang on!" She thrust the phone into Darla's lap and crawled partially into the car again. She reached up and gave the horn a hard blast.

This time the bullet came through the passenger door and thwacked into the driver's seat, not twelve inches from her head. She smacked a hand to her mouth to muffle her terrified scream and hit the horn again two more times, then slammed herself down onto the ground. She met Darla's wild, tear-filled eyes again. A bullet must have severed some wires because the horn continued to blare like a siren. Or was it the car alarm?

"Vera! *Vera!*"

She whipped her gaze to the phone in Darla's lap. But Conner's voice wasn't coming from there. It was coming from—

His car fishtailed around the boulder, blasting its horn and spraying gravel all around it like a machine-gun turret. Conner hung out of the driver's-side window shouting her name.

"Conner!" She jumped up and ran straight for him as he dove from the car, rolled and came up sprinting. Belatedly she realized running to him wasn't the smartest move. He grabbed her and lunged back behind the Lexus.

"Get the hell down!"

But no more bullets came at them. No more shots. As they held their breath, the only sounds to be heard were the distant cry of a hawk, the warm breeze rustling through the creosote bushes and the ticking of Conner's car engine.

"Is he gone?" Darla half sobbed in a pathetic whisper.

"Yeah," Conner finally said after a few more tense moments. "I think he is."

And that's when Vera lost it. Sinking down in his arms, she collapsed in a flood of tears.

Chapter 18

Agent Duncan wheeled up ten minutes after Conner in an unmarked SUV, followed closely by Conner's cousin Natalie, who wailed up in a LVMPD cruiser with lights spinning and sirens blaring. Thank God he'd called them when he did.

By now, Conner'd gotten Vera reassured and Darla's hysterics under control, and the three of them had managed to stop Henry's bleeding and make him comfortable until the ambulance could arrive. He was going in and out of consciousness, but Conner was pretty sure he'd live.

Before the cavalry arrived, Conner had refrained from asking more than two questions, since he knew they'd all just have to go through the story again with Duncan. But his mind burned with theories.

Especially after he found a newspaper clipping on the ground. It was an article about the charity fund-raiser held at Luke Montgomery's Janus Casino several months ago. Next to the column was a photo taken at the event, of Candace showing off the Tears of the Quetzal for the camera. On the night of her murder.

Coincidence?

He didn't think so.

That's what had prompted his two questions. That, along with Darla's badly bruised face.

"Did you beat up your sister?" he asked Henry during one of his lucid moments.

Pain flared in the other man's eyes, though Conner couldn't say if it was physical or mental. "No," Henry rasped. "I'd never hurt Darla."

Darla had gasped softly at the question and nodded at her brother's answer. "He wouldn't," she assured Conner brokenly. "Ever."

Satisfied, Conner accepted that and returned his gaze to Henry. "Did you kill Candace Rothchild?" he asked evenly.

Henry's eyes squeezed closed, and he hacked out a dry laugh. "No. She almost got *me* killed." He opened his eyes. "And my sister." He glanced at Vera apologetically. "And now almost my other sister, too."

Baffled, Conner furrowed his brow. "Candace is dead. How could she possibly be behind the shootings today?"

Okay, so three questions.

But Henry slipped into unconsciousness, his mouth going slack, and didn't answer.

"This wasn't Henry's fault, Conner," Vera said. "He was trying to save Darla's life."

But she didn't have a chance to explain further because just then Duncan and Natalie had gotten there and leaped from their vehicles, weapons drawn and shouting orders to their subordinates to fan out and start searching for the gunman Conner had alerted them to as soon as he'd heard the first shots fired.

"Conner! Are you okay?" His cousin Natalie came running up at full tilt, double-fisted grip on her service revolver, looking like a lean, mean cop on a mission.

Conner rose and swept one arm around her waist and gave her a big hug. "I'm good, Nat. Thanks for coming. I know it's not Metro jurisdiction."

She holstered her weapon and squeezed him back. "Are you kidding? Family's family."

It hadn't always been that way. Natalie was Candace's twin sister and had participated fully in the disparagement of young wrong-side-of-the-family Conner. However, Natalie had matured emotionally faster than her twin; she'd realized their taunting was wrong and hurtful and stopped her part of the torment around the time they graduated high school. Candace never had. But then, by that time, Conner had realized she was an equal-opportunity bitch. Family, foe, friend, stranger: she didn't care who she ripped apart. Anyway, over the past ten years or so, he and Natalie had actually become good friends.

Which was probably why her brows hit her hairline when she noticed that his *other* arm was firmly around Vera and that Vera was clinging to him like a limpet to a ship's hull.

Ah, hell.

He knew damned well that whatever Natalie knew, the whole damn Rothchild clan would soon know…which meant word would get back to his parents in about, oh, ten seconds flat.

He really wasn't prepared for this now.

"Natalie, this is Vera Mancuso. Vera, my cousin Natalie," he said to stave off any immediate pointed inquiries, and left it at that, despite Natalie's crazy eye gyrations, and the fact that he refused to let go of Vera even if it meant he was so freaking busted.

"Nice to meet you, Vera," Natalie said. "Wish these were more pleasant circumstances."

"Thanks, me, too," Vera murmured softly.

"Were you and Ms. St. Giles injured?" Natalie asked.

Vera swallowed and darted a glance at Darla, who was holding Henry's hand as the EMTs loaded him onto a stretcher. "I wasn't. Darla was beaten, but I don't have it exactly straight who did it. Not Henry, though," she said and looked up to Conner for support.

"That's what they both claim," he affirmed. "I believe them on that point. But they're obviously involved in some seriously bad stuff. And…" He dug in his pocket and wordlessly handed Natalie the newspaper clipping.

She froze, absorbed the implications in a nanosecond and motioned to Darla to hold out her wrists. "Sorry," she said, bringing out her handcuffs. "I've gotta do this."

"Whatever," Darla said bleakly.

"Come on. You can say goodbye to your brother before he's taken to the hospital."

"Wait!" Vera said and stepped away from Conner to give her sister a mutually tearful hug.

"Thanks, sis," Darla said, choking up. "He really was going to kill us. You saved our lives."

"No," she denied, wiping her tears. "It was Conner who saved the day. I just beeped the horn."

Nevertheless, Darla said, "You've always been my biggest hero," and kissed Vera's cheek as Natalie, for some reason, smiled at *him,* then led Darla away.

"Beeped the horn, my patoot," Conner said, turning back to Vera, who was suddenly preoccupied with wiping the dust off her ruined skirt. "You're far too humble." That's when he noticed she was barefoot. "And what *is* it with you and shoes?" he asked with a tender smile, and swept her up in his arms just to be able to hold her tight. He was so damn proud of her. "I always seem to be carrying you around. Not that I'm complaining," he added in a low murmur in her ear. "Gives me a chance to cop a feel."

She gifted him with a sweet, watery smile. "You really don't have to carry me. If it embarrasses you, I can—"

"Don't be silly. Why would it embarrass me?" Where had *that* come from? He started walking toward the car, then paused. "Um, listen, I'd like a quick word with Duncan. You want to come with? Or…?"

"Would you mind if I just sat in your car and waited?" she asked, nibbling on her lip. "My knees are still shaking so hard I don't know if they'll hold me up. And to be honest…it makes me cry to see my sister in handcuffs."

"My poor darling." He sneaked a kiss onto her hair, brought her to his car and deposited her gently in the passenger seat. "You just relax. There's a bottle of water behind the seat, if you want it."

She nodded, and he could feel her eyes on him as he made his way over to the ambulance where Natalie was still holding the newspaper clipping with her arms folded over her chest. Duncan was talking to Darla while Henry was loaded into the back of the bus.

Duncan turned to Conner as he came up. "I probably shouldn't tell you this…" His lips quirked in resignation. "But I figure you'll hear it all from Detective Rothchild, here, anyway. Besides, I owe you one…seems you've broken my case wide open for me."

"Always happy to be of service to our friends at the Bureau." He winked at Natalie.

Duncan snorted. "Anyway, Ms. St. Giles has corroborated Ms. Mancuso's statement as to how she came into possession of the stolen Tears of the Quetzal ring and has also absolved her sister of all involvement in any jewelry thefts."

Conner smiled. "Vera will be relieved to hear that. Listen,

would you mind if I asked Darla a question?" The ambulance carrying Henry pulled away, and Duncan turned back to Conner, looking uncertain. "I've already read Ms. St. Giles her rights. She doesn't have to say a word."

"I understand."

"Well. Then it's up to her."

"Ask me," Darla said. "I owe you that much for showing up when you did."

Since she'd been read her rights, he also assumed she'd waived her right to an attorney.

"Okay, your brother said *Candace* nearly killed you both. What did he mean by that?"

A dark shadow passed over her face. "As I've already told Special Agent Duncan…if it weren't for her, we wouldn't be in this mess. My brother and I may have stolen a few pieces of jewelry, but we've never hurt anyone. Jeez. We did it for the thrills, not to get ourselves shot at."

"So how'd that happen?"

She unconsciously worried the bandage on her arm. "This guy, Thomas Smythe, approached us maybe six months ago, wanted to join in our—" she shrugged "—you know, the jewelry thing. He and I hit it off at first and we hooked up for a while. But it turns out he was only using me to get close to Candace."

"Why?" Conner asked. Not that anyone ever needed a reason. Candace had been a force of nature, attracting all sorts of people—weirdos and saints alike. They all wanted to bask in the light of her stardust and notoriety. "What did this Thomas guy want with her?"

"Not her," Darla explained. "Thomas was obsessed with the Tears of the Quetzal. I'm telling you, the guy was bonkers. He talked Henry into trying to steal it." She shrugged again. "Hell, why not? Even cut up into smaller stones, it would bring millions. I'd finally be free to do anything I wanted. With or without the approval of my father."

Aha. So Conner's theory about her had been right.

"Anyway, since I was friends with Candace, my job was to persuade her to sneak it out of her daddy's safe." Darla rolled her eyes. "Talk about obsessive. Her old man is nearly as crazy as Thomas about that ring." Suddenly, she remembered who she was talking to and winced at Natalie. "Sorry. I forgot he's your dad, too."

"No, you're right. He does have a major bug up his nose about that ring. He's convinced it's cursed."

Darla nodded vigorously. "Yeah! So did Thomas. But he's got it in his head the ring will give him some sort of special powers. Something about revenge or some nonsense like that. He was never real coherent when he talked about that stuff." Her mouth turned downward. "I should have listened to my instincts. After a while I broke up with the nutcase and stopped baiting Candace to borrow the ring, but Henry still had this deal with him to fence the diamond if he stole it from her."

"So what went wrong?" Conner asked.

She covered her mouth with a trembling hand, then slid it down to unconsciously touch the bruises on her throat. "The night of that big charity deal at Luke Montgomery's casino, it was all over the local news. You know—" she made quote marks with her fingers "—'Film at six! Live from the red carpet!' God, and there she was, wearing the damn thing on national TV! I mean, we knew Thomas would go for it that night."

"Did he?" Duncan asked grimly.

Tears welled in Darla's eyes. "I honestly don't know. When we heard Candace had been murdered and the ring was missing…" She swallowed.

Natalie burst out accusingly, "My God, Darla! He killed her and you didn't come forward? She was your friend!"

"I would have, honest, but Thomas swore he didn't do it!" Darla wailed. "He was furious, and he didn't have the ring, so I believed him!"

That fit, unfortunately. The ring had disappeared after the murder, but then was found in the possession of Luke Montgomery's fiancée, Amanda, hidden in her purse unbeknownst to anyone. There was rampant speculation as to how it had gotten there, but as soon as it was found, Amanda Patterson had turned it over to the police. She hadn't even been in Las Vegas at the time of Candace's murder, so she was never a suspect.

"After the ring turned up in that woman's purse," Darla continued, "the papers all said the police were holding it as evidence. So Thomas hatched this crazy plan to disguise himself as a cop and walk right in there and check it out of the evidence room! And damned if it didn't work!" She sounded amazed.

Conner could see Natalie gritting her teeth. He knew heads had rolled over *that* one. He'd personally seen to it.

"So," Conner asked Darla, "why were you arguing with him outside the cop shop after he pulled it off?"

Her jaw dropped. "How did you know about that?"

"I saw you. I was on my way in."

"So *you're* the one who figured out so quickly he'd left the paste ring in its place!"

Conner nodded. "I recognized the copy. How did he get hold of it, anyway?"

"He claims he posed as a reporter to gain admittance into Harold Rothchild's mansion. Candace had once told him her stepmother kept an old paste copy of the Tears of the Quetzal in her jewelry case in the bedroom upstairs."

Naturally.

Harold's fourth wife was of the trophy variety and not the brightest bulb on the Christmas tree. It was hard to imagine a rational person keeping a million-dollar jewel in a box on the vanity. Oy. She probably thought just because it wasn't the original it wasn't valuable.

"Pretty clever of him," Conner conceded. "Might have worked, too, if Harold hadn't insisted I go and try to get the ring out of police custody."

"Dad never did trust cops," Natalie muttered. An understatement. Harold had not been happy when she became one.

"Apparently not just cops," Darla said. "Candace told us your father refuses to let anyone near the Tears of the Quetzal, ever."

"Yes, but it isn't about trust, it's about that stupid curse," Natalie said with a hint of annoyance.

"Anyway…" Darla cast her eyes downward again, looking honestly distressed. "If I thought for a minute he'd killed Candace, I would have called you, even though it meant getting heat on the jewelry thing. But he swore he didn't touch her." Her eyes welled. "But now, after he did this to me—" she looked up, gestured to her battered face, and her voice grew thready "—and trying to shoot us today…" Her tears spilled over her lashes.

"You think it was him doing the shooting?" Duncan asked.

"I *know* it was. Who else would it be? The man is a damn lunatic. He's *dangerous*. I'll sign a sworn statement, whatever you need to arrest this guy, but I want protection for Henry and me in exchange, until he's behind bars."

"I'll see what I can do to get you a deal," Duncan said. "Rothchild, you coming down to Metro? LVMPD is taking the suspects into custody for now. But I'll need your statement, along with Ms. Mancuso's."

"Sure thing." Hell, Conner'd gone *this* long without sleep, what was another few hours? He was on about his third…or maybe fourth wind, by now. "We'll meet you there."

Natalie waved to him as she led off her prisoner, then

darted a glance over to his car. "By the way, will we see you at dinner tomorrow, Conner?" she called.

"Not sure. I'll let you know," he called back, heading to the driver's-side door.

Lately he'd gotten into the habit of having dinner at the "other" Rothchilds' on Monday nights. But frankly, he'd rather spend the time with Vera. He slid into the car and smiled across at her, but…she was fast asleep. He leaned over and quietly snapped her belt over her lap, planting a kiss on her temple as he did so.

"Conner?" she murmured sleepily, her eyes still closed.

"Yeah, babe."

"You're not my Prince Charming anymore."

He raised his brows in amusement. Was she talking in her sleep? "No?"

"Nmn-mmnh. That was just for one night." She sighed dreamily. "Now you're my knight in shining armor."

He'd take it. "Okay."

"Know who that makes me?"

"No. Who?"

She giggled softly, still not opening her eyes. "Sleeping Beauty." She sighed and snuggled down into the soft leather of the bucket seat. Totally oblivious.

He laughed, marveling at the ability of this amazing woman to take a horrible situation and pluck the one positive note from its depths. Even in her sleep she was relentlessly optimistic and charmingly romantic.

God, he loved her.

Now if he could just get his family to love her the same way…to see all the good in her…to accept her as worthy of the Rothchild name.

Was that too much to ask?

Unfortunately, he feared it just might be.

Chapter 19

Vera was too wiped out to protest when Conner carried her up from his car to her penthouse.

"We've got to stop meeting like this," she murmured.

"Why?" he asked with a grin.

She couldn't think of a damn reason. So she reached up and kissed him. He winked back at her and carried her into the apartment. They were just here for a quick stop on the way to the police station. For shoes. And a change of clothes. The ones she had on were covered in dirt and blood.

"Maybe a quick shower, too?" she asked.

"Only if I can watch."

She smiled demurely. "Or you could join me."

"How quick are we talking here?"

"That all depends."

"On?"

"How good you are at lathering up."

He made a very male sound deep in his throat. "Oh, honey, I'm *real* good."

"I somehow knew that," she said, wrapping her arms around his neck and kissing him all the way to the bathroom.

He set her down and closed the door behind them with a firm click. Then advanced on her, murmuring, "Baby, prepare to be thoroughly lathered."

Conner's cousin Natalie, the homicide detective, only blinked once when he and Vera walked into Metro headquarters still damp from their not-quite-so-quick shower. She did, however, raise an eyebrow in salute to Vera.

Good thing *Conner* wasn't a detective, because he was totally clueless to the whole female-to-female exchange.

Vera was feeling so good, she couldn't help but smile back at the woman. She hoped there wouldn't be fallout because of Natalie's astute observation. She knew Conner's rich family would not be pleased he was dating someone like her. Her own father's ubiquitous "gold-digger" insults rang a constant reminder in her head of how people like the Rothchilds thought of people in her social class. As in poor. Dirt poor.

Whatever. She still had him for today, and that's all that mattered. What tomorrow brought, she'd deal with tomorrow.

Special Agent Duncan was there, too, and took Conner into a conference room to get his statement. Natalie led Vera over to her desk to take hers.

"Sorry about the luxurious accommodations," she quipped, snagging them each a cup of coffee along the way. "Interrogation rooms are all full. Sugar?"

"Just cream," Vera said. "Thanks. No problem."

Natalie very professionally went through the statement procedure, making sure she wrote everything down just right.

Then she handed the papers off to a junior officer to get them typed up for signature.

"So," she began, leaning back in her creaky office chair while they waited, "you and Conner, eh?"

"Um." Ho-boy. She should have known this was coming. Now what? "It's not serious," Vera echoed his words from yesterday morning to his dad, as much as she wished she dared say otherwise. "We just met, really."

Natalie nodded. "I figured as much. Since you weren't at the Lights of Las Vegas Charity Ball with him."

"Oh, I was there," she said without thinking. *Oops.* "Um. Just not *with* him."

Natalie stared at him. "So, you, like, met him there? Or earlier today?" She blinked again. "Please tell me not at the crime scene." She could tell the woman wanted to be scandalized but was only succeeding in being greatly amused. And trying valiantly to hide it.

"Not at the crime scene," Vera confirmed with a half smile. "Actually it was…four days ago." Had it been such a short time? It seemed like she'd known him a lifetime already. And yet…for only hours.

"Yeah? Where'd you meet?"

Vera felt like she was being interrogated.

Oh, wait. She *was* being interrogated. By a homicide detective concerning her favorite cousin. Territory didn't get much more dangerous than that.

Better play this straight, not only because Natalie would see right through lies, but…she may as well know the truth so she wouldn't get all excited about cuz's new girlfriend and blab to the family. Maybe this way she'd keep it to herself, and Conner wouldn't be embarrassed.

"He saw me dance," Vera said. She went to take a sip of

coffee. Except her hand was inexplicably shaking, so hot liquid sloshed over the rim. She hurriedly put it down again.

Natalie opened her top desk drawer and tossed her a napkin. "Can't take me anywhere, either," she said with a commiserating grin. Still trying to be friends. Vera wanted to cry. "So you're a showgirl. Cool. What show do you work?"

Oh. Crap.

She gave up, and looked Conner's cousin in the eyes. "The Diamond Lounge."

"Oh." Then it really registered. "Oh!" Natalie's eyes got wide. "You mean… A *dancer.* That's, um. Nice."

Yeah.

Thank God, the junior officer returned with her statement. She took as little time as possible to read and sign the thing, then rose and held out her hand. "Good to meet you, Detective. I should be going now. Got to get ready for work."

"Oh. Of course. Sure." She shook her hand, mumbled a thanks for the statement and escorted her back to the waiting area out front. "But you do know we shut down the Diamond Lounge last night, right?" she said as Vera was about to leave.

Vera halted. Frowned. "Closed down?"

Natalie said, "Yeah, Conner orchestrated this big sting of club managers over some call-girl deal, and the clubs all shut down until owners can get other management in place. It'll probably be a few days before the club reopens."

"Oh. I had no idea."

"Not surprising. Been a bit busy today," Natalie said wryly.

"Yeah. Well. Thanks for the heads-up. Guess I'll have the night off."

"Oh, and Vera?"

She paused. "Yes?"

"Conner's coming over to our house for dinner on Monday.

Kind of a new tradition, since…" She cleared her throat. "Anyway, we'd love for you to join us, too, if you can make it."

Disbelief sifted through her. Surely, she was kidding.

Just then, the desk sergeant called over to her, "Ms. Mancuso?"

She tore her gaze from Natalie. "Yes?"

"Can you wait for just a moment? There's someone who wants to speak with you before you go."

Rats. Conner must be finished, too. She wasn't sure she could handle being scrutinized next to him, not now that his cousin knew who she really was. Especially not after that unexpected invitation. *He'd* have to field that one. Vera dare not touch it with a ten-foot pole.

But it wasn't Conner who wanted to talk.

The door opened and out walked the last person on earth she wanted to see.

Her father.

No. No, no, *no*. Not here. Not right now.

She spun on a toe and practically sprinted for the door.

"Vera! Wait!" His voice boomed across the reception area.

She fought to hold back sudden tears. Of all days. Why did he *always* have to—

She fumbled with the door handle, unable to get it open. He reached her and put a hand on her shoulder. She stiffened, waiting for the verbal abuse to start.

"Vera. Please. I know I don't deserve it. But for the love of God, please let me say something to you."

He didn't deserve it? More like *she* didn't. Mutely, she took a cleansing breath and turned to face the barrage.

She was shocked at what she saw. His face was gray, haggard, his eyes bloodshot and rimmed with red. One of them was bruised by a half moon of purple.

He swallowed, his Adam's apple bobbing several times. "I just want to say…thank you," he said, shocking her even more.

Was this some kind of cruel trick? She felt her lips part but for the life of her couldn't think of what to say. It was like she'd landed in some kind of weird parallel universe. Dinner invitations from detectives. Thank-you's from her father. What next?

"Darla told me what you did," he choked out. "That you saved her life. And my son's. That they would both be dead now if it weren't for your calm thinking and unselfish bravery."

"She e-exaggerates," Vera stammered. Still waiting for the other shoe to drop.

"Somehow, I don't think so," he said, voice cracking. "I've been wrong about you, Vera. Your whole life, I've treated you like trash because of my own cowardly refusal to confront my feelings about—" He halted. Cleared his throat. "In any case…words can't express how truly sorry I am."

Wow.

Her throat tightened, almost squeezing the air from her windpipe and sending a flood of emotions cascading from her heart. Almost. But she would *not* let herself break down.

Nor would she fling herself into his arms and cry, "Daddy!"

Or even succumb to the shameful temptation of being as mean to him as he'd earned through his own despicable behavior over the years.

"Okay," she managed, thoroughly shell-shocked.

He looked at her desperately. "Please," he begged softly. "Forgive me?"

Tears stung the back of her eyelids, screaming to come out. This was so damn unfair. How could she forgive him after he'd caused her a lifetime of misery? *And* her mother?

How could she not?

"Sure," she rasped out. "I'll forgive you." Someday. "I've got to go now."

She turned, grabbed the entry door handle to escape, then turned back to Natalie, who'd been watching the entire exchange silently, with a studiously neutral look on her face. "Detective Rothchild," Vera said, her voice barely working. "About that dinner tomorrow? I think I'll have to send my regrets. But thanks."

Then she stumbled out the door, gasping down deep, stinging lungfuls of hot desert air as it surrounded her body.

My God. Her whole life she'd been waiting for this very moment. And now that it had come and gone, all she wanted to do was throw up.

She thought briefly of Conner. Oh, how she wanted his arms around her! But this was one thing she had to process on her own, without his nurturing cocoon of emotional protection.

She just needed to think.

"Ms. Mancuso?" A black-haired LVMPD officer waved and approached her.

Oh, God. *No more.* Please!

He smiled genially. "Ms. Mancuso, Detective Rothchild sent me out to give you a ride home. She said you don't have your car with you. Right?"

"Oh. That was thoughtful." Vera almost sagged with relief. Now she wouldn't have to stand here and flag down a taxi.

The officer led the way to a gray sedan parked on the street. "Sorry about the unmarked car. All the cruisers are out."

"It's okay. I'd just as soon not get dropped off at my building by a police car with lights flashing anyway," she said, making a stab at a normal conversation while her insides were still shaking and churning.

He chuckled and opened the passenger door for her, his strong cologne making her nose twitch. "I hear you."

She got in. But instead of going around to the other side,

he said, "I'm afraid I'm going to have to ask you to slide over and drive, Ms. Mancuso."

Her mind went blank. "What? Why?"

He drew his service revolver from its holster and pointed it at her head. "Because if you don't, I'll kill you."

Chapter 20

"Where's Vera?" Conner asked Natalie. He'd expected to see his lover chatting amiably with his cousin, waiting for Duncan and him to wind up their business. Of everyone in his family, he trusted Natalie not to prejudge a person based on her job, so he'd felt comfortable leaving Vera in her charge.

"She left a good while ago," Natalie said, sitting back in her squeaky chair to regard him.

"Oh. Okay." Disappointed, he poured himself another cup of coffee. It was his… Hell, he had no idea, he'd downed so many cups. He was wired, but at least he was awake. Duncan had kept him longer than anticipated…but he thought she'd wait for him anyway.

"There was an incident," Natalie reported.

Conner stopped mid-sip and held his cup still. *Ah, hell.* "Let me guess. Her father." He'd seen Maximillian gliding past the conference-room window, and hoped the bastard wouldn't run into Vera. Apparently hoped in vain.

"How'd you know?"

"The man is an ass. He should be tarred and feathered."

Natalie peered at him over her coffee cup. "The incident was not in the usual vein, from what I gathered."

Worse? Jeez. "Remind me again why I can't just shoot the jerk?" Conner asked her.

"Unspeakable acts in prison," she said without missing a beat. Then cocked her head. "Though, as a notorious defense attorney with close connections to the underworld, you might be spared the worst humiliations. Except by the guards, of course."

He chortled. "Okay, I get the drift. I'll be good. So. What was so unusual about the incident?"

"He apologized to her. Said she'd saved important lives, exhibited 'calm thinking and unselfish bravery,' I think were his exact words."

"*Seriously?* Max St. Giles?"

"Said he'd misjudged her."

"Wow. That's huge."

"So," Natalie said, eyeing him.

"Spit it out," he said.

"A *stripper?*"

"Please. Exotic dancer."

"Conner. Have you *lost* your mind?" she asked, lifting her cup to her lips.

"Possibly," he answered just as evenly. "Nat, I love her."

She sprayed coffee all over her desk.

He opened her top drawer and tossed her a couple of napkins. "What do I do?"

Her gaze said it all. Total, paralyzing astonishment. "Well…"

Just then her phone rang. Saved by the bell.

She grabbed it, bobbled it, recovered. "Rothchild." After a second, her eyes seemed to focus sharply. She stopped breathing—never a good sign. Her gaze sliced to him. "One moment." She handed him the receiver. "It's for you."

As soon as he took it, she jumped up and started making frantic hand movements at the officers across the room. What the—

Suddenly, his heart stalled.

"This is Conner," he barked into the receiver.

"I have something you want, *Conner,*" the male voice sneered. "And you have something I want. Trade?"

Conner's blood chilled. "What do—"

There was a muffled sound, and Vera's desperate voice came on. "Conner? Oh, my God, Conner, it's him, it's—"

"Do we have a deal?"

"What is it you want?" Conner forced himself to calmly ask while his pulse pounded through his body like a kettledrum. Natalie was still moving like a blur, listening in while organizing a trace, he assumed.

"The Tears of the Quetzal," he spat out. "You're at the police station, and I know they have it," he said. He, being Thomas Smythe. It had to be him.

The man's next words confirmed it. "One hour. Bring it to the same place you were this morning. Alone. No games. Or your little stripper dies." Then he hung up.

Conner let loose a string of violent curses.

Natalie, being the ever-practical one, swiped up the phone and punched in buttons like it was on fire. "Duncan!" she said. "Get out here. We have a situation."

"This isn't going to work."

Conner loosened his death grip on the steering wheel of the McLaren and flexed his fingers, taking another hairpin turn up the gravel road to the quarry where the shoot-out had taken place earlier.

"It'll work," came the muffled reply from the trunk, where Duncan was curled into a Kevlar ball, probably roasting in there like a pig at a luau. "It has to."

Tell him about it. He'd kill himself if anything happened to Vera because of this stupid, obnoxious ring.

Maybe Uncle Harold was right. Maybe it *was* cursed.

"Sure you can open the trunk from inside?" Conner asked for the dozenth time.

"Got the safety latch in my hand and my gun in the other, just in case."

"Okay." Conner took a deep breath. "Okay."

"Sitrep?" Duncan prodded.

"Almost there," Conner reported. "Just around the bend." He scanned the road and cliffs around him. "Don't see him yet."

"Vera?"

"No sign." All sorts of awful images flowed through Conner's head as he searched the mountain for any sign of anything.

He slowed to maneuver around the giant boulder, pulled up in front of the old mining hut and cut the engine. After the bustle, whistles and constant ka-ching of every venue in Vegas, the lonely mountaintop was disturbingly silent. Had it been this preternaturally quiet this morning?

He got out of the car. A dust devil twirled past. Nothing else moved.

"Smythe!" he shouted. "Thomas Smythe! I have the ring. Let Vera go!"

"Oh, I'll let her go, all right," came the maniacal reply.

Conner whirled toward the voice. Looked up. And his legs almost gave out from under him. "Vera!" he cried.

He could just make her out, dangling over the side of the cliff a hundred feet above them by a rope tied around her wrists. The rope had been threaded through the arm of an old, rickety piece of quarry equipment, a pulley-type affair on the top of the cliff, from which the rope pulled taut down the cliff to the front of the old hut, ending up winding around an old-fashioned hand crank and shaft. A black-haired Hispanic-looking man was holding on to the handle of the crank. For a split second Conner was confused. The man was dressed as a cop.

Then it hit him. Hell. How stupid could he get? Smythe had done it once and gotten away with it. Why not twice?

Sure enough, it was the same man he'd seen arguing with Darla in front of LVMPD. And who had attacked Vera on the street.

The bastard Thomas Smythe. Or whatever the hell his real name was. Duncan had run a check and found no one matching his description with that name. Figured.

In a flash, Conner saw that if Smythe let go of the rusty crank handle the rope would spin off like greased lightning and Vera would plunge down the cliff. To certain death.

Conner was rigid with fear. "Don't do anything rash, Smythe," he said as calmly as he could manage. "I told you I have the ring."

"Show it to me!"

Moving slowly away from his car, Conner reached carefully into his pocket and brought out the jewel. He held it up for the other man to see. Even in the dimming light of the setting sun, the stone glittered and shone, flashing green and blue and purple like a sparkler on the Fourth of July. Almost like the real thing.

For several seconds, Smythe seemed hypnotized by the sight, his eyes blinded with lust and greed, a look of ecstasy coming over his whole face. Conner took the opportunity to move closer. He had to get to that crankshaft before the deranged man let it go. Which Conner was absolutely certain he would do. Darla was right. He was already over the edge.

Conner cringed. Bad analogy. Really bad.

"Hand it over!" the man yelled, letting the crank unwind a whole revolution.

Vera screamed as she plunged several feet down the cliff.

Smythe's muscles strained to stop the movement. "Now! Or I let her go all the way!"

"All right, all right!" Conner said, taking a few steps closer. Close enough to see the gun tucked in the waistband of the man's jeans, the whites of his crazy-wild eyes, the beads of sweat drenching his face…and the deadly intent in his glazed expression as he started to let the handle go for good.

"Nooo!" Conner shouted, and threw the ring in a high arc over Smythe's head at the same time he made a flying leap for the crank's handle, just as it left the other man's hands.

He grabbed it. It whacked him in the chin going around, knocking him silly.

Vera screamed in terror.

He lunged for it again. This time it dug into his stomach, but he managed to hang on. Vera was still screaming and thrashing, making the rope pull all the harder on the handle. Conner could feel it slipping in his sweaty hands.

"Duncan!" he yelled in desperation. The plan had been for the FBI agent to chase Smythe down, shoot him or at least be able to tell the herd of Metro officers waiting below which direction he'd fled in. That wasn't going to happen. "I need your help!" he shouted.

In a flash, the agent was there, helping to hang on to the crank. Between the two of them they got it under control, then let the rope play out slowly to let Vera down without scraping her up too badly.

"Sorry," Conner grunted as they let out the rope. "I'm sorry I couldn't handle this myself. Now you've lost him again."

"Forget it. Vera's life is all that matters," Duncan said grimly. "Don't you worry. We'll get the bastard. And won't he be surprised when he realizes the ring he has is the fake."

They lowered Vera nearly to the ground, and at the last minute, Conner grabbed her. He hugged her fiercely to him, tears blurring his vision as she clung to him and let out a hiccoughed sob. She was shaking like a leaf.

Hell, so was he.

"You're okay now, you're okay now," he told her over and over, as much to convince himself as her.

She was so damn brave.

And at that moment he realized. It didn't matter what his family thought. Or the risk to his career. Or his social position.

Nothing else mattered.

She was his. And he would never, ever let her go.

Chapter 21

Conner didn't think he'd ever be alone again with Vera.

But after waiting an endless amount of time for the trackers to find Thomas Smythe—and failing—Lex Duncan decided they may as well go home for now.

Thank God.

Vera was on the verge of emotional collapse, and Conner hadn't had a wink of sleep in close to forty-eight hours, putting him near the limit of his endurance both physically and mentally. Lex seemed to recognize that.

"I'll take you two home," Natalie told him, looking more than exhausted herself after tramping up and down the steep mountains for hours. "Wouldn't want any more fake-cop incidents."

Vera glanced at her wide-eyed, and Conner managed a weary laugh, appreciating his cousin's stab at black humor.

"Thanks, Nat," he said, and turned over the McLaren's keys to an awestruck young officer. "Scratch it and you'll be washing my cars for the rest of your life," he warned the kid with mock seriousness. Okay, not so mock. Conner loved his car.

Almost as much as he loved the way Vera looked at him when he climbed into the back of Natalie's cruiser with her instead of getting in the front seat.

He just prayed they'd make it back to his place before he passed out. They did. Just barely.

"We'll be expecting you for dinner tomorrow night," Natalie said as a parting shot when they stumbled out onto his driveway. "*Both* of you."

"Nat—"

"Don't argue with me, boy," she said gruffly. "I have a gun, and I know how to use it."

He gave her a halfhearted grin and a tired wave, and she drove away. Ah, well. He could always cancel tomorrow.

He put his arm around Vera. "I'm about to fall over. How 'bout you?"

"I want to spend a week in bed."

And he had a feeling she meant actually to sleep. He'd probably be of a different opinion tomorrow, but right now that sounded like paradise. They went straight to his bedroom, shedding clothes along the way. Five minutes later they were in bed, snuggled up together like puppies in a basket.

Small tremors still sifted through her. He wrapped his body around her in a sheltering, protective shield. So she'd know without a doubt that, if anyone wanted to get to her, they'd have to go through him first.

She sighed, and finally her tense muscles began to relax. Skin to skin, warm and smooth, primal and visceral, he soaked in the feel of her, the smell of her, the sound of her soft, even breathing. And recognized on a soul-deep level that this was something special. Something once-in-a-lifetime. He kissed her brow, and she nestled closer. She put her lips to the curve of his neck, and whispered, "I love you, Conner Rothchild."

He looked down at the woman in his arms, his heart filling with an unexpected burst of joy and longing, and he wondered if she was talking in her sleep again. But then she opened her eyes and smiled up at him.

"Yeah?" he said.

"Yeah," she said.

"I'm glad," he said, and held her close. "So very glad, Vera Mancuso. Because I love you, too."

"We are well and truly screwed," Conner said, flopping back in the McLaren's bucket seat.

"Well," Vera mused, "not the most romantic way of putting it, but I suppose you could say that."

She thought back over the relaxing day. Without a doubt the happiest day of her life to date. They'd slept over twelve hours the night before, then slowly awoken to take advantage of their renewed energy, the glorious weather streaming in through the windows and the fact that Hildy did not put a single phone call through to his suite.

Well, until that last one. The *summons,* coming around midafternoon. Apparently *nobody* told Harold Rothchild he couldn't speak with his nephew. Whereupon he had told Conner in no uncertain terms he was to gather his "young lady" and bring her to dinner that night. Seven o'clock promptly.

They'd gotten ready and left at five o'clock. Conner had said he wanted to make a stop on the way. Something to give him the courage he needed to face his family with her on his arm. She hoped it had worked for him. *She* felt wonderful.

Vera followed Conner's gaze now as he surveyed the Rothchild driveway, brimming with Jaguars, Mercedes, Porsches and even a Lamborghini. "Looks like they've invited a few people over," he said nervously.

Poor Conner. He wasn't used to being the object of gossip or disapproval. "We can still leave," she told him. "Do this another time."

He glanced at her, pretending not to be scared. He was so sweet it made her heart ache with love. "Hell, no," he said. "If Uncle Harold wants to meet my young lady he's going to damn well meet my young lady." His mouth tilted up. Half of it, anyway.

She was still getting used to the thought of being Conner's anything, let alone romantically linked to him. *His young lady.* She glanced down at her hands. It had a certain ring to it.

He'd said he loved her. More than once. And as unreal as it felt, she believed him. Oh, how she believed him.

But inside, her heart was doing the quickstep. She had to say it. "What if they don't approve of me? What if they tell you you can't—"

"They won't." He cut her off. "And even if they did, I wouldn't care. I don't need their approval."

"But you want it."

He gazed at her. And nodded. "I want them to love you as much as I do. I have to believe they will."

Her heart swelled. "Okay, then let's go find out."

"Right."

He drove up to the house and left the car in the care of a young man who, a hundred years ago, would have been called a stable hand. She wondered vaguely what they called them nowadays…since they took care of cars, not horses.

God. She was mentally babbling again. It happened whenever she was nervous. She really had to quit wandering off into left field or she'd end up like Joe.

At the thought of her stepfather, a rush of warmth filled her. And wonder. The care facility had called her today, informing her that an anonymous donor had set up a fund to pay Joe's bills there for the rest of his life. She'd been shocked. And immediately assumed it was Conner, all set to hang up and tell him thanks but no thanks. But the director had told her in confidence the secret benefactor had been Maximillian St. Giles. After debating with herself all day, she was inclined to accept his generosity. After all, he owed Joe for taking over his role in her life for the past twenty-four years. This was small payment in recompense, but perhaps it would assuage his guilt just a tad. She could give him that much. Forgiveness would take longer, but this was a place to start at least.

"Ready?" Conner asked her.

She squared her shoulders and nodded. "If you are."

"Oh, I'm ready," he murmured, pulling her close to his side, leaning over and putting his lips to hers. He smiled down at her, and her heart did a perfect swan dive into the warm oases of his eyes.

And somehow she knew it would all be okay.

They walked into the Rothchild mansion arm in arm and were immediately surrounded by all of Conner's various cousins. Even his brother, Mike, with fiancée, Audra, were there—a first, apparently—invited by Natalie, whose skill as a detective Vera was growing to admire greatly. Natalie, it turned out, was getting married to her college sweetheart, Matt Shaffer, on June fourteenth, just two short weeks away. Matt was there standing next to her, looking all tall and lean and muscular like the security chief he was.

Hanging a bit back, observing the crowd, was another man, Austin Dearing, whom Vera immediately recognized from the tabloids. Brawny, tan, chiseled as a sculpture and built like a Delta Force god, he and Vera's friend Silver had created quite the scandal last month by announcing first their baby, and *then* their whirlwind marriage.

Silver was the first to come over and give Vera a big welcome hug. "You and Conner!" Silver exclaimed with a grin. "What a surprise!"

She had no idea.

They were immediately joined by the only cousin Vera hadn't already met. Jenna, the youngest of the half sisters, who was Vera's age. Jenna was an event planner, party princess, an absolute knockout and clearly the apple of her daddy's eye. Harold's gaze followed her proudly from the foot of the foyer staircase as she said hello to Vera then was drawn into the midst of the other arriving guests.

For a family dinner, there was quite a crowd gathering. Through which Conner expertly steered her, until they got to the staircase and Harold Rothchild, who'd been joined with perfect timing by his current wife, Rebecca.

Harold gave Conner a slap on the back. "Glad you could make it, boy. Come see who's here."

Vera saw Conner pale when he turned and found himself eye-to-eye with Michael and Emily Rothchild, his parents. Uh-oh. He *hadn't* been expecting that.

"Thought it was time to bury the hatchet," Harold said, then sobered. "When Candace died, I realized what was important in life. And that's family." He turned to Conner and lightened up. "Isn't that right, boy?" He slapped him on the back again.

Conner glanced over at her. She smiled, so filled with love for the man she was bursting at the seams. Even as he fought for his own happiness, he never forgot his love and duty to his parents and family. Never forgot that his decisions affected more than himself, or even her. It made her love him all the more to know he was willing to sacrifice for his family. She'd never known that kind of loyalty and was awed that it was now all directed toward her.

As was his attention. He held out his hand to her, she took it and he pulled her up the staircase a few steps, so he towered over the noisy throng crowding the massive foyer.

He let out a piercing whistle. The talking and laughing stopped abruptly. Everyone turned to stare at him in surprised expectation. Suddenly, her knees felt weak. *Oh, God.* This was worse than dangling a hundred feet over a cliff.

Okay, not really. But almost.

But his gaze met hers, and she could feel all the love and support she'd need for a whole lifetime pouring through them into her. He squeezed her hand. Then turned to the crowd.

"Before we go in to dinner, I'd like to introduce someone very special to me." He glanced at his parents and uncle. "Mom, Dad, this is Vera. Uncle Harold, you invited us here tonight because you wanted to meet my young lady. Well, I'm afraid that's not possible." Harold's bushy brows rose. "You see," Conner continued, "Vera is no longer my young lady. As of an hour ago, she's much more to me than that."

Gasps went through the room. He smiled down at her.

"Everyone, I'd like you to meet Vera Mancuso Rothchild. My new wife."

Epilogue

Two weeks later

Tears trickled down Vera's cheeks as she watched Natalie Rothchild and Matt Shaffer say their wedding vows. The church was packed, and there wasn't a dry eye in the house. Natalie and Matt had written the words themselves, and there was no doubt in Vera's mind that they meant every single word. It was movingly beautiful, the whole ceremony.

Afterward, as the organ music swelled and everyone stood wiping tears and cheering the bride and groom out of the church, Vera realized Conner, who'd held her left hand in both of his the whole time, was watching her instead.

She gave him a watery smile, dabbing with a tissue. "I'm such a sucker for weddings," she said with a happy sigh.

He raised her hand to his lips, kissing her ring finger, where two weeks ago he'd placed a simple gold band. "Are you sorry?" he asked softly, his eyes filled with emotion. "That I didn't give you a day like this? With flowers and a white dress and a big party? A day to remember for the rest of your life…"

She met his gaze, and her eyes brimmed over anew. Didn't he know stopping at that Vegas wedding chapel on the way to dinner at the Rothchilds had been the happiest moment of her entire life? The shock, the utter joy, the amazing realization that he truly loved her, wanted to spend his life with her, was worth more than anything in the universe.

"Oh, Conner. You *did* give me a day to remember for the rest of my life. I wouldn't have changed a thing. Not one. Not for the world."

He bent down and kissed her tenderly. "Sure?"

She gently touched his cheek. "Positive." She smiled. "And believe me, the white dress thing? Been there, done that. Not a big deal."

His lips curved up at that, as she'd hoped they would. She kissed him lovingly. "Conner, don't think for a single moment that—"

"Hey, you two," an amused male voice interrupted from behind Conner. "No smooching in church. You're holding up traffic."

She rolled her eyes at Lex Duncan, who'd sat next to them in the pew. It was their turn to exit. "You're just jealous because you didn't bring a date to smooch with."

He made a face. "Date? Remind me again what that is?" He followed them out of the church into the bright sunshine. "Aside from which, technically, I'm working."

Conner shook his head. "Buddy, you need to forget that job of yours for an afternoon and take advantage." He swept an appreciative glance around. "Check out all the gorgeous women, all dressed up and all choked up on love, just waiting for a handsome man such as yourself to make their dreams come true. Have you never seen *The Wedding Crashers?*"

Duncan gave a short laugh. "Funny. Anyway, I don't dare get distracted. Aside from keeping watch for our escaped stalker, I'm deathly afraid war is going to break out at any moment."

Conner winced. "You mean among the guests?"

Duncan nodded, surveying the large area in front of the church where the reception line was forming.

Vera looked, too. "What do you mean?"

Conner put his arm around her and squeezed. "Your new brother-in-law comes from the biggest mob family in Las Vegas. See all the hard-eyed men in dark suits? And you can't miss the sea of khaki uniforms."

True. Half the Metro force had turned out for the wedding of one of their own. And Matt had mentioned his notorious family on a couple of occasions.

"Yikes," she said. "I hadn't thought of that."

"I better get to work."

As Duncan left, Natalie's sister Jenna came up and gave Conner a kiss on the cheek. "Don't worry, cuz. Matt assures me his family will be on their best behavior."

Jenna had done an amazing job putting together the whole wedding. Her eyes scanned the proceedings critically, never resting, ready to head off any problem before it arose.

"The church flowers were lovely, Jenna," Vera said. "Everything was so gorgeous."

"Thanks. Wait'll you see the reception hall. Dad gave me an unlimited budget." She grinned. "I took blatant advantage. But speaking of receptions, you two are wanted in the reception line now. Get your butts over there."

"Us?" Vera asked in alarm.

"Favorite cousin, and all." Jenna's eyes landed on Duncan's

receding back. "Say, who was that guy? I thought I knew everyone on the guest list."

"Lex Duncan. The FBI agent who's been helping us with the Tears of the Quetzal. He just took over Candace's case, too."

Vera secretly winked at Conner. "Handsome, isn't he? And single, too."

Jenna's gaze lingered appreciatively on him for a second, then moved on distractedly. "Whatever. Come on, you two. Reception line."

Terrified at the prospect, Vera looked to Conner for support. "I really don't think—"

"Nonsense. It's time I introduced my wife to society. No time like the present."

Jenna smiled encouragingly. "It'll be fine."

And as it turned out, it was. More than fine.

When they joined the line right next to Conner's parents, his father shook Vera's hand and kissed her cheek, and his mother actually hugged her. The first couple of days after Conner's surprise announcement at dinner had been rocky. But they'd been more shell-shocked than disapproving. Once they accepted the idea of a married son, they'd made an honest effort to get to know his new wife. That was all Vera could ask, and it seemed like they had accepted her, too.

His parents weren't the only ones stunned by the news that Conner Rothchild had gotten married. He did, after all, have a reputation as a confirmed bachelor who played the field with gusto. She'd learned that was mostly media hype, a facade cultivated to help his tireless work for those less fortunate than himself. Nothing like society connections to change society. But even his close friends were surprised. When had a workaholic like him had time to fall in love?

Sixty seconds was all it took, he'd assured them all. One look, and he was a goner.

There were a few sideways glances at Vera from those guests who'd heard about her questionable background. But there were many more who'd read about the press conference Maximillian St. Giles had held about Darla and Henry, and his unexpected announcement that he'd discovered he had another daughter, one who had risked her life to save his other children. And that he'd acknowledged being her father and written her into his will as an equal heir to the other two.

Congratulations flowed from both sides, Conner couldn't stop beaming and her heart was filled with joy.

Talk about a Cinderella moment.

Things like this *did* happen to people like her!

"I am so incredibly happy," she said to Conner when they were in the Batmobile, driving to the reception, which was being held at the Rothchild Grand Hotel. "How did I get so lucky to find you?"

He grinned over at her. "Uncle Harold said it must be the curse of the Tears of the Quetzal. Or in this case, the blessing. Rothchilds are falling like dominoes. In love, that is."

She grinned back. "Well, it's true, I *was* wearing the ring the first time I saw you," she teased as they pulled in at the Grand.

"That's about *all* you were wearing," he teased back. "Who could help falling in love with you at first sight? Every last man in the room was in love with you." He pulled into the parking lot, leaned over to grasp her behind the neck and kissed her. "I was just the lucky guy who got you all for myself."

"Yes," she said, loving the taste of her new husband, loving the feel of his muscular body, loving the honor in his heart most of all. "You did."

The wedding party limo pulled up with a blare of horns and a rippling of crepe paper bunting. Natalie and Matt emerged, glowing and smiling and kissing like two people so in love the earth spun around the axis of it. Just like Vera and Conner.

She returned his kiss with all the love within her heart and soul. Then told him sincerely, "Flowers and white dresses and parties are wonderful, darling. But none of those things matter. We already have what's important. We have each other, and we have love. I love you so much, Conner. That's all I'll ever need."

His eyes looked down at her so tenderly her heart simply overflowed. "I love you, too, Vera. So very much."

Again, he raised her fingers to his lips and kissed them, and then he slipped another ring on next to her wedding band.

She looked down at it in surprise. A perfect diamond winked back at her, blazing with green, purple and blue sparkles. Just like a miniature Quetzal.

"So we can make our own magic," he whispered. And kissed her again.

Oh, yes. The magic of love.

* * * * *

HER 24-HOUR
PROTECTOR

BY
LORETH ANNE WHITE

Loreth Anne White was born and raised in southern Africa, but now lives in Whistler, a ski resort in the moody British Columbian Coast Mountain range. It's a place of vast, wild and often dangerous mountains, larger-than-life characters, epic adventure and romance —the perfect place to escape reality.

It's no wonder it was here she was inspired to abandon a sixteen-year career as a journalist to escape into a world of romantic fiction filled with dangerous men and adventurous women.

When she's not writing, you will find her long-distance running, biking or skiing on the trails, and generally trying to avoid the bears—albeit not very successfully. She calls this work, because it's when the best ideas come.

For a peek into her world visit her website at www. lorethannewhite.com. She'd love to hear from you.

To the wonderful crew at my publisher who pulled
this series together—it's been a real pleasure
working with you all.
And to my fellow authors: Marie Ferrarella,
Gail Barrett, Cindy Dees, Nina Bruhns and
Carla Cassidy—you guys are the best.

Prologue

The Nevada night was hot—no air-conditioning.

Lex clutched his teddy against his tummy even though it made him hotter, but he liked to hold his bear close when this particular TV program was on because sometimes the show made him scared. He was perched on the edge of his mom's bed wearing only his jammie shorts while he watched. His mother sat farther up, by the pillows, emptying the fat brown envelope that the man brought once a month.

Lex glanced at her during the commercial. She was counting out the cash onto the bed cover. His mom was always happy when the money came. She said it helped boost her croupier's income from the casino. Tomorrow she'd take him to the burger place for a special kids meal with a toy. It was their routine the day after the envelope arrived. Lex hoped that maybe when he turned six she'd take him to the steak house instead, where the chef cooked over big orange flames. He didn't need toys in his meal anymore, but he didn't want to tell her and hurt her feelings. He loved his mom. She was the prettiest woman he'd ever seen, too.

She caught him watching and smiled. He grinned back, getting that silly squeeze in his chest. But before he could turn back to his TV show, there was a crash downstairs in the hall. His mother tensed.

That made Lex scared.

A man's voice reached up the stairs. "Where's the kid, Sara!"

His mother's face went sheet-white. She pressed her index finger over her lips, telling Lex to stay quiet. Then she quickly gathered the money, reached for her purse and removed a small gun. Lex stared at it. His heart started to beat really fast. He clutched Mr. Teddy tighter.

"Where's the damn kid, Sara?" The voice—rough and raspy like Velcro tearing—was coming up the stairs. "He wants the boy!"

Lex's mother took his arm, dragged him to the closet. She got down to his eye level, grasped his shoulders tight. "Lexington," she whispered. She only called him Lexington when something was very serious, or he'd done something very wrong. "You get in that closet, d'you hear? Get in right behind the clothes. No matter what, do *not* move. Do *not* come out—"

"Sara!"

She shoved him quickly into the dark closet, shut the door, locked it. Lex peered through the louvered slats, but he could only see the bottom half of the room because of the way the slats were angled. He saw his mother's hand grabbing the telephone next to her bed.

The bedroom door crashed back against the wall. His mother screamed, aimed her gun at the man with one hand, holding the phone in her other. "Stay back! I'm calling the cops." She started to dial. That's when he heard the man hit his mother. A horrible sort of wet, crunching sound.

His mother gasped, dropping the receiver as she crumpled to the floor. Lex heard the gun skitter under the bed.

The man's hand—tanned with lots of dark hair on it—reached down and jerked the phone cord out of the wall. "Where is the damn kid, Sara?" he growled. Lex saw a knife glinting in his hand but couldn't see his top half, just his checkered pants.

"He…he's not here…" His mom was sobbing on the floor behind the bed. "I swear he's not."

"Lying bitch. I'll find him." He started to come toward the closet. Lex's little limbs began to shake. He wanted to smash out of the closet and kick the balls off that man, but he couldn't move.

"No! Please! He's not here!" He saw his mother had her gun again. She was on her knees by the bed. Her face was wet from tears. She aimed at the man, her hands shaking, and Lex heard a gunshot.

The man jerked, stumbled, swore something awful. "You… *shot me.*" He lunged forward, grabbed his mother by her hair and he cut his mother's throat. Blood went everywhere. Lex dropped Mr. Teddy and scooted right to the back, pulling his mother's dresses over him. He squeezed his eyes very tight, trying to shut out what he'd seen.

He heard the man's footsteps coming back to the closet. The door rattled, and Lex peed his pants. Then he heard police sirens—his mother's 911 call must have gone though. The man swore, staggered wildly out of the room. Lex heard tires screeching.

It fell silent in the room for a while before Lex heard the sirens growing really loud and stopping outside. There was noise again, lots of noise, all muddled up and not making sense—footsteps, yelling for paramedics. The girl from upstairs was sobbing, saying she'd heard fighting, a gunshot, someone running, a car fleeing. Then a male voice, deep like a drum, said an ambulance was no use.

His mother was dead.

Lex's whole body went cold, like ice. He couldn't think anymore. A big shadow came toward the closet door. And a little squeak of terror escaped Lex's chest as the door was rattled again. Someone said something about a key on the body. The door was unlocked, pulled open and the dresses covering him were yanked aside.

He blinked up into the sudden white glare of lights, saw the policeman's badge.

And that's how the cops found him. Stuffed into the back of the closet behind his mother's clothes. Mute with shock.

It took a full year before Lex could speak again. But his mother never came back.

And the police never found the man who'd cut his mother's throat.

Lex, however, would never, ever forget his voice. And he swore that one day he'd find that man. He would make him pay for what he'd done to his beautiful mother.

Chapter 1

FBI Special Agent Lex Duncan was due on stage right after the Vegas investment banker who was strutting down the runway with a long-stemmed rose clenched between his straight white teeth.

"Now this, ladies—" crooned the Bachelor Auction for Orphans emcee, a popular Las Vegas television host with dulcet tones of honey over gravel and butter-gold hair to match "—is an investment banker with *mutual* interest in mind. What red-blooded woman wouldn't want this macho money man to manage her *assets* for the night? Who knows, ladies—" the emcee lowered her voice conspiratorially. "There might just be some long-term profit for the right bidder…"

Shrieks and hoots erupted from the invitation-only crowd of almost one thousand very well-heeled Las Vegas women as Mr. Investment Banker shucked his pin-striped jacket, peeled off his crisply ironed shirt and got busy showing off some serious

sweat equity of his own, obviously earned by heavy capital investment in the gym. The bids started, kettle drums rolling
softly in the background heightening the tension.

Lex swore and shot a desperate glance toward the glowing
red Exit sign backstage. He felt edgier now than he had
during his first FBI takedown of a violent felon. Somehow
he'd ended up being slated as the last bachelor up for grabs
tonight, and he was feeling the pressure. The men ahead of
him had already driven bids all the way up to a whopping
$50,000, which went to a rugged foreign correspondent
whose "sword" was apparently mightier than his pen—a
comment that had brought the house down as the evening
eased into night, laughter oiled by the complimentary cocktails that were loosening the ladies' designer purse strings and
heating libidos.

Whoever had staged this event in Las Vegas's legendary
Ruby Room with its massive art deco clock, shimmering
chandeliers, red tones and old black-and-white photos that
alluded to the thrilling mystique of Vegas's dark mob past,
knew exactly what she was doing.

For more than an hour before the auction had started, women
clad in sleek barely there dresses with plunging necklines had
sipped free drinks as they mingled with men, sizing up the "mer-
chandise," whose duty it was to make small—and seductive—talk.

Lex had failed abysmally.

He was not one for platitudes, let alone parties. And volunteering for a bachelor auction rated way down there along
with…God knows what. He couldn't think of anything worse
right at this moment. Those sixty-three minutes of *schmin-
gling,* and yes, he'd counted every one of those minutes, had
been pure torture. Lex was not one for high-maintenance
women, either. Been there, done that, had the scars and divorce
papers to show for it. If he ever married again, he swore it was

going to be to a Stepford wife who understood his devotion to his job and charity work with at-risk kids.

The bidding out in the hall suddenly hit the $60,000 mark. The crowd of ladies exploded into raucous cheers, and the live band picked up the pace, ratcheting tension with a soft *boom, boom, boom* of drums. Lex tugged irritably to loosen his red tie.

His partner, Special Agent Rita Perez, had suggested red— to get the blood pumping, she'd chuckled. She told him the color was a good foil to the classic dark FBI suit and white shirt. He was going to kill Perez for this. She was the one who'd coerced him into it in the first place.

It's for a good cause, Duncan. All proceeds will go to the Nevada Orphans Fund. Think of how it will help your boys.

He adjusted his holster, his body heating under his jacket as the crowd thunderously applauded the top bidder who'd nabbed Mr. Investment Banker for an insane $62,500. Lex was up next, after the Clark County skydiving instructor standing beside him backstage.

Think of the Orphans Fund....

"You ever see so much cleavage in one place?" said Mr. Skydiver, eyes fixed on the shimmering crowd of women as he peered around the curtain. "Mostly pumas, I figure."

"Excuse me?"

"They're not all cougars over the age 45, check it out—" Mr. Skydiver edged the heavy curtain back. "See? Hot pumas, single or divorced females between the ages of 30 to 40, all with serious cash to blow. Best way to meet a prospective date if you ask me." He jutted his chin toward the audience. "Each one of those women out there has had her bank balance vetted—a marriage made in pure heaven."

Lex stared at him blankly. This guy thought he was going to find *commitment* here? "This is Vegas, buddy. Place of transience, slight of hand, trickery and sin."

"Ah, but magic happens in Vegas." Mr. Skydiver grinned, took a sharp swig from a small silver hip flask and offered the flask to Lex. "Dutch courage, in the name of Johnnie Walker?"

Lex shook his head.

Mr. Skydiver capped his flask. "Just ask any tourist," he said as he slipped the flask back into his pants pocket. "When that plane touches down at McCarran International, all rational thought goes clean out the window, and suddenly anything is possible. Yeah, Vegas will do that to you."

The guy had clearly gotten a little too intimate with Johnnie Walker. Lex made a mental note never to book a skydiving lesson with this dude, but he vaguely wished he had taken him up on the offer of a nip from the flask. The man looked enviably happy, and this was one time in his life Lex sure wouldn't mind numbing himself with a bit of false bravado. But before he could finish his thought, or change his mind and take up the flask, Mr. Skydiver was nudged abruptly forward by the bustling backstage coordinator taking his Johnnie Walker down the runway with him. And the next thing Lex knew, it was his turn.

"You're on, agent!" He was forced out from the protection of the curtain by the backstage boss.

His throat dried instantly.

Larger-than-life images of himself in various poses played out on a massive screen behind the emcee and the auctioneer. "Meet FBI Special Agent Lexington Duncan, girls!" Blinding stage spotlights swung his way.

Lex blinked into the glare. All he could see of the crowd was a dark blot stabbed by the occasional glitter of jewels and flash of sequins as women moved. He reached for his breast pocket and put on the sunglasses that Perez had insisted he bring.

"For the record," intoned the emcee. "Agent Duncan's weapon is disarmed. But who knows, he just might load his gun later for the right bidder." A murmur of excitement rippled through the women. Not quite the shrieks generated by Mr. Skydiver. Worry wormed into Lex as he took his first tentative steps down the runway. Maybe he was going to get lowballed. But the bids started instantly, flying fast and furious. *Oh geez.*

Heat prickled over his brow as he forced his legs toward the end of the ramp that jutted out into the sea of tables, a 007 theme tune mocking him. When he reached the end of the ramp, the music segued into a thumping sexy beast of a beat that thrummed up through his body from the soles of shined-up shoes making his heart constrict in time to the rhythm. His body grew hot. He yanked at his collar.

Oh, boy, was he ever going to kill Perez for getting him into this. He was going to get her right alongside with the mystery woman who'd organized this circus.

You don't have to do anything other than volunteer your time…yeah, well there was his pride on the line now.

He could just imagine the guys in the field office tomorrow morning. He shoved his shades higher onto his face with a scowl he made no attempt to hide. Patience he had in buckets— on a job. Not now. Now he'd lost every last ounce and wanted to get this the hell over.

Irritability powered his body movements as he strutted forward with the classic command presence of a cop. He got to the end of the ramp, flipped open his jacket, showing his holster and weapon.

The ladies went wild.

"Want to see Special Agent Lexington Duncan load that pistol, ladies? You've got to make those numbers real arresting in order to be taken down to the station, girls. Maybe he'll pat you down, or frisk you…"

Bids rose—higher, hotter, faster.

Lex stalked back up to the top of the runway, getting more and more steamed. He took off his jacket, draped it over the emcee's podium. It was his little intrusion into her space, a psychological ploy. Another wave of hoots and hollers burst from the crowd at this apparent audacity. Women began to leave their tables and line the runway, cheeks flushed, eyes bright, music loud. Their hands were waving with cash, trying to reach up to stuff it into his pants.

A strange sort of energy caught him. This was what crowd hysteria did to one, he thought, loosening his red tie, unbuttoning his white shirt, knowing his muscles were getting amped from the adrenaline and…well, yeah, the attention. He was male after all. Every man had his pride. And libido. Be damned if Lex's competitive edge didn't stab suddenly into his chest. Hell, if he was on the stage now, he might as well win, right? Why not get the top bid from that teeming excited mass of over a thousand women with more cash to burn than they knew what to do with.

For the orphans, Lex. Think of your boys. A small grin of satisfaction settled over his mouth. If "his boys" could see him now. He'd better do them proud. Yeah, he'd get his money's worth out of these pumas.

He slowed his swagger, put some muscle into it as he stripped off his shirt, tossed it to the crowd. His body was ripped and tanned—honed to peak perfection from daily training workouts, his twice-weekly coaching sessions with his kids under the hot desert sun, his eyes and reflexes keen from hours at the range. Under that conservative buttoned-up FBI exterior lurked a very different Lex Duncan, and it showed—in the exuberant reaction from the crowd.

"Take it all off! Take it all off! Take it all off!"

The chant rose in crescendo, and the live musicians, adept at playing to their audience, worked the energy. Lex thrust even more swagger into his walk, tightening his jaw, squaring his shoulders aggressively. Under the glaring spotlights his tanned skin began to glisten. Paddles continued to shoot up around the hall, bids going alarmingly high with one suddenly hitting an all-time record.

"*Ninety thousand dollars!* We have ninety thousand from the bidder in silver at the back of the hall. Going once…" The gavel was raised dramatically, poised to slam down with flourish. Lex squinted into the far recesses of the vast Ruby Room, trying to see who was prepared to plunk down such a serious chunk of change for a date with him, but the chandeliers had been dimmed and the spotlights blinded him.

"Wait! We now have…ninety-five thousand from the lady in red at the table in front!"

His heart beat faster, he strutted harder. The music went louder. Yeah. He was going to nail it—a top bid. Walk away from this with ego intact.

"Going once…going twice…" Called the auctioneer. "Oh, we have one hundred thousand! Again from the bidder in silver at the rear."

The atmosphere shifted suddenly, and a hot hush of tension pressed down over the crowd. The music all but stopped, just whispering kettle drums.

The auctioneer's voice took a quiet edge. "We have a bid of one hundred thousand dollars, ladies. Going once. Going twice…"

Adrenaline quickened through Lex as he tried again to squint beyond the glare of the spotlights. This was insane. Then again, this was Vegas. Where people believed that everything had a price, any dream could be bought. Anything could happen. Maybe Mr. Skydiver was right after all. A small ripple of hot pleasure coursed through him. Someone wanted him bad, and that was good, because this entire event, this bidding war over him right now was going to buy some real programs for his "kids." Besides, how bad could one date get anyway?

* * *

It was Jenna Jayne Rothchild's turn to get steamed. Someone at the back of the room was giving her one hell of a run for her money, and she had zero intention of losing Special Agent Lex Duncan to *anyone*. This whole damn extravagant event had been created solely so she could nab him.

"Who the hell *is* that back there?" she whispered angrily through her teeth, eyes remaining fixed on the auctioneer.

"Mercedes Epstein," said Cassie Mills excitedly. "And…oh, my God, Jenna, she's wearing Balduccio. A full-length silver Balduccio gown. It's like…oh God, it's stunning. Even at *her* age."

Jenna, Vegas event planner extraordinaire and organizer of the Bachelor Auction for Orphans, shot a hard, fast look to the back of the massive ballroom. The chandeliers had been dimmed over the crowd of over a thousand women—each one of them vetted and personally invited by Jenna because they had the wherewithal to plunk down substantial amounts of cash. But even in the darkness, Jenna could make out the shimmering silver-white chignon belonging to the gracious head of 62-year-old Mercedes Epstein. Diamonds glittered around the neck of the Vegas matriarch, and her gown was a silvery-lilac, like platinum. Like moonlight. The woman seemed to glow spectrally in the dark as if she possessed a mysterious inner phosphorescence.

"Crap," Jenna hissed, getting hot in her own low-cut designer gown. "What in hell does she want?"

"Your FBI agent, *obviously,*" Cassie said with her dimpled grin.

"I didn't send her an invite!"

"Is there any lady out there prepared to up the ante to one hundred five thousand dollars for a night of her design with Special Agent Lexington Duncan at her side, for her protection?"

Jenna shot her paddle up aggressively.

She didn't like to lose. Not ever. Especially not to Mercedes

Epstein. It was a female pride thing. Vegas may be chocked to the gills with transients and tourists, but Sin City still had it's hierarchy among the high-end Strip "locals." Mercedes, known for her charity largesse, especially when it came to child-related charities, was married to Frank Epstein, one of the most powerful men in Vegas—no, make that Nevada. No make that one of the most influential men in the United States. He was worth billions on Wall Street and had funded the campaigns of many a senator, local sheriff and Vegas city councilor.

A small fist of cold tension curled through Jenna's stomach as she clutched her paddle. Frank Epstein also had a long-standing rivalry with her dad, Harold Rothchild. Mercedes could outbid her anyday—and might just do it to annoy one of the Rothchild clan. But for whatever reason the matriarch was here, Jenna was *so* not losing to the woman.

This was *her* show.

"I don't give a damn what she's wearing," Jenna ground out through her teeth. "Or how much she has in her bank account. She can't have him. He's mine. He's the whole bloody point I organized this auction."

"One hundred ten thousand, going once to the lady in silver at the back…"

Again Jenna shot her paddle up, her heart beating faster.

"We now have one hundred twenty thousand from the young lady in red at the front…and oh, wait, was that a slight twitch of the paddle from the mystery bidder's assistant at the back of the room? Yes…yes…a twitch from the bidder in silver's assistant at the back. We now have a new bid of one hundred twenty-five thousand big cool ones, people. From our mystery lady at the rear."

There was a collective intake of breath. A kinetic energy began to pulse through the hall. The antique Egyptian fans turned slowly overhead, and the kettle drums started rolling softly. The FBI agent on stage inhaled deeply, and it expanded his chest.

A hot rush of adrenaline coursed through Jenna at the sight of him, and suddenly she wanted more than just to win him for Daddy's sake. She wanted him for her own sake. Getting close to Lex Duncan had, however, been her father's idea—his request, in fact.

Harold Rothchild had asked Jenna to try and seduce information out of the agent after he'd gotten wind that Lex Duncan was now the lead investigator in his daughter Candace's homicide case. The FBI had also seized an infamous Rothchild family heirloom—the legendary Tears of the Quetzal—a chameleon diamond worth millions that had been taken from Candace's finger the night of her murder—a rock Candace herself had appropriated from Daddy's safe and waved around inappropriately and, apparently, at the expense of her life.

A rock rumored to be cursed with an old Mayan legend.

Supposedly, in the right hands, The Tears of the Quetzal would bring great love to whoever held the ring, even momentarily. But in the wrong hands, grave misfortune would be sure to follow.

Jenna thought the legend was a bunch of hooey. Then again, Candace *had* died because of it. And after Jenna's attorney cousin, Conner, had failed to retrieve the infamous diamond, her father, clearly obsessed with the stone, now wanted it back at any cost. He'd asked Jenna to help find a way. He'd asked her to try and seduce the FBI agent into telling her where The Tears of the Quetzal was now being kept. And her casino mogul father had been uncharacteristically edgy and insistent in doing so. He hadn't even mentioned the plan to Conner for fear Conner might tip the agent who'd become something of a friend. Whatever— Jenna was happy to oblige her dad. She liked to make him happy.

Besides, she could pretty much seduce a monk. She didn't think twisting the buttoned-up, übercool FBI agent around her pinky finger would pose much problem at all.

She'd started by staging a little covert investigation of her own, and she'd learned that Lex Duncan was a keen supporter of the Nevada Orphans Fund. He volunteered for the organization twice a week, coaching at-risk teenage boys. It was clearly a charity Lex Duncan held close to his heart, so she'd come up with the idea a Bachelor Auction for Orphans as the best way to get her hands on him.

Her best friend, Cassie Mills, had then been co-opted into coercing Lex's partner, Special Agent Rita Perez, into twisting the reticent agent's considerably muscled arm. It was the perfect plan—Cassie was a student at Rita's martial arts class at the club, so she already had an in with Lex's partner.

Besides, organizing the event was fun. Parties, each with more bling and glitz than the next, were Jenna's forte, her way of escaping reality, her way of running from the dark questions surrounding her sister's murder.

She wasn't good at the dark stuff—she was good at escaping. Survival, Vegas-style.

Jenna inhaled deeply and got to her feet. Whispers rustled through the crowd like wind bending the tips of dry grass.

The 25-year-old Vegas casino princess—heiress to considerable Rothchild fortune, and daddy's girl—was making it clear she intended to lock horns with the grande doyenne of the casino empire. Despite the fact Mercedes was married to Frank Epstein, the grizzled old lion king of the Strip, Jenna wasn't going to be intimidated by the Vegas matriarch's pedigree. And the battle lines were drawn over the federal agent standing on the stage, his half naked, bronzed and ripped body gleaming under the spotlights.

Camera flashes popped everywhere, reporters smelling tomorrow's headlines. The kettle drums rolled softly, winding tension tighter.

"One hundred fifty thousand," Jenna called out coolly. The Ruby Room fell so silent one could hear a pin drop.

Mercedes tipped her coiffed head almost imperceptibly to the man seated beside her—a massive personal assistant-cum-bodyguard in a designer suit who then flipped her paddle silently for her, his pockmarked features unmoving.

"We have one hundred seventy-five thousand dollars for the Nevada Orphans Fund!" The auctioneer pointed to the back. "Going to our mystery lady in silver and her assistant at the rear."

Heads swiveled again, eyes blinking into the darkness.

The lighting technicians scrambled to spin a spotlight toward the back of the room in an effort to illuminate the holder of the big purse. But the beam didn't reach. One of the techs hurriedly began to remount the light.

Jenna swallowed. Daddy was just going to have to foot the bill on this one. "One eighty," she called out, squaring her shoulders, smiling seductively, telegraphing outward calm and control—fully aware of the camera lenses on her and her photogenic quality.

"We now have one eighty," echoed the auctioneer.

Camera flashes popped, making the shimmering zircon crystal beads on her dress glitter like an electric waterfall. Silence pushed down heavier onto the room. The fans circled slowly overhead. Jenna swallowed past the tension in her throat, waiting.

"And…yes, yes, we have one ninety! From the back!"

Jenna cursed violently under her breath, flicked her paddle, smiling sweetly. She didn't look around, wouldn't give her rival the pleasure. She was posing now, for the cameras, out to win. On all counts.

But her opponent remained steadfast and countered instantly.

"One ninety-five, to the back."

Her mind raced, doing the math, second-guessing her father's reaction. He was already on the hook for the organization of the event, never mind her personal bid.

"Going once. Going…" The auctioneer raised the gavel

theatrically. Everyone seemed to lean forward in collective anticipation.

"Two hundred fifty thousand," Jenna said, voice clear as a bell.

Silence expanded, stretched, vibrated and shimmered like a taut invisible thing in the room.

"We have two hundred fifty thousand dollars, going once... going twice..."

The tech finally managed to remount the spotlight, and he swung it abruptly around, forcing white light into the dim back reaches of the Ruby Room, illuminating the Vegas matriarch in her full glory. She rose majestically to her feet. Tall and elegant.

Then with a gracious tip of her head, Mercedes deferred to Jenna and touched her assistant's broad shoulder. At the matriarch's signal her bodyguard rose and escorted his charge toward the grand gilt-engraved doors. He held them open for Mercedes, and she seemed to float from the room. The doors swung slowly, silently shut.

"*Sold!* To the lady in red." The gavel hit the block, and the crowd erupted, music exploded and Jenna's heart thudded wildly. "Special Agent Lexington Duncan fetches a record winning bid for the night, ladies. Please come up and claim your man, 159," the auctioneer said, referring to the number on Jenna's paddle.

"Damn, that was close," she whispered into Cassie's ear as she bent down and took a deep gulp of champagne from her glass. She then pressed her palms down on her hips, trying to remove the dampness and straighten out her nerves as she walked up to the stage. Agent Duncan stood shirtless, waiting to see the lady in the red dress who'd bought his pleasure. He removed his shades as she neared.

Jenna reached her hand up to him, and he clasped it. His grip was hard, rough, all power as he jumped down from the stage, landing beside her with a thud. Jenna's heart did a crazy little squeeze that made her catch her breath. Must be the adrenaline, she thought. But when she looked up into his moss-green eyes she knew it was more. Lots more. He raised her hand slowly to his lips and kissed the backs of her fingers lightly. "Touché," he whispered. "I'm yours for a night." Heat arced along her arm and stabbed into her heart like a jolt of pure electric current. She felt as if she'd just been sucker punched. One look and FBI Agent Lex Duncan had rendered Jenna Jayne Rothchild utterly—and uncharacteristically—speechless.

Cameras flashed blindingly, adding to her strange and sudden sense of confusion.

He bent down, mouth near her ear. "Just name the time and place for our date, and then I can get the hell out of here," he growled.

A smile curled slowly over her mouth. "Why, but you sound pissed, Agent Duncan. Are you unhappy with your date?"

"Lex," he said. "And it's not you—this is not my thing."

"Jenna," she said softly. "Jenna Jayne Rothchild."

He stiffened, recognition suddenly hitting him square between the eyes. He swore viciously under his breath.

"What's the matter? You have something against the Rothchilds as well as bachelor auctions?"

Hell yeah!

He'd just been "bought" by the heiress of the family he was investigating in connection with murder—a professional conflict of interest that could blow the whole damn case. He was instantly furious. He had to extricate himself ASAP.

"Look," he said hastily. "There's been one huge mistake. I need to bow out—"

"Oh, but you can't, Agent Duncan," she crooned. "I've just paid two hundred fifty thousand dollars for the pleasure of your company. You signed an agreement."

"This is a conflict of interest, Ms. Rothchild. I'm handling the investigation into your sister's homicide. And you know it."

She placed her cool, smooth hand on his amped forearm. "Do you want the Nevada Orphans Fund to be a quarter of a million poorer than it is right now?" she asked with a soft and flirtatious smile, her big dark eyes twinkling. "That money could be targeted specifically to your at-risk coaching program—the one you volunteer for two days a week."

She knew. Damn her. She knew enough about him to...a dark thought suddenly hit Lex. Jenna Jayne Rothchild was the events planner at the Grand Hotel and Casino, her father's largest Strip operation. She was renowned for her parties, each one more extravagant than the next.

"Was it you who organized this auction event, Ms. Rothchild?"

"Jenna," she reminded him, smiling sweetly. "And yes. It went rather well, don't you think? We must have raised close on—"

"You set me up."

"And why would I do that?"

To compromise my investigation, to send my case down the legal tubes if it ever reached court. Hell alone knew. Whatever her motive was, Lex was going to find out. Sexy little Jenna Jayne Rothchild had just made herself a key person of interest in his homicide investigation. He removed a card from his back pocket, slapped it onto the white damask linen that covered her table. "Call me when you've decided whether you can afford the donation—*without* the date. Because the deal is off."

"But—"

"Sorry," he snapped. "Can't mix business with..." He hesitated as she moved her sexy body closer to his amped one.

"You were going to say...pleasure?"

He felt heat. Swallowed.

"Because it sure wasn't business that I had in mind, Agent Duncan."

His throat began to thicken, and his brain headed south. "Sorry, no can do." But be damned if right at this insane moment

Lex was suddenly feeling it was *all* he wanted to do. This woman, up close, was pure bewitchment. He had to get out of her aura, suck in a dose of desert air, figure out what the hell to do about this stunt she'd pulled. He turned to go, just as the dance music was heating up and lights began to pulse over the floor.

"Wait." She grasped his arm. "At least give me this one dance?"

Lex stilled at the sensation of her hand on his bare arm, cognizant of the fact that he was still naked from the waist up. Her hand moved a little higher, and his stomach tightened sharply. He turned, slowly, and looked down into her deep liquid-brown eyes. *Mistake.*

Because suddenly he couldn't seem to pull away. "It's…nearly midnight," he managed, his voice thick. He tried to tell himself it was the excitement, the adrenaline pounding through his system. But it wasn't. It was her. She was doing this to him.

She laughed. "What? You worried your SUV will turn into a pumpkin?" she said naughtily with a little pout on her red lips, and he knew he was going to be toast if he didn't move. Real soon.

"I…have to report to work early tomorrow."

"Is it always about the job for you, Lex?"

He studied her brown eyes, drowning in them for a long moment. "Pretty much."

And his orphans. That was his life right now. That was the way he liked it.

Her eyes flickered, a mischievous glint in them. "We'll have to do something about that, then."

Oh, boy. On impulse he snagged a tequila from a passing tray, swigged it back, felt the oily burn through his chest. Another mistake. It seemed to shoot straight to his groin. Making him hotter, not to mention hard.

She moved her curvaceous body closer, almost pressing up against him. He could smell her fragrance, her warmth. The lights dimmed. Colored spotlights played over the dance floor, the crystal in the chandeliers shimmering in dazzling small pinprick shards of light. A low primal beat began to swallow the dance floor.

"Come," she whispered against his cheek. He felt her hand sliding down his arm, her fingers gently encircling his wrist. He could feel the warm swell of her breast against his bare torso, the soft champagne breath from her lips against his face, and she lured him, as if manacled, drawing him onto the dance floor. "Just one dance," she said. "Then I'll let you know where to pick me up tomorrow night."

Lex glanced desperately at the massive art deco clock on the wall. The luminous hands showed three minutes to midnight—the average length of a song. He vowed he'd be outta here within those minutes. Then he'd find a way to weasel out of the date. He was convinced she'd set him up. Because what were the odds of this being a coincidence? She'd have to have been living under a rock not to know he was the lead agent on her sister's homicide case. And under a rock was the last place this casino princess would be.

Then again, as Mr. Skydiver had pointed out, this was Vegas. Weird stuff—magic—really did happen. A gambler could bet a single quarter and pull a slot machine handle, and it would spew out one million dollars. Another could plunk down his life savings and lose his entire fortune with the simple flick of a card.

Luck. Fate. Chance. The only sure thing about Las Vegas was that nothing was sure, nothing predetermined. No one ever knew what could happen next.

It's what made Sin City so exciting.

So dangerous.

Jenna placed her hands on his hips, guiding him to the rhythm of the beat, and Lex's brain went blank. His blood began to thump in time with the music. And before he knew it, the trademark Ruby Room clock began to chime. Midnight.

Music halted momentarily for effect, twirly strips of silver confetti shimmering down like crystal rain as the lights strobed white. Like silver, like money. Like magic. The Vegas sleight-of-hand. And Lex knew, on some level, he'd been witched, by a pair of big brown eyes and a goddess body in a shimmering red dress, and it had happened somewhere in those three minutes before the stroke of midnight.

In panic he snagged another shot of tequila, knocked it back, thinking of Dutch courage and skydiving. Because he sure was free-falling right now, out of control, and gaining speed each time Jenna batted those big browns and arched against him.

Chapter 2

The DJ amped the music, and the base pulsed deeper. Bodies gyrated, red strobes flashing off glass in the chandeliers, off the red crystals on Jenna's dress, and the tequila began to work on Lex's brain, along with his libido.

Truth was, the more Lex looked at her, the more bedazzled he was by Jenna Rothchild. She had the kind of looks that really did it for him—rich chestnut hair that fell in lustrous waves to well below her creamy shoulder blades. Full mouth, painted blood-red, high cheekbones that gave her an air of experienced sophistication—the kind that made a man forget about her youth—and a body worth every bit of wattage in Sin City. *That* made a man hot.

It wasn't easy to stand out in a place like Vegas—a town of lean, leggy showgirls with spotlight smiles—but this woman did. She was also big money and high maintenance, and for all those reasons, Lex wanted to avoid her like the plague. Never mind a conflict of interest. Jenna Jayne Rothchild was plain dangerous to him personally as well as professionally.

But as he was about to pull back and extricate himself while he still could, she leaned up and murmured against his cheek. "You feel a little stiff, agent."

Oh yeah, and she was going to find out just how stiff if she pressed her body any closer to his pelvis. The music wasn't the only thing hot and pulsing right now.

She used her hands to guide his body in time to the retro beat. "Come on, loosen up a little, move with me, agent. Or are you always wound this tight?"

Unsmiling, he allowed her to move his hips to the primal tempo of the music and be damned if all he could think about was getting her into bed, and moving with her like a real man, naked between the sheets, the way nature intended. It made his head thicker, it made his vision narrow, it made perspiration begin to gleam over his bare chest.

Lex tried to stay in focus, thinking he should never have downed those shots, because he was not feeling himself. Instead, he found himself fixated on her cleavage, the way the neckline of her dress plunged so low that the sparkling fabric seemingly just floated atop her breasts. He had no idea how it stayed there. And he found himself *waiting* for it to slip, lust winding so tight inside him he thought he'd bust. Then as she moved, the diamond teardrop pendant nestled between her smooth breasts at the end of a gold chain, winked at him.

And the thought of the big diamond rock in FBI lockdown suddenly slammed into him. The Tears of the Quetzal. The case he was working.

The homicide.

His job.

He leaned down to tell Jenna he was leaving, but she placed two fingers over his lips and shook her beautiful head. "No," she mouthed over the music. Then she leaned up again, whispering in his ear. "Don't think. Just dance with me. Find my rhythm." Her voice reverberated softly against his skin, breath warm in his ear as she swayed seductively against him. He felt her hands slide up the sides of his naked torso, lingering over ridges of muscle, exploring his body inch by inch as she moved. A shaft of heat shot clean to his groin and Lex's breath strangled in his chest. For some reason, Harold Rothchild's youngest daughter was really working him.

She was trapping him with her magic, and she knew it. And his lust was beginning to feed on itself like a forest fire. Lex was going to have one hell of a time trying to put this carnal genie that had been awakened back into its little bottle.

She moved her mouth toward his, brushing her red lips over his, allowing the barest tip of her tongue to enter his mouth and touch the inner seam of his top lip.

Lex's world swirled darkly. He opened his mouth, unable to stop himself from tasting her.

And suddenly, another camera flashed, capturing the moment.

Lex blinked, shocked instantly back to reality. He cursed viciously.

He could just see the headlines tomorrow: *Half-Naked FBI Agent in Charge of High-Profile Vegas Homicide Locks Lips on the Dance Floor with Victim's Younger Sister.*

He was toast.

He had to get the hell out of here—and fast.

Lex *lived* for his job. The Bureau, his "kids," the old Washoe County sheriff who'd pulled him back from the edge when he was being bounced from one foster home to the other—*those* things were his family. And he had no intention of blowing it all over a woman.

Especially *this* woman.

He grabbed her wrist firmly, his jaw tense as he escorted her brusquely toward the doors. The teeming, dancing crowd of bodies parting in front of him like the Red Sea. He ushered her out into the hall where it was quieter.

The doors shut sullenly behind them.

"You set me up, Jenna. Why?" he demanded. "Did you do this to compromise the case? What's in it for *you?*" The direct approach, all business, was the only way for Lex to steer himself clear of his own libido right now.

She blinked those impossibly big, sparkling eyes. "I had no idea you were on the case, Lex."

"You'd have to be living under a rock not to know!"

"I don't follow all that—" she waved her hand dismissively "—technical stuff."

He cupped her jaw, lifted it up. "Don't give me the bimbo spiel, Ms. Rothchild. I suspect you have more intellect stashed in your pretty little head than Mr. Investment Banker with the rose wilting in his teeth back there. What game are you playing? What're you trying to achieve here? If you're trying to mess with this case because you have something to hide, I promise you now, I *will* find it."

She swallowed, pupils darkening reflexively. Heat ribboned through him.

"Look," he said, his voice coming out an octave lower. "It's up to you what you do with that quarter million, but I'm outta here."

"You still owe me a date, Lex."

"I owe you nothing, Jenna."

"If you want that money to go to charity," she said with a defiant tilt of her head, "you'll spend a few hours with me."

He glared at her. "An ultimatum? Oh, that's rich."

"We had a deal."

"What we have, Jenna, is a conflict of interest."

"Not to my mind. And if you don't play, agent, I don't give."

She made a moue, and all he could think about was kissing those full, pouty red lips of hers.

Lex swallowed against the dryness in his throat. And before reengaging his brain, the words came out of his mouth. "One date. That's it. The money goes to my kids. Then this is done. Over. *Capiche?*"

"What ever made you think I wanted—" her eyes teased slowly over his bare chest "—anything more?" she whispered. "I did this purely for charity, Lex."

He muttered something unholy under his breath. Then spun, and stalked off toward the hotel lobby.

Jenna watched him go, admiring the view. His dark-blond hair glinted under the pinprick lights, and his neck was taut. The power in his shoulders transferred with each stride down the corded muscles of his broad back into the waistband of his tailored pants—pants that had been expertly cut to accommodate the rock-hard thighs she'd felt against her body while dancing. And suddenly, this really wasn't about Daddy and the diamond at all. Not even remotely. This was about Jenna. What *she* wanted…and she wanted him.

Except he appeared immune to her charms. And her money.

Lex Duncan had just tossed down the gauntlet, because Jenna never failed, *especially* when it came to men. She always got what she wanted from a guy, and this one was making her determined to prove her skill.

And Jenna had learned from early childhood how to manipulate the males in her life, starting with her dad.

Her mother, June Smith Rothchild, had died while giving birth to Jenna, and she'd always felt that others in her family, including her father, saw her as somehow responsible for June's death. And when Jenna and her older twin sisters—Candace and Natalie—had fought, Candace would get nasty and "remind" Jenna she "killed their mom." These attacks had made

Jenna feel like an outsider in her own family. Not to mention guilty. She'd become a sensitive and lonely child with a driving need to be loved, to please and to be liked.

And as she got older, Jenna sometimes caught her dad watching her in a certain way. It was at those times that Jenna knew she was reminding him of the wife he truly loved and missed. And although Jenna knew her father totally adored her, his feelings about his youngest daughter were complex. On occasion, especially after a few nighttime single malts, Harold would lash out irrationally at Jenna because she reminded him so painfully of June.

Those moments caused Jenna extreme hurt, and it became her goal to do anything she could to keep in her daddy's good graces. To be liked by him, to be his favorite daughter. He was her rock. Her defense against the twins, against the nasty friends at school, and she'd found that flattery worked. It was the beginning of where Jenna learned to charm males, with very real results. She'd come to realize she could get whatever she needed this way.

It was the same in high school. Because of her seductive beauty Jenna was automatically labeled as promiscuous. So, to stay "cool" and "liked" she pretended to be "bad," wore the sexy clothes, hung out with the in crowd. And she always managed to hide her giving heart, her sharp intelligence and her genuine sensitivity. No one had ever really gotten to know the real Jenna Rothchild.

And Jenna started to become the person she had so carefully fashioned. Because of this, she continued to attract the wrong sort of men post school, and she continued to escape with parties. Throwing fabulous events became her forte, her way to escape uncomfortable reality, to be the center of attraction— to be *liked*. And she was so good at the parties it grew into a business, her dad eventually hiring her as a key event planner for his major Strip casino—the Grand Hotel and Casino.

But deep down, something was missing. A pit was forming in Jenna's gut—a longing for a sense of worth, something real. Some value and relevance in the scope of the world. And she'd begun to harbor secret fears that maybe she really had no personality after all. Then with Candace's murder, the inner Jenna really began stirring, asking questions about what life and money were really all about when it couldn't buy the kind of happiness her poor beleaguered sister seemed to have been yearning for.

Her dad approaching her for help in Candace's case was a way to wrest some control of it all. To do *something*.

And now there was this bonus—Special Agent Lexington Duncan.

He was pure eye candy. She wanted him and was stunned he'd been able to resist her, especially after she'd coughed up a cool quarter million for his pet charity.

Damn cool solid hunk of granite.

It made her all the more determined and just a little bit vulnerable.

She pushed a wave of hair back from her face, watching him exit the hotel, shirtless. And she allowed amusement to whisper over her lips. Poor devil. He'd thrown his shirt to the crowd of bidding women, and now he was apparently too proud to go back inside to look for something to wear. The FBI agent was left with no choice but to go home half-naked.

Her smile deepened into a grin.

She'd get him.

She'd seal the seduction tomorrow, on their date.

This was just phase one, she told herself. She'd done her reconnaissance, and gotten him here—playing it smart, staging the event away from the Grand Hotel and Casino and keeping her own name off the event ticket.

Enlisting Cassie to approach Lex's partner, Rita Perez, at the gym where Rita gave martial arts classes two evenings a week had been the coup de grâce.

Yeah, the date itself would be phase two. And once she was done there, he'd be pure, warm putty in her hands. And that thought sent a hot little tingling zing of anticipation through her belly. She exhaled, pressing her hand against her stomach as she watched the glass revolving door spew him out into the hot desert night. The valet rushed over to him, called for his car.

As Lex passed by on the other side of the big glass windows making his way toward his black SUV he glanced up, caught her watching and scowled.

She smiled sweetly and gave a little wave.

Then she spun on her four-inch heels and sashayed back toward the pulsing Ruby Room. But as she pulled open the doors, she bumped into Cassie coming out.

"Uh-oh," Cassie said the minute she saw her friend. "You have that look."

"What look?"

Cassie glanced over Jenna's shoulder, saw the shirtless cop through the windows getting into his SUV. "Oh, come on, Jenna. Why do you want *him* so bad, when you could have any one of the guys back there?"

Jenna didn't answer for a minute.

"Ah, wait, I get it." Cassie's disarming chuckle bubbled up from her chest. "It's because he's immune to the infamous Jenna Rothchild charm, is that it? He doesn't want *you*. Because he can see right through you, girlfriend."

Jenna laughed, making light of it while she said goodbye to her friend. But Cassie's words left a niggling coolness inside her. Maybe Cass was right.

Maybe Lex did see right through her. And he saw there was nothing inside. Nothing under the money and superficial glitz.

Jenna wasn't sure how to handle this idea. It made her feel

more than just a little bit vulnerable—it made her feel worthless. Maybe she was wrong. Maybe Lex Duncan had nailed the game advantage and she hadn't won after all.

Lex was greeted by a chorus of adult males making the yipping sounds of a small dog as he walked into the bullpen at the FBI's Las Vegas field office Friday, the next morning.

He glanced at Rita Perez. "What the hell is going on here?"

"She has one of those little purse pooches," Perez said as Lex removed his jacket.

"What are you talking about?"

Perez slapped a copy of the *Las Vegas Sun* on Lex's desk. "You and *it-girl*." She folded her arms across her chest, looking too damn smug for her own Latina good. Lex glanced down and saw the photo he knew he would. The one that showed him half-naked, gleaming with perspiration and kissing the Vegas heiress who was also the youngest sister of his homicide case victim.

He swore under his breath.

More yips taunted him.

"What's a *purse pooch* anyway?" he said, glaring at the press photo, growing hot under his collar.

"One of those little it-girl dogs, you know? The kind that cost several grand and fit right inside a designer purse. Look—" Perez flipped the paper open to page four, tapped the page annoyingly with her finger. "There. A file photo of your casino princess on a little shopping spree with her pooch and daddy's money, no doubt. Note—" said Perez, bending forward for emphasis "—that the purse matches Rothchild's outfit, as does that cute little bow in the dog's hair."

"What the hell kind of dog is that anyway…look at it's teeth. It's got an underbite like it's permanently mad at the world."

"Shih-Tzu," said Rita.

"Shih-t-*what?*"

Guffaws of laughter burst from the room, and more yipping came from the far corner of the bull pen.

"Shih-Tzu," corrected Perez. "It's Vietnamese."

"Chinese!" called an agent from across the room.

Another crescendo of yips rose through the office.

"Geez," Lex muttered, shuffling papers off his desk. "Bunch of losers."

"Agent Duncan!"

He glanced up sharply to see Harry Quinn, FBI Special Agent in Charge, standing at the rail up a level at the offices. He was holding a copy of the *Las Vegas Sun,* the big black headline sticking out over his thumb: "Record Two Million Raised for Nevada Orphans Fund."

"Can I see you in my office." It wasn't a question.

"Ooh, he's in the shih tzu doo-doo now," someone cooed in a loud stage whisper. More raucous laughter rolled through the bullpen. Lex swore softly as he made his way into Quinn's office.

Quinn slapped the paper down on his desk. The photo of Lex, topless, partying down with a person of interest in his homicide investigation mocked him from the polished surface. From the look in his boss's eyes, Lex was about to hear that he was off the case. Or worse.

He cleared his throat. "I can explain—"

Quinn raised his hand. "Let me see if I've got this straight," he snapped. "Jenna Rothchild paid a quarter of a million? To date *you* for a night?"

Lex ran his tongue over his teeth. "Yes, sir."

His boss suddenly threw back his head and laughed. Hard, really hard. He slumped down into his chair, wiping a tear from his eyes.

"Geez, Quinn, I'm not that much of a dog," Lex muttered. "Besides, I told her to forget it. Mistake. Conflict of interest. This—" he wagged his hand at the newspaper on Quinn's desk

"—will all blow over by tomorrow." Why did he not sound more convincing to himself?

His boss sat forward suddenly, eyes dead serious again. He had a way of switching back and forth, unnerving people. It kept his agents on their feet. "No." His black eyes bored into Lex. "No. This is not over. We use this. We use *her*."

"Excuse me?"

"Play along."

Surprise rippled through Lex. He had zero intension of messing any further with Jenna for personal, never mind professional, reasons. "That's…ridiculous. It's a clear conflict of interest. It could pose a problem for the prosecution if they find a connection between me and Rothchild, especially if a defense attorney gets wind of—"

"Granted, yes, it's unorthodox." Quinn tapped his pen impatiently on his desk. "But *nothing* about this case to date has been orthodox. Consider it a covert operation, Duncan. A Rothchild infiltration." He leaned back in his chair as he spoke, and Lex detected a faint smirk of amusement on his superior's face.

"There's no way—"

"She's a tool, agent. She handed herself to us on a silver platter. *Use* that tool, leverage it to get to her father, to dig up information on that little trophy wife of his, on the dead sister, crack anyone or anything open, pry it loose. Play her game. One hundred percent. God knows we need some kind of break on this case."

"She set me up."

"So? Find out why."

"The media will—"

"I'll let the media know you're officially off the case. Unofficially, you're on it 24/7. We'll plug it as a covert op, and the legal stuff will be in the clear as long as you keep your hands off her."

"Look, I—"

His boss stood, making up in breadth what he lacked in Lex's height. "It's good to have you in the Vegas office, agent. I was more than happy to approve your request for transfer."

"Thank you, sir." That was a veiled threat if he ever saw one. Lex was no idiot. He'd put in for a post at this Las Vegas field office several times over the last couple of years, wanting to get out of Washington and back to the Reno-Vegas area for reasons of his own.

His application had been approved nine months ago, thanks in major part to Harry Quinn. And Lex had settled in fast, coaching troubled foster kids at football, volunteering for Nevada orphans-related charities. He'd landed himself a nice little house in one of the new subdivisions away from the hubbub of the Las Vegas Strip from where he could see the fire-red spring mountains. It was his springboard to the desert wilderness he'd always loved as a kid, yet not too far from the sort of pulse he'd grown up with in Reno. In many ways, Lex felt he'd come right home to Sin City. His mother had a past here, and it was here he'd come looking for answers. Lex was finally in a position to put everything into finding the man who had killed his mother.

He had no intention of being eased out now. If keeping this posting meant tangling with Jenna Rothchild, he'd have to bite the bullet and try to keep his libido in check. In spite of what moves she pulled on him.

Damn—he was between a rock and a hard place. He could already hear the snickers out in the bullpen.

He blew out a chestful of air as Quinn showed him out the office door. "And keep me briefed, Duncan. Let me know if you need anything. Perez remains your backup on this."

Perez was the one who got me into this.

He saw her smiling up at him as he neared his desk. "I wanted to kill you last night," he muttered as he approached.

She grinned, teeth bright-white against her dusky skin. "And now?"

"Even more so. You better watch your back, Perez."

She chuckled. "I'll be too busy watching yours. Just make sure you keep your shirt on this time, will you?"

He grunted as he took a seat at his desk.

"Did you actually read that article, Duncan?" she called over to him.

"You got any work to do there, Perez?"

"No, seriously, did you see who the hot competition was for your bod? Who the mystery bidder was that gave our little it-girl a run for her daddy's money?"

"Who?" He fussed with moving papers across his desk, feigning disinterest.

"Mercedes Epstein."

He went stone still then turned slowly to look at Perez.

"*Si, amigo,* that's right," she said, getting up and sauntering over to his desk to him with that devil-can-do look in her Latina eyes. "Wife of *the* Frank Epstein, who's currently under investigation with the FBI financial crimes unit in New York. Some junk bond scam, apparently."

Mercedes had bid on him? The wife of the man who had once employed his mother in his Vegas casino as a croupier? The man who'd fired Sara Duncan when she fell pregnant with him, necessitating her move to Reno, to start a new life. Just him and her.

"Interesting, huh?"

It was plain freaking weird. "Mmm," he said, opening a file, but his pulse had quickened.

"So, what d'you think the grand Vegas matriarch wanted with you? You think she pushed up the bidding just to get up Jenna's whatoot?"

He glanced up sharply. "Tell you what, Perez. Why don't

you and me go for a little drive and check out that new shooting range? And while we're there you can tell me how and why you signed me up for that bachelor auction while I try not to shoot you. Because I'm thinking it was *you* who set me up, not the Rothchild heiress."

"Sure," she shrugged. "We can go shoot. From that photo it looks like you could let off a few."

He grabbed his jacket angrily, took her elbow. "For starters," he growled as he led her out the door, "who approached you about the auction?"

"Cassie Mills. She takes a class at the club where I teach martial arts."

"She Jenna's friend?"

"How the hell would I know?"

Jenna was feeling an inescapable buzz. Being attracted to a man she was going to see that night was like a drug to her system, a welcome relief from all the sadness that had beset the Rothchild mansion since Candace's horrible death. "Good morning, Dad," Jenna said, as she bent down to kiss her father on the cheek. She set a bowl of doggie kibble down for Napoleon, poured coffee from the silver jug Mrs. Carrick, their cook, had left on the patio breakfast table and took a seat with a view of the pool.

The surface shimmered with refracted morning sunlight as Jones, their groundskeeper, cleaned the pool filter. A soft, hot desert breeze ruffled the tops of the garden palms. It was late June, Vegas peaking into summer, and today was going to be a scorcher.

"So?" Harold said over the top of his paper and his reading glasses, his Paul Newman-blue eyes twinkling. "Two mil for the orphan fund? Not bad, sweetheart."

She grinned. "The FBI agent is not too bad either."

"When is your date?"

"Tonight. I just sent him a text message asking for his address and to say my limo will be waiting outside his house at 10 p.m."

"Rather late for dinner?"

She shrugged. "He said he had some kind of evening coaching session with his at-risk teens or something. Anyway, I told him I wanted white flowers and that the rest of the evening was my treat—" she stirred her coffee, chinked the spoon on the side, smiling "—and my surprise."

Jenna liked this time with her dad. He was a flamboyant casino mogul with movie-star good looks, a much-noted temper, a passion for perfection and a shrewd eye for business. He liked to get up real early each morning, do work in his home office and then kick back for a while over breakfast. It was his time to catch up with Jenna and the newspapers and to drink his coffee. After that he'd go down to the Grand Hotel and Casino, where he often worked well after midnight. He was a driven entrepreneur, and he wasn't a man who needed much sleep.

But he'd always made time for her, since she was a kid, and Jenna loved him for it. She'd do just about anything for her father. He remained the solid center of her rarefied Vegas life. Her BlackBerry beeped suddenly, and Jenna set down her coffee cup, checked the message. It was from Cassie. FBI agent Perez had apparently just paid her friend an "official" visit, and Cassie wanted to know what Jenna had gotten her into.

"You'll ask him about the ring, of course."

Frowning, her eyes flashed up. "Of course." She hesitated. "Dad—you've always said that The Tears of the Quetzal came from granddad's South American operations, but where exactly?"

"Ah, sweetheart, I'm not one hundred percent sure. All I know for certain is that your grandfather had the diamond set down there, but otherwise, all the paperwork seems to have been lost in an old fire at the South American office."

She studied him. If there's one thing Harold always was, it was sure. A teensy icicle of doubt formed. "What exactly do you want me to get out of Lex Duncan?"

He chuckled, removed his reading glasses, blue eyes sparking like the broken surface of the pool catching sun behind him. Yet there was a sharp edge that lurked behind his smile—an edge that appeared whenever Harold spoke about The Tears of the Quetzal. "Anything you can, sweetheart. You could make a monk drop his habit, Jenna, and I have no doubt you can work your charms on this man. I want some idea of the FBI's thought process in connection with the case. And of course I want my ring back. I want to know where they are holding it. In the wrong hands it—"

"I know the drill—in the wrong hands great misfortune is sure to follow. In the right hands it brings true love. You don't honestly believe that old Mayan nonsense, do you?"

He gave her an odd glance. "Just look what happened when that lunatic Thomas Smythe got a taste for it. He almost killed Conner's Vera, not to mention her sister Darla and brother Henry. Although the cops haven't officially named Smythe as a suspect in Silver's near-fatal scaffolding accident, I wouldn't put it past him. And God only knows who killed Candace. That damn ring is cursed, I tell you. I just want it out of circulation, back in the vault where it belongs before it causes any more damage."

A small shiver passed through Jenna as she thought of what had happened to Candace after she'd removed the rock from daddy's safe. Her sister had gone and gotten herself bludgeoned to death after wagging it around at a charity event the night before her murder. That ring had been the one thing taken from Candace's apartment by the killer, only to turn up in the purse of a single mother named Amanda Patterson while she was visiting Luke Montgomery's casino.

Having possession of that ring had close to gotten Amanda killed as well. And then Luke had stepped up and proposed to her, of *all* people.

The ring had subsequently been taken into Las Vegas Metropolitan Police Department custody, and a man named Thomas was later ID'd as the thief who impersonated a LVMPD officer and stole the ring from the evidence room. Conner had discovered the paste copy left in its place when he'd been sent to retrieve the ring from the police department. He'd then tracked The Quetzal to an exotic dancer and landed bang in the middle of an FBI investigation into a cross-state jewelry thieving ring. Which is how Conner ended up defending—and falling for—a stripper named Vera Mancuso who'd been implicated in the diamond theft by her roommate. The jewel thieves had, however, been caught and that case closed, but it was at that point that the LVMPD and FBI investigation into Candace's murder had intersected, and how the whole shebang—both the ring and murder—had landed up under FBI jurisdiction.

And now her dad wanted that ring back at all costs.

Jenna shook off an uneasy sensation, reached down and picked up Napoleon. She stroked him absently on her lap. She suddenly wasn't so crystal clear on what she was doing with the lead investigator on her sister's murder case.

Or why her father wanted her involved at all.

Lex returned to the FBI field office building after his coaching session that evening to pick up some reports. He wanted to go through the file on The Tears of the Quetzal again, check out the ring's trail. Somehow, that rock was central to everything—including Candace Rothchild's death. And now that Thomas Smythe—Darla St. Giles's boyfriend—had disappeared, Lex was back at square one.

It was late and most of the offices were empty and dark. Lex flipped on the neon overheads. One of the bulbs flickered as he made his way down the corridor to evidence lockup. He hesitated outside the door, a sense of coolness settling over his skin. Damn AC thermostat was on the fritz again, turning the place into a virtual meat locker. He unlocked the heavy door, creaked it open. He hadn't noticed the creak previously—must be the quietness in the building at this time of night.

Lex picked up the box containing the rock that had caused so much trouble and opened it. He took the ring between his thumb and forefinger, holding the massive stone up to the dim light, he swiveled it.

He was momentarily blinded by a flash of green, violet, then blue light. His pulse accelerated slightly. He'd never seen the rock in this light before. It was magical. He turned it more slowly in his fingers, the facets of light bouncing electrically as it moved. The Tears of the Quetzal. Even the name seemed sad. Somehow poignant. Yet beautiful at the same time. Seven carats of chameleon diamond. Set in gold.

The colors were dazzling. The strange luminous shafts of light emanating from the stone were like the ectoplasmic fingers of some ghost, reaching out to curl back and retreat suddenly as he moved the ring. The play of luminosity absorbed Lex's attention so fully, so totally, that he was no longer aware of any sound at all in the office, or the fact he was standing alone in near dark under the flickering blue lighting of the evidence room. A band of sensation tightened across his chest as an incredible thought shimmered into his mind.

What if the legend was true?

Natalie, the LVMPD cop—Jenna's sister and Candace's twin—had fallen in love while investigating the ring's disappearance. Then Amanda Patterson, whose purse it was found in, ended up marrying Luke Montgomery in a true Cinderella series of events. After which Silver Hesse Rothchild, a stepsister of Jenna's, had found true love with her bodyguard after a mere passing acquaintance with the ring. Even defense lawyer Conner Rothchild had fallen head over heels for Vera Mancuso, an exotic dancer, after he'd spotted her flashing the ring during a steamy striptease. Vera was probably the most inappropriate woman a man like Rothchild could possibly end up with.

Enduring love—it was one of the promises of The Tears of the Quetzal.

Given the odd series of romantic events in the preceding months one might actually be forgiven for thinking this ring held mysterious power, thought Lex, watching the light curl into itself in the stone, as if a sentient thing. Alive. Shimmering. All-knowing. He snorted softly, trying to brush aside the hypnotic power the thing seemed to be exerting over him.

Then he thought of Candace and the flip side to the supposed Mayan curse on this stone. And a cold chill rippled over his skin again as he stared at it, his heart beginning to beat even faster, a strange sensation beginning to settle through him. Lex couldn't say why or what possessed him but he suddenly pocketed the ring, leaving the box empty as he locked the evidence door.

Chapter 3

"So, what are you doing in Sin City, Lex?"

Lex regarded Jenna warily, his body language defensive as he sat across the table from her. His job tonight was to work Jenna Rothchild for whatever information he could. And then get out fast.

But things were already going sideways.

Jenna was clearly in the driver's seat. Having her limo pull up at his humble suburban driveway was no doubt a power play on her part. So was her "request" to be greeted with a bouquet of white flowers.

During the limo ride Jenna had plied him with top Scotch en route to one of the most opulent establishments in a city already renowned for excess. More cocktails awaited at the restaurant, which she'd reserved solely for the two of them—an octagonal, glassed-in affair that revolved slowly over the Vegas skyline. Candles shimmered in crystal holders on every table, a silvery sheet of water cascaded over a rock feature into a pool of lilies in the center of the room, while staff, dressed in black and white, stood discreetly in the shadows. And sitting at a baby grand, tinkling ivories for them alone, was a renowned singer from New Orleans with husky jazz vocals to rival the best of Nina Simone.

Lex would bet his last red casino chip that Jenna's choice of music was intentional. Somehow she'd known he loved jazz.

That meant she knew way too much about him.

"I hear you've been in town nine months now, Lex, and that you put in for the transfer to the Vegas field office from your post in Washington."

Definitely too much.

Jenna smiled the smile of a woman who knew exactly what wattage she generated. She was dressed in pure, virginal white and looked anything but virginal. Her blouse was low-cut, sheer. Her palazzo pants were silky. She wore them over impossibly high strappy gold sandals, and Lex had been unable to stop himself from fixating on the way the fabric had swished around her long legs when she walked. Or was that sashayed? Jenna didn't do anything ordinary like "walk."

In contrast to the white silk, her butter-smooth skin was tanned a soft biscuit-brown, and her limbs were taut—a woman with time for the pool and the gym. She looked vibrant, athletic, radiantly alive. And somehow sophisticated at the same time. Pure privileged casino princess. And way out of his league. Hell, she was out of his freaking hemisphere.

Her eyes glinted with some secret amusement as she waited for him to answer. Lex wondered if it was his obvious discomfort that she found so entertaining. "And you got this information from who?" he said guardedly.

She swiveled the stem of the crystal glass. "Let's just say I mounted a little covert investigation of my own." Her eyes slanted up. "I learned quite a few things about you, agent."

"Including the fact I like jazz?"

"Maybe." She smiled.

"Cassie Mills? Did she wheedle it out of my partner, Perez, at the gym?"

"Perhaps." She took a slow sip of champagne, eyes fixed on his with a directness that made him think of sex. "Is that why the feds paid Cassie a visit today?"

He leaned forward, irritation beginning to lance dangerously through the lust burning a hot and persistent coal into his gut. "How about we just cut to the chase, Jenna? Are you trying to compromise the investigation? Is that what the auction stunt was about?"

Maybe he'd just blown his chance at getting anything out of princess here, but he'd had his fill. Spending any more time with Jenna Rothchild was going to be real bad for his health. And quite possibly his job. Because no matter what Quinn had ordered, Lex could see himself taking the fall if this so-called "under the covers" operation—a farce if he ever saw one—went downhill. And because this murder and this Vegas family was so high-profile, FBI top brass would need to make an example of him. He could smell it all from a mile away.

And it stunk.

She cast her eyes down, tracing her fingertips slowly, seductively along the silver knife alongside her plate. Lex felt his body go hot.

"No, Lex," she said finally. "I did not set you up to mess with the investigation." She lifted her eyes. "I'll concede, though, that I did know you were the lead in the investigation, but when I glimpsed you at Natalie's wedding and saw your photo in the paper, I also knew you'd be the star of my bachelor auction, *if* I could get you. I also figured it would be a tough sell to get you to play because of your involvement with the case, so I kept my name out of it and sent Cassie to talk to Rita instead. We learned you had a thing for the Nevada Orphans Fund, so I swung the entire event around you. And then, when I saw you up on that stage, half-naked and getting all hot under your tie, well—" she paused, watching him intently "—I just had to have you for myself." She placed her cool hand over his. "Does that make you angry, Special Agent Duncan?"

Lex tried not to flush. Crap, he didn't even know where to look for a moment. She was flat out, shamelessly, seducing him. Or mocking him.

How far did she really want to go? He glanced down at her hand, her slender fingers splaying slowly over his, and perspiration prickled under his dress shirt. The idea he could have sex, tonight, with this intensely gorgeous young heiress—*if* he so chose—lodged hot and fast and sharp in his very male mind. And Lex knew he wasn't going to get the image out of his head any time soon. His gut turned molten, and his brain felt thick. Quinn's words crawled into his mind.

The legal stuff will be in the clear as long as you keep your hands off her.

Yeah, sex was the last thing he needed.

"Look, I don't know what game you're playing, Rothchild, but I'm not buying the fact you just felt like raising money for an arbitrary charity, for fun."

She made a moue. "You *are* angry." She feathered the back of his hand softly with her long red nails. "But you do look rather cute when you're worked up." Leaning forward, she lowered her voice to a whisper. "I knew there was a fire buried somewhere inside that buttoned-up suit of yours." She slipped her manicured nails gently between his fingers as she spoke.

Heat arrowed straight to his groin. "I don't like being played, Jenna," he said, his voice thick. "You know what I think? The real reason behind this whole auction gig is to have my case thrown out of court down the road, when Rothchild lawyers start pointing out I was having a relationship with the victim's sister. Maybe you want to see my career tank right along with the case, too?"

Her eyes flared.

He leaned forward. "And what *I* want, is to know why? What's in it for *you,* Jenna Rothchild? Is it because you're trying to hide some personal involvement in Candace's murder by obfuscating things like this? Because this is not some party trick, some amusing distraction for a bored young socialite. This is serious. This, Jenna, is life and death, because there's still a killer out there." He paused. "One who could very well strike again."

Her eyes flickered sharply, and a blush started to rise up her neck. Lex went for the gap. "Do you not want to find your sister's killer, Jenna? Do you not want a murderer punished?"

She withdrew her hand, glanced away for a moment. "I'm not trying to hide anything," she said very quietly. "Of course I want Candace's killer brought to justice."

Lex zeroed in on the crack forming in her facade. "What is it with you people anyway?"

Her eyes shot back to him. "What do you mean *'you people'*?"

"You people who live in this rarefied Vegas air," he said with a wave of his hand, indicating the extravagance of the empty restaurant. "You people have none of the touchstones normal, everyday folk do. You live in your daddy's casino castle, Jenna, playing with your glittery toys, fancy parties, little dogs. You're immune to the world. To reality. I don't think Candace's death means a whole lot to you."

Jenna's cheeks went red, his comments cutting to the quick and infuriating her. Lex clearly didn't like a single thing about her or her family. And quite honestly, when her father had asked her to come up with the auction shenanigan, Jenna hadn't thought of the ripple effects—the very real and dark implications down the road. Like having Lex's case thrown out of court and a killer walking free because of her. Or him losing his job.

Jenna couldn't help wondering what her dad *had* been thinking when he persuaded her to mess with Lex Duncan. Harold was renowned for his sharklike business acumen—he used people. God, was her own father using her, too? And why wouldn't he come clean about the provenance of that damn ring?

Jenna was convinced he wasn't telling her everything he knew about the history of that stone.

She suddenly felt scared and small. And stupid.

Like she used to as a kid.

Lex was right—she didn't have normal touchstones. She'd never had them. She'd been born into a family that always led her to believe the same rules that applied to everyone else did not apply to them. They were the Rothchilds, special, above it all.

"Wow, you really do have a problem with my family." She reached for her glass, took a deep sip of champagne, trying to hide her hurt. She'd be damned if she was going to let him see how badly he'd rattled her.

Guilt pinged through Lex.

He was lashing out at Jenna, making it personal, mostly because he was irritated with himself for being so damn attracted to this woman. For being weak. For falling under her bewitching spell.

He moved uncomfortably in his chair and suddenly felt the hard shape of The Tears of the Quetzal in his pocket. His pulse quickened at the reminder he still had it. What the hell had possessed him to take it? He had to get it back into lockup ASAP. Never mind Jenna and her games—if he lost a piece of evidence, a rock worth millions, he'd tank his own career all by himself.

The ring began to burn a hole into his conscience—and into his pocket—and an insane thought suddenly struck him. What if the ring had made him pocket it?

That was absurd. He was losing it. His body temperature elevated as the urgency to get out of this place and return the darn thing wound him tighter.

"You read me wrong, Lex," Jenna said sweetly, feeling anything but. He'd taken a mean jab at her, below the belt and personal. And now in her mounting anger, Jenna was growing even more determined to win. Because now this went straight to the core of her self-image, her secret vulnerabilities. There was just no way she was going to accept she couldn't seduce this man. And she sure wasn't going to leave here empty-handed, either. She was going to get the information her daddy wanted.

"I want Candace's homicide solved as much as you do, Lex. But I wasn't thinking about the investigation at all when I arranged the auction. I was thinking solely about charity, and entertainment. It's what I do—entertain. It's my job, and I'm good at it. And you saw what kind of money I raised." She smiled flirtatiously. "So why can't you just accept that and put business aside and enjoy a meal with me on behalf of your orphans?"

His gaze held hers, and the air between them began to vibrate with hot, dark tension. Something tightened in Jenna's stomach. Apparently he wasn't immune to her after all. And she felt a hot rush of pleasure. It fueled her determination. Heat began to pulse low in her belly, a shimmering excitement, anticipation welling inside her as she met the intensity in his sparkling, moss-green eyes. Right now, in the candlelight, they gleamed with the same hints of color she knew existed in the facets of The Tears of the Quetzal, if you held the stone just right. A strange, overly powerful sensation, came over her. It was so bizarre, so potent, she felt dizzy. Goosebumps broke out over her arms, and her heart began racing.

"Jenna? Are you all right?"

"I…um, yeah. I…I'm fine." She laughed lightly, unconvincingly. "For a second, I just felt as though…" *Some kind of ghost had walked over my grave.* "It was nothing. I just felt a little…dizzy. That's all." She blew out air, placing a hand on her chest, gathering herself. "To tell you the truth, I was thinking about The Tears of the Quetzal."

His brow lowered instantly, and his eyes sharpened forcefully. "What about it?"

"I—I was wondering where you're keeping it? Where is it now?"

He leaned back, studying her, the pulse at his jawline throbbing. He looked suddenly edgy. Dark and dangerous. "I thought you said no business. No more games."

She met his gaze, unflinching. God, he really was gorgeous. Suddenly she couldn't get the idea of sleeping with him out of her head. All she could think about was wrapping her legs around him, feeling his body against hers…inside hers. It was like she was possessed by a force beyond her control. "You know what I think, Lex," she whispered, her voice going husky as she leaned forward, showing him her cleavage, watching his eyes flicker downward with a small hot flare of female satisfaction. "I think you really do like to play games. You're a consummate poker player, aren't you, Lex?"

He forced his eyes away from her low-cut blouse, cleared his throat. "What makes you say that?"

"Because you're a watcher. I think you like to study people from the shadows, the sidelines, assessing weaknesses, while showing nothing of yourself. Then you suddenly take them by surprise." She sipped from her champagne glass, and his eyes dipped down to her lips. Jenna moved her fingers lightly down the stem of the glass, slanting her eyes back to his. "I suspect you know exactly how much a man can lose by carrying emotion in his eyes."

"You get this on *Dr. Phil?* I'm a cop, Jenna. Not a poker player."

"Same psychological posturing, same strategy, right? Whether it's casino chips or criminals."

He said nothing. Because she was right. Lex chose not to wear his heart on his sleeve, a skill honed from a very young age, right from that day in the closet. The day he saw his mother's throat being slit. The first day of his life alone.

Lex had come to realize that no matter what a man did in life, no matter what friends he made, no matter what women he slept with—or married—he'd always be alone. People were born alone and they died alone. Pain was suffered alone. Sure, he'd tried to convince himself otherwise. He'd gone and gotten himself hitched to a beautiful woman who'd said she loved him, tried the whole classic nuclear family thing. Been there. Done that. Didn't work.

It was a farce.

Now he just tried to be there for his at-risk kids whenever he could. But inside, Lex knew that, like him, they'd always be orphans. They'd always march alone. All he was doing was keeping them marching somewhere near the right track. Just like the old sheriff from Washoe County who'd stepped in to put him back on track when he'd started to run afoul of the law. That man had shown Lex he could take back control of his life.

Sheriff Tom McCall was *the* reason Lex had gone into law enforcement, a career Jenna Rothchild could end up costing him if he wasn't careful tonight. These thoughts suddenly chilled the edge off the lust simmering inside him. Sleeping with Jenna was not worth losing his life over. Because, in truth, that's what his job was—his life. It's all he really had, along with his charity work. Even his friends were all tied to law enforcement one way or another.

The food arrived, and a sommelier brought wine. They sat in awkward silence until the servers left again.

Lex took a deep slug of what was obviously a very fine merlot, but he was more interested in the numbing effect and getting this dinner over with than the vintage. It had taken strange turns and felt oddly personal.

Personal was not a place he cared to go.

"You still haven't told me what brought you back to Nevada, Lex," Jenna said between mouthfuls.

He stopped chewing. "Back?"

"I know you grew up in Reno."

"Rita told Cassie this?"

She nodded.

I swear I'm going to kill Perez.

Jenna dabbed her mouth with her napkin. "Cassie can be rather persuasive."

He grunted, chewing. The food was excellent, and Lex realized he was famished. "I was born in Reno," he said, slicing into his fillet. "My mother was a Vegas native."

"She's deceased, then?"

He held her eyes for a moment. "Yeah." He cleared his throat. "But I guess you know all that, too." He took another swig of merlot.

"I don't," she said, her big brown eyes softening with a genuine compassion. It made her more beautiful, and Lex had to tamp down a strange impulse to tell her this, to let her know that when she dropped the act, he actually saw something he really liked, beyond her body. "She died when I was five," he said, a weird compulsion driving him to tell Jenna things he'd really had no intention of revealing. "She was working at the Sun Sands Casino in Reno at the time, as a croupier. Before that, she worked here in Vegas, at Epstein's old place."

"As in *Mercedes* Epstein?"

"One and the same. Frank Epstein used to own the old Front-line Casino before he razed it to make way for the Desert Lion."

Jenna frowned. "It was Mercedes who forced your price sky-high at the auction, you know."

"And why do you think she did that, Jenna?"

"Probably to rattle the chains of the Rothchild clan—there's an old rivalry between Frank Epstein and my dad. She likely wanted to force me to fork over top dollar for her precious orphan charity. I mean—" she flushed. "I'm sorry, Lex, I know the charity is special to you. It is to Mercedes as well. She's known for her largesse when it comes to the Nevada Orphans Fund."

"So the Epstein-Rothchild feud runs deep. Why?"

She looked a little flustered. "I...I don't know. Honestly. My dad used to do business with Epstein back in the seventies. They had some kind of partnership deal. Then when my father wanted to move toward the construction of a couple of family-friendly super casinos, they had a falling out and parted ways. They won't speak to each other now. Not even in public." She brushed it aside with a quick wave of her hand. "But that's Vegas," she said, as if it explained everything.

Lex digested this information, wondering if the rivalry between the two casino moguls should be factored into his investigation. The FBI was looking for a motive—any motive—in Candace's death. It was the one thing the LVMPD, and now the FBI, could not get a handle on. At first they'd thought she was killed because of The Tears of the Quetzal, but then the ring had mysteriously shown up again in the purse of a single mother. Nothing about this case was making sense.

But Jenna artfully swung the focus back to him. "What happened to you, Lex, after your mother died? Did you stay with your dad?"

He snorted, a little light-headed from all the alcohol. "I have no idea who my father is. He might be alive, somewhere here in Vegas. He might be anywhere in the world or deceased himself."

Jenna studied him in silence for several beats. "I know what it's like," she said softly. "I mean, to lose a parent. I never knew my mother, either," she said. "She died giving birth to me."

"That must be some cross to bear."

She laughed, making light of it, but a telltale glimmer in her eyes gave her away. Lex felt a soft blush of affection, which startled him.

"Candace never let me forget it, either," Jenna said. "She was the mean twin. Natalie was cool, but when we were kids, and Candace and I fought, Candace would accuse me of 'killing' our mom." She shrugged. "I'm close to my dad, though. It makes up for it. Except…sometimes I think I remind him too much of June, my mother. I look a lot like her."

This was good, thought Lex. He was finally getting what he'd come for tonight—a better sense of family mechanics, of connections, of possible motives.

"So you didn't get along with Candace—you fought often?"

"Ah, don't think you can go looking at me for a murder motive, Agent Duncan." Her lips curved. "No business, just dinner, remember?"

"Touché." He smiled, in spite of himself.

"But *your* personal life we *can* talk about." She placed her hand over his. Nerves and heat skittered though him. Little warning bells began to clang at the back of his brain, but he found himself ignoring them as he turned his hand face-up under hers and traced his thumb across her palm. "I suspect," he said in a dark whisper. "That you're still playing me, Ms. Rothchild. And I'm still wondering why."

Her eyelids dipped. She moistened her lips, swallowed. "Would you like to go somewhere for dessert, Agent Duncan?" she whispered.

His heart kicked, then jackhammered. "You're proposi- tioning me?"

She said nothing, just looked direct into his eyes.

Heat speared into his groin. Panic circled.

He had to extricate himself. Fast. Before he did something real stupid.

He pulled his hand away abruptly. "It's late. I think I've upheld my end of the bargain." He plunked his napkin on the table, intending to get up.

"Wait." She grabbed his arm, forcing him back into his chair. He stared at her fingers on his arm, anxiety torquing. If he looked back into her eyes he'd be toast, and he knew it.

"You can't just leave like that."

"Why not? Or did you think plunking down a quarter of a million would buy bonus extras, Jenna? Like sex?"

She stared at him in stunned silence for several beats. "Oh, that's…harsh," she whispered.

"Well, then tell me exactly what you're doing here? Because you've been playing me like some high-class trick roller."

She opened her mouth, at a loss for words. *"Trick roller?"* She cursed softly. "That is *so* low."

"Then what the hell *do* you want from me?"

Raw hurt, then anger flared in her eyes. "You are so damn presumptuous!" she snapped. "I don't need to pay for sex with…with an uptight hunk of frigid granite." She pushed her chair back and got to her feet, taking the upper hand. "And don't think I'm going to let you be the one to walk on *me,* Duncan."

Jenna leaned down over the table, making sure he could see all the way down her shirt to her belly button, and liquid fire burned between his legs at the sight of her tight rose-brown nipples, firm breasts, flat stomach. She brushed her mouth angrily over his, aggressively parting his lips, flicking her tongue, ever so slightly, between them. A battle salvo.

Lex's heart raced. Her lips were soft. She tasted of wine. Dangerous. His world began to spin wildly.

"That—" she said, standing up, eyes flashing with fury…

and dark-hot desire "—is for free. Just so you know what you're missing, Agent Duncan."

"High-maintenance may be pretty on the outside, Jenna," he whispered, voice hoarse, his sudden erection straining against his pants. All he wanted to do was take her right here, right now, on this table. "Been there, done that. And I'll tell you something, Ms. Rothchild. It's not worth it."

She swore softly at him again. But it didn't hide the raw hurt glimmering in her eyes.

Then she swiveled and stormed out.

Lex slumped back in his chair. Beaten, hot and throbbing like he'd never been in his life. Angry as all hell at what he'd allowed to come out of his mouth. He'd been lashing out at himself for even being tempted. She was right. What he said was way below the belt. He didn't mean it. He watched her disappear into the restaurant elevator, silk pants swishing in smooth flow around her ankles. Dark hair swinging across her back. Head held proud.

The elevator doors slid shut, and the gentleman in him kicked back in.

Who the hell did he think he was?

He got up, ran after her, jabbed repeatedly at the elevator button, cursing the car to rise faster.

Jenna was shaking, hurt, aroused. Her eyes filled with tears. Never had she been through such a maelstrom, or been so humiliated. She was like a frustrated firecracker ready to detonate by the time she stormed through and out the lobby into the steaming Vegas night.

No one—*no one*—hurt her pride and dignity like that! But what really burned was the fact he didn't want her. That he'd been able to rein himself in. The coldhearted jerk was actually immune to her tried-and-true seductive ploys. To her wealth, to her looks.

She'd always gotten everything this way.

What cut even deeper were his comments about her lifestyle, her family. About who she was inside.

It made her want to prove him wrong. It made her want him even more, damn it. And that made her scared. Because she was beginning to see that if she really wanted to win Agent Lexington Duncan, she was going to have to try something completely foreign. She was going to have to be herself. That old self she'd buried at school so very many years ago.

So long ago that Jenna didn't know if that person even existed anymore.

What if there was nothing under her facade?

What if *this* was who she'd truly become?

She slumped back into the limo seat as her driver pulled into the street. Wouldn't that be ironic, she thought, if the one man in her life that she might actually end up wanting—really wanting—would be the one she couldn't have.

Lex rushed out under the myriad of gold bulbs just as Jenna's limo pulled out of the valet area and into the palm-lined boulevard of the sweltering Las Vegas night. He stared at the red brake lights flaring, then fading down the road. He swore, kicked a tire.

The valet came at him instantly. "Sir? Please—"

He raised his hands, backing off. "Sorry, sorry, no worries. I'm outta here," he muttered as he made his way to the line of waiting cabs. But as he stole another glance at the vanishing white limo, a dark sedan, plates obscured, pulled out fast, tucked in behind it.

Lex stilled, a sixth sense whispering inside him. The limo turned left off the boulevard. The dark sedan followed.

He shook off the sensation. It was Jenna's affect on his body—and it was the ring in his pocket messing with his head, making him paranoid. He climbed into a taxi, almost telling the driver to take him straight to the Vegas FBI field office before his brain kicked back into gear. He should go home first, get his own vehicle, then return the legendary ring ASAP. He'd be a fool to make the cabbie an outside witness to the fact he'd even been to the FBI offices this time of night.

But as Lex sank back into the car seat, hand in his pocket, fingering Harold Rothchild's diamond, he realized he'd crossed the line. Big time.

What in heaven had he gone and gotten himself into?

The Avenger.

That was his tag tonight, how he was going to think of himself for this leg of his mission. He tucked in behind the white limo, slowing as it turned into the driveway of the Rothchild mansion. The security guard Harold Rothchild had hired since the murder of his daughter waved the limo in through the gates.

The Avenger cut his engine and lights, watched from darkness across the street.

He now knew the FBI agent heading up the Candace Rothchild homicide investigation was seeing the youngest Rothchild heiress. This could get interesting. It held real potential—in any number of ways. Hot deliciousness snaked through him, making him hard. Death, he'd discovered, excited him. Ever since he'd taken the life of that Candace slut.

Killing her had made him powerful. Invincible. Determined to systematically wipe out the rest of the Rothchild scum from the earth, to get his hands on The Tears of the Quetzal. He wanted that ring, *needed* it.

For his father.

And in doing this, his father's death would finally be avenged.

The fact that Agent Duncan had a personal interest in Jenna Rothchild made him feel even more righteous about it all. Duncan had become his key opposing force. His enemy, stoppage—ever since Duncan had thwarted him, conspiring with that lawyer Conner Rothchild to throw him a fake ring to save a cheap stripper.

He turned the ignition. Vegas was all a game. A gamble. Somebody won.

Somebody lost.

This time the winner would be him.

And this week, Jenna Jayne Rothchild would be the one to die.

Chapter 4

It was almost midday, temperatures spiking at 105 degrees. Oscillating waves of heat shimmered up from the road as Lex pulled his SUV into the palm-lined driveway of the Rothchild mansion, braking at the security booth at the gates.

He wound down his window, showed his shield. "FBI, for Mr. Rothchild." The security guard pressed a button on a newly installed intercom system, announcing the federal agent's presence. So much for the element of surprise, thought Lex as the gates rolled open.

He drove up the sun-bleached driveway, the Rothchild mansion looming into view. The architecture was Spanish-influenced—Moorish arches, red tiles, stuccoed walls that echoed the sun-baked tones of the surrounding Mojave Desert. Palms flanking the entrance rustled softly in the hot breeze.

A wall of heat slammed Lex as he got out of his vehicle. He made his way up the steps to the massive front door, noting a small security camera tucked into the portico, another aimed around the side of the house. All new since his last visit. Harold Rothchild was clearly feeling a tad nervous these days, perhaps taking the threat that had been made to the powerful Rothchild clan after Candace's murder a little more seriously but not so seriously that he'd hired bodyguards. Lex rang the doorbell.

His goal today was to interview Harold without encountering Jenna. Harry Quinn be damned.

According to Jenna, Harold had old business connections with Frank Epstein. Epstein, in turn, had Vegas mob associations that went back to the early seventies, and he was currently the subject of an SEC and FBI commercial crimes probe into an apparent New York Stock Exchange junk bond scam. If there were connections between the Epsteins and Rothchilds it could go to the heart of motive for murder. At this point, Lex wasn't ruling anything out.

He also wanted to press Harold again about the provenance of The Tears of the Quetzal. Lex was convinced the man was not coming clean on the history of the diamond for some reason.

Hot wind gusted, crackling through the ragged palm fronds as the big door to the mansion swung open wide. And there stood the one person he was seeking to avoid, wearing nothing but a scrap of bikini the colors of a Tequila Sunset, and just as damn intoxicating as a shot of the liquor to his system. The sight of her clean took his breath away.

"Jenna. I was…expecting your butler."

Jenna's lips curved, but no light reached into her eyes. "I didn't think I'd see you again so soon, Lex."

His eyes skimmed hungrily over her—couldn't help it. She was wearing crazy high heels that put a killer curve into her calves, seductive arches into her feet and a powerful punch to his gut. In her navel, a small little emerald green jewel winked. It took an embarrassing moment before he could wrench his attention away from it. He cursed softly to himself as the latent tension from last night's date quickly began to shimmer between them again.

"I presume you're here to apologize?" she asked.

He cleared his throat. "Actually, I'm here on business. I understand your father is in?"

Her mouth flattened slightly, some of the glimmer leaving her. "Fine." She stepped back, holding the door open but not far back enough so he didn't have to brush against her barely covered chest as he entered.

"Harold is out by the pool. Go through the hall and then through the wet bar over there," she said coolly, with a tilt of her chin.

It wasn't the first time Lex had been inside the Rothchild lair, but again, he couldn't help musing his entire house would pretty much fit inside just the hall alone. He started to make his way over the gleaming tiles but paused. "Look, Jenna," he said, swinging around. Mistake.

She was too close.

His brain headed completely south, and she could see it. A whisper of amusement toyed briefly with her mouth. Yet a hint of insecurity remained in her eyes. An insecurity that wasn't apparent last night.

He'd put it there.

Again, guilt twisted.

He cleared his throat again. "I am sorry about last night. I…I want to say thank you for all the trouble you went to, with the dinner, the restaurant, your very generous contribution to a charity I—"

"It was my pleasure, Lex." But no pleasure showed in her features. "I just wish…" Her voice faded slightly. "Sorry it was such torture for you."

Oh, boy, she didn't know the half of it. He ran his hand over his hair, feeling sweat prickle along his scalp, and was thankfully saved by the appearance of the Rothchild butler.

"Ah, Clive," Jenna said, clearly relieved herself. "Special Agent Lexington Duncan is here to see Harold. Can you please show him to the pool?"

Harold Rothchild had movie-star good looks, thought Lex as he shook the flamboyant casino mogul's hand and took a seat on the designer rattan furniture in the shade on the pool deck. It was cooler by the water, a sparkling oasis surrounded by palms, thick-leaved shrubs, carefully tended blooms of exotic color and scent. A sprinkler shot staccato arcs over the greenery.

"Nice out here," Lex said.

"I like working by the pool," Harold answered dryly, taking a seat himself. "So, a personal visit? Must be important. What can I do for you Special Agent Duncan?"

Lex cut to the point. "What can you tell me about the provenance of The Tears of the Quetzal?"

Harold sat back with a deep sigh. "We've been through this."

"I thought maybe your memory might have been jogged since the last time we spoke."

He studied Lex for a long moment. "It hasn't. I can't add anything to what I mentioned to the FBI before. The Tears of the Quetzal was handed down by my father, Joseph Rothchild. The stone apparently came from one of his South American operations."

"But you have no paperwork to show this?"

"Not a thing. All lost in a fire in his South American office, way back."

Jenna had been right about one thing last night: Lex was a consummate poker player. Reading people—every flicker of an eye, body movement, inflection of voice—was a skill he'd sharpened to almost sixth sense perfection as a homicide investigator. And that gut sense was telling him that while Harold might be a good liar he was not *that* good. And he was lying now. Lex made a mental note to check out the story around the alleged fire. There'd have to be a record somewhere.

Jenna appeared carrying a tray of iced teas, cubes of frozen water with mint clinking against sweating glass, distracting Lex instantly. He thanked the heavens she'd tossed a skimpy pool robe over her bikini, but it still hung open down the front.

He couldn't blame her for showing off her body. A figure like hers required effort, probably honed to perfection with daddy's health club membership. It wasn't a thing to be hidden.

But it sure didn't help his focus.

A hairy little dog scampered at her heels, and for the first time Lex laid eyes on the subject that had provided so much amusement and yipping back at the FBI office. Ugly thing, he thought, glancing down at it. The animal settled at Jenna's feet, the movement drawing Lex's attention down to her immaculately painted red toenails. They matched her fingernails, the ones that had trailed over his hand the night before. His pulse quickened at the memory, and he concentrated on the dog instead. The pedigreed mutt had a row of sharp little white teeth along the bottom of his jaw that jutted out over his top ones. And its black beady dog eyes were trained on him. A growl began at the back of the ugly animal's throat as Lex met its stare.

"Oh shush, Napoleon, it's just the police," Jenna chided, at the same time managing to put Lex in his place on the social ladder. "Iced tea, gentlemen?" she said with flourish and a dazzling smile. She'd recovered her composure—game clearly back on. Lex felt his adrenaline spike. Another hot gust crackled through dry palm fronds.

"Looks like he's mad," Lex said to the dog, trying to avoid staring as Jenna leaned forward to set a glass of tea in front of him.

"Oh, Napoleon? He can't help it. He always looks like that, even when we have company we *do* like." She set a glass beaded with perspiration in front of her father. "You shouldn't judge someone on their DNA, Lex. That's prejudice in my book. People can't help what they're born to look like. They don't pick the financial status of the families into which they're born, either."

She was digging at him for his comments about her family last night.

"It's a dog, not a person."

"Napoleon is a 'he.' Not an 'it.' Aren't you my little poochi-kins?" She bent down and scratched under that mean little chin, then looked up. "And Naps is as good as human to me. More affectionate and understanding than some people I've recently met." She was back to provocatively taunting him.

Lex glanced at Harold in growing desperation. "Is there somewhere we can…talk?"

"I keep no secrets from my daughter," Harold said, reaching for his glass of iced tea. "She might even have something to add." He sipped, watching Lex, shrewd blue eyes set in creased, tanned features as he calculated the situation. He was a dangerous man, thought Lex. And the only help Harold's daughter was going to be was in distracting him from the reason he'd come here.

Lex stole another glance at her. She was settling into a deck chair in the sun just near the table and well within his direct line of sight. The little jewel in her belly twinkled in the sunlight as she wiggled her fine butt into position and readjusted her bikini bottoms. Napoleon scuttled into the shade under her chair and glared at Lex.

She began to rub in sunscreen.

His blood pressure began to rise.

Harold smiled—the smug, knowing male smile of a powerful patriarch who knew exactly what a fine genetic specimen of daughter he had under his mansion roof. And what effect she was having on the FBI agent who had deigned to come question him.

That smile hardened something in Lex.

He was going to find something to nail this mogul, even if it went way back into the 1970s and had nothing to do with his daughter's murder, or that spooky ring. "You were saying…you have absolutely no paper trail to prove the origin of the ring."

"I have nothing I need to prove, Agent Duncan. I know where The Tears of the Quetzal came from, and that's good enough for me. I'm not looking to sell or have it appraised. Mostly I'd like it back in my safe. Where it belongs. It's caused enough trouble already."

"Can you tell me what year the fire was that destroyed The Tears of the Quetzal's paper trail?"

"Give my lawyer a call. He might have that on record somewhere."

Lex caught Jenna glance sharply at her dad and sensed a flare of tension between them. He filed this away.

"So all you do have in connection with the ring is some…mumbo jumbo about a curse?" Lex said, allowing a hint of derision into his voice.

"A Mayan legend that was passed down with the diamond. In the right hands, instant and true love follows. In the wrong hands—"

"Yeah, I heard, grave misfortune."

"You had any misfortune down at the field office yet, Agent Duncan?"

"If you're implying the ring is in the wrong hands, it's exactly where it needs to be, Mr. Rothchild, until this case is resolved."

A darkness flickered, very briefly, through Harold's eyes. Lex felt the tension wind tighter between Jenna and her father as Jenna stirred on the deck chair, eyes now fixed on her father.

The hot wind blew a little harder, ruffling fine strands of hair over her beautiful features. And Lex couldn't help but think of how the ring had actually felt hot in his pocket at dinner, and again the thought of sex with Jenna crawled through his mind.

If he didn't know better, he'd swear he'd been under the damn Mayan curse himself, unable to resist the power of her charms in the ring's presence. He was relieved to have been able to return it to lockup without further incident. Damn stupid move that was.

He glanced at his watch, changing tactics. "We asked you a while back if there was anyone you could think of who might have a motive to harm your daughter, Mr. Rothchild. You gave us a long list of Candace's boyfriends, exes, married men and the spouses who might have felt cheated by your daughter's various high-profile love affairs. Has anyone else come to mind since?"

"No," he said, too quickly. "No one. Apart from that Thomas Smythe."

"I see you've installed quite a bit of additional home security recently."

"The security measures are past due. Should have done it ages ago."

"So you haven't received any more notes threatening the Rothchilds?"

Again, that darkness seemed to shadow Harold's eyes, and his body stiffened slightly. "What're you implying? That I'd hide threats from the police? I wouldn't jeopardize my family that way."

"Just doing my job."

"If you were doing your job, Agent Duncan, you'd have found the man who sent the first note. And you'd have located Smythe and questioned him."

First note. It did imply more than one. Again, Lex filed the information, and again, he ignored the jab over Smythe.

"We have no indication at this point it was even a male who wrote the note," said Lex, removing his notebook. He flipped it open, jotted down a few notes of his own. He'd get Perez to dig up whatever she could on Harold's Las Vegas business history from the 1970s onward, looking for ties to Epstein and his mob cartel in particular. He'd also get Perez to check into Harold's allegations of a fire at his father's old South American mining headquarters. "You ever had a business partnership with Frank Epstein, Mr. Rothchild?" he asked as he jotted in his book.

Harold said nothing.

Lex looked up, waited.

"What does my personal business have to do with my daughter's murder or the ring theft?" His voice remained civil but slightly quieter. A small vein had risen along his temple. Lex had angered the notoriously quick-tempered mogul.

"Just covering the bases. I understand you've had some history with the old Epstein cartel."

Silence.

"And that you and Epstein parted on bad terms?"

Harold stood abruptly. "My business is not on the table for discussion. This interview is over."

"Doesn't matter what's on the table, Mr. Rothchild. If there is a vendetta against your family for some reason, bad business blood may be behind it. It could spell motive for murder. Revenge." Lex paused for effect, cool as trademark granite on the outside. "Wouldn't be the first time in Las Vegas history, now would it? We all know what kind of secrets were once buried out in that desert. Secrets that people might even to this day kill to keep buried. Epstein had…rather interesting connections."

Harold's voice was now dangerously quiet, the controlled expression on his face belied by the small bulging vein, the cords of tension at his neck. "If you're alluding to a Mafia past, I—"

Jenna sat up suddenly, swiveling her tanned legs over the side of the deck chair. "It *was* strange that Mercedes Epstein crashed my auction and bid against me like that, Dad."

Harold Rothchild cast his daughter a withering look.

Jenna met her father's eyes, a little pulse at her neck beating in pace with her heart, a small droplet of perspiration at the hollow of her throat glimmering in the sunlight.

Now, *this* was interesting.

Lex watched, still seated, while Harold stood glowering down at his daughter, but neither Jenna nor her father moved. It was then that Lex noticed the shadowy form of Harold's young trophy wife, Rebecca Lynn Rothchild, standing with a drink in her hand just inside the door of the wet bar, out of Harold's line of sight. Listening.

Rebecca Lynn caught Lex looking and moved quickly back into the cool shadows of the house.

Even more interesting.

Unfortunately this little domestic interplay was going to force Lex into further contact with Jenna. She looked to be a possible weak link in the family facade right now. A chink into which he was going to need to force his crowbar and leverage open. Just as Quinn wanted him to.

Lex already knew there'd been no love lost between Rebecca Lynn and Candace, who'd been close in age to Harold's newest wife. The LVMPD had looked closely at Rebecca Lynn as a possible person of interest in Candace's homicide because of it, but had uncovered nothing but a latent hostility. Lex wondered how well Jenna got on with her daddy's latest Mrs. Rothchild.

And by the look in Jenna eyes, not all was peaches between her and her daddy, right now, either.

Lex got to his feet, pocketing his notebook. "Thank you for your time, Jenna, Mr. Rothchild. I'll show myself out."

Harold moved in front of him, swift as a predatory mountain lion in spite of his age. He motioned with his hand, and Clive appeared as if from nowhere. "Actually, Agent Duncan, Clive will show you the door." He dismissed Lex with a curt nod of his silver head.

But as Lex entered the house, Harold called out behind him. "And you can forget pug-nosed mafiosos, Agent Duncan. Las Vegas cleaned up its mob act a long time ago, in case you hadn't noticed. The new Vegas has risen."

Yeah, right on top of dirty old mob money, thought Lex as Clive shut the massive front door behind him. The ghosts and secrets were buried in the same foundations.

Same snakes, different skin.

He was going to get Perez right onto checking with the FBI's economic crimes division in New York to see what they were digging up on Epstein. Might find more than one skeleton. More than one closet.

And he was beginning to think one of them might just belong to Harold Rothchild.

"You *do* know where The Tears of the Quetzal came from." Jenna glared at her father. "I swear I can tell by the way you answered Agent Duncan."

"I told you, Jenna, I can't say where it comes from."

"Can't, or *won't*? What's the deal with that rock, Dad? What're you trying to hide from me? And why?"

He checked his watch. "Are you going to be home for dinner, sweetheart? We can chat then. I've got a conference call coming in at—"

"Don't brush me off. Not this time. You were the one who asked me to get involved in this."

"Jenna, sweetheart—"

"That's always it, isn't it—Jenna, *sweetheart*. Your sweet

little Jenna Jayne, your youngest daughter who hero-worships her daddy and will do anything for him. Including seduce the cop on his case. Yet you won't treat me like an equal, like a damn adult, like you treat and talk to every other member of this godforsaken family!"

"Jenna!"

She stalked off on her heels, Napoleon scuttling after her.

"Jenna! Get back here! Where in hell is all this coming from all of a sudden?" He muttered a curse as she slammed the patio door shut behind her.

Jenna cinched her pool robe tightly across her waist as she stalked across the hall tiles and swung open the front door. She ran over the shimmering-hot driveway, reaching Lex's black SUV just as he was about to pull off. Banging on his driver's side window, she made a motion for him to open the window. A blast of cool air-conditioned air hit her face as he did. Jenna leaned forward into his window, the respite from heat welcome.

She'd set out to tempt and fluster him at the pool in retaliation for last night. And it had been working. But after listening to her dad, Jenna was feeling oddly vulnerable. Lex was right. While her auction stunt had started out as a stupid lark in her mind, it was no longer a game. And her dad wasn't being totally honest with her. Jenna was worried that even she was starting to look like a suspect to Lex. And if Lex ever found out that she had been at Candace's apartment—

Lex regarded her warily through the window, his green eyes crackling with suppressed fire, and suddenly Jenna was thrown right back to thoughts of the ring, the mysterious tones of burning green trapped inside the stone, and she clean lost her train of thought.

"What is it, Jenna?"

God, for the life of her she couldn't recall what she was going to say. Her head started to pound crazily, some magic in his eyes possessing her. And all she could think of was making a connection with him, seeking some reassurance from him that she'd see him again. "I…I know you don't approve of me, or my family, Lex. But…will you give me a second chance?"

His brow cocked up, confusion marring his rugged features. "That's why you came out here?"

She inhaled. "Let's just say I'd like to start over."

"There's nothing to start over, Jenna." He paused. "Is there?"

She swallowed, feeling compelled along this course now like a speeding car just waiting to hit the wrong hairpin bend. "Look, last night was not your thing, and neither was I. You made that pretty clear. But what *is* your thing, Lex. What makes you tick?"

A ghost of a smile toyed with the corners of his mouth. "You really don't like to lose, do you, Ms. Rothchild?"

She smiled. "Not if I can help it."

He studied her for several beats. "I tell you what. I'll show you my thing."

She flushed.

His hint of a smile cut suddenly into a wicked grin that made her heart do a slow tumble through her chest. It was the first time he'd actually smiled at her, and the effect was devastating. It totally blanked Jenna's mind of anything other than thoughts of being with him. Up close. Very close.

"I'll pick you up here tomorrow at noon."

"Where are we going?"

"That's when I'll show you what 'my thing' is." He put his vehicle in gear.

"But I'm working tomorrow."

He shrugged. "Too bad." He put his vehicle into drive. "It might've been fun."

"Wait!" She clasped her hands over the window edge of his door. "Okay…okay, I'll be here. Noon."

"Don't be late. I won't wait. Oh, and do me a favor, leave

little old Groucho Marx behind, will you." He shot a look at
Napoleon. "I have a reputation to uphold."

Lex wheeled out of the estate gate wondering what he'd just
let himself in for. He'd come up this driveway intent on keeping
away from Jenna Jayne Rothchild. Now he was leaving, having
made a date with her.

*She's a tool. She handed herself to us on a silver platter with
bonus cash to spare. You use that tool...*

Yeah—but right now Lex felt that "tool" was somehow
using him.

But in spite of that thought, as he neared the outskirts of town
and drove down Lake Mead Boulevard toward the FBI building,
he found himself grinning again.

Then he chuckled out loud at the thought of what he was
going to show Jenna tomorrow. He was going to take princess
out of her comfort zone, and he sure was going to enjoy seeing
her as a fish out of water for a change. He'd purposefully not
told her to dress real casual, either. That in itself was going to
be entertaining—seeing her on his turf in those crazy whatever-
inch heels.

A man needed every edge he could get.

Lex slowed his vehicle as he approached the guard hut at the
FBI parking compound, realizing with mild surprise that Jenna's
sense of fun, her sense of game, had actually infected him.

In spite of his caseload, in spite of everything else, he was
feeling just a little lighter in his heart.

Jenna watched his SUV disappearing down the drive and ran
her hands through her hair.

"Damn, what just happened here, Naps?" She stooped to
pick up the one thing she trusted most in her world, and carried
him inside. "Guess you better stay home and guard the fort for

me tomorrow, because it looks like I have a real date with Agent Lex, and he doesn't want to share me."

She stopped suddenly, glanced up, thinking she'd caught a movement in one of the upstairs windows.

The drapes stirred. Then nothing.

Jenna frowned. *Must be the air-conditioning*, she thought. But as she started towards the stairs leading up to the front porch, Jenna caught a sudden glimpse of Rebecca Lynn ducking away from the window.

Jenna stilled and stared up at the window, a fusion of anger and disquiet rustling through her. *Daddy's obnoxious little trophy wife was spying on her again.*

Why?

The idea unsettled Jenna more than she cared to admit.

She climbed the stairs and let herself back inside. Despite her rush at being invited out by Lex, a cool sense of foreboding whispered through her.

Chapter 5

When they entered a rough neighborhood of housing projects, Jenna finally capitulated and asked, "Where are we going?"

"Right here," Lex said, turning into the parking lot of a school. He drove around the back of the building, came to a stop on a slab of cracked pavement under a lifeless tree, and killed the engine.

Jenna stared at Lex, then out the window.

A few banged-up old beaters were parked in the lot up against a chain-link fence in serious need of repair. Beyond the broken fence, on a field of drought-dry grass, a group of male teens, most of them built rough and tough, save for one real skinny guy, were running and tossing a football to each other under a scorching desert sun.

"The field is rutted, irrigation shot to hell," Lex said, opening his SUV door. "And a couple of the kids have to bus a fair way to get out here, but they do come. Twice a week." He came around to her door and opened it for her.

"Coming?"

A wave of sauna-like heat body-slammed into Jenna, clean sucking breath from her lungs, making her skin instantly damp. The white-hot glare of the midday sun was ferocious. She put on her massive designer shades. "You mean they come all the way out to this dead piece of field in this area of the city because of you?"

"Because of what *we* have built—a team. A sense of purpose. A friendship outside of their sometimes harsh lives. Those guys out there relate to each other, Jenna. They've all been through a similar thing—loss of family. Or they never really had one to begin with."

"So this is your volunteer job?"

"Not a job—" he began to walk towards a gate in the fence, his sports bag in hand "—I do it for love." He called back over his shoulder, "Coming?"

Jenna hesitated, loathe to leave the air-conditioned SUV. "So *this* is your 'thing'?" she called after him.

He stopped, turned to face her—rugged, tall, hair glinting in the hot sun. His rock-hard thighs were tanned, dusky, his calves powerful. In his shorts and workout gear, Jenna could see he was built just as rough and tough as any one of those young adult males out on the scorched field. He literally telegraphed physical prowess. Confidence. Leadership. And already his skin was sheened by a glow of perspiration. He looked even better than he had up on the stage that night. Bigger. Sexier. *Real.*

And way more at home.

"Yeah, Jenna. This is my thing. So? You gonna come meet the guys, watch us do some drills? Or d'you want to sit in the SUV?"

She stared at the dry field beyond the ugly fence, taking in the sandy patches among dead grass, the football posts. "It must be like 106 degrees out there, Lex," she said, pushing her thick fall of hair back from her face. "Why?"

"Why is it hot?"

"No, I mean, why do you coach at this time of year, this time of day? It's almost July. Midday. It's insane. People *die* exercising in weather like this."

A smirk played over his mouth as he raked his eyes slowly and purposefully over her short, tight skirt, her very high heels, the way her halter top was already wet with sweat under her breasts. "Can't stand the heat, sweetheart?"

Irritation flared. "Oh, please. I'm serious. People really do die in stuff like this."

"This is the only time we can get access to a field free of charge. No one uses these grounds at this time of day or on weekends. We take what we can get."

She thought of her quarter million donation. Of how it could help. Of why Lex had actually subjected himself to strutting on stage. While it had been a mercenary ploy on her part to help her father get his hands back on his precious ring, Lex had done it for those guys out there under the scorching sun on a burned-out field. His orphans.

He'd done it for love.

And she felt a little spurt of affection and of purpose. She—Jenna Rothchild—could actually help make a difference. A *real* difference.

To these lives.

To his.

She slammed the SUV door closed behind her, started toward him, careful not to catch her heels on the cracked concrete. "I still can't believe anyone actually physically exerts themselves in this heat," she muttered.

Lex grinned, and took her hand. As he did, a sharp jolt of energy whipped up her arm and slammed into her chest. Shocked, Jenna stopped dead, stared at him. And she could see in his unshaded eyes that he'd felt it, too. Again, thoughts of The

Tears of the Quetzal shimmered eerily into her mind as she stared into his green eyes. She felt shaken. And oh so out of place.

He glanced away sharply, equally rattled, and he started to lead her around the fence, making for a stand of metal risers along the perimeter of the field. Jenna stumbled after him, her sharp heels sinking deeply, awkwardly into bone-dry sand.

Jenna loved heels. They made her feel feminine. They made her feel complete when she dressed. But for the first time in her life, be damned, Lex was making her feel wrong in her own clothes. In her own city.

"You could have at least told me what to wear," she grumbled.

That smirk played over his mouth again, but he said nothing.

She stopped again, withdrawing her hand from his. "Oh, wait, I get it." She scooted her oversized designer shades higher up her nose. "You did this on purpose, didn't you?"

"What? You mean taking daddy's little casino princess out of her shiny tower and putting her down in the dirt? Showing her how real folk live on the other end of town? Now why would I want to do that?"

She glared at him.

His eyes sparkled, naked against the harsh glare.

The sound of a boot resounding off pigskin echoed over the field as one of the guys kicked the football, his skin gleaming ebony with sweat under the relentless sun. Another teen caught it, absorbing impact with his body, then ran. The others were doing exercise drills. But they all stopped, began milling about, watching from the distance as Lex and Jenna approached the risers.

She knew they had to be wondering who she was, why she was here. And for the first time since elementary school, before the girls decided she was "cool," Jenna actually felt self-conscious.

"Hey, Coach!" The guy with the ball yelled, punching his arm high into the sky.

Lex raised his hand. "Be right there!" He stopped at the risers. "You want to watch from here?"

She shielded her eyes. There was nowhere else, no shade in sight. "A hat, Lex. You could have suggested I bring a hat. And sunscreen."

He held out his duffel bag. "All in here. Ball cap, sunscreen, sports drink, water. Camera. The guys would love some shots of practice, if you're up to it."

Jenna wasn't sure whether to curse at him, call her father's chauffeur to come fetch her, or just show Lex that she could suck it up and take whatever curveball he was going to throw at her next. She grabbed the bag handles. "So, now I know what turns you on, Agent Duncan—making fun of *me*."

His gaze skimmed brazenly over her body. "It's just *one* of the things—" he said, lowering his voice "—that turns me on, Jenna."

Her nipples hardened in spite of the heat, and she swallowed. "Guess I asked for it, huh?" she said softly.

A delicious smile curved over his lips. "I guess you did, princess." He hooked his knuckle gently under her chin. "Would you prefer I take you home?"

"If I said yes, would you?"

He laughed—a glorious sound deep and throaty, from somewhere in his broad chest. It rippled over her skin, unsettling her further.

"What is so damn hilarious? Why are you laughing?"

"Because, Jenna." He tilted her chin up gently. "I *know* you won't say yes."

"A gambling man are you then?"

"Just an astute reader of personality. I think you pointed that out yourself over dinner. And you, Jenna, are a fighter. In your own sweet way."

"And you, Lex, are annoyingly patronizing," she snapped, as she yanked the bag from his hand and turned to climb the bleachers before realizing that in her tight skirt, she was going nowhere up. She was going to be relegated to the bottom rung. The universe was trying to tell her something today.

"Glad you find me so amusing," she said, dumping his bag down on the bottom riser. She rummaged through it, finding his water bottle, and she took a deep and thirsty swallow, wiping a spill from her mouth with the back of her wrist. "Still can't believe anyone can handle physical exertion in this hellish weather. I'll be the one sitting here saying I-told-you-so when one of your guys collapses and dies."

Lex pulled off his shirt, abs rippling, and Jenna stared while he wasn't looking. "My boys are built to take the knocks in life," he said, pulling on a fresh gray T-shirt that molded to his hard lines. "They wouldn't be here today if they weren't. Some of those guys have had a really rough shake, Jenna. They're lucky to even be alive."

"And they're all orphans?" She offered the water bottle to him.

He took a swig. "Yeah. Some are in foster homes now, being bounced around by the system. Others are on their own."

"Is that what happened to you, after your mother died? Were you bounced around the system?"

"Yup." He capped the bottle. "Until I ran afoul of the law in a minor way. I was on a one-way track to trouble until Tom McCall, the Washoe County sheriff at the time, took me aside and helped me pull my act together. He said he saw something in me." Lex hesitated for a moment, the darkness of some memory entering his eyes. "I ended up going into law enforcement because of Tom. He showed me that if I worked with the system, instead of against it, I could take charge. Hit back. Fix things."

"And catch bad guys."

He looked at her, silent for a beat, darkness consuming his eyes. "Yeah. And catch bad guys."

Jenna studied him, sensing a hidden story between his

words. She wondered which bad guy in particular might have fired up the young Lex and what it was he'd so badly needed to fix back then.

Lex turned to look at his boys out on the field. "I owe that sheriff," he said quietly, watching them for a moment. "Big time."

"And helping those kids is your way of paying back?"

He grunted, tossing the water bottle back into his bag. "We'll be out there for a couple hours. If you start to wilt, go wait in the car." He began to jog out onto the grass.

She swore at him, only partly in jest. He turned, jogging backward, a big grin back on his face. "Hey, Rothchild—I *like* fighters," he said. And he turned, jogged out onto the hot field to join his guys.

Jenna forced out a lungful of air as she plunked herself down on the metal bench. Yelping, she jumped right back up as the hot metal seared the backs of her legs under her short skirt. She cursed again, yanked Lex's shirt out of his bag and sat on it, thinking it was a darn good thing she'd listened to him and left Napoleon at home. Poor Naps would have perished of heatstroke out here. She might just die herself, she thought, wiping sweat from her brow with the back of her wrist.

As the minutes ticked by the day pressed more heavily down on Jenna. Her face grew flushed and red, her hair springy. Sweat trickled irritatingly between her breasts, down her stomach. But she was not going to let Lex win—she was *not* going to crawl back into his air-conditioned SUV with her tail between her legs. She refused to give him that satisfaction. She lifted the hem of her halter away from her belly and fluttered her shirt, trying to let air in and dry herself.

Nothing worked.

Jenna finally just gave in to the sweltering temperature, stopped worrying about what the humidity was doing to her hair, and how beet-red her face must be—no one cared what she looked like out here, anyway. So she let the heat swallow her as she watched the guys play.

Lex repeatedly threw the ball, neat spiraling rockets as the guys peeled off a line, one by one, to run and catch it. While they sweated they traded cheerful insults, bantering. Guy stuff. The day grew hotter, more intense.

Jenna shaded her eyes and squinted toward the distant mountains. The red haze over them was gathering into a dark bank of purple cloud, signs of a looming summer electrical storm. No wonder the air pressure felt so heavy.

Lex ran backward, received the ball and was tackled hard. She heard him thud to the ground.

Jenna winced.

But he was up, running and throwing again, his muscles getting pumped, his hair damp. His skin glistened, and his T-shirt molded wet to his torso. They played hard like that for almost a full hour, zigzagging over the field, doing different drills. Lex looked so different out there compared to the dry FBI suit who'd visited their home yesterday. On that field he was in his element, gripped by a sense of free spirit, joy even. It was fascinating to watch.

Jenna got over herself and into the spirit. She found Lex's camera in his bag, fiddled with it until she figured out how to use it. Then she kicked off her sandals and worked the sidelines barefoot, the grass hard and sharp underfoot in some places and pocked with small stones in others. But it was easier than having her spiked heels sinking erratically into soil—she was so not going to break her ankle. She could just imagine the hilarity that would invoke. He was asking for her to make a fool of herself, and she knew it.

Well, she was going to prove him wrong.

Jenna got down on her knee, her skirt riding high up her thigh. She zoomed in with the lens, clicked. Good shot, she thought, trying for a different angle.

Lex waved, suddenly distracted by her and what she was doing. It cost him—he took the full brunt of a barreling kid in the gut, blew backward into the dirt, landing with a hard bounce that made her scrunch up her face.

Ouch.

But he laughed—that great big infectious laugh. And she caught the moment on camera. Then she lowered her lens, stilled. He watched her for a moment, an energy transferring between them over the length of the field, crackling with soft electrical potential.

"Coach! Heads up! Incoming!"

He spun, caught the football just in time and the game was back on.

Jenna smiled.

Lex ducked his head under an outside tap, sun hot on his back as a barefooted Jenna watched. He stood, flicked back his wet hair. "Pass my shirt, will you?"

She handed him his clean T-shirt with a warm smile and a happy lightness in her eyes.

He stilled as he took his shirt. Something had shifted in Jenna. His princess had easily shed her Vegas glitz. She looked *real*—her hair a sexy wild mass, skin aglow, cheeks kissed soft pink from the sun, her blouse molded to her breasts, damp with perspiration—and Lex's world narrowed as his attention was drawn along the curves of her body. He slowly took his shirt from her hand, forgetting why he'd brought her out here in the first place. He forgot the homicide case, The Tears of the Quetzal, the FBI…it all flowed in a dim viscous river to some place deep down at the back of his mind as his skin connected with hers.

She came a little closer, eyelids lowering. "Lex—" her voice come out a low whisper "—I understand."

Lex tried to swallow. "Understand what?"

"What you don't like in me." Her eyes held his with a bright directness that made him turn to throbbing molten lead down low in his gut. The sun burned down on his head.

"I can see why I am not your thing," she said.

Right this minute, babe, you're exactly like my thing.

He cupped the side of her face suddenly, thumb under her jaw. And he tilted her full mouth up to him, meeting her lips with his, fast and hard before he could think. Her curvaceous body softened instantly against his. He drew her close to his naked chest, tasting her, drawing her scent in deep as he opened her soft, sweet mouth under his.

She ran her hand down his torso to his waist, urgency mounting in her body, and she reached the band of his shorts. A raw lust bottled and swelled inside him like it was going to blow. He wanted her bad. All of her. Now. Here. In his car, wherever. But this was wrong, so wrong…*the legal stuff will be in the clear as long as you keep your hands off her.*

He pulled back instantly, breathing hard, trying to align everything in his head—he was supposed to be working her for information, and he'd just crossed the line, damn it.

Quinn would have his balls if he found out. The system would eat him alive.

Lex swore to himself. No one needed to know this had happened between them. He just had to make damn sure it didn't happen again, and that he kept his lust in check. Besides, how could he be sure that Jenna wasn't still playing him on behalf of her father? He wouldn't put anything past that family.

Lex quickly pulled his shirt over his head, cleared his throat. "We should get into the shade. It's…hot."

"It sure is." She grinned. Genuine. Affectionate. Definitely not calculated. And deep down Lex wanted to believe that what he saw in her face, in her eyes, was real. And that's when he knew he was in real trouble. "Do…uh…you want to go get an ice cream…or something?" *Like a cold shower.*

"Love to."

"Hey, Coach!" The skinny kid suddenly came trotting back around the corner, all toothy smile and sweaty gear. "I lost my bus money."

"Again?"

"Could you maybe loan me some?"

Lex peeled off a couple of notes from his wallet and handed them to the kid. "You gotta watch your cash, Slim."

He shuffled on his feet. "Hey, I'll pay you back, just like I did last time."

"Yeah. Take it. Go." Lex slapped him playfully on the back. "Get yourself some dinner while you're at it. Put some meat on those skinny bones of yours."

"Thanks, Coach! Thanks a ton."

"Go!"

He spun and jogged off.

And in that moment, Jenna thought she could fall head over heels in love with this man. He was the furthest thing from any of the guys she'd ever dated, and way out of her social circle, but he did something to her. He'd make a terrific father, and that made her think that maybe she wanted a family of her own someday. Something real, built on love. And the notion shocked her. Jenna had never, ever thought along these lines before.

"Come," he said, taking her hand in his and leading her back to his car. "You surprised me back there, you know?"

"Because you thought I'd melt?"

"You did," he chuckled, holding the car door open for her.

Jenna flushed. He was right—she had melted. Her hair had frizzed out all over the place. She'd gotten sunburned and sweaty.

And she didn't give a damn. Because *he* thought she looked gorgeous. She could see it in his eyes. She'd tasted it in his kiss.

And that's all that mattered right now.

Afternoon was segueing into evening and wads of purplish-red clouds were now scudding in from across the Mojave as they entered an industrial part of the city. Jenna felt fatigue creeping up on her. With the low feeling came a sense of regret.

After watching Lex give of himself to those kids, after having seen him suffer on stage at her auction because he cared for them, Jenna was beginning to feel she was a flake. Truth be told, she'd wasted a good chunk of her life shopping and partying. Moving from one pseudoevent to the next. She was surprised Lex had even bothered to bring her out here, that he'd actually given her a second chance.

Why had he?

She glanced at his strong profile as he drove, and Jenna found herself wishing it was because he'd glimpsed something in her. More likely it was because he was interested in her connection to Candace—and his case—and he wanted to keep plying her for information.

He shot her a look. "Hey, what's up? You've gone quiet on me."

She shook her head, feeling a weird burn of emotion in her eyes. "It's nothing."

"Jenna?"

She looked out the window.

He drove in silence for a moment. "I'm sorry," he said. "For what happened back there."

"Oh, no, Lex…that's not it."

"You sure?" His eyes were vulnerable, and she felt a sharp stab of affection. It bloomed soft and warm through her chest. She tried to smile. "I was just thinking…about how I've wasted my life, my money. How I could've been doing so much more.

Seeing what you did in one afternoon, how you create a sense of family for those kids…" Her voice faded as she thought of her own dysfunctional family, that stupid woman her dad had gone and married. About how she wished she'd had her real mom around. "It's nothing."

"Hey, you haven't had a normal life, either, Jenna. Growing up in Vegas, imprisoned by your father in that—"

Defensiveness flared in her. "Imprisoned? Hardly. And my father has always been good to me."

"I know, I know. I'm sorry."

She shook her head, pulling a face. "It's okay. Lord knows I probably deserve some payback considering the hell I put you through at that auction."

Lex turned down a deserted street. The sky was lowering, darkening over them, a strange kinetic energy filling in the air. The torn fronds of a lone palm fluttered in the hot, mounting wind. Litter scattered in squalls across the streets.

This section of town was a far cry from the glittering epicenter of Jenna's existence. She began to feel nervous as they passed lowbrow gambling halls, dim bars, a few homeless people huddled in a corner, sharing a smoke. The streets seemed strangely empty for a Saturday evening, compared to the 24/7 buzz that was the Strip.

Lex swerved to the curb suddenly and slammed on brakes, his tires screeching.

"What is it?"

"I saw someone—" he rammed his SUV into reverse, backed up a block, fast. Across the street an older woman in a gypsy skirt walked briskly down the sidewalk, black shawl fluttering in the wind. She turned and abruptly vanished into a narrow alley.

"It's *her!*" He reversed farther.

"*Who?*"

He turned the ignition off. "Jenna, I need to check something out. Can you wait?"

Nerves fluttered irrationally in her stomach. She glanced out the window at the darkening street. The first fat plops of rain were beginning to fall. "What is it, Lex? Who was that woman?"

"Someone I've been looking to question for months. Every time I come out this way, I seem to miss her, like ships that pass in the night. I won't be long."

Jenna sat in the SUV as he jogged across the road and disappeared down the same alley that had swallowed the woman. Craning her neck to see over the backseat, Jenna tried to peer down the alley and caught the flutter of the woman's shawl as she vanished into a tiny storefront that had a broken pink neon sign over the door. Jenna could make out the first two words: Lucky Lady. The *c* was missing.

Hot wind gusted outside more fiercely. Bits of newspaper swirled off the sidewalk and danced up in a wicked little dervish. The sky turned a deeper purple. A man pushing a shopping cart wandered by, stared at her.

Jenna double-checked that the doors were locked.

But after a few minutes, she was feeling real uneasy. The streets were growing eerie with the dusky dark orange glow of the coming storm. Heavier drops of rain bulleted down onto the car.

Jenna reached for the door handle. There was no way she was going to sit here alone in a full-blown storm. Then she hesitated. Few places in the world had tighter security than the big resort hotels clustered in downtown Vegas. But outside those populated tourist areas Sin City had the same urban ills and muggings as any other big metropolis. Common sense had always had Jenna sticking to the busy parts of town, the well-lit streets.

These were not.

She removed her ostentatious emerald bracelet and the

diamond pendant around her neck, then opened Lex's glove compartment. But as she was about to stuff them in, she saw a plastic sleeve containing old newspaper cuttings. One headline immediately caught her eye: "Reno Mother Brutally Slain While Son Hid in Closet."

Curiosity quickened through her. Wind rocked the vehicle slightly, and Jenna grew edgy as she scanned the news cutting. But as the words of the report sunk in, her blood turned to ice.

It was a story printed in the *Reno Daily* thirty years ago about a croupier named Sara Duncan—a single mother aged twenty-seven who'd been slain in her own home while her five-year-old son, Lexington Duncan, had hidden in the bedroom closet.

Jenna quickly read the second article contained in the plastic sleeve. Sara's child had actually witnessed his mother's throat being slit through the louvered slats of the door, but had not been able to speak for well over a year. And when he had started speaking again, Reno police learned he was unable to identify his mother's killer. He'd only seen the man's pant legs and hands. And the knife—the murder weapon used to cut Sara Duncan's throat.

Jenna sat back in her seat, numb.

Lex wasn't just an orphan. His mother had been taken from him in the most brutal way possible.

And he'd *seen* it.

Suddenly she felt scared. Alone. And beyond curious. She opened the car door quickly. Rain was coming down hard now, the kind of torrential summer downpour that flash flooded Vegas streets notorious for bad drainage, snarling traffic up along the city arteries.

She ran across the street and ducked down the alley.

Chapter 6

Small bells chinked as Lex entered the Lucky Lady psychic store, tendrils of incense smoke curling in the wake of his movement. It was dim inside—no air-conditioning. Shelves cluttered with silver dragons, cards, dice, engraved boxes, fetishes, crystal balls and fat little Buddhas lined the walls.

This was obviously the Lucky Lady's game—peddling fortune, fate, magic. Selling a chance to beat the odds, win the dream. Parting cash from those who believed they could control such things. Lex's eyes adjusted to the light, his gaze settling on a faded old poster that hung on the far wall. It promoted a topless, psychic act at the old Frontline Casino circa 1970s, the same casino his mother worked at. The "psychic" on the poster was a busty, leggy redhead in a belly-dancer costume, shown seductively stripping copious veils.

"Hello!" Lex called out. "Is there anyone here?"

A parrot squawked somewhere in the back. Lex tensed. "Hello?"

Suddenly, from behind a heavy curtain sewn with a myriad of tiny silver stars, the old gypsy woman he'd seen on the street materialized. Lex's pulse quickened. She came slowly forward, huge false eyelashes making her unblinking eyes seem surreal. Gold hoop earrings dangled from her ears and small spots of rouge looked comical on her parched cheeks. Her wrinkled eyelids were heavily lacquered with blue-green eye shadow, the color collecting into darker rivers in the creases of her aging skin. Lex realized with a start that she was the woman depicted in the old poster, faded and crumpled and made sadly comical by time as she tried to hold on to the thinning threads of the past.

"Marion Robb?" he asked.

She blinked. "Who's asking?"

"I'm Lex Duncan," he said, wondering what this woman could possibly tell him. "A friend of mine, Tom McCall—the old Washoe County sheriff—said I might find you here. He… suggested I come talk to you."

Her features grew guarded. "What does the sheriff's office want?" Her voice was husky, the sound of possibly too many cigarettes, cheap whiskey and loud bars.

"McCall is retired. He doesn't want anything, it's me who—"

"You a cop?"

"I'm here for personal reasons."

"You are a cop then."

"FBI."

"What? You want a reading?" She jerked her head toward her rate board. "I'm about to close up shop, but I can maybe do a fifteen-minute session."

The parrot squawked again, and thunder rumbled low and close outside. Lex could hear the splat of rain coming down heavily out in the street. A gust of moisture-tinged air chased through the store, and a door somewhere banged upstairs.

Lex cleared his throat. "I didn't come for a reading, ma'am. Tom McCall told me that you once knew Sara Duncan, a croupier who worked at the old Frontline Casino about thirty years ago."

Her face remained expressionless, but he detected a shift in her body tension. "What you say your name was?"

"Lex Duncan."

She stared at him for a long while, and as Lex watched, her features seemed to melt, and her hand went to her neck. "My oath," she whispered, voice hoarse and low. "You're her boy."

Lex's chest constricted, his mouth going dry. "I...wanted to ask you some questions about Sara, about my mother. Sheriff McCall helped work my mother's homicide case along with the Reno police all those years ago. He mentioned you had been a friend of my mother's, that you and her used to work together at Frank Epstein's Frontline Casino."

She nodded. "Before it was razed to make way for the Desert Lion. Yes. Yes, I worked there at the same time Sara was there." She drew the curtain back hastily, hooking it up into a silver loop. She pulled out a chair at a small round table that was draped in midnight-blue velvet. "Sit." She fluttered her hand full of rings at the chair.

He held up his palms. "I didn't come for a reading—"

"No, no...you must sit."

Lex edged awkwardly onto the tiny chair at the little round séance table. The old woman seated herself opposite him, reached over the table, clasped both his hands in hers, her skin papery, dry, her fingers bony. "I can't believe it," she whispered. "Sara Duncan's boy." Moisture filled her eyes as she considered him intently. "You have her features, you know? And the color of your eyes, it's the same green as hers. Sara, she turned the head of many a man...you've come looking for your father."

Lex shook the chill she gave him. It would be obvious that he'd be looking. "Yes," he said.

Always, he was looking.

She narrowed her eyes. "But mostly you want the man who killed your mother."

He said nothing.

She sighed heavily. "Son, you're seeking a past in a city that holds no memory. Not only that but there are still people in this town who will go to great lengths to ensure that the past stays where it belongs—buried." She leaned forward, bony fingers tightening around his. "You go trying to mess with that, and you're looking to be messing with some real bad ghosts."

"I'm looking for truth. Not ghosts."

She shook her head. "Honey, what you're looking for is trouble."

Lex heard the storefront bells tinkle suddenly, as if someone had entered the store. He couldn't see the door from where he was sitting—he was tucked behind the curtain. Besides, he couldn't tear his eyes away from the woman's strange, lined face. Probably just another gust from the storm, he told himself. The bells blew again in the wind. Thunder clapped right overhead. Candles shimmered, sputtered in wax. His pulse quickened. "What are you trying to tell me?" he said quietly.

She closed her eyes, began to rock backward and forward, her voice taking on a strange and dissonant monotone. "A past…buried in the Mojave sands. Sands of time…a grave…"

"What *exactly* are you saying?"

She rocked some more. Then her eyes suddenly flared open. "Bodies!" she hissed.

Tension wedged into Lex's throat. "Look, I didn't want any reading. I just wanted to ask you some questions about my mother."

Her eyes refocused on him. "People used to bury bodies

out there, in the desert, you know? Before the feds ran them out of town."

People? Feds? Was she alluding to the fact he was a federal agent, or was she referring to Las Vegas's dark mob past? Lex thought of the fat envelope of cash that used to arrive for his mother, delivered by a guy in a shiny blue Cadillac convertible. "Are you trying to say my mother might have been involved with organized crime?"

"Everyone—" she whispered "—was touched by those tendrils of evil. Everyone."

Lex grew agitated. He didn't believe in this woo woo crap, yet this woman was managing to rattle his cage nevertheless. He tried to get back on track. "Did Frank Epstein ever mess with my mother, while she was working there?"

She shook her head. "Don't even go thinking about it. Epstein is not your father. He used to bed a different woman every night, but once he met his Mercedes, then a showgirl from the Flamingo Club, his whole world changed. From the moment he laid eyes on Mercedes he never, ever touched another dame. And he never touched your mother."

"Why did Sara leave Vegas after she was fired from the Frontline?"

"I honestly don't know. She just packed up one day and vanished." A sadness filtered into the Lucky Lady's eyes. "I figured it was because you were on the way. Maybe she wanted a fresh start."

"She wasn't seeing someone special in Vegas at the time?"

"Lexington, I loved your mother. We were close, real close. Like sisters. You need friends in a town like this, and she was mine. But not once did she talk about a special man in her life, and I never saw her with anyone who might be special to her."

Lex was startled by her use of his full name. No one but his mother had ever called him Lexington.

"Sara broke my heart, you know, when she left? Took me almost a year to learn she'd actually ended up in Reno. By then you were born. I visited her a couple times, but she was different…distant. She was getting regular money from some place. I reckon she must've had a decent gig going because she bought her own house in a Reno suburb, never talked about Vegas." She inhaled deeply. "Look, maybe she was seeing a married guy and he was paying her to keep quiet about his kid. Or maybe she was hooking again, high-class stuff." She met his eyes. "I would tell you if I knew who your father might be, Lexington. It was terrible what happened to her. Just terrible."

"You think my father might have killed her?"

"I don't know. And that's what I told the cops when they came to question me. They came because I was her friend."

Lex leaned forward. "Marion, my mother used to get cash, once a month, delivered by some guy in a pale metallic-blue Cadillac convertible. The car had a little sticker on the bumper, like a logo. It looked like cartoon lion standing up, with a crown on his head? Do you recall anyone who drove a car with a sticker like that? Maybe from the Frontline?" It wasn't something Lex had thought to tell the police when he was five. He hadn't even remembered that bumper sticker until very recently when he'd gone to see a woman the FBI occasionally used as a forensic hypnotist to aid witnesses in recalling crime detail. He'd done it because there was this hole in his life—this need to know what had happened that day, thirty years ago, and why. Because not once since that horrific moment had Lex stopped searching for the man with the sandpapery voice who'd slaughtered his beautiful young mother.

It had become a driving force in him.

It was why he was back in Vegas. And while he was here, he was going to keep looking. Until he found that man.

Dead or alive.

And this time, if that killer was still alive, Lex *would* be able to move. Instead of being frozen with fear in a cupboard. He now had a badge, and he had a gun. And he had the power to take the man's freedom. He was going to fix what he hadn't been able to fix three decades ago.

But the woman's face had suddenly shuttered at the mention of the Cadillac and bumper sticker. Her eyes grew flat. "That's all I know."

Lex sensed there was more. A lot more. He also sensed he wasn't going to get it by pushing. He'd come back again in a few days, win her confidence in increments. He had time on his side now. As long as he held this Vegas post.

He jutted his chin toward the faded old poster behind the woman, the one promoting the sexy topless psychic act at the Frontline Casino. "Is that you?"

"Back in the day."

"Nice."

She didn't smile.

Lex placed a wad of cash on the table. The woman stared at it.

"Please, Marion, take it. And thank you." He placed his hand on the wad, pushed it closer to her.

She closed her eyes suddenly and slapped her hand down hard over his, on top of the wad of notes, making him jolt. "A diamond!"

"What?"

"I see a diamond…a *big* diamond. Tears."

An ice-cold shiver rippled over Lex's skin. Damn, this woman really was psychic. "What about a diamond?" His voice came out slightly hoarse.

"Very, very powerful stone…" She began rocking again, faster, harder. "Great danger…. No! Great love. A curse and a promise wrapped in…*death*…" Her voice started to fade to a thin papery whisper. "Death…buried in sands…sands of time…death to be *avenged*…" Her eyes opened. She said

nothing more. Just stared at him, features a blank slate. It was
as if the woman inside the body was gone.

Hiding his uneasiness, he got up. "Uh…thank you."

"Be careful," she hissed.

"I…I don't believe in this stuff." He felt compelled to say
it. To convince himself, more than her. Being involved with that
Mayan rock of the Rothchilds' was getting to him.

"You can't *not* believe," she whispered. "You can't work in
Vegas for any length of time without coming to believe, at
some point, that luck, fortune, fetish, fate play a role in all of
our lives. No matter how you try to control your destiny, Lexington, you can't not believe in magic. Not in Vegas."

Oh, yeah, he could not believe if he wanted to.

But his blood still ran cold as he stalked toward the store exit,
needing to get the hell out of here, and fast. But he did a sharp
double take when he saw Jenna standing wide-eyed near the door.

He grabbed her arm. "Geez, Jenna, how long have you been
standing there listening?" he snapped.

"Did you hear what she said? About The Tears of the Quetzal?"

"Keep your voice down," he growled as he ushered her out
into the pelting sheet of rain. They ducked their heads against
the deluge, ran hand in hand to the car, got in breathless and
wet. Both sat in silence for a moment.

Jenna turned to him. "Lex, she *had* to be talking about The
Tears of the Quetzal."

"It was nonsense," he said brusquely. "And even if she was
referring to the ring, it was probably because she read about
Candace's murder and the diamond in the papers. Damn it—"
he ran his hand over his rain-soaked hair "—she probably
recognized me from the newspapers the minute I walked in
there, played me all along. And then *you* go and walk in."
Anger stirred, and he swore again. "If she goes to the press with
this now, if she tells the media that you and I were together in

that place, after they splashed me kissing you on that front cover—" Lex slapped the steering wheel.

"Lex—".

He turned the ignition. "You should have stayed in the damn SUV."

He pulled into the street, incensed. It was dark now, wipers smearing rain across the windshield. He'd be a fool to believe a word of what the Lucky Lady had said about his mother. The woman was a charlatan, a fake, like the rest of this place and everyone else in it.

Hands tight on the wheel, Lex replayed the scene in his mind, thinking of when exactly he'd heard the chink of bells and sensed another presence in the store. "You heard everything, didn't you? You heard me talk about my mother." His words came out bitter. He didn't want Jenna to know.

It was personal. Maybe a part of him felt humiliated by his past, the fact his mother had once been a hooker before she'd cleaned up her act and gone to dealers' school. Maybe a part of him really wanted all the ugliness of Sara's murder to stay buried, not associated with him. Hell knew. He'd never analyzed it.

"I already knew about your mother, Lex," Jenna said softly as she opened the glove compartment. "I saw these."

"Oh, you went snooping around my—"

"I didn't want to get mugged wearing my emerald bracelet and diamond pendant, okay? So I took them off to stash in here." She removed her bracelet from the glove compartment, clasping it back on while she spoke. "And I couldn't help seeing these newspaper cuttings."

"So you just read them."

"Wouldn't you?" she snapped.

He shot her a hard look. "Put them back."

She stared at him in silence for a moment, then shoved the

articles back into the glove compartment, slapped it closed. Lex noticed her hands were trembling.

They drove in tense silence, entering thickening traffic, water writhing little snakes over the windshield, refracting the brake lights ahead.

Then suddenly, in the dark, he felt her hand move onto his knee. Just a gentle touch. No pressure. Reassuring. Compassionate. As if to let him know she was there for him, that she understood.

Moisture burned suddenly into his eyes. His jaw tightened. He clenched his fists around the wheel. He needed to get her home, dump her outside her fancy mansion and get her the hell out of his life.

Because he was scared. He was starting to feel like leaning on her, sharing.

His deep down private stuff.

He didn't want another relationship, marriage. He didn't want to start falling for a woman—not in that way. *Especially* not Jenna Rothchild.

He remained silent as he drove sharply into her driveway. Waved on by the security guard, he drove right up to the portico, stopped, but did not kill the engine.

"I can let myself out."

He nodded.

She reached for the door handle, hesitated. "That's why you really came back to Vegas, isn't it, Lex?" she said. "That's why you put in for the transfer. You came to find your father. To learn who killed your mother." Her voice was thick, full of emotion and compassion. Lex just wanted to stay on safe, uncommitted territory. He wanted to cruise in his emotionally neutral zone. He wanted her to get out. Leave him alone.

"Yeah," he said, not looking at her. "That's why I put in for the transfer."

"Do you think that Mercedes Epstein bidding on you at the

auction had anything to do with…with the past, with your mother's job at the Frontline?"

"Why the hell should it?" Truth was, that question really unsettled him. "Mercedes showing up at your auction probably has more to do with the old business your father had with Frank Epstein, Jenna, than anything to do with me."

She stared at him in silence, opened the door. The interior light flared on and droplets of rain blew inside. But she wavered again.

"Lex?"

"What?"

"Thank you."

"For what?"

"For showing me something about myself that I'd forgotten today. It meant a lot to me, being with you. And those kids."

Lex didn't trust himself to speak right now, so he said nothing.

She leaned forward suddenly, kissed him fast and light on the mouth, and was gone, door slamming shut as she ducked through the rain and ran up the stairs. Clive swung open the door for her, and she was swallowed by her mansion as it closed.

Lex shut his eyes for a nanosecond, still tasting her on this mouth. He inhaled deep.

He was a cop.

He'd acted like an idiot.

Enough games.

He'd crossed too many lines, and now he had to pull back. But as he drove out of the Rothchild driveway in the pelting storm, he knew that he'd already gone too far.

Because deep, deep down, a part of him knew that he was falling for Jenna.

In spite of himself.

Jenna crouched down in the hallway to ruffle Napoleon's fur as he squiggled about her feet, happy to have her home. But as she petted her dog, she sensed a presence, someone watching from within the darkened interior of the adjacent living room.

She stilled, got slowly to her feet, walked into the dark room. "Hello?" she said, reaching for the switch of a lamp.

"Jenna." Rebecca Lynn's voice came from near the bar.

Jenna flicked on the lamp, saw her so-called stepmother sitting in a chair in front of the floor-to-ceiling window. From that window she'd have seen Lex's SUV, possibly even Jenna kissing the agent, illuminated by the vehicle's interior light because the door had been partially open at that point.

"Rebecca Lynn," Jenna said coolly. "Why are you sitting in the dark? Is Ricky in bed already?"

Ricky was Harold's newest child, his first with Rebecca Lynn, and his only son. Little Ricky was a spoiled kid, constantly being used as a bargaining chip in the relationship between Harold and his latest wife. A relationship that was going sour. Already.

"I was watching…the storm," Rebecca Lynn said.

Jenna realized from the studied delivery of Rebecca Lynn's words that her stepmother had already been drinking. Quite a bit.

"Was that the federal agent who dropped you off?" she asked. "The one on Candace's case?"

"Why do ask?" Jenna said, recalling the movement in the drapes upstairs after she'd dashed out to Lex's SUV yesterday.

She sighed dramatically. "Your father is hiding things from you, Jenna. Do you know that?"

Here we go again, trying to drive a wedge between me and my dad. "Look, I don't have time for this, Rebecca—"

"Oh, I think you do." She pushed herself up out of the chair, wobbled, smiled, then teetered over to the bar. She poured a heavy shot of gin, topped it with tonic and plopped a slice of lemon in, stirring it with her pinky. "I'd be surprised if that FBI agent doesn't think *you* could have done it."

"Done what?"

"Murdered Candace."

"Oh, for God's sake, are you insane? Or is that the gin talking again?"

"Hmm." She sucked the moisture off her pinky. "I did happen to tell the FBI there was no love lost between you and Candace, you know? I told them that when they questioned me the first time around. And then—" she took a sip from her glass "—Agent Duncan came to see me at work this morning. He asked me again about your relationship with Candace. Did he tell you *that*, Jenna?"

A cold chill seeped through her. Lex hadn't mentioned it.

"He didn't, did he?"

The feeling deepened. "Why should he? It's his case, he can't talk about the details with me."

"He's using you, Jenna Jayne, to get inside the Rothchild cloak of secrecy." She made a woo woo motion with her hands.

"Nonsense—I was the one who set him up at the auction remember?"

"At whose request, I wonder?"

"Well, that should prove a point, shouldn't it? The Rothchilds are the ones using him, not vice versa." Hell, why had she even said that? Rebecca Lynn was baiting her and fool that Jenna was, she'd taken the lure. Hook, line and sinker.

"I forgot to mention *that* fact to Agent Duncan this morning. Maybe," Rebecca Lynn said slowly, her words slurring, "I'll give him a call later and tell him that Harold requested you to go all out to seduce him for information on The Tears of the Quetzal."

Anger began to mushroom inside Jenna. "Do what the hell you like, Rebecca! You're drunk, and I'm going to change. I'm soaked." She turned to leave.

"I also know that you went to visit Candace on the night she was killed," she called out.

Jenna froze.

"Maybe, Jenna Jayne, if I was truly malicious, I might suggest the FBI try and match your DNA to the scene. Who knows what the feds could come up with."

Her heart jackhammering, Jenna turned slowly to face her wicked little stepmother. "You don't know what you're saying—"

"Jenna, I *know* you were there."

Jenna stared at Rebecca Lynn for several beats, feeling increasingly ill. Slowly, she sunk down into a chair, Napoleon at her feet. "How?" she whispered, scared now, wondering what Lex really knew about the night of the murder, wondering if this reviled stepmother of hers had already told Lex that she'd been at Candace's apartment mere hours before her sister was killed.

"*How* do you know?"

Rebecca Lynn started sashaying theatrically out of the room.

"Rebecca Lynn!"

She stopped in the doorway, smiling crookedly.

"Did you have me followed that night?"

"No, I went to visit Candace myself that night, Jenna. When I got there, I saw your car was already parked outside. So I just sat in my vehicle for a while, waiting for you to come out. Watching."

"What on earth were you doing there?"

"I needed to talk to Candace, alone. About…an issue between us. But then I saw you two up in front of the big lighted window, arguing. I saw Candace throw the vase at you, and you ducked. You began to pick up the broken pieces. It looked, Jenna, like you might have cut your finger, because you sucked it quickly. Do you think you might have left blood on one of those vase pieces? Your DNA, perhaps?"

Jenna swallowed against the thickness ballooning in her throat. She should have told the cops right away that she'd gone to try and talk Candace into a rehab program. But there was such a media circus around the murder she didn't want to smear her dead sister's name further into the mire. As much as she and Candace had squabbled, Candace was still her blood. Her *sister.* And there were her boys to think about. Jenna had been raised to close ranks at times of family trouble.

Besides, she knew she hadn't killed her sister, so what difference did it make, truly, that she'd been there a few hours earlier? Except now Lex would see it as a lie by omission. Another reason not to trust her.

God, he might even think she'd done it.

"Are you going to tell Agent Duncan?" she whispered.

"Don't think I need to. Your sexy bachelor agent probably already knows that you're a lying little bitch. It's probably why he's escorting you around town, plying you for information so he can nail you." She snorted derisively at Jenna's expression. "What? You thought he actually fancied you?"

Nausea slicked through Jenna's stomach.

If what Rebecca Lynn said was true—and Lex *had* been playing her—it meant the fragile bond she'd felt dawning between her and Lex today had been a complete farce. And that hurt more than anything.

Rebecca Lynn had just stomped her stiletto into Jenna's fragile burgeoning emotions, grinding them right into the dirt. And Jenna hated her more than ever. "You know I didn't hurt Candace," she said quietly. "If you were watching, you'd have seen me leave, while she was still alive. You're a witness to my innocence."

"Hmm," Rebecca Lynn said, putting the glass to her mouth, wetting her lips with gin. "Not sure I can recall those little details."

Jenna launched to her feet. "For all I know *you* did it! You've just told me you were there. *After* I was."

"I never went into her apartment. It would've been pointless to try and talk to Candace when she was in a drunken rage, so I drove home."

Jenna glowered at Rebecca Lynn, all sorts of dark suspicions suddenly growing in her mind.

Rebecca Lynn sighed theatrically, as if suddenly bored out of her skull. "I didn't hurt Candace, my dear, as much as I would've liked to," she said. "And I certainly didn't send all those threatening notes."

"There was only one note. A typed one, left in Dad's mailbox."

"Oh, really?" Rebecca Lynn glanced pointedly at Harold's study door. Jenna followed her gaze and noticed that the door was ajar. It was never open. Harold always kept that door shut. And through the open door Jenna could see the top drawer of his desk was partially open. Harold was meticulous about such things. He'd never have left it like that.

Had Rebecca Lynn been in there? Jenna shot a hard look at her inebriated stepmother. Rebecca grinned lopsidedly, held up her glass in cheers and sauntered out into the hallway, listing like a drunken sailor.

Whatever had possessed her father to marry that 34-year-old witch was beyond Jenna. She waited until she heard Rebecca Lynn's heels on the marble stairs, then Jenna went to her dad's office.

She clicked on the tiny desk light, worried that if her father returned, he'd see a brighter light from the bottom of the driveway.

She pulled the top drawer open wider. Wind lashed outside suddenly, drumming rain against the window in waves. The palm trees swished eerily against glass panes and the curtain billowed. Jenna tensed, her heart racing.

She was feeling spooked, guilty for being in here at all.

Quickly, she removed an unmarked yellow file folder from the drawer, opened it and stared in shock.

The folder contained five more notes—death threats—against the entire Rothchild family.

Notes her father had *not* given to the police.

These were not typed, either, like the first threat. They'd been created from letters cut from magazines and newspapers. Jenna was careful not to touch them as she read the words, horrified.

Whoever had crafted and sent these was threatening to systematically kill off Rothchild "trash," eliminating family members one by one after Candace. Each of the notes was dated, and every one alluded to the infamous Tears of the Quetzal, in increasing detail. And all five spoke of an old deed that needed to be avenged.

The last one was even signed, The Avenger.

A shudder washed over her as the rain lashed against the windows again, and fronds swished against the panes.

Why was her dad hiding these?

Had he kept these notes even from Natalie, her LVMPD sister and Candace's twin? Just as Jenna herself hadn't told anyone, including Nat, that she'd been to visit her sister the night of the murder?

Jenna was really afraid now. She needed to come clean, tell Lex everything that had happened the night of Candace's death.

And she needed to inform him about the existence of these notes.

But that would mean betraying her father. Maybe Harold had good reason to have withheld these from the cops. Maybe these notes weren't even from the killer—they were a completely different style to the first one.

She needed to speak to her dad, find a way to broach the subject of the death threats, and she'd make her decision from there. But as Jenna closed the file the headlights of a car swept up the driveway, and she heard the distinct crackle of tires approaching on wet driveway. She glanced up. She had to get out of here, fast. Quickly shoving the file back into the drawer, she closed it and flipped off the light.

Jenna couldn't face her father now…she needed to think.

Rebecca Lynn had set her up to find these. Why? And how had Rebecca Lynn known about them in the first place? Had Harold told Rebecca Lynn himself? And, if so, why not tell the rest of the family? Her stepmother had succeeded in her goal tonight—she'd driven a needle of mistrust into Jenna. Mistrust of her own father.

Carefully shutting his office door, she made her way quickly through the living room and up the marble stairs. She reached the landing just as the front door opened.

Heart thudding, Jenna peered down over the banister, saw her dad's distinguished silver head. And with a sick feeling, Jenna knew. She just knew that she was going to be forced right up against the fence, and she was going to have to pick a side.

The side of her family, a place of murky allegiances and mixed-up love, a place she'd always felt secure, the only place she'd ever really known.

Or the side of law—Lex's side.

Chapter 7

It was late Sunday afternoon, and both Lex and Rita Perez were still in the FBI office. Perez was meticulously combing through public records of Rothchild real estate dealings, putting together a detailed timeline of transactions. She was looking, in particular, for links between Harold and Frank Epstein's old cartel. Lex, on the other hand, was focusing on Frank Epstein himself.

The two families seemed to be intersecting in relation to himself and to this case, and Lex didn't believe in coincidence.

He was finding it tough to accept Mercedes Epstein had shown up at Jenna's auction, uninvited, and started a bidding war on him purely by chance. Or was he just trying to read too much into it all because Mercedes had worked at the Frontline at the same time as his mother? And because Frank Epstein had been the one to both hire—and fire—Sara Duncan.

Lex rubbed his eyes and pinched the bridge of his nose. He was also troubled by the fortune-teller's allusion to his mother being connected to the old Vegas underworld. Or was he also giving too much weight to the Lucky Lady's strange words?

There was no doubt in most minds that Frank Epstein did once have ties to the Chicago mob and subsequently to organized crime in Las Vegas. Epstein, now in his seventies, would have been in his late twenties in the late 1950s—a time when gangsters still owned and ran all the big Vegas joints. Epstein was reputed to have had a sharp eye for a deal, even at a very young age, and he'd made connections and climbed fast, eventually forming a powerful business cartel that had bought the old Frontline Casino. It was a mob-owned, Chicago-based union pension fund that had enabled Epstein to finance the razing of the Frontline and the subsequent construction of his massive Desert Lion—the sheer scope of his new casino unprecedented at the time.

Those were the days when no bank or legitimate investor would've come near the gambling business. Without mob money, the Vegas boom would have never happened. They were the days before Howard Hughes had started investing massive proceeds from his airline sale into Vegas property, giving gambling its first positive image, opening the doors to corporate ownership of hotel-casinos. After Hughes, Wall Street investors had finally sat up and started taking notice—and gambling had become acceptable to mainstream America. It was about that time that the federal government had started a massive crackdown on organized crime in Las Vegas, running most of the old gangsters out of town.

Epstein, however, had managed to elude the dragnet. He'd given the feds nothing they could pin on him. But they'd continued to watch him. They'd kept files on him, looking, in particular, to connect him with some of the brutal murders alleged to have been carried out by a man named Tony Ciccone.

A mob enforcer.

Lex continued to scroll down through the old microfiche files the FBI had compiled on Epstein dating back to the 1970s, noting that Epstein had hired Ciccone from Chicago to handle security at the Frontline.

He sat back, reached absently for his coffee mug, sipped. It was cold. He pulled a face, shoved the mug aside, thinking that one needed to understand the context of Vegas at the time. It was a period when the mob literally ruled Sin City. And people like Ciccone—who took orders from men like Epstein—commonly got away with murder. Murder and gangsters even added to the edgy glamour and allure that was Las Vegas in that era.

But when Ciccone had eventually come under investigation for a run of increasingly violent homicides, Epstein seemed to have severed ties with him. Lex scrolled further through the files, noting it was around this same time that some sort of rivalry had developed between Ciccone and Epstein. And Ciccone had broken away from Epstein, forming his own camp, and allegedly muscling into Epstein's business, on Epstein's turf.

It was also around this period that Lex's mother had been murdered.

Lex rubbed his brow. Was he insane for even thinking along these lines? What on earth could Sara Duncan have had to do with any of these people? The fortune-teller's words snaked back into his mind. *"Everyone was touched by those tendrils of evil. Everyone..."*

He shook off the thought, turned back to the files.

Apparently, before the feds had been able to pin the homicides on Ciccone, the Italian-American had simply vanished. Dematerialized into the ether. The FBI had mounted one of the country's biggest manhunts for the violent mob enforcer, but no one ever found a clue what had happened to him. It remained an unsolved mystery to this day.

And from the point of Ciccone's disappearance, Frank

Epstein's business seemed to have suddenly gone squeaky clean, Epstein apparently transitioning seamlessly into the new corporate era of Las Vegas.

The new Vegas has risen...

However, the FBI files on Epstein had remained open, and the feds continued to keep him in their sight. Now, decades later, the U.S. Securities and Exchange Commission, and the FBI's financial crimes unit, finally had a small lead on Epstein's alleged involvement in a massive junk bond scam. And now an undercover investigation into some of Epstein's other holdings and New York Stock Exchange transactions was currently under way.

Lex reached for his coffee, almost taking another swallow before he recalled how cold it was. He set the mug back down, turned to Perez. "You got any idea yet when exactly Harold and Frank were on good business terms, and when things went sour between them?"

Perez flipped through her notebook. "I got here that in the early 1980s, they were still in business. Seems things went sideways in the mid-80s when they dissolved a formal partnership."

"Does the dissolution revolve around any deal in particular?"

"Still looking into that."

Lex chewed on the inside of his cheek, thinking. Harold was a little younger than Epstein; still he'd been around and doing business in Las Vegas long enough to have been tainted by the organized crime that had once ruled Sin City.

"What are you thinking?" asked Perez.

About who could have killed my mother, and why.

"Just can't help wondering what happened to Tony Ciccone, you know?"

Perez twisted her thick, dark hair round a pencil and made it into a bun, the pencil sticking out the top. She did that when she was getting tired and needed to keep focus. "You think Epstein had Ciccone whacked or something?"

Lex shrugged. "A lot of people apparently thought so at the time. Ciccone was in Epstein's employ, and when Ciccone started drawing too much federal heat to Epstein during the crackdown, it looks like Epstein tried to sideline him, send him back to Chicago. It appears Ciccone didn't want to go home. He dug in, started trying to muscle in on some of Epstein's Vegas business himself. Then, poof, suddenly he's gone." Lex snapped his fingers. "Just like that. And Epstein goes clean as a whistle."

Perez got up, stretched her back. "I'm beat. Want some food? I'm going to get takeout."

"Uh…yeah, sure. Did you manage to get those records on Mercedes Epstein I asked you about yesterday?"

Perez rummaged through the growing pile of papers on her desk, extracted a file. She slapped it down on Lex's desk, reached for her jacket. "Pizza or Chinese?"

"Whatever," Lex said, opening the file.

"Oh—" she stopped at the door "—that fire in South America, at Joseph Rothchild's old offices? No record of it."

"No surprise, either," Lex muttered as Perez left the room. But what Lex saw when he opened the file *did* come as a surprise—Mercedes was not her real name. It was a stage name. She'd been born Mary Roberts and had officially changed her name when she'd arrived in Vegas and started dancing. And what Lex read next chased a strange shiver over his skin.

Mary Roberts, aka Mercedes Epstein, originally hailed from bluegrass country, a Kentucky girl who'd run away from home at the age of seventeen. In the file that Perez had compiled were copies of newspaper stories about a distraught couple searching for their missing teenage daughter. But it was the next line that had chilled Lex.

The city Mary Roberts hailed from was *Lexington,* Kentucky. He sat back, feeling vaguely shaky. Not many people had the name *Lexington*. Personally he didn't know one. This meant nothing, of course, just *another* coincidence that a woman who had bid a fortune on him hailed from Lexington, Kentucky, and that she was the wife of a one-time mob man who had sacked his mother for being pregnant with *him*. And that she shared Lex's passion for orphan-related charities.

He dragged his hand though his hair, cursed softly. Perhaps the Lucky Lady was right. Perhaps Las Vegas was rubbing off on him, and now he was starting to look for signs, for connections. For omens.

He thought again of The Tears of the Quetzal, of the legendary curse.

Of Jenna.

He shook it all off. Superstition was ludicrous. He was a cop. He dealt in cold hard facts. Logic.

Still, it felt weird. He felt off, and no matter how freaking nuts it all was, somehow it *was* all dovetailing. On impulse, he grabbed the phone, dialed the FBI's financial crimes unit in New York, asked to speak to someone on the Epstein investigation.

It was late Sunday evening and Harold was still holed up in his study. Jenna paced impatiently outside her father's door. She'd been trying to find an opportunity to speak to him all day, and now she was dressed up and due at Cassie's big birthday bash being held at the Desert Lion.

But she couldn't go without speaking to her dad first. She just could not leave this for another day. She stopped outside his door, sucked in her breath, knocked. Harold detested being bothered in his study.

Jenna waited impatiently, getting tense. She rapped again, harder.

"What is it?" her father barked from inside.

She opened the door. The lights were dimmed, and Harold

Rothchild was sitting in his great leather chair with his back to her, feet up on an ottoman, whiskey tumbler balanced on the arm rest, as he listened to female vocals with the clear voice of a bird. He did this sometimes when he was brainstorming a particularly thorny problem.

He glanced round. *"Jenna?"*

"I need to talk to you." She set her purse down, struggling suddenly for a way to broach the issue.

He studied her for a long moment. "Why don't you take a seat and—"

"I don't want to sit. I want the truth, Dad. You're hiding things from me, and I want to know why." She gestured in the direction of his desk drawer. "Why didn't you tell me about the additional death threats to our family? Why did you keep those other five notes from the police? And what's all that stuff about revenge for a past deed and The Tears of the Quetzal? What was it, *really,* Dad, that got Candace killed?"

His face, usually so controlled, his blue eyes usually so deceptively friendly, suddenly turned dark and thunderous.

A warning to be cautious whispered through Jenna. She'd intended to broach the issue delicately, but she'd already botched it in her frustration. And she could see her father had already had a couple of Scotches. It was at times like this, loosened by alcohol, that Harold could get mean, and she'd become a little afraid of him, even though she loved him so much. Because of his power to hurt and reject her.

Because of her own need to be loved.

All those old childish emotions suddenly began twisting into a thorny braid in Jenna's chest now.

"You saw the notes?" he asked quietly.

"I saw them," she said. "Why did you hide them, Dad?"

He said nothing.

Anger began to bubble deep in her gut, fueled by her conflicting emotions. Jenna tried to keep her cool, but control was elusive. "Candace died, Dad—she was *murdered*. And those notes threaten our entire family with the same fate. That includes *me*. But you didn't think to let me know, did you? Oh no, the great Harold Rothchild is immune from death threats. Little Jenna doesn't need to know anything. Just use her to play with the FBI agent and mess up his homicide investigation so it can all be thrown out of court later—"

"Jenna, that's not—"

"Not true? Why should I believe a thing you say now? I think Lex was right—I think you *do* want to use me to obfuscate this whole business." Her heart was racing, moisture now filling her eyes. "Why? Why are you doing this? Why do you not want the police to solve this thing? Why are you putting us all in danger?"

He swung his feet down off the ottoman, took a deep slug of his drink, set it down and glared at her. "What were you doing in my office?"

"Is *that* all you care about?"

"What—" he repeated, cold and slow "—were you doing in my office?"

"The…door was open and so was the desk drawer—"

He got swiftly to his feet. Even in her four-inch heels, Harold positively towered over Jenna. She instinctively cringed inside but refused to take a step back. "Rebecca Lynn had been in here, Dad. *She* left the door ajar, and she left that top drawer open with the file sticking out."

A fleeting unreadable look shadowed his features.

"Rebecca Lynn knew about those death threats, Dad, and she purposefully set me up to see them." Jenna wasn't going to mince things now. She wanted to poke at him, about Rebecca Lynn, about everything.

Harold regarded her for a long moment, as if trying to control his rage before he spoke again. Jenna felt Napoleon nudge against her ankles, but she resisted the powerful urge to scoop up her little dog, hold him tight. Instead she met her father's glare head-on.

"They're idle threats, Jenna." He watched her eyes carefully as he spoke. "They're simply designed to unnerve us. My belief is that someone read in the papers about Candace, the ring, the legendary curse and just wanted to jump in on the whole Rothchild media circus. I will *not* allow the sender of the notes that pleasure."

"Is that not a conclusion the FBI should be making?"

"Does this mean you're going to tell your FBI agent about this?" His voice was ominously quiet.

"Why shouldn't I?"

He picked up his glass, walked over to his private bar, uncapped his bottle of prized whiskey, poured a glass—neat, no ice—turned back to face her. "Jenna, for all I know, Rebecca Lynn could have left those notes herself."

"Excuse me?"

"We're having…relationship issues. Rebecca Lynn wants attention. She could have done this to get it. Those notes you saw are clearly different from the first one, and the fact Rebecca Lynn showed them to you would seem to confirm my suspicions. You see? I kept those notes secret, therefore Rebecca Lynn did not get the attention she was seeking, and now she wants you to cause a fuss with me." He sipped his drink. "She wants to drive a wedge between you and I, sweetheart."

"So…you didn't speak to Rebecca Lynn about them at all?"

"No."

Jenna brushed her hand over her hair, suddenly unsure. "I…I still think this is something for the FBI to decide."

"Absolutely not. I will not have them messing around in my personal issues. Can you just imagine the media finding out my own wife left me death threats? I don't want the feds looking into my business dealings, either. Candace's murder has nothing to do with all that. It'll just cause trouble." He paused. "Untold trouble. Look, Jenna, you're not naive. Some of my dealings, like those with the Schaeffers, were not exactly kosher. An investigation into my private business could bring us *all* down, the entire Rothchild empire."

"Maybe it was Frank Epstein who sent the notes," Jenna said, pushing. "Maybe Lex was right, and bad business blood had Epstein wanting to avenge some old deed." She took a step closer to her father. "You don't want the feds digging into your relations with Epstein, either. Why? Because of old mob ties?"

He stilled. The color of his eyes seemed to fade, flat and hard as ice.

"Epstein didn't do this. He had nothing to do with Candace."

"How do you know?"

"Trust me. I *know*."

She frowned. "What exactly—" she said, taking another step toward her father "—happened in the past with Frank Epstein, Dad? What makes you so darn sure about him now?"

Harold's neck corded, and a hint of nervousness seemed to flicker through his features. Which scared Jenna.

"You—" he pointed with his index finger off his whiskey tumbler "—have to understand, Jenna Jayne, that messing around with that FBI agent, leading him to look into Rothchild business dealings is going to end up bad news."

"You," she said, meeting his pointed glare, "were the one who set me up to get involved with Lex Duncan in the first place."

"Solely for information about the ring."

Again, the ring.

"You set me up to seduce him, Dad."

"Not be seduced *by* him," he snapped.

"Oh, like you can control the whole damn world! My emotions to boot."

He set his glass down slowly, seriously registering for the

first time that his daughter might actually have some real and very dangerous personal allegiances with the federal agent. His daughter was falling for the cop who could take him down. *If* she let him.

"It's gone too far with him, Jenna. End it."

She swallowed, shaking inside with fury. "You don't control me," she whispered. "You don't tell me to switch my feelings on and off at your own whim, for your own personal gain."

"Pick a side, Jenna Jayne. Choose your family, everything we own, or pick that man—a blue-collar federal agent," he spat the words out derisively. "For what? One night of hot sex, for the novelty of sleeping with a law enforcement officer?"

"No," she whispered. "For something *real,* Dad."

"Consider your actions very, very carefully, Jenna Jayne."

"Oh, I am."

"Consider, too, that your agent friend might know that you went to visit Candace the night of her murder and that he may have pegged you as a suspect, too."

Shock rocketed through her. "Rebecca Lynn told you?" she whispered.

He said nothing.

Hatred rustled like an ugly thing under Jenna's skin. Rebecca Lynn wasn't just trying to drive a wedge between her and her father; she wanted to see Jenna go down.

A very dark and dangerous thought occurred to her—was Rebecca Lynn crazy enough to commit murder? Could she actually be behind all of this?

"Special Agent Lex Duncan is using you, Jenna. Once he is through, you will be left with nothing, because you will have alienated *me.*"

"Is that a threat, Dad?"

He glared at her for several beats. "No, Jenna. That's a fact."

Chapter 8

Vibrating with anger, Jenna got into her car. "Damn him," she muttered to Napoleon, who was sitting in the passenger seat on buttery leather. She slammed her hand down on the dash. "How could my *own father* threaten me like that?" Jenna clenched her teeth, turned on the ignition, setting her convertible engine to a smooth, low growl. She didn't want to feel hurt. Vulnerable.

For the first time in her twenty-five years of life she wasn't going to give in to her dad, to her own subterranean need for her father's affection.

But that meant she was alone.

She should go find Lex, tell him everything. She should let him know that she'd gone to Candace's apartment that night to try and talk her impossible sister into a rehab program—if not for her own sake, for the sake of her two toddler sons. But Candace had wanted nothing of it. Sky-high on a cocktail of drinks and drugs, she'd launched a Ming vase at Jenna's head.

And yes, Jenna had cut her finger picking up the pieces. It had bled pretty badly. Her blood very likely had been left at the scene. Rebecca Lynn might be right. Perhaps Lex *was* spending time with her solely to glean information that could secure him a warrant for her DNA, or something, so he could match her to the blood. Jenna didn't want to deal with that thought right now.

She'd tackle it all tomorrow, because right at this moment, she was falling into her tried and true coping mechanism. And she knew it. She inhaled deeply, glanced at Napoleon. "Ready, Naps? Because we're going to partay. We're going to the Desert Lion, and we're going to make sure Cassie has the best damn birthday celebration of her life."

And with that, she drove out of the garage, the automatic door sliding smoothly shut behind her. As Jenna headed down the driveway she registered in the back of her mind that Rebecca Lynn's slate-gray BMW hadn't been parked in its spot in the garage.

Daddy's little trophy bitch was out.

She shoved ugly thoughts of violence toward Rebecca Lynn from her mind. The night was clear, the moon high and she was going back to the twenty-four hour buzz that was Las Vegas. Where she felt safe. Where she felt herself. Where the lights and the laughter and the frenetic pace spelled freedom.

And as she neared the metropolis, the dusky gold glow of Sin City shimmered like a beckoning halo in the hot desert night, and Jenna felt her spirits lift.

She didn't notice the dark sedan that pulled out of the shadows and followed her into town.

Cassie's birthday celebration was a glittering event that had attracted the A-list of young Vegas natives, along with special guests and family who had been flown in from around the country. The party was being hosted at the Desert Lion, Frank

Epstein's massive temple to excess, because Cassie's uncle was a friend of the Epsteins, and Frank was generously returning a favor.

But no matter how she tried, Jenna could not put her heart into having fun. Her champagne martini sat untouched on the bar, and Napoleon, perched on the stool beside her, glowered at the crowds from the security of his little designer purse.

The fact Jenna was in Epstein's opulent establishment didn't help her mood. All she could think of was Lex, his questions about Frank and her dad. Which in turn lodged thoughts of Lex himself fast and firm in her mind. And now Jenna couldn't shake the images of his body in the sun, or the memory of kissing him, his scent, the green sparkle in his eyes when he smiled. The way those eyes had looked so haunted when he'd heard about his mother from the Lucky Lady fortune-teller.

She wondered again about a possible connection between Sara Duncan and Mercedes Epstein. They'd have been roughly the same age when they'd both worked at the Frontline—Sara as a croupier, Mercedes as the leggy showgirl who'd won the hand and heart of the big Frontline boss himself. Jenna found herself scanning the crowds half expecting to see the sleek silver chignon of the elegant Vegas matriarch drifting by. That's what Mercedes did—she floated. It was those long legs. She must have been truly stunning in her day as a dancer. Jenna wondered what Lex's mother had looked like.

"Hey, hon, why so glum?" Cassie said as she came up to Jenna and Napoleon at the bar.

She sighed. "Just need to wind up I guess."

"Well, drink that martini, and you'll feel way more yourself." Concern tinged Cassie's bright hazel eyes. "Never known you not to sparkle at an event, Jenna. What's going on?"

Jenna couldn't even muster a grin. "I'm sorry, Cass. It's

just…this whole Candace thing not being solved. It has me…edgy."

Cassie crooked up her brow quizzically. "So, it's not going so well with Mr. Sexy FBI Agent, then?"

Too well.

"I really don't want to talk about it."

Cassie gave her a long and knowing look. "It backfired, didn't it? He's gotten to you."

Jenna said nothing.

Cassie threw back her head and laughed. "*The* Jenna Jayne Rothchild has fallen for a federal agent investigating her family for homicide."

"I fail to see the humor, Cass."

Her friend's smile sobered. "Come on, let's try our hand at blackjack. I feel lucky tonight."

Jenna slid onto a seat alongside her friend at the blackjack table and stacked a pile of chips on the green felt, but all she could think about was losing…her dad, the bedrock foundation of her life. Lex.

Jenna played her hand, flipped over her card. A bust. The dealer raked in her chips.

Frank Epstein pointed to the top left screen along a bank of monitors. "Take camera seven in closer. Zero in on the blackjack table."

The technician zoomed into the pit.

"There, see that woman in green at the table? Closer."

The image of the woman filled the screen. Frank's pulse quickened. He stepped forward, attention riveted by the beautiful young siren in a low-cut shimmering emerald-green gown. Dark hair fell in thick waves down her bare back, and her lush lips were painted a ruby-red, the precise shade of her nails. A red ruby pendant hung at her throat. Even the mutt's purse matched her outfit—emerald-green with little ruby-red accents.

Frank's security head, Roman Markowitz, came up beside him. "It's Jenna Rothchild," he said in his characteristic sand-papery voice, a result of damaged vocal chords in his youth.

Frank nodded slightly. So Harold's pretty young daughter was playing in his casino.

From the monitors in his Desert Lion security room, Frank could spy on nearly all activity in his establishment. Virtually every corner of his hotel was watched by these cameras—his eye-in-the-sky—including elevators. Select hotel rooms had also been out-fitted with hidden cameras, which could be activated if necessary. Frank had gone so far as to install hidden filming devices in his own private penthouse where he lived with Mercedes, but those feeds only Frank could see, from a private setup in his office.

It wasn't that he was spying on his wife but he did like to record the activities of staff who serviced his penthouse. One never knew when a problem might arise and visual evidence could come in handy, perhaps even in a court case, for example. Information was currency in his business.

And in Vegas, everybody watched everyone else. 24/7.

Frank himself liked to spend several hours per day up here in the Desert Lion security room, mostly at this time of night when the action really started happening on his floors. And he never ceased to tire of the Vegas drama that unfolded nightly.

In one twenty-four hour period, at one of his blackjack tables alone, fortunes could be made and lost several times over. He'd see hearts broken, dreams shattered. People being seduced by luck and parted from their money by the shimmering illusion—the promise of a dream—that he was selling.

And all the while, he got richer.

Such was the game.

His security nerve hub was located adjacent to his private

office, and Frank felt that in standing up here, he was at the pulsing core of his happening hotel at the very heart of the Strip. Quite simply, he felt like a king.

Which, in many ways, he was.

It wasn't an accident years ago that his inner circle had started referring to him as the Vegas Lion, or Lion King. He held power most men could only dream of.

Harold Rothchild, however, was one man who had the wherewithal to take it all away. Harold remained one of those annoying, ever-present fault lines in the otherwise solid foundation of Frank's existence, a rival from Frank's past who had something on him—and on whom Frank had something in return. It was not a situation Frank liked to be in.

But he also couldn't simply make Harold go away—as much as he'd like to. He *could* kill Harold, but it would require some serious planning and risk. Frank was all about risk. Gambling, betting, odds—they were his business. Even so, the odds needed to be in his favor. The risk needed to be calculated, and resorting to murdering Harold definitely had the odds fully stacked against.

This was because Harold had "insurance," a videotape showing an illegal business transaction between Frank and himself. That tape was being held in a bank safety deposit box. It was evidence that would incriminate Epstein in a much broader range of illegal affairs and provide the FBI with the tools to start dismantling his entire empire. Harold had made it quite clear that should anything "untoward" happen to him, his will would ensure the tape was released into the custody of federal agents.

Epstein felt fairly secure that Harold would never take the video to the authorities prior to his own demise, because the tape would implicate Harold as well. Hence, keeping his rival alive was playing the best odds. For now.

Ciccone, of course, had wanted to eliminate Harold years ago—said he'd become a problem down the road. And Ciccone was right. He *had* become a problem. But when Ciccone had presented his plan to whack Harold Rothchild the climate in Vegas had already shifted, and simply offing people Ciccone-mob-style had come to hold serious consequences, especially during a period Frank was trying to get respectable for stock market investors. It became a time that Frank desperately needed to distance himself from Ciccone. But trying to hold the mob enforcer at arms' length hadn't been easy.

Frank had once liked Ciccone—but he'd have liked him even better with his hairy butt back in Chicago, doing the mob's union work. But Ciccone wouldn't leave Vegas. Instead, the stocky little Italian with a vile temper had accused Frank of betrayal, and he'd gone renegade, doing unnecessary violence as he'd tried to muscle in on Frank's turf. It turned into a bitter vendetta.

And things began to look real bad for Frank.

The feds had moved into Vegas in a big sweep to clean out Sin City and Ciccone was drawing serious heat to Frank—heat he didn't need.

Turns out, he didn't have to worry.

Ciccone "disappeared."

He'd been whacked, and Frank knew who'd done it.

"Rothchild's daughter is seeing the FBI agent assigned to the Rothchild homicide case," Markowitz rasped as he studied the gorgeous young woman down at the blackjack table. "He's the same guy Mercedes bid on at that auction."

Frank nodded slowly. He knew his wife had bid fiercely on Special Agent Lexington Duncan. He also knew why. He knew a lot of things that his wife didn't know that he knew. He was appraised of Mercedes's illness, too. It burned Frank, to think she was dying and hiding it from him. He loved her more than anything. For Mercedes, he'd literally move mountains.

He'd kill people.

"Could get interesting," Frank said, eyes fixed on Jenna. He wondered what game she was playing with the federal agent, how Harold might possibly be involved and how it could all potentially backfire on him—or Mercedes.

"Put a tail on her," he told Markowitz. "I want to know what she's up to. Get photographic records, anything that shows her and the federal agent in a compromising position."

One could never underestimate how useful those could be.

Frank and his security head exited the room together. "Did you take care of that fortune-teller at the Lucky Lady?" Frank asked quietly as they walked toward the elevators.

"Accomplished," rasped the security head, inserting his elevator card and keying in his code. "But Agent Duncan had already been there."

Frank's temperature rose slightly. "How do you know?"

"We made her talk first."

"She tell him anything?"

"Nothing that will bring him here."

They entered the elevator. Frank watched lights flicking down from floor to floor. As fast as he was moving to plug up holes, the past still seemed to be seeping up into the present, somehow triggered by that Candace Rothchild murder.

Frank for one wouldn't mind knowing who had killed the rich slut. She'd had it coming—that didn't concern him. What did concern him was the way it was filtering into his life.

He didn't like it.

Not one bit.

He clasped his hands behind his back as the elevator descended to the casino floor level, flexing his fingers in controlled irritation. This could not touch Mercedes. Not now. Not ever.

Especially when she had so little time left.

Jenna left the party at the Desert Lion early, looking forward to a hot bath and mind-numbing sleep. As she drove she was, as usual, grateful for Napoleon's company. She reached over and scratched his head fondly. A pet had always been the one constant in her life. Perhaps her only true friend.

"There's nothing like a pooch, you know, boy?" she told him. "No judgment, no worries if your hair looks like crap, just pure unadulterated love, and respect—" she hesitated as errant headlights from a car suddenly blinded her in the rearview mirror. The dark sedan behind her was coming a tad too close for comfort.

Jenna sped up a little, but the sedan kept pace. A cool sense of unease trickled through her. She didn't like the way the driver kept his brights aimed high. She changed lanes, weaving deftly between a big SUV and a delivery truck in an effort to avoid him. The dark vehicle swerved after her.

Was it *following* her?

Panic whispered through Jenna.

She recalled the warning notes in her father's desk drawer…*eliminating Rothchild trash, one by one.* She glanced up, trying to determine the model of the vehicle, but all she could make out was that it was a dark sedan.

The headlights loomed closer again, high beams blazing into her rearview mirror, making her eyes water. Jenna tightened her hands on the wheel. She saw an off-ramp looming ahead. It led off the freeway. On instinct, she swerved down onto the ramp, praying that the car would not follow, that she was just imagining it was tailing her.

It swerved after her.

The first dark tendrils of terror clawed through her. She *was* being pursued. The road fed into a quieter, secluded community near the deserted desert fringe. The sedan sped up behind her. Jenna's heart began to pound.

"Hold on, Naps," she whispered, hitting the gas, causing her tires to skid as she wheeled sharply round a corner.

But the sedan kept pace. The streets grew darker, more empty. Narrower. Raw fear tightened her throat. "What does that freaking idiot want with us?" she whispered to Napoleon.

As she headed over a long bridge, the headlights began to loom closer again. With one hand fisted on the wheel, eyes fixed on the road, Jenna groped under the dash for her purse. She pulled out her phone, began to dial, but the sedan drew up suddenly and smacked her bumper from behind. Her car lurched violently forward. She gasped, dropping her phone, as she clutched at the wheel with both hands.

It hit again, more at an angle.

This time her car slammed against the bridge railing on the passenger side, metal sparking against metal, tires screeching. She bounced back into the lane, swerving, managing to re-steady her vehicle, heart slamming in her throat, her body wet with perspiration. She saw the dark sedan speeding up again and veering wide out to her left, coming in for a sideswipe on the driver's side.

Oh, God, he was going to try and push her over the bridge railing!

She saw a highway on-ramp up ahead. She *had* to get back onto that freeway, where there were more cars, people. She gritted her teeth, punching down on the gas just as the sedan smacked sideways into her. She bounced off a median, swerving violently back onto the road. She was almost to the on-ramp, *almost!*

Jenna flattened the accelerator to the floor, screeching up the on-ramp as the sedan closed the distance gap at incredible speed behind her. It drew almost level with her as the road narrowed, forcing her vehicle to scrape against the concrete abutment, throwing sparks.

The passenger window of the sedan slid down. Then she heard it, something thudding into her car. He was shooting at her! Oh, dear God, *someone was trying to kill her!* Another bullet sparked off metal.

Adrenaline dumped into her system, firing every synapse in her body as she kept her foot flat on the gas, focusing dead ahead where she wanted to go. And Jenna careered from the on-ramp onto the highway, bouncing and shooting diagonally across four lanes. Cars screeched everywhere, radiating out from her, but she had her fists clamped on the wheel, and she aimed for the gaps between vehicles. A small truck swerved madly, narrowly missing Jenna. But in doing so it connected the back bumper of an old station wagon, sending it into an instant 360 degree spin behind her. Cars and trucks swerved outward from the spinning station wagon, tires shrieking, horns blaring…and she heard the sickening thud and crunches of metal against metal. But she *couldn't* look back. She kept speeding down the highway, hands fisted on her wheel, limbs shaking, tears streaming down her face. Soon the sound of sirens began to wail, coming at her along the highway from the opposite direction.

She passed the flashing lights and the screaming fire engines and ambulances.

Shaking violently now, mouth bone dry, her body drenched with sweat, Jenna drove for the one solid thing—the one person in her world who would know exactly what to do, how to keep her safe. Even if he was using her.

She pulled up outside Lex's modest suburban house, relief washing through her chest when she saw that his lights were still on inside. Jenna cut the engine, glanced up into her rearview mirror, saw nothing but empty street.

She peered out the side windows. It was dark, the shrubbery and trees moving in a hot breeze. Ominously writhing shapes. Jenna was convinced she could see malicious intent in every shadow, in every movement. She was terrified that whoever had murdered Candace, whoever had said that one by one, they would eliminate the Rothchild trash, was now trying to kill her. And even though the distance to Lex's door was short, she was too afraid to get out, cross the dark space.

"Are…are you okay, Naps?" she said on a harsh sob, reaching with trembling hands for her dog who was cowering on the floor. Napoleon made a small whine and climbed up into her lap, and Jenna began to cry, hard. She couldn't stay here, but she couldn't move, either.

The front door of Lex's house suddenly swung open. Warm gold light pooled out into the night, and the agent, dressed only in faded jeans, stepped barefoot onto his porch. Jenna scooped Napoleon up, rammed open her battered car door and bolted for his front door.

"Jenna?"

She hurled herself into his arms. Lex drew her quickly into his home, shutting the door to the night, and he just held her until she began to calm down. Jenna sobbed against his bare chest, clutching Napoleon, and not ever in her life had arms felt so warm, so welcome. So capably solid and protective.

So safe.

He titled her chin up, concern—real genuine care—softening his gorgeous green eyes. "Hey," he said softly. "What happened, Jenna? What's going on?"

"Some—someone just tried to kill me."

Chapter 9

Jenna cradled a mug of sweet tea in both hands, her face wan and hair disheveled, her mascara smudged. A band of tension strapped viselike across Lex's chest, and a quiet rage began to hum inside him.

She'd told him about being followed, the chase, the pileup on the freeway, and he'd called in her description of the dark sedan. Lex could not begin to articulate the relief he felt that she'd come through unscathed, save for a dark bruise forming on her left cheek where her face must have hit the driver's side window. He got up, wrapped some ice in a cloth. "Here," he said. "Hold this against your cheek. It'll keep the swelling down."

She took it from him, eyes dark vulnerable hollows. Her hands trembled. He'd wanted to take her to the emergency room. She was clearly in shock. But she'd refused. She did not want to leave his house or him.

He also wanted to get crime scene techs to look at her car—paint scrapes, bullet holes. She'd need to make a statement also.

Lex swallowed against the emotion burning his throat and took a seat on the couch opposite her. He was disturbed by the fierce power rising in his chest, the wave of protective compassion that threatened to overwhelm him when he touched her. Afraid of what was happening to him.

Geez, he even had little Groucho Marx eating cat food from a bowl in his kitchen. He scrubbed his hands over his face. It was almost 3:00 a.m. Neither of them had had any sleep.

"Why don't you take my bed, Jenna, get some sleep, and then I can take you down to the station in the morning so we can file a full report."

"Lex—"

"You need rest."

"Would…could you…just hold me?"

He stared at her, pulse racing, Quinn's words humming in his brain. *We'll plug it as a covert op, and the legal stuff will be in the clear as long as you keep your hands off her.*

"Please?"

He got up, sat beside her on the sofa and put his arm awkwardly around her shoulders. His body warmed. Her skin was so smooth. She cuddled down into the cushions and leaned into him, closing her eyes. A small tremor shuddered through her, as if she was finally letting go of something she'd been bottling inside. He tentatively touched her hair with his fingers. It was soft. He stroked it gently with his palm, his heart swelling painfully in his chest with a sensation alien to him. His eyes began to burn.

They sat like that for a long while, in silence. Groucho came in from the kitchen, glowered up at Lex with his beady black eyes and evil little line of jutting-out teeth, then promptly curled himself at his feet. Lex snorted. He figured he'd just sunk to a new kind of low. Mostly because he really didn't mind the dog sleeping at his feet. He was kinda cute, in his ugliness.

"I…I need to tell you something, Lex," Jenna whispered against his chest. "About my father."

Lex tensed slightly at the tone in her voice. "What about him?"

She sat up, nervously pushing a thick tangle of hair back from her face. "He…he's…" she got to her feet suddenly, began to pace, eyes filling with moisture.

Apprehension deepened. "Jenna, what is it?"

She stilled, faced him square. "He got five more death threats against our family."

Lex took a second to process. *"When?"*

"Over the past few months. He didn't tell the police."

"Why the hell not?"

"He doesn't think they're important. But I…I think whoever left those notes tried to kill me tonight."

Rage began to vibrate dangerously in Lex. "Why didn't you tell me this before, Jenna?" he said as calmly, quietly as he could. "This is absolutely relevant to what happened to you tonight."

"I *am* telling you. Now."

"What do these notes say?" Pressure built inside him like a cooker.

She exhaled shakily. "Have you got something stronger than tea?"

He got up, poured her a Scotch, handed it to her. She took a deep sip and exhaled slowly. "Whoever sent the notes is threatening to take out the 'Rothchild trash' one at a time, after Candace. All of the notes alluded to some historic deed that needed to be atoned for, and all mentioned The Tears of the Quetzal. The last one was signed *The Avenger.*"

"How do you know which was the last one? Were they dated?"

She nodded. "And made up of letters cut from magazines and newspapers, not like the first one that came right after

Candace was killed." She took another slug of her drink, her eyes watering and nose going pink as it went down. "Dad said they were just some hoax, someone trying to get in on the Rothchild media hype after Candace's death. He said Rebecca Lynn could even have left them, seeking attention. But I think that whatever is going down is tied to that diamond and something that happened a long time ago, maybe even in South America."

Cool anger directed at Harold Rothchild arrowed through Lex. The bastard had put his entire family in jeopardy by not reporting those death threats, by not coming clean on the provenance of the ring. Because now, more than ever, Lex was certain Harold knew exactly where that cursed stone had come from. By not putting all his cards on the table, Harold Rothchild had left law enforcement chasing shadows, possibly costing months in lost time hunting down a killer. He reached for his phone. "I need a warrant," he said, crisply. "I need those notes. And I want to see what else he's hiding."

Panic shot across Jenna's face. She grabbed his arm. "Lex—wait!"

"What for?"

She couldn't speak for a moment and looked terrified.

"Jenna? You're not afraid of your own father, are you? Do you realize what danger he put you in? You could have been killed."

She cast her eyes down. "I…I love him, Lex. He's my dad. He's…all I really have."

Lex stilled, seeing in Jenna something he hadn't noticed before—a vulnerable young woman. In spite of all her sophistication and seductive glitz, underneath it hid a beautiful, sensitive creature who'd been born into the rarefied air of the Rothchild empire, a woman who had zero exposure to the normal touchstones of life. A lonely woman, even, who'd armored herself with a bright, breezy smile and who sought self-validation through attracting men. A woman who needed—*depended*—on the love and goodwill of her tyrant sociopathic father.

And in turning to Lex, Jenna clearly felt she was betraying her own father—one of the most powerful men in Nevada. She'd come to Lex's home, and in a sense Lex could see she wasn't going to be able to go back to her casino castle after this. He put the handset back down.

She glanced up, and his heart clenched. "There's more Lex. I…I was at Candace's apartment the night she was killed."

"You were *what?*"

"I…" She dragged shaking hands through her hair. "I should've reported it, and I didn't."

"What are you trying to say, Jenna?"

"You didn't know I was there?"

"No."

"So you weren't playing me, trying to get more information? Maybe find a reason to get my DNA so you could match it to my blood at the scene."

"Your *blood?*"

"I…I cut my finger on a piece of the vase Candace threw at my head. It bled pretty badly."

He swore. "Sit. Tell me. Everything."

"Lex—"

"Now!" He was furious.

She sunk slowly down onto the sofa.

He waited, stomach knotted.

"I…I went to try and talk Candace into going to rehab that night, for her children's sake, for my little nephews. Those toddlers are—"

"Stick to the facts," he said crisply.

She swallowed. "Candace was high, drunk, whatever, and when I mentioned rehab, she flew into a blind rage. She hurled a Ming vase at me. It smashed against the coffee table, and I tried to pick up some of the pieces and cut my finger on one, and then she threatened me with a fire poker if I didn't leave at once. So I did."

He glared at her, a vein thrumming in his forehead. "And you didn't report this, why?"

"I didn't think her drug problems and my personal issues with my sister were relevant to the homicide, or to the media circus that ensued. I…I thought it was a robbery gone wrong."

"You *thought?*"

"You have to understand, Lex, that every time the press got hold of something Candace did, the whole sordid business was splashed all over the papers and picked up by trashy tabloids nationwide. And it was her two little children who were ultimately going to suffer. Not her. She didn't give a damn. I just wanted it all to stop. For *their* sakes. Growing up knowing their mother was brutally murdered is going to be bad enough, damn it!"

"Geez, Jenna, don't you see? That vase, that argument of yours, it impacted a homicide scene. How in the hell were crime scene techs to know that broken vase wasn't part of the brutal attack on your sister? What you held back from the police has helped obfuscate an already confounding investigation! Who do you people think you are? Above the law, or what?"

Her mouth flattened. "It was a mistake, okay? I'm really sorry. I thought the Vegas police would catch the killer quickly. I thought it was just someone after the diamond, and that her latest drug binges wouldn't need to come out. Then the longer it took to find her killer, the more complicated it became to even mention I was there. I…I started to get scared."

Lex swore, raked his hand through his hair. "What, Jenna, makes this any different from what your father did in withholding critical evidence? Don't you see? You're playing the *same* game. And how am I supposed to do *my* job when you deceive me, hamstring me like this, huh? What're you trying to do, make a mockery of what I do?"

"Lex, no, it's not like that—"

"What's it like then?"

She lurched up off the chair, two hot spots forming on her cheeks. "I'll tell you what it's like. I have just betrayed my father! What I've told you could take—"

"Hey, you hid evidence, also."

"Yes, I did. And in confessing to you, in telling you what my father has done, I could take my whole family down, including my innocent nephews. I have just alienated myself from everything I know, Lex. My father said if I told you about those notes I'd have nothing. If he finds out I have done this, I won't even be able to go home. Because he—" she jabbed her finger toward the window "—owns the roof over my head. He owns my job. He owns who I *am,* Lex, and I've turned my back on him, on it all. I am on your side, damn it! Can't you see? I *am* telling you this, and I'll do everything I can to help you catch that killer." Her voice caught, emotion filling her eyes.

"You're only telling me this because you were attacked, and now you're scared," he said bluntly. "Otherwise you'd have come forward earlier." *Like when I kissed you, like when you put your hand on my knee in the dark car...*

She slumped down into a chair, burying her hands into her face. "I was going to tell you before I was attacked, Lex. I had made a decision to come clean, about everything. I...I knew I had to pick a side." She glanced up slowly, tears, mascara streaking her face. "And I did. I picked your side," she said, her voice small.

His heart constricted sharply. He crouched down in front of her, tilted her face to his. "You picked the right side, Jenna," he said softly. "You did the right thing." She began to sob, and he gathered her into his arms. She felt so good, so right.

And she'd picked *him.*

Jenna had put herself in his hands, and no matter his conflict over her actions, Lex was determined to do right by her. To keep her safe. But what were the implications—for him, his case, his job? Could he risk involvement?

He closed his eyes. God, was it even remotely possible that she could be with him long-term, that he, the orphan son of a hooker-turned-croupier mother who'd been brutally murdered, could have some kind of future with this Las Vegas princess?

Would it be such a terrible mistake to even try?

Jenna slid her hand up the back of his neck and drew his mouth to hers. He felt her tongue against his lips, and his consciousness spiraled liked a wild, dizzying fairground ride, shades of red and darkness swirling behind his eyes as heat arrowed straight to his groin. He moved his mouth over her lips, parting them. They were wet, warm, salty with tears and the lingering notes of Scotch. She opened under him inviting, vulnerable. Lex's heart began to pound as he teased the inner seam of her lips with his tongue. She moaned softly, sinking herself back into the cushions, drawing him on top of her. Her emerald evening gown slipped sideways off her breast and Lex's breath clean stopped. He moved his mouth along the smooth column of her neck to the firm swell of her breast, and he teased her nipple, feeling it bead tight and hard under his tongue. It sent blood rushing between his legs, and he began to throb, hard, with exquisitely painful, urgent need.

Jenna pressed her body up into his, kissing him deeper, wrapping her arms around him, wanting him, enveloping him. Breathing hard, Lex pulled back. While he could.

While he had a shred of sanity left in his brain.

She looked up at him, her lips swollen from his kiss, eyes dazed.

"Jenna…this is…I mean…the case. I can't—"

She sat up, pulling the fabric of her dress back over her chest.

"I'm tired," she said simply. "I...I'm not thinking things through. I'm sorry."

Lex stared at her, his entire body, every damn molecule pounding a tattoo that said *take her, take her now, she wants you, she's yours...*

But he couldn't.

Not without removing himself from this investigation first. Not without thinking through the repercussions first, while he still could. Lex didn't want to hurt Jenna. And he did not want to deny Candace Rothchild justice by having this case tossed out of court because of his actions.

And Lord knew, he didn't want to mess up his own life. Again. He couldn't afford to lose his career.

He swore to himself. This was exactly what he'd been afraid of. *This* was what he'd been running from when he'd tried to dump her outside her mansion in the pouring rain.

"Come," he said, helping her up from the couch. "You take my bed, upstairs."

"What about you?"

He cleared his throat. "I'm going to work some things out down here."

Lex flipped off the bedroom light, hesitating at the door. She was asleep already, out almost the moment her head hit the pillow. And there she was, in her shimmering green dress. In his bed. Jenna Jayne Rothchild, the Vegas princess. His lips curved, his heart feeling a rushing expansive sensation. He couldn't abandon her now. She was going to be in for a rough ride when he went after her father. How in the hell was all that going to work out? *Yeah, bro, never mind thinking things through—you're already well and truly sunk.*

He closed the door with a soft snick, blew out a lungful of air and then went downstairs.

Snagging an ice-cold beer from the fridge, Lex went to sit out on his porch, the hot night air silky against his bare chest. He took a deep swallow from the bottle and exhaled slowly as alcohol crept through his body.

He put his head back, looked up at the sky—crystal clear and splattered with desert stars. A gentle warm wind rustled the leaves in his small garden. Lex felt alive, more alive than he had in years. He took another drink, and a small spark of excitement began to shimmer inside him. What if—after this all cleared up—they gave it their best shot? What if she really *did* want him? Long-term.

Or was she just turning to him now because he was in the right place at her time of need? Maybe once things calmed down she'd scoff at what she'd done, tire of her blue-collar federal agent. Move on. To bigger and brighter things. To men who moved easily in her social sphere.

Lex swore softly. He was a freaking nut job to think Jenna Rothchild was going to want the kind of life he could offer. What was he doing thinking of commitment, anyway? Most men he knew would sleep with the woman and be done with it.

Besides, he reminded himself, he'd tried this road before. The orphan in him had craved family—a real one of his own. But he'd chosen the wrong woman, a high-maintenance social climber who had zero time or respect for his charity and volunteer commitments. Toss in a life-consuming law enforcement career, and that was a recipe for disaster Lex had no intention of repeating again.

He snorted, took another swig of beer, feeling the soft explosion of bubbles in his mouth. He was a pretty big flake to even think of trying to make a family again. It was probably the furthest thing from Jenna's mind.

He drained his bottle, got up, paused as he heard something rustling in the foliage along the boundary of his yard. Lex

narrowed his eyes, peering into dark shadows, the interplay of
moonlight and shrubbery and soft wind toying with his mind.
He couldn't see anything, yet he felt an uneasy sensation. He
went inside, slid the glass door shut and locked it. Then he went
upstairs to check on Jenna.

Jenna blinked into the darkness as she felt Lex enter the
bedroom. The room was full of moving shadows shaped by pale
beams of moonlight streaming through the slats of the blinds,
the wind in the tree outside his bedroom window. He came to
the bedside, sat beside her, his bare torso a powerful silhouette
in the surreal interplay of light.

She felt his hand, warm, strong and gentle as he brushed her
sleep-tangled hair back from her forehead. She was hot, had
tossed the sheet off, her evening dress slipping off her breasts
again. But she didn't move to cover herself up. She wanted him
to see her.

Jenna closed her eyes, savoring the sensation of his touch,
his care. Because that's what she felt—care. It was what she'd
glimpsed, briefly, in his eyes. And all Jenna was certain of
right now was that she wanted him. All of him. All the time.

He was the first real thing she'd ever truly known in her
strange whacked-up life. Lex was putting her in touch with the
self she'd lost so many years ago, and Jenna was finding that she
wanted something deeper than her shallow, glittering existence.

She was prepared to give it up for a shot at making it work
with Lex. A gamble, yes, but this was Vegas. And the odds were
that if she won, it would be worth it.

He caressed the side of her face, his thumb gentle against
her bruise. A small shiver tightened her nipples and angled
down into her belly. Jenna ached to wrap her hot body around
his hard one.

"You okay?" he whispered.

Jenna swallowed, almost hurting with need, exquisitely conscious of every part of her body. She sat up, slid the straps of her dress off her shoulders so that the shimmering fabric fell to her waist, her breasts feeling suddenly heavy, swollen under his scrutiny. "You tell me—" Jenna whispered, reaching for his hand "—if I'm okay." She guided his hand to her breast. Lex inhaled sharply as his skin connected with hers. He cupped her roughly, drawing her closer.

Kissing her hard, he opened her mouth, his tongue hungry, aggressive. Jenna's world spun. She grabbed his hand, moved it down her abdomen, sliding it beneath her dress so he could feel the small silk triangle of her G-string. He groaned softly, moved closer, kissing her deeper, the sensation of his hand more urgent, more firm. Jenna parted her legs. He moved the fabric of her G-string aside, and she felt his finger on bare skin. Hot. Delicious. She opened her legs wider.

"Jenna—" his voice was hoarse "—this is…"

But she held his hand firmly between her legs, parting her thighs, drawing his body down on top of hers, as she sunk back on the bed. "I want you, Lex…" she murmured against his lips, her mind blind to anything but the sensation of his weight on top of her, his hand against her.

He gave in with a small moan as he thrust his finger up into her. Jenna arched her hips up desperate for more.

He began to move his hand, sliding another finger into her, teasing her sensitive swollen nub with his thumb until a pressure began to build low in her chest, screaming for release. And Lex lost any last shred of control. His breathing ragged, he yanked her dress down over her hips, tearing her scrap of G-string aside as she fumbled urgently with his zipper, her tongue slicking and tangling with his.

He positioned himself between her legs, his knees opening her thighs wide, and with one sharp thrust, he was inside her.

Jenna gasped, arching her back as her body accommodated him, and she smiled against his mouth. "Mmm, that emcee sure wasn't kidding about your loaded weapon, agent," she murmured, moving her pelvis against his.

He watched the upstairs window from the bushes.

He knew they were in there. He'd seen their shadows against the blinds earlier, before the agent came outside to drink beer.

Probably screwing each other now.

The idea agitated him, made him hard. Hot.

It had taken him some time to get around the highway pileup she'd left in her wake. Bitch. He'd guessed she would run straight here, to her cop. Well, she got away this time.

He'd have to find another way now, be smarter. He grew even hotter, harder at the thought—because when he did get her, he was going to do a lot more than just kill her. He was going to have her just like that cop was probably doing her now.

Chapter 10

Jenna met his fervor, arching her pelvis to him as he thrust deep into her, heightening every nerve in his body, driving him higher, hotter, until she stiffened suddenly, then shattered around him with a cry, her nails digging into his back. It drove Lex past the point of restraint—he yanked her hips up hard against his, and released into her, his vision spiraling in a wild vortex of dark sensual pleasure as she wrapped her legs tight around him.

They lay hot in the moonlit shadows, tangled in sheets, entwined with each other, Lex going soft inside her. And in his heart he felt whole. At the same time, he knew he'd failed.

He'd allowed himself to be sucked over the cliff edge, and he was wildly free-falling. Because now that he'd done this, now that he'd made love to Jenna, he wanted more.

He wanted it all.

And that scared him. Because maybe she didn't.

The darkness turned to dawn, and the morning sun began to stream lemon-yellow through the blinds, another hot desert day dawning, and Lex had to get to work. He was going straight to talk to Quinn and have himself removed from this homicide investigation. Lex prayed it wasn't too late already, that he could still hide from Quinn, from prosecutors and defense lawyers down the road, what had transpired between him and Jenna Rothchild while he was still assigned to the case.

He'd tell Quinn he'd elicited information from Jenna about her father that would secure a warrant to search Harold Rothchild's estate and bring him in for further formal questioning. Quinn would be good with that.

And Lex would need to step back from Jenna for a while in order to maintain the charade.

But at the same time, she was going to need him. The road ahead was going to be real rough because she was going to be a witness to the fact her father was obstructing justice. Lex *couldn't* leave her alone now as much as he *had* to step away for the case to proceed successfully.

He cursed to himself.

Excusing himself from this high-profile homicide investigation was also going to be a career killer. That he'd have to swallow. But Jenna, he had no idea how to handle. He swore again—what in the hell had he done?

One choice was clear—the first move. Get reassigned.

"Jenna—"

She opened her eyes, smiled up at him, brown eyes twinkling. Sated, naked, warm and beautiful. In his bed, his home. And she'd sneaked her way right into his heart—jaded old fool that he was, Lex couldn't believe he was daring to hope.

"What is it, Lex?"

He was going to tell her he wanted to make a go of it. But suddenly anxiety wedged into his throat, and he didn't know how to say it all and felt like an ass. What if she really wasn't on the same page as him? Maybe she was too young for him, had too much life in front of her yet to commit to him. And how stupid it would sound to tell her he loved her after a few days. Who fell in love after a few days?

Seems he did.

He got up, wrapped a towel around his waist, sun already warm on his skin. "Want some breakfast?" was all he could think of to say.

Something shifted in her eyes. She watched him, as if waiting for him to say something more, deeper, something about what had transpired physically between them. Anything.

"I need to get dressed," he said, instead. "Got to get into the office." He wavered. "I make a good omelet—" But before he could complete the sentence, angry barking erupted from downstairs. They both looked at each other, shocked almost, to remember that Napoleon was still in the house. Jenna jerked up in the bed, pulling the sheet over herself. "Napoleon?" she called.

He growled and barked again. Jenna's eyes shot to Lex. "Someone's down there. Naps never barks like that unless something has spooked him."

Lex charged downstairs. Napoleon was growling and yipping along the glass door that looked out onto the porch. Lex took his weapon from his gun safe, slotted in a clip, chambered a round and slid the door open. He stepped barefoot onto the porch. Napoleon bulleted out at his feet, rushing over the grass to a line of trees and shrubs along the boundary. He started growling and snuffling exactly where Lex thought he'd heard something rustling the night before. Jenna appeared on the porch behind him, his robe wrapped around her. He motioned for her to get back inside quickly.

Lex made his way over the grass, crouched down and examined the soft dry soil under the trees. Prints. And they looked to have been made by a male, about a size eleven shoe. Someone had been standing here. Lex glanced back at the house.

Whoever had been lurking under this tree would've seen him on the porch last night. He needed to get someone to look at these prints. He dragged his hand over his hair. What was he going to say? That he'd been making love to Jenna Rothchild instead of bringing her in after the attack on her life last night?

God, he'd been a fool. This could have been her attacker, right here, watching.

Lex swore softly, made his way back over the grass to the house.

"What was it?" she asked, her eyes wide.

"Nothing."

"But Napoleon never—"

"I want you to get dressed, Jenna. Take some of my clothes. And I'm going to call Perez to come pick you up. She can take you in, help you file a report—"

"What about you?"

"I'm going to get myself off this case."

"What…do you mean?"

He took her shoulders. "Jenna, this is going to get real complicated between me and you. It appears your father not only withheld those death threats but he also lied about the fire at your grandfather's South American office. We're likely going to see him being charged for obstruction of justice at minimum. And depending on how this all plays out down the road, and what else we learn from him in questioning, you may end up being a witness for the prosecution—"

She blanched, reaching for the back of a chair, the implications—the full brunt of what she'd done—hitting her square in the harsh light of morning. She wiped her brow with the back of her wrist, shaking slightly. She was also perspiring, probably still in shock. Geez, he should never have slept with her. "Jenna, listen—"

She jerked out from under his touch. "Look, intellectually, I know this all has to happen, Lex. But…can you…maybe leave me out of it? I mean, get a warrant for those notes without naming me or letting him know I betrayed him?"

"I can't do that, Jenna."

Panic mounted in her face. "Lex, you have to, please. I told you everything. I came clean. I just don't want him to know I—"

"Do you realize what you are asking me to do? I'm a law enforcement agent, Jenna."

She grasped his hand. "*Please,* Lex. For me."

"Listen, we need you, Jenna. Your father is withholding serious evidence in connection with murder. What he did, what he hid from police, could have gotten you killed. For all we know, he's up to something that *did* get Candace killed. He needs to tell us what happened in the past, with that ring, or more people could get hurt. And we're going to need your testimony to do what we need to."

She looked nauseous. "And…and you're taking yourself off the case?"

"I must."

"So you're just handing me over to your partner, who will take me to talk to agents who don't know me, who don't understand me like you do? What are *they* going to do to me when they find out I was at Candace's place the night she was murdered? I told *you,* Lex, because I trust you. I need you on my side now."

"Jenna, this way I *can* be there for—"

She shook her head. "I was a total fool, wasn't I? You were using me, just like my dad and Rebecca Lynn said you were. You were baiting me, setting me up to betray my family."

"That's not true!"

"Isn't it?"

He hesitated. "Look, Jenna, it might have started out that way—"

She glared at him, then swore and made for the stairs.

"Jenna!" he called after her. "Can you honestly tell me you weren't setting me up at that bachelor auction? Can you swear your father had *nothing* to do with that?"

She wavered on the bottom stair but didn't turn around.

"See? We both *started* out on the wrong foot, Jenna. But things have changed."

"Have they really, Lex?" she said softly, turning to face him, her big dark eyes hollow. "Because the way I see it, you're still a cop first." And with that she disappeared up the stairs.

"Jenna!" Lex cursed, turned in a circle. Damn. He wanted to kick something. He'd wanted to say he thought he was falling in love with her, that the core reason he was taking himself off the case was so that he could distance himself from the homicide and give their relationship a living chance.

She came down the stairs wearing his oversize gym shorts and a large white T-shirt that swam on her. Her evening gown was bundled under her arm, and her fingers were hooked through the straps of her high-heel sandals. Napoleon scuttled at her bare feet as she marched straight for his front door.

He grabbed her arm, swung her around. "Where d'you think you're going?"

"Back where I belong. Where I should have stayed. The only godforsaken place I know!" She jerked free of his touch.

"You've got to wait."

"For what, *Perez?*" She yanked open his front door and stomped barefoot down his small driveway toward her beat-up sports car. She wrenched the door open, and Napoleon bounded onto the passenger seat.

Lex followed her to the car, wearing his towel. "Jenna! Stop!" He grasped her wrist.

"What? You going to arrest me now?" Her voice was cool, her eyes defiant.

"I will if you make me."

"I dare you," she whispered angrily. "I dare you to tell your Special Agent in Charge you were screwing me, instead of just pumping me for information. Because if you don't, I will. And I'll tell the papers, too. Don't think I'm afraid to do it, either. Got nothing to lose now, have I?"

He clamped his hand over her door, stopping her from getting in. Anger bubbled inside him. "So you got what you wanted, did you, Jenna? You bought me at your auction, seduced me. And now you're going to use it to screw my case—is that how it goes?"

Her eyes flickered, filling with moisture.

"Think about it," he said, voice low and controlled. "You go to the papers with this story and you'll be doing exactly what your were seeking to avoid when you didn't tell the police that you were at Candace's apartment. You will once again drag the media circus down on top of your family—a nice legacy for those little toddler nephews you were trying to protect. And you'll be dancing to your father's tune again. Because I will now bet my last chip that he set you up to do that auction. He *wants* this case to go down the tubes for some reason, and he's *using* you to do it, Jenna."

"Let go of my door."

"I can't let you drive. You're not thinking straight. You're still in shock, Jenna. You did the right thing in telling me about those notes. Now you've got to find the courage to see it through. You've crossed that line, and you said it yourself—there's no going back now."

Tears glimmered in her eyes.

"Look, Jenna I *know* you're scared." He lifted her chin gently, but she jerked away.

She shoved past him, got into her car, slammed the door and started the engine.

"Jenna, don't do this." He banged on her window. "Geez, I...love you," he yelled. "I want to make this work, damn it!"

Her eyes flared, her mouth opened slightly. She cursed at him and hit the gas. Fishtailing down his road.

Lex swore, kicked the curb, then rushed inside to grab his phone.

"Perez, it's Duncan. I need you to get someone on Jenna Rothchild's tail ASAP. She's heading home right now. No—" he hesitated, sliding further over to the dark side. "I don't want you to bring her in. Just have her followed, make sure whoever you put on her tail has backup on call. Don't leave her alone for one second, understand? I..." He slipped even deeper into gray ethical muck. "She was followed last night, and...she might lead us to our target. Or flush him out." He shut his eyes for a moment, praying he was doing the right thing.

"You want me to tail her myself?"

"No. I need you in the office. I'm coming in—I'll explain." He needed Perez to keep working the angles they'd started, and he was going to have to talk to Quinn.

Lex hung up, wondering how in the hell he'd gotten to this point. Perhaps he should've chased after Jenna himself. But she was so strung out it might have driven her to excess speed, and a dangerous accident involving not only her life but others. Once she was inside the Rothchild mansion, she should be safe with all Harold's security and an FBI agent at the bottom of the drive.

A chorus of yipping rose the instant Lex walked into the bullpen. "Shut the hell up, would you?"

"Feeling a little rough, are we, Duncan?"

"Did you get someone on Rothchild's tail?" he asked Perez, removing his jacket.

Concern showed in Rita Perez's eyes. She got up from her desk, came up to him, talking quietly. "What's going down, partner?"

"They're freaking idiots, that's what. Where's Quinn?" he said, noticing the door to his office was shut.

"He's in Washington, gone for two days. You going to tell me what's going down with Rothchild?"

Lex sighed and swore. His little chat with the boss was going to have to wait. He was going to have to remain on the case, status quo, for another forty-eight hours.

"What you want Quinn for?"

"Just needed to speak to him about something personal."

Perez put her hands on her hips. "What you need is to speak to me, partner. You need to tell me what the hell is going on between you and that Rothchild woman."

"Nothing is going on."

"Oh? Apart from the fact she was followed last night, caused a major highway pileup and you didn't bring her in?"

"Executive decision," he said crisply, pulling out his chair.

Her brow tweaked up, and she regarded him suspiciously. "Let's hope it's the right one. For your sake."

"Haven't you got some work to do, Perez?"

"Yeah. I got work. I'm just wondering if we're like, still a team here, you know?"

Lex grunted.

She remained, arms akimbo, looking at him.

"Look." He glanced around the office, lowered his voice. "I'll explain it all, I promise. Between you and me, I got myself messed up personally with this woman, and I need to get myself off this case. And I will as soon as Quinn gets back."

She studied him for a few beats. "You gonna be okay?"

"Yeah, as long as you quit hassling me and get off my back for a few minutes."

Perez sat at her desk, began busying herself irritably with

her computer, and Lex felt bad. Rita Perez had worked for the FBI for twenty years now, and she'd always been there for her partners. She had that kind of rep, never fussed about stuff like tenure, and who'd been where longer. She was one of the most decent, fair, equality-minded people he knew. And apart from the recent bachelor auction fiasco, he trusted her with his life. "Everything okay with your niece?" he muttered.

She glanced up, that dark all-knowing brow of hers crooking higher. "What? You want to be my friend now?"

"Whatever. Don't worry about it."

"Marisa is fine," she snapped. "Better than fine—she's got a new man in her life."

"Who?"

"Patrick Moore, an accountant and a really decent guy who came out of nowhere into her life. I'm happy for her. She's had a rough haul since her miscarriage. She's opening up her own nanny agency now."

"That's great, Perez. Tell her I'm happy for her." And he was, genuinely so.

Perez hesitated. "I'm having them both over for dinner next weekend. Want to come?"

"Thanks. Maybe I will. I—" The phone on his desk rang, and he snagged the receiver. "Special Agent Duncan," he barked.

It was his contact from the financial crimes unit in New York returning his earlier call. And what Lex heard next made him sit forward sharply.

The New York unit apparently now had an informer, a retired personal accountant of Frank Epstein's from the old Frontline days who'd kept copious copies of records—payroll, budgets, tax files, receipts—all because he feared he might one day need "insurance" against Epstein. And among those records was a mention of a business deal with Harold Rothchild.

"Can you fax those pages through, the ones that pertain to Rothchild?"

"It's just two pages—a copy of a letter from Epstein's desk to Rothchild, outlining the parameters of a pending partnership in a property deal. I'm sending them as we speak."

Lex walked over to the fax machine, phone still to his ear. "They're coming through now—" He stilled when he saw Epstein's letterhead inching out of the machine, his mind veering wildly off track and back into time. Because next to Frank Epstein's name was a little logo—a cartoon lion with a crown on its head. *The same logo Lex had seen on the bumper of the metallic-blue Cadillac that used to bring the brown envelope of cash to his mother's house in Reno each month.*

Heart thudding, Lex removed the fax, stared at the logo. "That little drawing—"

"It was Epstein's logo for a while, back in the day," said the New York agent. "It's on all his personal correspondence from that period. Apparently those in Epstein's inner circle used to call him the Vegas Lion, or the Lion King, a bit of egotistical motivation that led him to dub his next big casino project the Desert Lion."

Lex hung up, feeling light-headed.

"What was that?" asked Perez.

"FBI New York." He bit his lip, thinking.

"Do they have something on Harold and Epstein?" She came over to his desk. "What's the fax say?" she asked.

Lex reached for his jacket. "I need to pay Epstein a visit. I'm going to the Desert Lion."

She cursed. *"Duncan—"*

He held up his hand. "I promise, I'll explain. Later. But where I'm going now has nothing to do with this case. This is personal."

"What about the fax?"

"On my desk."

She glowered at him for several beats, then threw up her hands and muttered something in Spanish as he left.

Jenna stormed into the hallway, Napoleon's little doggie nails clicking on the marble behind her. She was insanely relieved no one appeared to be home. But as she headed for the stairs, aiming for a hot shower, and some serious thinking, she caught sight of the headline on one of the morning papers that Clive routinely placed on the hall table.

The main story and photo was of the big auto pileup on the freeway last night. Her mouth went dry. Jenna snagged the paper, quickly scanned the story.

Thank God, there was nothing about any deaths or terribly serious injuries. There was also no mention of who had caused the pileup. Yet. She flipped the page and read the continuation of the article, a smaller headline underneath the story suddenly snaring her attention. And her blood ran cold.

There'd been a murder.

The owner of the Lucky Lady, a fortune-teller named Marion Robb, was found early this morning, her throat slit.

Jenna folded the paper, numb. Afraid. Somehow everything was connecting, and she couldn't see the patterns. She climbed the stairs, mechanically going through the motions of showering, dressing, feeding Napoleon. But all she could think of was Lex, of what the Lucky Lady had told him about his mother, and how the fortune-teller had alluded to Vegas's dark mob past and Sara Duncan's possible involvement.

Sara's throat also had been slit.

Had that dark mob past finally caught up with the present in that murky psychic store that sold dreams?

Jenna thought of her own father and his possible ties to Epstein, and of the stories about Epstein's old links with Vegas Mafia. She thought of the death threats in her dad's drawer—how they promised to avenge a past deed, how they all referred to The Tears of the Quetzal and how Candace was the "first" to be taken out. How her dad had lied about the fire in South America.

Jenna sagged onto her bed, inhaling deeply. Lex was the one person in her life that remained a lighthouse through this maelstrom. And she'd run from him. She'd pushed him away.

And he'd said he loved her.

Her eyes misted.

She couldn't begin to articulate how messed up that made her feel. Being with him last night, having him make love to her in his bed, was like nothing she'd ever experienced. He'd made her feel whole. As if she'd come home somehow.

More home than she felt here in the Rothchild mansion now.

She angrily brushed away an errant tear.

She'd been overwhelmed by it all—along with the shock of almost being killed and by the gravity of what she must now do to her own father. To her family. But in truth, Jenna knew the course was the right one, and she had to find the courage to go through with it.

Candace was, after all, family, too. She needed justice, too.

Jenna wondered if Lex was even aware of the Lucky Lady's murder. It wouldn't be an FBI case, as far as she knew, so he might still be unaware. She needed to talk to him.

She dialed his cell phone, but it went straight to voice mail.

She tried his office number, again voice mail. Jenna walked to the window, looked down into their beautiful garden, their wealth visible, tangible. She thought of Lex, his orphans. His mother. His strong sense of allegiance. Honor.

Of course he couldn't lie about her finding the death threats—she'd basically asked Lex to go against everything he was. She needed to see him. Talk to him. *Now.*

She grabbed her keys off her dresser and ran down the stairs.

* * *

Perez found Jenna Rothchild in a small FBI waiting area, not looking at all like the Jenna Rothchild she knew. Sweet little dress, flat sandals, hair all loose and unstyled, no jewelry. Jenna had asked to see Lex, and Perez was vaguely amused by the idea that the tail she'd put on Jenna Rothchild this morning had been led right back to the FBI field office. It appealed to her twisted sense of humor. "Agent Duncan isn't in, Ms. Rothchild. I'm Agent Perez, his partner. Is there anything I can help you with?"

She got up, looking nervous.

"You okay, Ms. Rothchild?"

"I…I'm fine."

"You got a pretty bad bruise on your cheek there. Did someone hurt you?"

She swallowed, tensing, arousing Perez's veteran instincts. Something weird was up. First Duncan. Now this woman. Acting odd. They were in on something, and Perez had a feeling it was more than just sex. Perez would do anything for her partner, even if it meant crossing the line, just a little. Because that's what partners were for, right? They had each other's backs. And Rita Perez was sensing something deep under the surface here. Something not so good. Something that maybe involved the Desert Lion.

"I…walked into a door," she said, touching her bruise.

"Duncan says you were followed last night."

Rothchild's eyes flickered fast. She turned and looked as though she was about to hightail it out of the place, skittish as a damn deer. But then she wavered. "Is Lex maybe out investigating what happened with that psychic murder?"

"Psychic?"

"I…it's nothing. Thank you for seeing me." She spun and began to stride out the building.

"You want me to tell him you stopped by, Ms. Rothchild?" she called after her.

Jenna wavered, turned. "Could you tell me where he went instead?"

Perez chewed on the inside of her cheek, very curious now about a psychic, a little plot of her own hatching. "Yeah," she said suddenly. "He went to the Desert Lion to see Frank Epstein."

Jenna's eyes widened for a moment. "Thanks." And she was gone.

Perez returned quickly to her desk, snagged her phone and called the tail she had on Jenna. "Hey, you just cut a break, Savalas. I'm taking over your babysitting duties, okay?"

"All yours. Fill your boots, Perez."

"Hey, Savalas—" she said before she hung up "—you hear anything about a psychic being murdered?"

"It's an LVMPD case. Happened last night. A woman who owns the Lucky Lady psychic store had her throat slit. Guess she didn't see it coming." He chuckled at his own sick joke. "So much for being psychic."

Or lucky.

"Careful you don't choke on your lollipop there, Kojak." Perez hung up and made for her vehicle. If Duncan wasn't going to tell her what was up his butt, she'd find out herself.

"Men," she muttered. "They need a damn mother half the time."

Chapter 11

Frank Epstein was not in the building. Lex asked to see Mrs. Epstein instead. It was a personal visit, but he wanted results, so he showed his badge. The receptionist picked up the phone, spoke to Mercedes, then handed Lex a special key card and pointed to a private elevator on the far side of the bank of main elevators. "She's in the penthouse apartment, thirty-third floor. She'll be expecting you."

Lex watched the lights blink as the car climbed to the top of the luxurious five-diamond casino hotel thinking that the little Lion King logo circa three decades ago, stuck onto the bumper of the pale-blue Cadillac might mean nothing. Anyone could have put that sticker on his car—it didn't necessarily mean that the man who drove it worked for either the Frontline or Frank Epstein. Or had anything to do with killing his mother. And the man who regularly brought the money certainly had not been the one with the hairy hand and raspy voice.

But the sticker in conjunction with the fact that Sara Duncan did at one point work for Epstein, and then mysteriously packed her bags and left in the quiet of night for Reno after allegedly being sacked by Epstein, is what had now brought Lex here. He wanted to hear from Frank Epstein's mouth the circumstances around the firing of his mother. And in Epstein's absence, Lex planned to ask Mercedes flat out if she'd known Sara Duncan and who might have been visiting her in Reno once a month in a blue Cadillac convertible. With a brown envelope full of cash. And her husband's Lion King logo on his bumper.

The elevator car stopped on the twenty-ninth floor, and two suits got in. Both sported Desert Lion name tags. The older man's tag decreed him Roman Markowitz, security head. Lex judged him to be in his sixties, but still a powerful man with darkly tanned olive skin and a thick head of pepper-gray hair. He threw an odd glance at Lex, then pressed the button for the thirtieth floor. Hairy hands, Lex noted. The doors slid closed, and the car began to ride up again.

It stopped, and as the two men exited the car, the older one turned to the younger. "Should be a long night."

The blood in Lex's veins turned instantly to ice.

The voice!

The doors slid closed.

He stared at them in a moment of raw shock. He'd know that distinct sandpapery voice anywhere—a sound that had haunted his childhood dreams. And lived in his adult ones.

The voice of the man who'd killed his mother.

Lex lurched forward and punched the Open Door button, but it was too late. The car had started to climb again. He hit the button for the thirty-second floor instead. Pushing through the gap in the doors as they started to open, he dashed down the passage, twisting and turning through the mazelike layout, looking for fire exit stairs. He bashed through the fire exit door, an alarm going off as he clattered down two floors, hit the bar to open the door to the thirtieth floor. But his weight slammed solid up against the door. It was locked from the inside of the stairwell. A security measure.

He swore. Then he heard footfalls clattering down the fire escape stairs. He'd set off the alarm. They were probably watching him right now from the cameras up in the security room—the omnipresent Vegas eye-in-the-sky. Lex squared his shoulders, and pulling his jacket straight, he began to calmly climb back up the stairs. Two security men stopped him. "Excuse me, sir—"

Lex held up his badge. "I'm on my way up to see Mrs. Epstein. Looks like I must have gotten off on the wrong floor."

The security guards exchanged sharp glances.

"You can check with Mrs. Epstein's receptionist if you like, she's expecting me," he said casually as he pushed past them. "I'll just head back up the way I came."

As Lex went back through the fire door the guards had left propped open, he heard one of the men key his radio, checking Lex's story and clearing him with reception. He made for the private elevator, heart slamming.

He'd bet his life that the security head for the Desert Lion was the same man he'd glimpsed through the louvered slats of the closet, wielding the knife that had slit his mother's throat. The voice, skin tone, age, hair, his association and current position with Epstein's casino all fit.

And now he had a name—Roman Markowitz.

Lex wondered if Markowitz knew who he was—that Special Agent Lex Duncan was actually the child of Sara Duncan, the child he'd come looking for on that fateful day in Reno thirty years ago.

Even if Markowitz didn't know, Lex had little doubt he'd be watching him right now via the security camera in the elevator, especially after the little incident on the stairs. And he'd be checking Lex's credentials, asking himself why a federal agent was visiting Mercedes Epstein.

It occurred to Lex, as the elevator bell dinged on the penthouse floor, that either way, Markowitz probably felt safe. Because he had no idea that Lex had recognized him or even could. After all, Lex had not been able to describe his mother's assailant to the police all those years ago. All he had was the memory of a voice. But no one understood just how indelibly that distinct voice had been burned into his brain.

The doors slid open, and Lex stepped into the penthouse lobby.

A butler showed him into a living room with elevated ceilings and a massive wall of tinted glass that overlooked the Las Vegas Strip below. The decor was all done in shades of cream and white. Even the orchids were white, the only contrast being the glossy black Chinese vases that contained them, and the black granite bar in the corner.

Mercedes was standing at the windows, her back to him as Lex entered the room. She was dressed in cream as if to match her decor—a sleek image of matriarchal elegance.

"Lexington," she said, looking out the window. "I was hoping you'd come."

For a second Lex was at a loss for words. No one had called him Lexington since his mother—and then the Lucky Lady.

She turned slowly, smiled, holding out her hand. "It's so good to see you. Take a seat. Can I offer you something to drink?"

He ran his tongue over his teeth, stepped forward. "No, thank you. What do you mean you were hoping I'd come?"

"We have so very much to catch up on."

"I beg your pardon?"

She nodded. "I understand, it's confusing."

An unspecified tension tightened like a wire around his chest. "I came to see your husband, Mrs. Epstein. But Frank

Epstein was not available, so I was hoping you'd help me out by answering a few questions."

She raised her elegant brow. "Is it a federal matter?"

"A personal one."

She looked at him for a long time, something strange and unreadable in her features, something that made him real uneasy. "What is it that I can help you with?" she said finally.

"Did you once know a young woman, a croupier, by the name of Sara Duncan?" he asked. "She would have been working at the old Frontline Casino around the same time you were there."

Several beats of silence thickened the air.

"Please," she said, very quietly. "Will you sit?"

Lex glanced at the virginal cream sofa, the matching chairs. "I'd prefer to stand—this shouldn't take long." He didn't like the look in her eyes, the unease he was feeling. Something big was coming down the pike here, and he had no idea what it was.

She walked to the bar counter, moving smoothly on impossibly high heels. She reached for a bottle of mineral water, uncapped it. "I knew Sara," she said as she poured a glass. "What do you want to know about her?"

"She was my mother."

Mercedes put the glass to her painted lips, sipped slowly, eyes intent on his. She set the glass down, a small chink of crystal on the black granite surface of the counter. "No, she wasn't, Lexington."

"I…excuse me?"

"Sara Duncan was not your mother."

He stared at her blankly.

She inhaled. "I'd really prefer you to sit, Lexington."

"Right about now, I really don't want to sit."

She nodded, turned away from him, looked down on the activity on the Strip thirty-three stories below. "It's been such a long time, so much in between. A lifetime really." She paused. "I had a one-night stand, Lexington. Just over thirty-five years ago."

Roman Markowitz had called Frank Epstein immediately upon encountering Special Agent Duncan in the private elevator. Epstein's driver had rushed Frank back to his hotel. He now sat in his private viewing room, watching the video feed into his own penthouse apartment. Markowitz stood at his side.

"You think he recognized you?" said Epstein, eyes glued to the monitor.

"Not a chance. He has no idea who I am."

Epstein nodded his head. "Keep it that way."

"How do you want to play this?"

Epstein studied his beautiful wife. "Let's hear what she tells him and see how he reacts. We'll take it from there," he said quietly. "What happened the other night with the tail on the Rothchild heiress by the way?"

"We lost her in a car chase. Someone else was following her. Caused the freeway pileup."

"You see who it was following her?"

"Negative."

"Interesting," Epstein mused.

"What does your one-night stand have to do with Sara Duncan?" Lex wasn't sure he wanted to hear what was going to come out of Mercedes Epstein's mouth next.

She ignored his question. "It was a crazy, impulsive and very dangerous thing to do, because I had recently married Frank, and Frank was a very, very possessive man." She was quiet for a few seconds, staring down at the tiny cars far down in the street. "I'm sure you know the rumors about Frank in those days."

She spun round suddenly. "I fell pregnant that night, Lex-

ington. And do you want to know what the irony is? The irony
is that Frank has always been unable to sire children. As much
as I needed to hide the affair, I couldn't even begin to think of
passing off my baby as his. And I couldn't get rid of my unborn
child. It was not in me to do so."

Nausea rose in Lex as the meaning behind her words
burrowed into his brain. "Who…did you have this affair with?
Who was the father of your child?" His voice came out hoarse.

"A man by the name of Tony Ciccone. He worked for
Frank. He was—"

"I know who he was."

Pain twisted into her features, and her eyes glimmered.
"Tony told me to get rid of the child. He said Frank would
murder us both if he found out, and I believed him. But I could
not go through with an abortion. I…" Her voice hitched. "I…I
just couldn't."

Lex didn't trust himself to speak.

"So I arranged to go on an extended tour. I was a dancer back
then, and Frank was very busy with a major project at the time
and wanted to keep me happy. He'd have given me the world
if he could. He has given me so much—"

"The baby?"

She moistened her lips, nodded. "I timed my tour so that I
could carry my child to term, and I gave birth in secret, where
Frank wouldn't find out."

"A boy."

"Yes," she said quietly. "And I named him Lexington." Her
eyes misted over, and her voice grew thick. "I named him for
my hometown in Kentucky because I had a desperate need to
root my son with some part of myself, my history, before I had
to give him away."

Lex ran his hands over his hair. Feeling hot. He needed air.
He needed to get the hell out of this place. He didn't want to

hear what he was hearing. Didn't want to believe it…couldn't process it. "I…I am that son."

She nodded. "I entrusted you to Sara Duncan's care."

"You *gave* me to Sara Duncan?"

"She was a good person, Lexington. And she needed the kind of money that Tony and I could give her to do this for us."

He closed his eyes for a moment. This woman was trying to tell him that he—a federal law enforcement agent—was the son of one of the most notorious and violent gangsters in the country? That *she* was his mother?

Right about now, he needed a drink. No, he needed to get blind freaking inebriated. He needed to smash something. Disbelief, anger—he couldn't even articulate what—was building like a Molotov cocktail inside him. But he remained rooted to the spot. It was like watching a train wreck, the train wreck of his life, and he couldn't tear himself away.

"Tony Ciccone is—"

"Your father."

He swore. Violently.

"Lexington, I know this must—"

He held up both hands, palms out, keeping her at bay, not wanting to hear more, yet compelled to stay and hear it all. "Just…just give me the facts, keep it simple."

She had the audacity to look hurt. "Tony went ballistic when he found out I refused to terminate my pregnancy. He had a terrible temper, and he was convinced Frank would tear him apart limb by limb with his bare hands. I was afraid of Frank, too. As much as I love him, he can be a fearful man when crossed. But I do love him, above all else—"

"Please, Mrs. Epstein." Lex couldn't even call her by her first name now. "The facts."

"We paid Sara handsomely to take you as a newborn and to register you as her own child in Reno. She feigned pregnancy while I was away on tour, making herself look progressively advanced. It was a policy of Frank's that no visibly pregnant women could work his casino floor, and Sara caused a scene over it, as we had planned, and got herself fired. She then left for Reno, where we delivered the baby to her."

"*The* baby," he said, almost inaudibly.

"You."

"And then?"

"And then Sara had enough money to buy herself a house and to raise you on her own. We continued to pay her a monthly stipend, cash, organized by Tony. Non-traceable, of course."

Apart from the pale-blue Cadillac that came like clockwork to their house. "Who brought her the cash each month?"

"Jackie Winston, a man in Tony's employ."

"Did this Jackie Winston work for Frank Epstein as well as run personal errands for Tony Ciccone?"

"Why do you ask?"

"Just answer the question."

"Yes, he did work for Frank, but Tony put Jackie on a separate payroll as well. Frank didn't know this. You see, Tony was trying to coax several of Frank's men over to his side at that time. Frank and Tony were in a battle over…certain things in their…business relationship."

That would explain the frontline logo on Winston's blue Cadillac. "Do you know who killed my mother, Mrs. Epstein?" He couldn't *not* think of Sara as his mother. As far as Lex was concerned, she was the beautiful young woman who had held him, loved him, laughed with him, praised him when he came home from school with good marks. Made his lunches, found Mr. Teddy when his bear got lost…held him tight when he was sad. He didn't give a rat's ass what anyone said—Sara Duncan *was* his mom. And no one was his father. Not as far as he was concerned.

"I don't know who killed her, Lex," she almost whispered. Fear, or some other emotion darkening her eyes and blanching her skin.

"Don't lie to me. Not now."

"All I can tell you, Lexington, is that it was one of Tony's henchmen who did it, one who routinely handled Tony's dirty—or as he called it—wet work."

The one with a raspy voice who was inside this casino hotel this very minute. Still alive and kicking while his mother had been stone-cold dead for thirty years.

She inhaled shakily. "The first I heard of Sara's death was when I opened the newspapers the morning after she was killed. I called Tony right away. As I mentioned, this was at a time when Frank and Tony were having a very serious falling out. Frank was insisting Tony return to Chicago, and Tony was refusing. It made for some very bad blood. Frank, however, had the upper hand…it's a long story, but Tony figured he was going to get leverage by sending someone to kidnap you, and he was going to hold you—and me—ransom to get me to twist Frank's arm. He said if I failed to change Frank's mind, he was going to deliver the kid—you—to Frank in person. You were going to be the living flesh and blood proof of my infidelity and how I'd cheated him all those years."

Mercedes took a deep swallow of water, and Lex noticed her hands were trembling. "It…it was a really foolish thing for Tony to do, but he was growing more and more irrational, and violent, and the excessive drinking and drugs he was taking didn't help." She hesitated, looked Lex directly in the eyes. "If you know who Tony Ciccone was, Lexington, as you say you do, then you'll know the history and the rumors that circulated around him. You will know what people say he did. Frank needed to distance himself from all that, because he ran a clean operation."

Like hell. Lex glared at her. "Go on."

"But the kidnapping went wrong. Sara apparently hid you and shot and injured Tony's man, and he fled when he heard the police coming."

"Did this…man survive his gunshot injury?" Lex asked, seeing in his mind a replay…the checkered pants, the man's hairy hands, the glint of the knife. His mother's blood.

"I don't know."

"You're not telling the truth."

"I have nothing I want to hide, Lexington. I am telling you this because I need to. I am ill—seriously ill—and the prognosis is grave. I might have only days left, weeks at the most. When things start to go wrong in my body, it will be fast. My husband doesn't know I am sick. He doesn't know any of what I am telling you."

"Then why *are* you telling me."

"I need to," she said simply. She walked across the room, almost took a seat on a white chair, but restrained herself from showing weakness. Instead she forced her spine straight again. A proud woman, no doubt, but now that Lex looked carefully, under it, he could see a frailty. Under her artfully applied makeup was a face that was pale. Sick.

"When you approach the end of life, Lexington, and you look back over all that you have done…I…I just need to make peace with my God." Her eyes glimmered again. "And to do this, I needed to see you, to look into the eyes of my son, and to tell you the truth. It's my atonement. My absolution. This one thing I must do before I pass from this world."

"So it's for your own satisfaction. Because it's clearly not for mine."

"The truth, Lexington, it sets one free."

"And this truth of your affair, what do you expect it will do to Frank?"

"You don't need to tell him," she stated.

"So the truth sets only certain people free?"

She said nothing.

Lex walked to the window, looked down at the city of sin and light. Of illusions, deception. Of promise, fate, fortune. And ruin.

"Will you tell him?" she asked very quietly.

"I'm a federal agent, Mrs. Epstein. You've just told me who is behind the unsolved murder of a woman. It's a thirty-year-old cold case that could now, finally, find its way to closure. Frank will become part of that investigation, given his alliances with Ciccone, and the fact he is your husband."

"Frank had nothing to do with Sara's murder."

"He did, Mrs. Epstein. He was the target of the kidnapping attempt that went wrong. He was the reason for it all."

"And who would you see prosecuted at the end of it?" she asked. "Exactly who would stand trial—a dead man?"

"Justice must be done."

"Tony Ciccone is *dead*, Lexington. Gone. There's no one to arrest, no one to try in court. No need to bring it all up."

"It never ceases to amaze me," Lex said slowly, "how the Epsteins, the Rothchilds, the Schaeffers of this world truly think the rules apply differently to them—that you're somehow above it all."

She glanced at the street way below. "We are above it, Lexington," she said softly. "It's the way the world works. Money is power. Especially if you know how to use it."

"Like Frank does."

"Yes, like my husband. And all you will do is hurt him if you tell him about my infidelity. And he has infinite—and I mean *infinite*—power to hurt you back."

"A threat?" Lex snorted derisively. "You have this desperate need to tell me that I am your son, to atone with your God, but you must threaten me at the same time?" He spun, strode toward the exit. "You people make me sick. Besides, you have no proof you are my mother. I have no reason to believe it."

"DNA will prove—"

"There's no way in hell I'm taking a DNA test to find out *you* are my mother." He stalked into the lobby, rammed the elevator button.

"Would it help if I told you where Tony Ciccone's body is?" she called out.

Lex froze. He turned slowly, stepped back into the living room. "How do you know where he is? Did Frank kill him?"

"I did. I shot and killed the father of my child."

Lex stared at her, heart pounding. "Why?"

"Because of what he did to Sara," she said, the steel returning to her eyes, her neck corded tense. "And because his henchman allowed you to witness the horror. Because he allowed *my son* to become an orphan. The remorse, the guilt, it has been horrific to bear. It's why I have always supported the Nevada Orphans Fund, Lexington. And until you left Reno, I always knew where you were. And then when I saw your name in the paper in connection with the Rothchild homicide case, I knew you'd come back to Nevada."

She inhaled deeply. "Then I saw your name on that bachelor auction list, and I…" Her voice faded and tears began to stream down her cheeks. "It's why I came to see you with my own eyes and why I bid on you that night. I pushed the bidding sky high because…because I couldn't stop myself. I wanted that young Rothchild heiress to know just how much my boy was worth, and I wanted the orphans fund to get as much of her cash as she could give."

Lex shook his head, staring at the woman who said she was his mother.

"You can't put a dollar value on a person, on a baby."

"This is Vegas, Lexington. People can buy what they like."

Including a fake mother.

"Where's Ciccone's body?" he said coolly. "What did you do to him?"

Mercedes steadied herself by reaching for the back of a chair. "When I read about Sara's murder in the paper, I phoned Tony right away, and I learned what he'd done. I set it up to meet him at a place in the desert, an isolated spot that Tony and I had been together before, a ghost town where they used to mine silver. I said I had something important to tell him about Frank, and that I was worried about being followed, so he had to be careful not to tell anyone or bring anyone. He trusted me, Lexington. Tony, in his way, adored me, and he had no idea just how much hatred he'd put into me. I shot him, out in that desert. I rolled his body down the mine shaft. He didn't see it coming."

The words of the Lucky Lady psychic sifted into his mind. *A past…death…buried in the Mojave sands…sands of time…death to be avenged…*

Lex tried to swallow, trying to absorb what she was telling him—that she knew the answer to a mystery that gripped the nation thirty years ago, that she had killed a notorious Vegas gangster…and that gangster was his father.

"Why should I believe this?"

"Because I'll tell you exactly in which mine shaft you will find Tony Ciccone's remains, if there's anything left of him."

"Then, Mrs. Epstein, I'll see that you are brought in and charged with homicide."

A sad smile curled over her mouth. "I very much doubt, Lexington, that I will live long enough to see that."

"Where's the body?"

"At a small ghost town thirty miles southwest of Vegas, down a shaft in the old Conair silver mine. There's a main headframe, easy to spot. Next to it is an old metal-sided building. If you go about two hundred yards east of that, you'll find another shaft opening covered with a metal grate. He's down there."

Lex studied her. This woman, this proud Vegas matriarch, an ex-showgirl, was supposed to be his mother and a cold-blooded murderer?

"Why'd you sleep with him, with Ciccone?"

"It was a wild time, Lexington. We were all young, flush with cash, liquor, drugs. We felt like gods. We *were* gods, in our world. Las Vegas was our oasis, our desert kingdom. And Tony was rough, sexy. He had an edge that women liked. You have his Mediterranean complexion—"

Lex shot up his hand. He didn't want to hear that he resembled Ciccone in any way whatsoever. "One thing I still don't understand is that you have so much to lose by telling me this. And so little to gain. Why? Why tell me at all? Maybe you'd have done me a favor keeping quiet."

She shook her head. "I don't think you'll ever understand just how much I have gained, Lexington. Looking at you, right here, in front of me, in my home. My *son*. Whom I have thought about every waking day for thirty-five years. It clean broke my heart, Lexington, to hand over that small, warm bundle the day I gave birth. I have never, ever felt so proud as when I bore you into this world. The sky had never looked brighter, and I had never grasped so keenly the meaning and sense of life." She wavered. "And I've never, ever felt so lonely, so hollow and empty, as when I had to place you into the hands of another woman."

Lex scrubbed his hand hard over his brow. Crap, this was a messy tangle of love, adultery, murder, and revenge—old Las Vegas mob-style. And the only reason he'd stumbled upon this dark and dirty truth about his own past was because Harold Rothchild's old connection with Frank Epstein had led him here.

"*...there are still people in town who will go to great lengths* *to ensure that the past stays where it belongs—buried. You go trying to mess with that, and you're looking to be messing with some real bad ghosts…"*

Yeah, well now he knew just how bad those ghosts really were.

"What is your illness?" he asked calmly.

"An advanced form of leukemia. When my system starts to fail, it will be very fast. And it could happen anytime. Today. Tomorrow, next week."

Lex stared at her for several beats, then turned and exited the penthouse without looking back, his heart stone-cold numb.

His soul empty.

Mechanically, he pressed the elevator button for the lobby and began the ride back to ground level.

He finally had one answer he'd been searching a lifetime for—he knew the name of his father. And he felt more alone than ever, more at a loss as to who he really was. Because in a way, he'd just lost his mother. He'd just lost everything he thought he'd ever known.

Empty, emotionless, alone, he exited the elevator.

And there she was—Jenna—pacing agitatedly in front of the elevators, wearing an innocent summer dress with a small floral print, flat sandals, loose-flowing hair. Her eyes lit brightly when she saw him, and she ran to him.

Lex took her in his arms, wrapped himself around her. Held tight. As tight as he dared without hurting her. She was suddenly a buffer against the overwhelming emotion threatening to crack out of him, the only thing stopping him from crumbling. The only thing in this world that mattered to him right at this moment.

She looked up, eyes warm, soft and caring. "I wanted to say I'm sorry," she whispered. "I should never have asked you to go against your job, your principles."

He closed his eyes against a sudden sharp burn, put his head back, battling to keep it all inside. But she cupped the back of his head, made him look at her, and she leaned up on tiptoe and kissed him.

Through her summer dress he could feel her breasts, her nipples hardening, and he felt himself implode. He had to make love to her. Right now. In Epstein's hotel. Jenna's mouth opened warm, soft under his. Kissing her, Lex backed toward the check-in desk. "A room," he murmured against her lips. "We need a room."

They started up in the elevator, his tongue tangling with hers as he slipped his hand under her dress. He lifted her bare leg, smooth as silk, hooked it around him, finding her panties damp. His heart began to race, his breath coming short. Knowing the cameras, the eye-in-the-sky was watching, he thrust his fingers inside her, began to move them. Jenna sagged against him, sinking down onto his fingers, deepening his reach as she hooked her leg higher. He felt her undoing his fly, taking his erection into her hands.

She hurriedly guided him into herself, and Lex grabbed her buttocks as she curled her other leg around his hips and they crashed back against the mirror. With near-blind passionate hunger, a desperate need to find himself, to find her, he thrust up into her. She threw her head back, hair cascading down her back as she clung her arms around his neck.

This was one thing that felt true, real, right…and he pumped into her, fast, repeatedly, supporting her weight as she gasped, one hand sliding on the steamy mirror the other flying back to grip the railing as she came with a sharp cry, just as the bell clanged onto their floor.

Chapter 12

Stumbling backward into the room, kissing, they backed clumsily toward the bed, door slamming shut behind them. Lex dropped Jenna onto the covers, lifted her dress over her head and removed her panties. She moved her hands to his hips, slid his pants down his powerful thighs, exhilaration burning in her chest. "All of you," she whispered. "I want to see all of you."

It was turning to dusk outside, the vibrant flickering wattage of Vegas pulsing hotter as the sky over the desert dimmed to mute purples and browns. The light from the window was surreal, and it made him look like something from an erotic dream—Mediterranean skin olive and smooth, his muscles pumped with energy, literally vibrating for the same kind of release she'd had in the elevator. His hair hung in a loose lick over his forehead, and his features were predatory, etched with hunger for her, eyes fierce dark emeralds—something had shifted in him. Something had been set loose—primal and aggressive. And hot damn, she liked it.

Jenna grasped his wrists, yanked him down onto the bed and straddled him, hair falling wild over her shoulders. His eyes grew smoky, lids lowering as she sunk down onto his erection like a hot, wet glove, moving her hips until he groaned, grabbed her buttocks hard with powerful hands. He was still rock-hard from the elevator, and she was heating, tingling, for release all over again.

And with sudden shock, Jenna came, an explosion of muscular contractions that seized her body with glorious, gut-punching power. Lex couldn't hold back a second longer. He swung her roughly around onto all fours, took her from behind, squeezing her breasts, pulling her into his pelvis as he thrust and she arched her back, lustrous hair dark against creamy skin.

Lex's world shifted as he came with such fierce release that it shattered his body and mind, obliterating everything he'd just learned upstairs, and they fell back, breathless, sated. Lex held her, stroking her hair, his body still shimmering with latent energy, knowing, at the same time, that he'd never be the same. He'd found truth. In more ways than one. And not in the way he'd expected. Because the real truth lay right here in his arms, and so did his future—if he played it all right. And he realized, with irony, that while he'd come to Vegas seeking his past, instead he'd found the road that led ahead. Perhaps that's what he'd wanted all along.

Jenna rolled onto her side and traced her fingers over his abs, down the thick line of hair that ran to his groin, and she smiled wickedly as he began to swell again in front of her eyes.

"Careful," he whispered.

"Why?" she tickled the backs of her nails a little lower.

"Because I'm not done with you yet."

Jenna moved her hand to his groin, took hold of him, slid her knee up over his legs. Rolling closer, she moved her lips close to his, breasts pressing against his chest. "Did you mean it, Lex?" she murmured against his mouth.

"Mean what?"

She inhaled sharply as she felt him enter her.

"When…you said—" her voice came out thick, breathy as he moved, slow strokes that made her eyes roll back into her head "—that…you loved me? Was it true?"

He swung himself on top of her, deepened his thrust. She couldn't concentrate.

"Jenna—" his voice was husky "—you are the one thing in my life right now that is true."

"Boy, you're one sorry puppy, Lex Duncan, considering… *ah*—" He thrust hard and she arched. He came quickly. And they sank back, glowing with perspiration.

"Yes," he whispered up to the ceiling in the growing dark. "It is true."

He did love her.

He felt her hand slip into his, squeeze, and Lex's heart swelled to busting point.

"It's this," Lex said, tilting his chin toward the skyline. "This has got to be what people love about this place." They were sitting immersed in a hot tub full of bubbles, drinking from champagne flutes, looking out the floor-to-ceiling window at the Vegas night.

"Making love?" she said with a smile, hair piled loosely up on her head, tendrils wet, skin flushed.

He slanted his eyes to hers. "No, the fact that magic *can* happen," he whispered.

She studied him in silence. "What happened to you today, Lex?"

"What makes you think anything happened?

"You're…different. I don't know how to describe it. Intense. Edgy. Alive in a way that almost feels…dangerous."

His features turned serious. He trailed his fingers along her collarbone. "I found out who my father was today, Jenna," he said softly.

"What?"

He turned to look out over the view again, silent. "I was also informed that Sara Duncan was not my real mother."

She sat up. "Lex?"

He smiled ruefully. "You're so beautiful, Jenna." He glanced up into her eyes. "Do you think we could make it work? Do you think we could try?"

Emotion burned fast and sharp into her eyes. "Is…is this a proposal of some kind?" she whispered.

"Do you think you could love me, Jenna?"

She looked at him for several long moments, and his eyes grew worried.

"I think," she whispered, "that I fell in love with you the first time I saw you on—"

"Please, do not say on that god-awful auction stage."

"No, Lex, on that drought-brown football field. With your boys. I saw a leader, a man with an incredibly strong moral compass. And…" Emotion tightened her throat. "You made me think I…might want a family of my own one day. I'd never thought that before. You made me want more, Lex, something very different to what I have."

He glanced away sharply, features twisting, and Jenna saw tears glisten in his eyes…real damn tears. In her FBI agent. "God," he whispered, not daring to look at her. "You have no idea…absolutely no idea what that does to me."

"Tell me," she said softly, reaching out, cupping his jaw, turning his face back to hers. "Tell me about your mother, Lex. About your father."

He inhaled deeply. "Mercedes Epstein claims to be my mother, Jenna."

"What?"

"She said she paid Sara Duncan to register me in Reno and to raise me as her own son."

Her mouth fell open. "I…I don't understand. Does that mean Frank Epstein is—"

"My father? No. Mercedes apparently had an affair with a man named Tony Ciccone. You ever heard of him, Jenna?"

"Yes," she said very quietly. "He was the gangster who disappeared, the subject of one of the FBI's biggest manhunts at the time. He had a crazy temper, was a violent mob enforcer."

"And he was my father."

She looked at him, dumbstruck.

"Yeah," he said with a wry twist in his mouth. "Ironic, huh? The straight-shooting, button-up law enforcement officer has one of the most infamous mobsters in Nevada history as his dad. How's that supposed to make me feel, Jenna? What of that monster lurks in my DNA, under my skin, in the beat of my heart?"

"Lex, listen to me. That single-mindedness, that ferocity that was apparently Tony Ciccone, you might have it in you, but you chose to use it for good, for justice."

"It's weird, isn't it? They say that the profile of a cop is often closest to that of a criminal."

"But one is for good and the other bad."

He snorted. "If it were so simple."

"Hey," she said, leaning forward. "I know how blurred those lines get, remember? I was the one hiding stuff from homicide investigators. You showed me there *was* a line though and that I had to pick a side. I did, Lex. And you yourself, long ago, picked your side, too—the side of justice, when that Reno sheriff…what was his name?"

"Tom McCall, Washoe Country sheriff."

"Yes, when Tom pulled you back from trouble, he showed you where that line lay, Lex. He set you on track, and just think of all those kids that you've done the same for. You might have your father's genes in you, but maybe he never got the same chance that you did back in his own childhood." She gazed at him intently "Maybe he didn't find a Tom McCall, but he found a Frank Epstein and mob family instead. What you do, Lex, is honorable. And you told me yourself that you do it because you love."

And God he loved *her* for reminding him of this, telling him what he so desperately needed to hear. For being here for him, nothing to hide between them any longer.

"Tell me, Lex. Everything."

She sat quietly and listened to the rest of his story, the whole story, including how he'd seen the man he believed had murdered Sara Duncan.

"How come you didn't go after him right away?"

"Because I need to do it right—I want a charge of murder, and I want it to stick. For that to happen, I still need evidence. All I have is a memory of a voice, and a conviction that Markowitz is the man I saw."

"What about Mercedes's story?"

"She could deny she said anything. Besides, she doesn't know who actually killed Sara, or so she says."

"What are you going to do?"

"First I see if Ciccone's remains really are down in that mine shaft. That's step one, hard evidence that can be used to have the Sara Duncan homicide case reopened. Then I hand this case over, because I am a victim and a witness. Next Ciccone's body goes for autopsy, and Mercedes is brought in for questioning based on what she told me. It'll have to be done soon if she's as ill as she claims to be."

"So Epstein doesn't know any of this?"

"Mercedes says she kept it from him."

Jenna snorted softly. "That's so ironic—Roman Markowitz, Tony Ciccone's old henchman, now working for Epstein as his security head…and neither Mercedes or Frank Epstein know."

"It looks that way."

"It's weird. Because I know a little about Roman Markowitz through the event planning business," said Jenna. "And from what I understand, Markowitz got his break in the security business at the old Frontline."

"Well, if he was working for Epstein back then, he'd have had to have been doing Ciccone's bidding on the sly, the bastard."

Jenna shook her head. "Mercedes is your mother… I still can't believe it. Do you think that's why she came to my auction, to see you?"

"So she says."

"And it's why she supports all those orphan charities?"

"Again, it's what she claims."

"I feel sorry for her, Lex, in a way."

"Why, she gave her kid away? Basically paid cash to get rid of me, because she didn't have the stomach for an abortion?"

"And she's been haunted by guilt ever since. I think deep down she's a good woman, Lex."

"You know something, Jenna—you're generous. With your heart. To a fault, even. You don't need money when you have real wealth like yours."

Her eyes filled with tears. "Lex, not one person in my life has ever said anything so beautiful, so meaningful to me. Thank you," she whispered.

He took her into his arms, all slippery soap bubbles and fragrance, and crushed his mouth to hers. "Jenna—" he said pulling back abruptly as it dawned on him. "How'd you know I'd be here, at the Desert Lion?"

"Rita told me. I went to find you, to…" Her eyes darkened.

"Geez, Lex, I almost forgot. I wanted to know if you'd heard about the Lucky Lady, Marion Robb. I read about her in the morning paper."

"What about her?"

"She was murdered. Last night. Her throat was slit."

He sat up abruptly. *"What?"*

"Yes, I thought—"

Urgency crackled through him. "I've got to get you out of this hotel, Jenna. Get dressed, at once. When we walk out that door, you act like nothing is wrong. Understand?"

"What are you saying, Lex?"

"Marion Robb's death cannot be coincidence. Someone must have been following us, learned I was looking for answers and was worried because Lucky Lady knew something. Something that would lead me back *here,* to Markowitz. Quick, move!"

"You…you think Markowitz knows you're onto him?" she said, stepping out of the tub, grabbing a towel.

"God alone knows." Lex pulled on his pants. "Marion didn't give me anything other than a hint at old mob connections, but I believe she had more to tell. She clammed up suddenly when I told her about that cartoon logo on the Cadillac—she *knew* something, Jenna, and it scared her. I was going to go back, build her trust, ease her into talking, over time."

Time that had just run out for her.

Lex grabbed his shirt. *"If* Markowitz is responsible for slitting her throat, he either believes I got something out of her, or she might have told him she'd stayed mum, and he killed her to keep it that way. Markowitz might still believe he is safe from me, as long as he doesn't make a stupid move. But I'm not taking chances, Jenna. I want you out of this hotel, *now.*"

He buttoned up his shirt as he called Perez. "I need you at the Desert Lion."

"I'm here, right outside. Followed Rothchild after telling her where you were." She yawned theatrically into the phone. "What's taking you two so long? What in the hell are you up to, Duncan?"

"I'll explain—"

"Heard that one before, partner. Not buying it again."

"Perez," he said urgently. "I'm into something. I want you to take Jenna home, far away from me. Close protection detail. Understand?"

"Duncan—"

"I believe I know who killed my mother. He's in this hotel, and he might get wind I'm onto him. That'll make him a very dangerous man, and I don't want Jenna anywhere near me if and when that happens. I think he's behind the death of Marion Robb, owner of the Lucky Lady psychic store on East—"

"Duncan, this is—"

"Just listen to me, Perez. Contact the LVMPD. Tell them the Lucky Lady homicide case is ours. Then get someone to look into a man named Roman Markowitz. He's security head at the Desert Lion. He apparently goes way back with Epstein, to the Tony Ciccone days. Maybe Markowitz whacked the psychic himself or had someone do it for him. Tell whoever takes the case to see if they can link Markowitz to that homicide. DNA, whatever. Anything."

"And where are you going?" Her tone had changed. She was sensing the seriousness in him.

"To find Ciccone's body."

Silence.

"You still there, Perez?"

"Are you okay, Duncan? You haven't lost it on me have you?"

"Jenna will fill you in." He hung up, felt for his weapon, chambered a round and held it ready, under his jacket, knowing the eye-in-the-sky would be on them the instant they exited the door. He took Jenna's arm, ushered her out the door and they started moving swiftly along soft carpet to the elevators.

Two suits appeared at the other end of the passage. Security. The men started to move toward them.

Lex had to force a smooth, casual pace. He pressed the elevator button, watching the men nearing in his peripheral vision. The elevator bell pinged, doors opening painfully slowly. He ushered Jenna in, jabbed the lobby button, pulse accelerating.

The elevator doors closed just as the security men passed by.

Two floors down, another security employee got into the car, but so did a middle-aged couple. Lex positioned Jenna behind the couple, using them as cover. Tense, they stood in silence as the car hummed slowly down. The doors opened. Lex put his arm around Jenna, sticking very close to the middle-aged couple, keeping them between the security employee and Jenna.

They exited the massive hotel doors and were hit by a wall of dark, damp heat. Perez was there, in her SUV, engine running. She leaned over and flung open the passenger door.

"Do you think any of this has anything to do with The Tears of the Quetzal, or Candace's death?" Jenna asked quietly as Lex held the door open for her.

"All I know is that ring led me down this road, Jenna." In more ways than one. Lex glanced at his partner, his eyes saying it all: *Be careful. Candace Rothchild's killer is still out there and someone still wants to hurt Jenna.*

"Lex—" Jenna's eyes were big, dark. A man could lose himself in those eyes "—be careful, okay? I…I have plans for us."

"Hey, I'm not going anywhere," he bent down to kiss her quickly. "I've got some plans of my own."

"Agent Duncan forgets—" Frank Epstein said quietly, observing Lex and Jenna exit his hotel "—that everyone watches everyone in Vegas, all the time. And," he added, "some men even watch their wives."

Roman Markowitz studied his boss in silence, his posture rigid.

Frank pinched the bridge of his nose, replaying in his mind what he'd witnessed on the monitor through the private feed into his own living room. None of what had transpired between Mercedes and Lex Duncan was news to him. Frank knew his wife was dying—he was in touch with Mercedes's doctor and paid him very well to keep him informed. He'd also known from day one that Tony Ciccone had been screwing his wife, that she'd tried to hide the pregnancy from him. He'd have whacked the little Italian bastard himself if Mercedes hadn't done it for him. And he loved her for it.

Besides, it had solved a very thorny little problem for him. Ciccone's mysterious vanishing act had kept the FBI off his back.

He'd always wanted Mercedes to have an illusion of freedom, but in effect, he controlled every aspect of her life. His sleight-of-hand, his trickery, had always been for her own good. He'd always protected her. Yet to the world she was independent, proud, regal—his Vegas queen. And he wanted her to die proud. On her terms. Under her own illusions. He loved her that much, that fiercely.

She'd become much more deeply religious and spiritual since she'd learned of her terminal illness. And in doing so, she'd become even more poignantly beautiful to him. So fragile in so many ways.

But now Lex Duncan knew her truth.

He knew Mercedes had shot and killed a man.

And the look Frank had glimpsed in the agent's eyes when Mercedes had confessed this—he'd seen that intent look before in another man. In the eyes of mob enforcer Tony Ciccone.

A bit of the father in the son, he thought to himself. You can't get away from that, Lexington.

A man like Lex Duncan, Frank could use on his side. On the wrong side… "He's dangerous now," he whispered.

Markowitz held his hand toward the monitor. "He still doesn't know who whacked his mother," he rasped. "You saw him on camera, and I saw him in that elevator. He doesn't know who I am. He has no idea."

Frank whipped to him, fury expressing violently through his blood. "It's not you I'm worried about, Roman," he said calmly. He looked at his nails, trying to defuse the pressure fizzing inside him. "You might have been working for Ciccone as my spy into his inner machinations at a time I really needed to know the extent of his operations, and what he might use against me. But—" he looked up "—you never should have killed that woman when he chose to send you to kidnap the boy."

"The bitch shot me."

"And your temper remains too short for your own good. No, Roman, it's not you I'm concerned about, it's my wife. It's *me*— I don't want this ancient Ciccone crap coming back to sit on me now. And I simply cannot allow my wife to suffer at the hands of the FBI, be taken in, interrogated, possibly charged for murder in her last days."

She needed to go in peace. And Frank was prepared to kill to ensure this.

Markowitz cleared his throat. "You want me to take him out, sir?"

"It's imperative." He breathed his words out softly, like he so often did when he was about to blow. "My regret is that we did not have them put into one of our rooms wired with camera and sound. We have no idea what Duncan told the Rothchild woman while he was screwing her."

He inhaled deeply, trying to ease the hammering in his skull, his skin heating at the thought of them fornicating in his own elevator, under sight of his cameras. And Duncan doing it with a daughter of Harold Rothchild of all women. It was the ultimate slap in his face, in the face of his wife and his entire establishment. If he wasn't going to have the man killed, Frank would have his badge. He'd release the sexual footage to the mainstream media—a federal agent screwing the sister of a homicide victim, a case on which he was the lead investigator. Duncan had to know he was being watched. The bastard. It was like he no longer cared…which worried Frank. A little.

"So we do her, too," said Markowitz in his scratchy voice. "Just in case."

Frank tilted his chin slightly toward the monitor. "That's an FBI vehicle he's putting her into."

"I can have someone on that SUV in seconds. Just say it, boss, and I give the order."

"Do it."

Markowitz reached for a special cell, one he used only for very discreet jobs. Like the contract killing of a casino heiress and her FBI bodyguard. Like the elimination of a psychic with too much knowledge.

"It's me," he rasped into the phone. "This one must look like an accident. Affirmative—all occupants of the vehicle. Same payment structure."

He looked up, flipping his phone shut. "Done."

"Good. Now come with me. We're taking a little drive into the Mojave to remove Ciccone's remains. This time, the ghost of Ciccone will vanish for good."

"What about Duncan?"

"Trust me, he'll go straight out there to look for Ciccone's body. We'll be there waiting for him, take care of him ourselves."

"I can send someone—"

"No. We do it. You and me. No more loose ends."

Roman eyed his boss. Warily. A cold fist of tension curling in his abdomen.

* * *

Lex closed the door, stood back, banged the roof of the vehicle. "Go!"

The SUV moved on. Lex exhaled, dragging his hand over his hair as he watched the vehicle disappearing into the soaking hot, airless night, sweat already forming on his skin.

Geez, was he being overly paranoid? But he couldn't bear the idea off losing her. Not now.

Not ever.

Jenna had just given him a glimpse into a future, shown him what he really wanted, what they could have together. But that meant he now had everything to lose.

He told himself she'd be safe with Perez until he got back. Perez was a top agent, experienced. Sharp. He breathed out a hot sigh, allowing tension to ease just a little as he made for his own vehicle.

When Lex left the rambling city perimeter, taking the road that would lead to the old ghost town, the desert night grew thick and dark. Stars spattered the black dome of sky. And tension torqued inside him. He felt under the dash for his flashlight and an extra clip for his weapon.

Chapter 13

Rita Perez drew her SUV up to the security booth at the Roth-child mansion. She depressed the brakes, scrolling her window down as she reached for her badge.

But before either Jenna or Rita could even register what was happening, a man dressed completely in black with a balaclava pulled over his head stepped in front of Rita's passenger window. He aimed a gun fitted with a suppressor into the car. Behind him, lying on the driveway, dark blood glistening in her car headlights, Jenna saw the limp body of her dad's security guard.

She screamed.

As she did, Rita reached for her weapon, ducking and push-ing Jenna below the dash in the same motion. But as Rita moved, the man fired.

The shot was quiet, like in an assassin movie.

Jenna felt Rita's body jerk hard, and then shudder. The agent slumped limply on top of her. Hot blood came gushing from a wound on her head. Terror dumped through Jenna's nerves. She pushed Rita's body off her and stared in sheer horror at the ragged wound in the agent's skull, the way her mouth hung slack and open. The man with the black balaclava was moving quickly round to Jenna's door. He yanked it open, his gun now aimed at her. "You! Get in the back!" he hissed, grabbing her upper arm.

A small squeak came from somewhere low in Jenna's throat as she tried to scream and jerk free of his grasp. But the man raised his pistol and struck a glancing blow off her temple.

Her world went black.

When she came round, she felt nauseous. It took a few sickening, dizzying moments to realize she was bound tightly with rope and lying in the back of Rita's SUV. Rita's body lay limp and bloody beside her.

And the car was moving, somewhere dark. In the desert, no lights anywhere around them.

Headlights cut through blackness along a faraway ridge. The beams were then swallowed as the vehicle emitting them dipped into a canyon. There was only one road up ahead as far as Lex knew, and it led to the ghost town.

A sense of foreboding rustled through him.

Could be teens, out for a party, he thought. Or something more sinister.

He pulled abruptly over to the side of the road and examined his map with his flashlight. There was a much older disused track that led around the back of the abandoned town. It was several miles longer, but if he used that track, he could approach the town from the rear unanticipated. He could park his SUV below a ridge to the west, cut his lights, climb up and over the ridge, advancing in silence. If there was anyone in that old ghost town, he'd have the advantage of being able to see who they were, where they were and what they were up to.

He quickly removed his white shirt, reached back into the passenger seat and extracted a dark long-sleeved T-shirt from his gym bag. He pulled it over his head, checked his weapon and restarted the ignition.

Lex crept up the back of the ridge. The night was cloaked thick with heat, dead silent. The uncanny quietness set him on edge, heightened his senses. He could smell sand, stone, feel residual heat radiating up from sand that had blistered under the desert sun. He crested the ridge.

Below him silver moonlight glowed eerily over ruined buildings that squatted in a valley of dry scrub. A knotted ball of tumbleweed lodged at the facade of a crumbling structure, shades of gray and black playing tricks with his eyes. Lex could make out the shape of an old oil drum, a rusted old truck—remains of a life, an industry. Long gone. A mine headframe loomed above the abandoned structures, throwing long distorted shadows over the landscape.

There's a main headframe, easy to spot. Next to it is an old metal-sided building. If you go about two hundred yards east of that, you'll find another shaft opening covered with metal grate. He's down there…

Lex shifted his gaze eastward, and suddenly he saw it—an SUV parked at the far end of the buildings, moonlight glinting off chrome.

Sliding his pistol from its holster, he scrambled sideways down the steep drop, dislodging a shower of small pebbles that went skittering down the bank ahead of him, sound disproportionately loud. Lex stilled at the bottom, pulse quickening. He waited. Silence descended back on the ghost town, and he crept stealthily toward the hulking buildings.

The sudden creak and groan of metal grating cut through the stillness, and again Lex froze. He edged further along the front of the metal-sided building, gun held down and in front of his body, making his way two hundred yards east of the rusting headframe as per Mercedes's directions. He stopped. He could hear voices now. Males. Two.

He crept closer, ducked down behind a rusted drum, listened.

And he heard the sound that had haunted his boyhood dreams—the distinct sandpapery voice of Roman Markowitz. Lex peered cautiously around the wall. And he saw Frank Epstein in the pale moonlight.

They'd come ahead of him.

But how had they known? This was supposed to be Mercedes's dark secret from her husband. The thought struck him suddenly…could Epstein have had a camera in his own penthouse, been watching her whole confession? Was Mercedes in trouble now—or worse? Lex's heart began to slam as an even more chilling thought scrambled goose bumps over his skin—what if Epstein had a camera planted in his and Jenna's hotel room? If so, Epstein would know that Jenna knew everything.

Had Lex put *her* life in danger?

His head began to swim. *Focus.* Jenna was with Perez. If he made a rash move now, he could end up dead. And dead wasn't going to help Jenna. He couldn't phone her now, either. The men would hear. Nor could he call for back-up.

Lex inched farther forward, lowering himself behind the cover of a rusting boxcar. From there he watched Markowitz descend into the mine shaft using rungs grafted against the wall.

Markowitz's granular voice carried eerily up the mine shaft, which seemed to function as a large bullhorn. "He's down here, all right, boss, I see bones." Markowitz swore. "He's like a freaking mummy. D'you want to throw that bag, and I'll package him, bring him up?"

Lex peered farther around the boxcar, saw the dark shape of

Frank Epstein directing a powerful flashlight down the shaft. The heavy grate that had covered it lay to one side. Pulling back that grate must have been what caused the sound Lex had heard earlier.

"You sure it's him?" Epstein called down the shaft.

"Yeah, yeah the ring…it's Ciccone's ring, the one with the gold seal." He swore. "Geez, his finger bones just fell off when I touched him."

"I want to see for myself. Wait there—I'm coming down."

Another wave of goose bumps chased over Lex's skin as he saw Epstein draw a handgun from a holster at his ankle, check it, chamber a round and replace his weapon. Damn, the bastard was going to kill Markowitz? When? Once they got the bones bagged and back up into the SUV?

Lex's brain raced.

He needed the evidence to remain where it was. And he couldn't call for backup now. They'd hear. He needed to find a way to incapacitate these two, maybe trap them down in the shaft with the remains of Ciccone. Hold them until help arrived.

Epstein began to lower himself carefully into the shaft, the beam of his flashlight catching dust that floated up from the disturbed tomb below.

"Careful, Mr. Epstein. It's steep and not very secure. Are you sure?"

"Of course I'm sure."

"What about Duncan—what if he arrives while we're down here?"

"We'd already have seen him coming miles away on that road. We can set an ambush for him once we've got Ciccone bagged."

Lex waited for Epstein's head to sink below ground level. The minute he was down there, Lex would make for the heavy grate, seal them in from the top.

But just before Epstein was swallowed by the earth, Lex's phone buzzed loudly in his pocket. He swore to himself, jerked back, fumbled quickly in his pocket. He was about to click it off but saw the number in the green glow. Lex put the phone to his ear. "Yes," he whispered, quiet as he could.

"Special Agent Duncan, it's Agent Savalas. We've got a situation—"

Lex tensed.

"There's a security guard down at the Rothchild mansion, and security footage shows a man in a black balaclava firing a weapon into Agent Perez's vehicle. He then got into the vehicle and left the scene."

His heart twisted violently. "Jenna? Perez?"

"He's got them."

"Are they injured?" Lex whispered, hoarse. In the back of his mind he heard the men in the mineshaft go quiet—God, they'd heard him!

"We don't know. And we have no fix on the vehicle—"

"Perez's vehicle is fitted with GPS. Track it. Call me as soon as you have a location. I'm coming in."

He killed the call.

Silence rung loud in his ears. Just the thud of his heart.

Lex swore to himself, panic whispering seductively at the edges of his consciousness. Was it the same man who'd fired at her during the car chase?

Footfalls crunched in dirt, advancing. *The two men were coming for him.* They must have scrambled back out of the shaft when they'd heard him, and he'd been distracted.

Lex heard the rack of a rifle.

Fire boiled into his blood. He refused to lose. If he did, Jenna would die.

A gunshot pinged suddenly off the side of the boxcar, near his head.

Lex ducked down. They definitely knew he was here. Alone

in the desert. Two against one. Lex scurried along the base of the boxcar, dashed in a crouch across a gap and tucked in behind a shed, staying low and quiet. Those two men were a good deal older than him. And he was now fired with raw determination like nothing he'd known, a passion that was consuming him whole. All those men were to Lex now was an obstacle in his way to saving Jenna.

She was his priority.

Not Epstein.

Not the man who'd killed his mother—not any longer.

Lex had reached a tipping point, and he'd gone over the edge, seen what lay on the other side. A future. With a woman who'd bewitched him within three minutes flat—the duration of the song that had played on the dance floor only four nights ago, before the big clock in the Ruby Room had struck twelve. Lex had known it back then, deep down, that he was toast.

Blame it on The Tears of the Quetzal curse. Blame it on Vegas fate, chance, luck, magic. Whatever it was, he wasn't going to let Jenna go now. He was going to be her protector 24/7. For the rest of his life. And these bastards were simply in his way.

Another shot pinged off the boxcar where Lex had been just seconds ago. It gave the gunman's position away. Lex peered round the shed, squeezed off two shots. Immediately gunfire returned. Lex ducked, aimed again, this time the shooter went down with a grunt and thud in the dirt. It was Markowitz.

Lex now aimed for Epstein, who was running for his vehicle. He fired into dirt at this feet. Dust kicked up in a small explosion. Epstein kept running. Lex stepped out from his cover, weapon aimed at Epstein. "Halt! FBI!"

But Epstein kept moving. Lex squeezed off another round, aiming for the sand at his feet.

Panting, Epstein stopped. He raised both hands, turned slowly round. "Don't. Shoot."

Lex didn't waste time even acknowledging the bastard. His weapon trained on Epstein, he moved quickly toward the bag and length of rope they'd been going to use to raise Ciccone up from the shaft. He snagged the rope, approached Epstein, grabbed the old man, and shoved him brusquely onto his stomach in the sand.

"Wait…think this through, Duncan. I've got enough cash to—"

"You bastard," Lex snapped as he wrenched the grizzled old lion king's hands behind his back with the rope and hauled him to his feet. "When are you going to learn you can't buy everything, Epstein?" He shoved the stumbling, heavily-breathing man towards the SUV as he spoke.

"I can give you what you want—"

"I already got what I want. I'm going to see your entire empire go down into the dirt. Where are the keys?"

"I swear, you're going to regret this, Duncan. I have connections in places that—"

"Get in!" Lex barked as he yanked open the back hatch. "On your stomach."

"Duncan—"

He pressed the muzzle of his gun into the old mobster's back. "Do it! Now!"

Once the old man was humiliatingly bundled into his own trunk, Lex hogtied him, looping the rope so that Epstein's feet were bound to his hands. This desert king wasn't going anywhere but down.

Lex climbed into the driver's seat, dialing dispatch as he started the ignition. "Connect me with someone who can give me a fix on the GPS in Agent Perez's vehicle!" he barked. "And I need backup as soon as we get a reading on where she is." He hit the gas as he spoke, giving dispatch a rundown of the situation. And with Epstein swearing in the back, he raced back toward the city of Las Vegas, toward the gold halo of light in the desert, dust boiling in a dark cone behind him. Lex had no idea which direction to go, but this was a start until he had a fix on Perez's location. There was no way he could just sit and do nothing while he waited.

He called both Jenna's and Perez's phones as he drove. Both kept flipping to voice mail. Tension torqued like a vise in him.

His phone buzzed. Lex snapped it to his ear. "Yes!"

"We have a location. Perez's vehicle is stationary at a place called Bucktooth Ranch, an old property that was sold and slated for demolition two years ago, but redevelopment permits have been on hold because of legal issues—"

"I know it!" Lex hit the brakes, wheeling sharply as he pulled a 180 degree turn off-road. The car fishtailed into sand, dust billowing in a cloud around him as he bounced wildly over rugged terrain, dry scrub scraping the undercarriage of the SUV as he aimed for an intersecting road about a mile ahead. "I'm not far out. I can be there in a few minutes," he yelled into his phone. "Get that tactical team out there stat!"

The SUV tires bit suddenly into harder packed dirt as his vehicle hit the intersecting road. He punched down on the gas, increasing speed. "I'm about eight miles out now. Can you give me the ranch specs? How many buildings?"

"A bunch of old cabins…seven to the left of a main building, which is derelict."

"Approach road?"

"One road in, dirt. There's also an old horse trail that hooks around to the west."

"Wide enough for an SUV?"

"Affirmative."

"I'm going in that way."

Lex cut his lights and engine.

In the distance a yellow glow spilled from a window in one

of the old log cabins. The dark shape of Perez's SUV was tucked in alongside the west wall of the cabin, facing outward, as if ready for a quick getaway.

Leaving Epstein hog-tied in the vehicle, Lex ran in a crouch through a stand of dry scrub. He came up under the window, peered carefully up through broken, dusty glass. A flickering lantern stood on an old wood table, cell phone lying next to it. He shifted his gaze to the left, and his heart stalled.

Jenna! Arms above her head, hands tied from the rafters. Her face sheet-white, streaked with dirt, tears, mascara, hair a wild tangle. A man in a black balaclava held a knife to the exposed column of her neck. He was trailing the hooked tip down to the hollow at the base of her throat.

Although the man's face was masked, he was familiar in height and build to Thomas Smythe, the man who'd threatened the life of exotic dancer Vera Mancuso.

He peered up a little higher, caught sight of Perez's body lying in a small heap in the darkened corner of the cabin. Lex struggled to draw in a breath, to hold his position. It was not known if Smythe was the same guy who'd murdered Candace, but Lex had seen enough during the standoff over Mancuso's life to know that if this was Smythe, he was no rational man. Smythe had wanted that ring. And he'd probably do anything first and foremost for The Quetzal. Lex ducked down, checked his watch, mentally calculating how long it would take for backup to reach this remote ranch.

Too long.

Especially if Perez was still hanging onto life, needing medical attention. Lex *had* to move. But if he did act now, without backup, he could cost Jenna's life. He peered up again.

The man tilted Jenna's chin up with the hooked blade of his knife. Fresh tears shimmered down her face. Lex saw blood on her dress. Was she injured? Was it Perez's blood?

The man began to trail the blade back down the column of her throat, moving his body closer to hers. Jenna tried to shrink away from him, arms straining visibly above her head. But the man hooked the knife tip into the top of her dress and jerked it down hard. The fabric split in a ragged gash, flaying open at her sides to reveal bare breasts and her skimpy scrap of a silky G-string. The man touched her nipple with his knife.

Blinding rage erupted in Lex.

He launched up, shouldered through the door. It smashed back with an explosive crash as he barreled into the room, his weapon aimed at the man. "Get back from her, now, you bastard, or you're dead," he growled, shaking inside, his arms steady as granite.

"Lex! Oh, God..." Tears poured down Jenna's face. She began shaking. Perez still lay lifeless in the far corner, blood congealing dark under her head, glistening in the lamplight.

The man swiftly pressed his blade to Jenna's neck. "Put the gun down," he ordered, a faint hint of Spanish accent coming out under stress. "Or I *will* cut her throat before you can squeeze off a shot."

Lex swallowed, the shaking inside turning his gut to jelly, but he remained calm on the outside—as controlled as he could possibly be. He stared into the man's eyes, dark-brown like Smythe's. "I brought the ring," he said quietly. "I have The Tears of the Quetzal. I think you want that diamond more than you want her."

Agitation rippled visibly through the man. He pressed the knife tighter against Jenna's throat, sweat glistening around his eyes. With his free hand he slid a handgun out from the back of his jeans and aimed it at Lex. "Put the ring and gun on the table."

"Easy, buddy. Release her first, and then you get the ring."

His eyes narrowed in his balaclava slit. "How'd you find me?

How'd you know to bring The Tears of the Quetzal? I didn't give you directions yet."

"I tracked Agent Perez's vehicle," Lex said coolly, forcing himself not to look at his partner lying in an unconscious heap in the corner. He needed to get her to a hospital. The seconds were ticking down, time running out. Yet he had to stretch time out perhaps until backup arrived, in order to save Jenna. Tension cinched like a vise inside Lex. "Now, why don't you step back, put your weapons down, and like I said, I will give you the ring."

"No, *you* put your gun down, and place the ring on the table."

Lex could hear the nerves increasing in the man's voice. Warning bells began to clang.

"That's not how it's going to work," said Lex. "And don't think of pulling that trigger, because you'll be a dead man before I even hit the ground."

The man pressed the blade of his knife tighter against Jenna's throat. She whimpered, shivering, half-naked, tears streaming all the way down her breasts now. Lex trembled with bottled rage inside.

"If you hurt her—" Lex said, voice ice cool, his mind racing and thinking of what Jenna told him about the death threats her father had hidden "—then I will kill you, and you will get nothing. No ring. No revenge for the old deed you mentioned in those notes to Harold Rothchild."

The man wavered.

Good, *this* was his guy, Smythe, and Lex had made a connection. "That's why you want the ring, isn't it? To fix some past wrong. The ring that is more important to you than the 'Rothchild trash,' am I right? You need that ring first. Without the ring, you have nothing."

The man's dark-brown eyes flickered. "Just…just put it on the table." The Spanish accent that had crept into his voice as tension and fear got to him was thickening. His hands were beginning to shake. The warning bells in the back of Lex's mind clanged louder.

"Something happened back in South America didn't it…an old deed that needs to be avenged?"

"The Rothchilds must pay!"

"Harold Rothchild? Or someone older perhaps? Like his father, Joseph Rothchild, maybe?"

Agitation suddenly grew very marked in the man. Sweat began to pool around his eyes. Big damp patches were forming under the arms of his black shirt. "Just put the damn ring on the table!"

"And if I do, what guarantee do I have that you won't do something stupid, like try to kill us both once you have The Tears of the Quetzal?" Lex kept repeating the name of the cursed stone. It clearly had an effect on Jenna's assailant.

The man's eyes darted to his right, and flicked back to the door. Lex followed his gaze, saw the trip wire. And another one. His heart began to slam. *Smythe had rigged the whole cabin.* This place was set to blow the minute he left here.

"Did you rig this place? Is that your plan?"

The man's eyes shot to the cell phone that lay on the table. So, thought Lex, that's probably how he was going to detonate his explosives once he'd left. Using the cell phone.

"Okay," Lex said slowly. "I'm going to put the ring down on the table now."

"Gun first."

"No. I keep my gun." Lex moved his hand to his pocket, and the guy got instantly jumpy, shoving his knife tight against Jenna's throat.

"Easy, buddy, I'm just reaching for the ring, okay?" Lex extracted his wallet from his pocket, leaned forward, placed it on the table. "It's in there."

"Take it out."

"No. You take it out."

The man's eyes were fixated on the wallet. His whole body began to shake with desperation to snatch the ring he believed was in the wallet. They were locked in a standoff now.

Then Lex heard it, the distant sound of approaching vehicles.

The man picked up the sound, too. Panic flared in his dark eyes behind the mask. And Lex saw him struggling mentally, pulled by the powerful lure of the ring. Abruptly the man swung his gun, fired at the lantern. The glass exploded, lantern flying back and clattering to the floor. The room went dark, small flames licking through spilled lantern fuel.

Lex saw the man lunge for the wallet and cell phone, but he couldn't risk shooting in the flickering shadows from this angle. Instead, he moved on instinct to block Jenna's body should the man fire.

Headlights suddenly illuminated the desert outside as FBI vehicles crested the distant ridge, and Lex saw the shadow of the assailant as he fled out the door. Flames were licking into dry wood, smoke filling the cabin. Lex quickly groped on the floor for the blade the man had dropped in his desperation to grab the ring, and he cut Jenna free. She collapsed into his arms. "Oh, thank God," she whispered, her face wet against his neck, her body soft and beautiful in his arms. "Jenna, you okay? Are you hurt anywhere?"

"I'm fine, but Perez—"

Lex moved quickly over to his partner's limp form, felt her neck. "She has a pulse! Get out there, Jenna! Tell them we need an ambulance. Bomb squad. And get as far away from this building as you can!"

Holding her ripped dress together, Jenna ran outside to warn the FBI team as Lex gathered Perez in his arms, and staggered out of the smoke-filled burning cabin.

It exploded behind him in a whoosh of orange, sparks brilliant in the desert sky. Fire began to crackle fiercely, and black smoke billowed up to blot the stars.

Lex stood in the dark desert with his arm around Jenna as they watched firefighters extinguish what was left of the blazing cabins. Jenna was wearing a tracksuit provided to her by a female member of the tactical response team, and had a blanket draped over her shoulders. Paramedics had checked her out, and crime scene techs had taken evidence from beneath her nails—she'd managed to gouge her assailant's neck as he'd fought to truss her up to the rafters.

Her attacker had, however, managed to slip like a ghost into the Nevada night. He was in for a small surprise when he learned there was no diamond in Lex's wallet.

Meanwhile, Epstein had been taken into custody, and Perez had been rushed to hospital after being stabilized on the scene.

"You think Rita is going to be okay?" Jenna said.

"I believe it with all my heart," said Lex. "The paramedics said she was lucky. The bullet just grazed her skull. She lost a lot of blood and received a bad concussion, but she was already starting to regain consciousness when the ambulance left." Too bad Perez hadn't managed to get a glimpse of her assailant, thought Lex. They had no definite proof it was Smythe.

Jenna slipped her arms around his waist, holding him so tight, like she never wanted to let him go. And Lex knew immediately what he must do—take her away. Get off the case. Get the hell out of Vegas until that maniac was caught.

Until his woman was safe.

He didn't care if it cost his job, his career, anything else, as long as he kept her.

Forever.

He was not going to allow Jenna out of his sight for a minute. His heart brimming with emotion—and purpose—Lex turned

to face her. Cupping the back of her neck, he threaded his
fingers up into her thick lustrous tangle of hair and tilted her
jaw up with his thumb. "Jenna, I may not have had The Tears
of the Quetzal on me, but I *do* have a diamond," he whispered.

"What…do you mean?"

"I can see it, in my mind. So real. Small—tiny in fact—
nothing like The Tears of Quetzal. But it's pure, Jenna. A tiny
faultless blue-white. As clean and real and enduring as I want
things to be for us. And when I do find that little stone, I…"
His voice caught. "I want you to wear it."

She stared up at him, eyes beginning to mist in the darkness.

"Will you, Jenna? Just try it on for size while you see if you
want to be my wife?"

He felt a small tremor shudder through her body. Tears
began streaming down her face again. "Lex—"

Worry wedged into his heart.

"Only while we try, Jenna. Promise me—"

"Lex," she whispered. "You're pumped on adrenaline,
anger…maybe…maybe this should wait until—"

"I don't need to wait."

"It's only been four days, how…how can you *possibly* be
sure?"

"I'm as sure, Jenna, as I was when that clock struck midnight
in the great Ruby Room, that I wanted nothing else but my
casino princess. But if you're not ready—" he hesitated, unsure
of what the hell he'd do if she said no.

"Oh, God, no I *am* ready, Lex. I've been waiting for you all
my life. I…I just didn't know it. I just couldn't believe that…
you…that you would want me."

"Is that a yes?"

She leaned up on tiptoe, met his lips with hers. "That, Agent
Duncan, would be a yes."

He kissed her, hard and fast and desperate in the thick desert night, and Jenna thought her heart would burst with sheer love. He'd freed her, come riding into her rarefied life like a knight in shining armor, and he'd shown her how to be real.

How to be true to the self she'd so long ago buried inside.

He'd given her herself.

Himself.

And the promise that came with a small true blue diamond— a future, together.

"Do you think it's true, Lex?" she whispered, lips burning from the raw possessive passion in his kiss.

"What?"

"The legend…the curse of The Tears of the Quetzal."

Lex laughed, feeling a strange tingling chill even as he did, recalling the words of the skydiver. "It's Vegas," he said softly. "Anything can happen here."

Even magic.

And he kissed her again under the desert stars, the quietly strobing lights of police vehicles nearby, the glow of a burning building.

And he'd never felt more centered. More whole. More at home, than with this woman in his arms. He'd found family. His own.

Epilogue

With Lex and Jenna off celebrating their engagement on a small and isolated Caribbean island with no electricity, no glitz, no glam—simple and real like they'd said they wanted it, Rita Perez had been asked to temporarily take over as lead agent on the Candace Rothchild homicide case.

Harold Rothchild's lawyers had cut a deal with the feds, handing over the notes he'd kept hidden from police, along with an earth-shattering old video of Frank Epstein brokering a mob deal back in the 1980s—evidence that would ultimately help the FBI dismantle the entire Epstein empire.

In turn, Rothchild's lawyers were seeking immunity for their client on other possible charges. It looked like Rothchild would walk free.

People with money got away with murder, thought Rita as she hung up her dishcloth, and put the last of her dinner dishes away. It also turned out that Rothchild's little trophy wife,

Rebecca Lynn, while acting suspiciously, had just been gunning for Jenna, insanely jealous of Harold's affection for his youngest daughter.

Mercedes Epstein, on the other hand, was in the hospital, the prognosis not good. But she had confessed to the murder of Tony Ciccone. And Frank Epstein, in trying to save his own neck, had given up everything he had on the dead Roman Markowitz. The 30-year-old cold case—Sara Duncan's homicide— was thus finally solved.

Epstein had also offered up the names of two contract killers who'd handled several jobs for Markowitz—including the murder of Marion Robb, aka Lucky Lady.

Rita flipped off the kitchen light, her head beginning to hurt again. Dinner with her niece Marisa and her man Patrick Moore had been wonderful, and Rita was real happy for Marisa, but she was worn out and needed sleep.

But before going to bed, she unlocked her gun safe and removed a small box. She just needed to see the contents just one more time.

Pulse quickening, Rita opened the box…and an ice-cold nausea swept into her chest.

The diamond was gone!

Rita stared at the empty box, her heart jackhammering, sweat forming over her body. She should never have brought The Tears of the Quetzal home. She couldn't even articulate why she'd done it, but she had.

She'd gone into that evidence room compelled by some strange force to take a look at the mysterious stone. And when she'd lifted the diamond out of the box and held it to the light, luminous shafts had darted out, picking up a rainbow of colors from green to gold to champagne. It had clean stolen her breath.

Along with her mind.

Overcome by a strangely powerful impulse, Rita had

slipped The Tears of the Quetzal into her pocket, locked the
door and gone home.

And now The Tears of the Quetzal was missing…

* * * * *

5 MINUTES TO MARRIAGE

BY
CARLA CASSIDY

Carla Cassidy is an award-winning author who has written more than fifty books. Carla believes the only thing better than curling up with a good book to read is sitting down at the computer with a good story to write. She's looking forward to writing many more books and bringing hours of pleasure to readers.

Prologue

He stood on the curb across the street from the casino with its glittering lights and flashy marquee, and the ball of hatred inside him expanded to make him half-breathless.

Harold Rothchild owned this casino, the same Harold Rothchild who had built his fortune on the destruction and blood of others, the same Harold who had destroyed his life.

A small smile curved his lips. Poor Harold's life had taken a turn for the worse. "And it's all because of me," he whispered to himself.

He'd killed Harold's daughter and he now had in his possession the invaluable Tears of the Quetzal diamond ring. He'd done everything he'd set out to do, but as he started at the grand entrance of the casino, he realized it wasn't enough.

That was the funny thing about revenge—just when you thought you'd achieved it, that gnawing hunger for more rose inside you.

He felt it now, burgeoning in his chest, and he clenched his hands into fists at his sides. Rage. It roared through him like a hot wind, stirring his need to inflict more pain, more heartache.

He wasn't through with the Rothchilds, not yet, not by a long shot. He wouldn't be through until Harold Rothchild and his family fell to their knees and wept for all they had lost.

Chapter 1

The evening began with such promise. The house was in order, the kids had been bathed and dressed in matching outfits and Jack Cortland was looking forward to his date.

He'd met Heidi Gray in the grocery store on one of his rare trips into town. The sophisticated, attractive blonde had smiled at him, and before they'd left the produce section, they'd made a date. Since that time they'd been out three times, and tonight was the first time she would meet his children.

Ten minutes before she was set to arrive, he sat down with his two sons on the sofa. Four-year-old

Mick sat on one side of him and three-year-old David was on the other.

"Now, boys, this is a really important night. I want you both to be on your best behavior and be nice to Miss Heidi when she gets here," he said.

"Heidi tighty whitey," Mick exclaimed.

"Heidi tighty whitey," David echoed, and the two broke into gales of laughter.

"Now, now, boys," Jack said in an effort to gain control, but it was too late. Their giggles increased in volume, and Jack sat and waited until finally they'd worn their giggles out.

"I do not want to hear you say that again," Jack said as firmly as possible.

David frowned at him. "Bad Jack," he said. "No yelling."

"I wasn't yelling," Jack protested, and then sighed. "Why don't the two of you go play in your room until our guest arrives."

He watched as they raced out of the living room and down the hallway toward the bedroom. When they disappeared out of sight, he released a sigh of exhaustion.

The boys had been in his custody for a little over four months, ever since their mother, his ex-wife, Candace, had been murdered. And in those months he'd realized they were undisciplined, wild and had absolutely zero respect for him.

Jack knew how to beat a rhythm on the drums to

stir the blood. He could sing the rock and roll that was in his soul. He knew how to entertain a stadium of fans with his music. There had been a time not so long ago when he'd also known how to drink and drug himself into oblivion, but he didn't know anything about parenting.

He pulled himself up from the sofa and went into the kitchen, where the delicious scents of pot roast wafted in the air. Betty, his cook, stood before the sink, washing the last of the dishes before she left for the day.

"Everything is done and in the oven waiting to go on the table," she said as she turned away from the sink and dried her hands on a towel.

"Sure you don't want to stick around?" Jack asked hopefully.

She gave him one of her dour gazes. "I told you when you hired me that I cook and that's it. I don't serve, I don't clean house and I definitely don't babysit." She grabbed her purse from the top of the counter. "I'll see you tomorrow morning, Mr. Cortland."

As she headed for the back door, Jack squashed the panic that threatened to rise in his chest. He told himself that the night was going to be a rousing success.

He wandered into the dining room, where Betty had set the table with the good dishes and linen napkins. It was probably a mistake to share the meal with both his date and his sons, but it was important to him that whatever woman he invited into his life knew that his sons were part of the package deal.

For a year following his divorce from Candace, Jack had rarely seen his sons. Candace has spent much of that year globe-trotting, and Jack had been in no condition, either financially or emotionally, to chase after her.

When Candace had been murdered the boys had come to live with him, but Jack knew Harold Rothchild, Candace's father, was just waiting for him to make a mistake so he could swoop in and take the boys away.

Jack's stomach tightened at the thought of Harold. There was no question the wealthy, powerful Las Vegas mogul wanted his grandsons, but the only way he could take custody away from Jack was to prove that he was an unfit father. Jack was doing everything in his power to make sure that didn't happen. He was determined to be the best father he could be.

The doorbell rang, signaling the arrival of Heidi, and Jack hurried to the door to welcome her. From the direction of the bedroom came the sounds of the boys laughing, and once again he mentally muttered a prayer that the evening went well.

The first thirty minutes were relatively successful. On their previous dates Jack had found Heidi to be a good conversationalist, and it didn't hurt that she was jaw-droppingly gorgeous. He was male enough to enjoy the scent of her perfume in the air and the hint of cleavage that her V-neck blouse offered him.

After a brief introduction to the boys, they returned to playing in their room, giving Jack and Heidi time alone.

When it was time to move into the dining room for the meal, there were several minutes of chaos as Jack got the boys settled in their booster seats at the table, then hurried into the kitchen to bring out the meal that Betty had prepared.

Pot roast and potatoes, broccoli florets with cheese, homemade dinner rolls and a Jell-O salad all went to the table, and after filling the boys' plates, Jack returned to his seat.

"This looks yummy," Heidi said. "Did you do all this?"

"I wish I could take credit for it, but no. I have a local woman who comes in to cook for us." He smiled at her, then blinked as a piece of cheesy broccoli smacked her chest and slowly slid downward before falling into the vee of her blouse.

Mick giggled.

Jack stared at his son in horror. "Mick!" He turned back to Heidi. "I'm so sorry."

Another cheese-covered floret struck her in the head, and this time it was David who laughed uproariously. Suddenly the broccoli was flying and

Jack was yelling. Heidi jumped up from the table in an effort to escape the onslaught of food, her features tight with aggravation.

"Mick, David! Stop it right now," Jack exclaimed.

"Bad Jack," Mick yelled.

"I'm out of here," Heidi exclaimed. "I wasn't sure that I was at a place in my life to be an instant mother, and now I know the answer. I'm definitely not ready for this. Your children are undisciplined little boys, and you all need more than I can offer." She grabbed her purse and marched out of the dining room. Jack ran after her, muttering apologies that she obviously didn't want to hear.

As she slammed out of the front door, Jack leaned against the wall and closed his eyes. She was right. His boys were unruly animals, and he didn't know what to do about it, but something had to be done.

He could just see the tabloid headlines now: "Rock Star Children Belong in a Zoo." He hoped Heidi wasn't the type to cash in by selling the tale of the evening to the tabloids.

By ten that evening the boys had finally fallen asleep, David on the living-room floor and Mick on the sofa. Jack carried them into their room and put them into their beds, then returned to the living room and called his lifelong buddy, Kent Goodall.

Within fifteen minutes Kent was at the house and the two men were seated at the kitchen table sipping coffee as Jack told Kent about the disastrous date.

"I need help," Jack said. "Heidi was right. The boys are out of control, and I don't know how to fix things."

Kent swept a strand of his long blond hair behind one pierced ear. "I know a woman, a professional nanny. Her name is Marisa Perez, and she lives right here in Las Vegas."

"How do you know her?" Jack asked. Kent had no children. He wasn't even married.

"Remember the woman I dated? Ramona with the big hair and bigger chest? She's a friend of Marisa's. Last I heard Marisa was saving money to open up her own nanny agency."

Jack frowned. He didn't want to just invite anyone into his home and into the lives of his sons. As he recalled, Ramona with the big hair also had a pea brain. She'd been working as a showgirl in one of the casinos. He wasn't sure being a friend to Ramona was necessarily a good qualification for interacting with his children.

"I'm not sure Ramona vouching for somebody makes me comfortable," he finally said.

Kent grinned. "Trust me, I hear you, but it wouldn't hurt for you to interview Marisa and see if she's everything Ramona said she was. I'll call Ramona and get her number for you."

Jack wrapped his hands around his coffee mug and nodded. "I have to do something. If Harold gets wind of how badly I'm mangling the parenting stuff, he'll have me back in court fighting for custody." A painful knot formed in Jack's chest as he thought of the possibility of losing his boys.

For the next few minutes the men talked music and bands. When Kent and Jack had been teenagers, they'd formed a band that had played local clubs and at weddings. The band had been successful on a regional level, but Jack had hungered for more.

At the age of twenty-two he'd left Las Vegas for Los Angeles and eventually had hooked up with a group of musicians who had become the rock band Creation.

While Jack had ridden the rise of fame and fortune, then eventually crashed and burned, Kent had remained in Las Vegas with his band members, playing local gigs whenever they could get them.

It was after midnight when Kent finally left, and Jack had finished clearing the dishes from the dining-room table.

When he was finished he went down the hallway toward the bedrooms. The first one he stopped in was the boys' bedroom, and he stood in the doorway and stared at his sons.

Mick slept on his side, his legs and arms curled into a fetal position. David lay sprawled on his back, arms and legs thrown to his sides as if he'd fallen asleep in the middle of a leap off a building.

A surge of tenderness flowed through him as he watched them sleep. The love he felt for his sons was like nothing he'd ever experienced before.

Although he didn't want to think ill of the dead, Candace had possessed the maternal instincts of a rock. Jack had hoped that the birth of the boys would somehow domesticate the wild, beautiful woman he'd married—and for a while it had worked. But it didn't take long for the novelty of motherhood to wear off and for their marriage to self-destruct.

The boys had so many strikes against them. A mother who had been murdered and a father who was a recovering addict and knew nothing about being a dad.

They needed somebody else in their life, a nanny who could teach them how to be good boys—and the sooner the better.

"You are stupid to even consider this," Marisa Perez said aloud to herself as she drove down the dusty Nevada road in the direction of Jack Cortland's ranch.

He'd called her earlier that morning and asked her about her services as a nanny. Against her better judgment she'd agreed to meet with him at his house.

It had been big news when Jack had moved back to his family home two years ago following a very public divorce from Candace Rothchild.

For years Jack and Candace had been a favorite topic of gossip in the tabloids. Their lifestyle of excess and drugs and alcohol had been legendary.

The public had loved stories of the hard-rock star and his beautiful heiress wife.

From everything Marisa knew about Jack Cortland, she was not impressed. She glanced out her side window, passing land that her parents probably owned.

Like Candace, Marisa had come from wealth, but unlike Candace, Marisa had decided early on that she wanted to make her own way. She didn't want to work for the family in their real estate ventures. What she loved was working with children.

She tightened her grip on the steering wheel as she turned into the long, dusty driveway that led to the Cortland ranch.

This visit was more to satisfy her curiosity than for any other reason. Since moving back here Jack had kept a low profile, rarely being seen out of his home.

She'd read the stories about Candace's tragic murder and knew there were two little boys in Jack's custody. More than anything she'd been driven to come out here to check on those boys.

She might not think much of Jack Cortland as a person, but he had a low, deep voice that could weaken the knees of a soldier. After talking to him on the phone that morning, it had taken her several minutes to get that sexy voice out of her head.

The farmhouse came into view, and as she pulled up front and parked, she saw a towheaded tot wearing only a diaper racing across the grass and heading toward a large barn in the distance.

Marisa turned off her engine and expected at any moment some adult to come running out of the house to collect the child. When that didn't immediately happen, she jumped out of her car and hurried toward the little tot.

"Hi," she said when she caught up with him.

He stopped and smiled at her, and her heart crunched in her chest. He looked like a little angel with his pale hair and bright blue eyes. "Hi," he replied.

"What's your name?" she asked.

"David." He glanced toward the barn, as if eager to be on his way.

"I'm Marisa. You want to play a game?" His eyes lit up and he nodded. "Do you know how to jump on one foot?" He nodded again and began to jump up and down. "Let's see who can jump on one foot all the way to the house."

He took off, alternately hopping and running. Marisa followed after him, silently seething over the fact that a baby was outside alone with no adult supervision in sight.

David's laughter rang in the air as he hurried toward the house with Marisa at his heels. They had just reached the porch when the front door exploded open and Jack Cortland flew outside.

His gray eyes were wide with alarm as he took

the stairs of the porch two at a time. "David! Thank God." He grabbed the boy up in his arms, then stared at Marisa, panic still gleaming in his eyes.

She said nothing, merely stood drinking in the sight of the infamous Jack. She'd expected a man who looked dissipated, a man with sallow skin and the lines of debauchery slashed deep in his face. Instead his dark hair gleamed richly in the overhead sunshine. He sported a healthy tan and arm muscles that looked as if he wasn't a stranger to hard work.

He was hot…and for just a few seconds, Marisa forgot what she was doing here. It was only when David squealed in protest and struggled to get out of his father's arms that her brain reengaged.

"I'd say you have a problem with basic safety issues," she said.

"He's Houdini reincarnated," Jack said with obvious frustration. "I assume you're Marisa?" She gave him a brief nod, and he gestured her toward the front door. "Welcome to the zoo."

"I need to get some things from my car," she said. "I jumped out when I saw David racing across the grass and no adult in sight." She couldn't keep the thick disapproval from her voice.

"I didn't know he'd escaped," he replied with a grimace. "Get whatever you need and come on in." He didn't wait for her reply, but instead disappeared into the house.

Marisa headed back to her car and tried to still the

crazy butterflies that had gone dancing in her stomach at the sight of him. She couldn't remember when just looking at a man had caused such a visceral reaction. Certainly when she'd first met Patrick she hadn't felt the burst of heat that the sight of Jack had evoked.

The man was a mess, she reminded herself as she grabbed her purse and briefcase from the passenger seat.

Still, as she headed toward the front door she steeled herself against his obvious attractiveness. She was here to contemplate a job and nothing more. She had a boyfriend, her life was on track and the last thing she needed was for some thirty-year-old drummer with a disastrous history rocking her world.

She swept through the front door and into a small entry and then into a large living room that was obviously the heart of the house.

Jack stood in the center of the room, which was littered with toys and kids' clothes and had the faint scent of a dirty diaper. The boys were wrestling on the floor, and as Jack looked at her, once again his soft gray eyes held an appeal. "I need help."

She felt her resolve not to get involved fading away. He looked so utterly helpless in the midst of the chaos. "Is there someplace we can sit and chat?" she asked.

"Boys, why don't you go to your room and play," Jack said.

David jumped up and smiled at Marisa. "Watch," he said, then hopped on one foot down the hallway. The other boy followed his brother, and the two of them disappeared from view.

Jack swept a handful of blocks and toy trucks off the sofa and gestured her to have a seat. Then he sat in the chair opposite the sofa.

"I've had the boys in my custody for almost four months," he said. "They came to me undisciplined and wild, and as you can see, I haven't managed to change things much in the time that I've had them."

"Exactly what are you looking for from me, Mr. Cortland?" she asked.

"Jack, please make it Jack." He smiled, but the gesture didn't quite erase the worry from his eyes. "Isn't it obvious that I need somebody to train the boys and to teach them how to behave?"

Marisa didn't think Jack was ready to hear that. In her experience it was usually the parents who needed training, not the children.

At the moment she saw nothing of the hard-rock star. What she saw was a concerned father worried about his sons. She held on to her heart. There was something about Jack Cortland that made her think that if she allowed it, it would take about five minutes for her to fall crazy in love with him.

But of course she wouldn't allow it. She wasn't even sure she was going to take this job. Just because Jack had beautiful gray eyes fringed with sinfully long lashes, just because he had lips that looked as if they could drive a woman wild didn't mean she was eager to work as a nanny for him.

She opened her briefcase and pulled out a sheath of papers. "Here are my credentials and references," she said as she held them out toward him.

He waved his hand in the air. "Trust me, I've already checked you out, Ms. Perez. I wasn't about to allow just anyone into my home with my boys." He shot her a level gaze. "You graduated from college with a degree in early childhood education. You're twenty-seven years old, live alone and you're particularly close to your aunt Rita, who has worked as an FBI agent for the last twenty years."

Marisa raised an eyebrow. "Please, call me Marisa," she said, impressed by the fact that he'd done his homework where she was concerned. "How many other people do you have working for you here in the home?" she asked. "I need to know who the children interact with on a daily basis."

"I have a cook who comes in the morning and leaves right after she fixes the evening meal. Other than that, it's pretty much just me. The nanny Candace had used for the boys got another job."

"No housekeeper?" she asked.

One corner of his mouth turned up in a rueful grin as he looked pointedly around the room. "If I had a housekeeper, I would have definitely fired her by now."

"You understand this would be a live-in position," she said.

"There's a spare bedroom across from the boys' room. You'd have your own private bath and of course free access to the rest of the house." He leaned forward in his chair. "Tell me you'll take the job, Marisa. You have no idea how important this is to me."

But she did see how important it was to him. A frantic desperation shone from his eyes, something that looked remarkably like fear.

There was more going on here than just his need for her to teach the boys to be well-behaved. She was definitely intrigued.

The fee she collected from this job would put the final dollars in her bank account that she needed to start her business, but she had no idea how far Jack had come from the bad-boy rocker he had once been. Was this really a man she wanted to work for?

"Okay," she heard herself saying before she even knew she'd made a conscious decision. "But I have a condition."

"Just name it," he exclaimed.

"We agree to a weeklong probationary period. If at the end of that week you wish to terminate me, or I decide to leave, then you pay me for the week and I'm on my way. At the end of that week if we're both agreeable, then I have a contract to sign that will assure me two months here."

"Just two months?" he asked.

"I'm a troubleshooter. I only work temporary positions. If you're looking for somebody for long-term, then when I finish my two months I'll help you hire somebody for a permanent position."

"Sounds reasonable to me. When can you start?"

"Tomorrow morning around nine?"

"Perfect," he said with a sigh of relief. She stood and so did he.

She was far too aware of him just behind her as she walked back to the front door. She turned back to him, finding him standing ridiculously close to her. The scent of him washed over her, a clean scent coupled with the faint remnants of a spicy cologne.

She stepped back, her breath catching in her chest as that crazy surge of heat swept through her. He held out his hand, and she stared at it for a long moment, almost afraid to touch him, afraid of how that touch might make her feel.

"I'll see you in the morning," she said as he awkwardly dropped his hand to his side. She flew out the door and hurried toward her car.

Dear God, what was wrong with her? She was acting like some silly, empty-headed fan—and she hadn't even liked his music or his band.

She was doing this strictly for the kids. It was obvious they needed some loving attention and a firm hand. Still, as she thought about moving into

Jack Cortland's home the next morning, she couldn't help feeling that it might just be the biggest mistake she'd ever made in her life.

Chapter 2

"What's he like?" Marisa's aunt Rita asked. Rita had invited Marisa and Marisa's current boyfriend, Patrick Moore, for dinner that evening. They were all seated around the dining table in Rita's apartment.

Marisa picked up her glass of ice water, as if needing the cold against her skin as she talked about Jack Cortland. "Desperate," she replied. "The little boys are a mess and from all appearances are the ones running things."

"I still don't like it," Patrick exclaimed. "That man has a terrible reputation. I don't like the idea of you living in that house with him."

Marisa smiled at the handsome man across from her at the table. "Initially it's just for a week. If I see behavior that makes me uncomfortable, then after that week I'll be done."

There were times she thought Patrick was too good to be true. Not only was he incredibly handsome and charming but he also had a good job as an accountant and seemed to have fallen head over heels in love with her.

They'd been dating only a couple of weeks, but Patrick had already made it clear that he believed she was the woman he wanted to spend the rest of his life with.

Although Marisa liked him a great deal, she wasn't about to fall into a hot, passionate affair with a man she'd been dating only a brief time. She'd done that once before in her life, and the results had been devastating.

She took a sip of her water and wondered why thoughts of a hot affair automatically brought a vision of Jack to her mind.

"I was a fan of Jack's band for a while," Patrick said. "Creation did some awesome songs, but once he married Candace Rothchild the band seemed to go straight downhill."

"Such a shame about her," Marisa said. She looked at her aunt. "You were working that murder case for a while, weren't you?"

"Still am," Rita replied. "Unfortunately, there

aren't many leads to follow." Rita shook her head. "I can't imagine having to bury a child, even a child who was thirty years old at the time of her murder."

"It doesn't seem to have slowed down her father. What's he on now—his third or fourth wife?" Patrick asked.

"Third wife," Rita replied. "This current one is a former showgirl considerably younger than him. Rumor has it that the thrill is gone and the marriage is in trouble."

"I'm sorry that Harold lost a daughter, but I'm even sorrier that David and Mick lost their mother," Marisa said.

Patrick smiled ruefully. "From all accounts, she wasn't much of a mother."

"I know, but I still feel bad for those little boys," Marisa replied.

"Just don't get too emotionally involved," Rita said with a gentle smile.

Marisa laughed. "Aunt Rita, I've been a nanny for quite some time now. I know how to separate myself from my little charges. I never lose track of the fact that I'm only in their lives temporarily."

Rita was the only person on the face of the earth who knew what had happened to Marisa in college. Eventually if she and Patrick decided to marry, she'd have to tell him before any vows were exchanged. But it was far too early in their relationship for deep, dark secrets to be exposed.

The rest of the dinner was pleasant, and when they were finished Patrick excused himself from the table and disappeared down the hallway toward the bathroom while Marisa and Rita began to clear the table.

"I like him," Rita said as she rinsed off one of the dinner plates. This was only the second time Patrick and Rita had shared any real quality time together. Rita had entertained them over dinner a week earlier.

"He is great, isn't he?" Marisa handed her another plate. "He couldn't wait to get to know you better. He knows how important you are to me."

Although Marisa's parents were lovely people, they'd never really understood their daughter's desire to make her own way in the world rather than follow them into the very lucrative family real estate business.

Marisa had always been particularly close to her father's sister, Rita. It had been Rita who Marisa had confided in when her world had fallen apart in college.

"How are you doing?" Marisa asked and gestured to the bandage on the side of Rita's head. She and Jenna Rothchild had been kidnapped, and Rita had suffered a gunshot wound to the head. It had rendered her unconscious, and although she and Jenna had managed to get away neither of them had been able to identify the man responsible or why they had been kidnapped in the first place.

"I'm okay—a little headache now and then, but that's all," Rita replied. "You're taking things slow with Patrick?"

"Absolutely. I want to marry once in my life. I'm not about to jump into anything too intense too fast."

Rita smiled. "I think Patrick has other ideas. He seems quite smitten with you."

At that moment he walked back into the kitchen and any further conversation with him as the topic halted.

After cleaning up the kitchen, the three of them moved into the living room where the conversation revolved around Las Vegas life, Patrick's work and a new casino that had opened in town. Rita never discussed her work, but she was a charming hostess who kept the conversation flowing until Patrick and Marisa decided to call it a night.

It was just after nine when Patrick pulled up in front of the small house Marisa rented. "I like your aunt," he said.

"She liked you, too," Marisa replied.

"What's not to like?" He flashed her a bright smile.

"I'd invite you in, but I really want to get a good night's sleep before the morning," she said as he parked the car.

"Am I going to see you at all over the next week?" he asked.

"Probably not," Marisa admitted. "The first week

in a new position is always pretty intense. But it's just for a week, Patrick." She opened the passenger door and got out.

Patrick got out of the car as well and fell into step next to her. He grabbed her hand in his as they walked to her front porch. "And what happens after the first week? What if you take the position for the next couple months? Does that mean I won't be able to see you the whole time?"

She disentangled her hand from his to reach into her purse for her keys. "Not at all. If Jack Cortland and I agree that he needs my services for that long, then I always make sure I have most weekends off."

She unlocked her door then turned back to face him. "Good night, Patrick." She reached up and kissed him on his smooth cheek, but he quickly pulled her into his arms for a real kiss.

It was pleasant, but it didn't curl her toes or weaken her knees. When the kiss ended he reluctantly released her. "Then I guess I'll see you in a week or so?"

"I'll call you and let you know how things are going," she replied.

"You know I'll be waiting for your calls," he replied.

She watched as he walked back to his car. He was a man who could easily turn female heads. Tall and slim, with the dark features of his Hispanic heritage, he always dressed with an understated elegance and looked both handsome and successful.

Minutes later as she undressed in her bedroom she thought of that kiss and Patrick. Maybe one of the reasons she was attracted to Patrick was because there weren't wild fireworks when they kissed, there wasn't that sizzle that came from a simple touch and the breathlessness of a mere glance.

She'd experienced that crazy hot passion once in her life and never wanted it again. It had destroyed her life, and the thought of feeling that way again frightened her.

She pulled her red silk nightgown over her head, turned out the light and crawled into bed. Maybe real love was just that faint warmth that filled her when Patrick smiled at her or the quiet friendship they were building together.

She frowned as she thought of Jack Cortland. So what was it about him that had caused that sizzle inside her? Why did a man she had little respect for, given his past, fill her with a wild sense of anticipation at the very thought of seeing him again?

Jack worked until almost three in the morning cleaning the house. The boys had finally fallen asleep around eleven. He'd moved them into their bedroom, then had tackled the living room with a vengeance.

Toys went back into the boys' room, dirty plates and cups carried back to the kitchen. He polished and washed and vacuumed until the room looked presentable. Then he went into the guest room that Marisa would call home and cleaned it as well.

It had needed to be done for the past couple months, but the days were so full with keeping the boys occupied and trying to oversee the work being done on the ranch. By the time the boys fell asleep at night Jack was comatose, and cleaning was the last thing on his mind.

He'd considered hiring more help but had put it off, hoping to get the boys better acclimated to him before bringing other people into their lives.

When he finally fell into bed he thought sleep would come quickly, but instead he found himself thinking of Marisa Perez.

He hadn't expected her to be so sexy. Even though he'd known before he'd met her that she was twenty-seven years old, he'd expected a maternal type, someone who was overweight and not particularly attractive.

Marisa had been more than attractive. Her long, dark brown hair had sparkled with honey highlights and dark, sexy lashes fringed her large chocolate brown eyes. She had the bone structure of a model, but her body wasn't model thin; rather, it was lush with curves in all the right places.

He'd eventually fallen asleep and dreamed of her…and in those dreams she'd been soft and yielding in his arms. Her kisses had stirred him like none had ever done.

He awoke at dawn and hurried into the shower, eager to get dressed and maybe choke down a cup of coffee before the boys awoke.

Betty wouldn't arrive for another hour so he made the coffee, poured himself a cup and sat at the table, trying not to remember the dreams that had bordered on downright erotic.

He breathed in the peace and quiet of the morning and stared out the window where his herd of cattle grazed on whatever vegetation they could find in the hard, dry earth.

His father had raised cattle here, as had his father before him. Jack's dad had wanted Jack to follow in his footsteps, to take over the ranch and continue producing quality cattle. He'd wanted Jack to live by the values they'd tried to teach him instead of the ones Jack had learned on his way to fame and fortune.

It would always grieve Jack that both his parents had died before he had returned here. Worse than that, he suspected that they had died brokenhearted by the bad choices their son had made in his life as a rock star.

He wouldn't make the same mistakes now. He wanted his boys to grow up and be proud of him. He wanted to give them a solid foundation of love and good values. More than anything he wanted to be the man his parents had known that he could be.

By eight-thirty Jack looked forward to the arrival

of Marisa. The boys had been fed their breakfast and were dressed in clean clothes.

The living room was still relatively clean, and the boys were playing quietly with their trucks in the middle of the floor.

Jack was grateful that he was going to get some parenting tips from Marisa, but he also recognized that his interest in her wasn't solely that of a father needing help with his kids.

It had been a man's interest that had kept him awake the night before, and it had been a shocking desire for her that had filled his dreams, reminding him that he'd been alone for a very long time.

At exactly nine o'clock his doorbell rang and he hurried to greet her, surprised that his heart was pumping harder than it had in months.

He opened the door, and she offered him a bright smile that made him believe that this was going to be a very fine day. "Good morning, come on in."

As she walked past him into the living room he caught her scent, a floral spice that seemed to shoot right to his brain. "What a pleasant surprise," she said. "You've cleaned."

He gave her a sheepish grin. "I didn't realize how bad things had gotten until I saw them through your eyes. Here, let me take that." He gestured to the suitcase she held in her hand. "I'll just take it to your room."

"Thanks," she replied.

He took the case and hurried down the hall. When he returned she was in the middle of the floor with David and Mick. The boys were showing her the trucks that were their favorite toys.

"So how does this work?" he asked. "You just teach them what they need to do?"

She smiled and rose from the floor with a sinuous grace. "It's not quite that easy, Jack. What I'd like to do this morning is just kind of sit back and observe what would be a normal morning for you and the boys. Then at lunch we'll sit down with a game plan."

"Oh, okay." He shoved his hands in his jeans pockets and stared down at his sons, then back at her. "All of a sudden I'm feeling very self-conscious," he admitted.

At that moment Mick hit David with one of the trucks, and within seconds both boys were crying and Jack was yelling. He grabbed Mick up into his arms. "You don't hit, Mick. That's not nice."

"Bad Jack," Mick cried and wiggled to get out of his arms.

"Bad Jack," David yelled, obviously forgetting that it was his brother, not his father, who had hit him in the head.

"Both of you go to your room," Jack exclaimed as he set Mick back on his feet. "Go on. You're both in trouble."

As the boys went running down the hallway, Jack

slicked a hand through his hair in frustration then looked at Marisa. "I handled that badly, right?"

"We'll talk at lunch," she said, her beautiful features giving nothing away of her emotions.

The morning passed excruciatingly slow for Jack. The boys seemed to be on their worst behavior, and he was overly conscious of Marisa watching his every move.

Then, right before lunchtime, while he was in the bathroom with Mick, David climbed through the window in his bedroom and snuck out of the house. As soon as he realized what had happened, Jack raced down the front porch to grab David. Marisa and Mick stood in the doorway and watched him.

Jack was exhausted and his patience was wearing thin. He hadn't hired the lovely nanny to stand around and observe. She was supposed to be fixing things, not watching from the sidelines.

When Betty announced that lunch was ready, Jack had never been so happy for a meal. He set the boys in their booster seats at the dining-room table then gestured Marisa into the chair opposite his as he introduced her to the cook.

"About time you did something," she said to Jack, then glared at Marisa. "I don't babysit, and I don't clean. I don't leave this kitchen except to serve the breakfast and lunch meals. I don't serve dinner. I just cook. That's all I do."

"That's good to know," Marisa replied with a friendly smile. Betty harrumphed and disappeared back into the kitchen.

"I pay her for her cooking skills, not her sparkling personality," Jack said with a dry chuckle.

Marisa laughed, and the sound of her laughter filled a space in him that had been silent for a very long time.

He couldn't remember the last time he'd shared any laughter with anyone. For the past couple months everything had been so tense; the stakes had been so incredibly high.

"One of the first things we need to address is David's ability to escape out any door and window," she said. David smiled at her, his mouth smeared with mustard from his ham sandwich. "You need to purchase childproof locks for every door," she continued.

"I agree. It's only been in the past week or so that he's developed this new skill," Jack replied.

The afternoon sun drifting through the window played on those golden highlights in her hair, making it look incredibly soft and touchable. Her lipstick had worn off by midmorning, but she had naturally plump, rosy lips that he found incredibly sexy.

"What's bedtime like?" she asked.

"Bedtime?" Memories of the visions he'd had of her the night before in his sleep exploded in his head, and he felt a warm wave seep through his veins.

"Do the boys have a regular bedtime?"

He shoved the visions away. "It's regular in that their bedtime is whenever they fall asleep."

"And they fall asleep in their beds?"

"They sleep wherever they happen to fall," he replied.

"They're bright, beautiful boys," she said.

Her words swelled a ball of pride in his chest. "Thanks. I just want them to be good boys as well."

"Good boys," David quipped and nodded his head with an angelic smile, then threw a potato chip in Jack's direction.

After lunch the boys played for a little while, then both of them fell asleep on the floor. Jack carried each of them into their room, put them in bed for their afternoon nap and then returned to where Marisa sat on the sofa.

He sat on the opposite end from her, close enough that he could smell the enticing scent of her perfume. "They should sleep for about an hour," he said.

"What's in the barn?"

He blinked at the question that seemed to come out of nowhere. "What?"

"Both times David got out of the house he was heading for the barn. What's inside?"

"A small recording studio, memorabilia from my old band, my drum set." He shrugged. "My past."

"You miss it?" she asked.

He considered the question before immediately replying. "Some of it," he admitted. "I miss making music, but I don't miss everything that came with it. Why do you ask?"

Her dark eyes considered him thoughtfully. "I need to know that you're in this for the long haul, that the number one priority in your life is your boys. I don't want to spend a month or two of my time helping you here only to have you decide fatherhood is too boring and you'd rather be out on the road making music."

There was a touch of censure in her voice that stirred a hint of irritation inside him. "Nothing in my life means more to me than David and Mick. When Candace and I divorced I rarely got to see the boys. Usually the only time I saw them or heard about them was if they were mentioned in an article in a tabloid." He exhaled sharply. "I'm sorry Candace is dead, but I'm glad the boys are with me now—and I intend to do right by them not just for a month or two but for the rest of their lives."

Warmth leaped into her eyes, and that warmth shot straight into the pit of his stomach. He couldn't remember the last time a woman had affected him so intensely. He wanted to reach out and tangle his hands in her long hair. He wanted to press his lips against hers and taste her.

"It's not going to be easy to turn things around here," she warned.

He smiled. "Over the past couple of years I've fought some pretty strong personal demons. Two little boys aren't going to get the best of me."

"'Bad Jack.' Where did they learn that?"

Jack's smile fell and he frowned instead. "I suppose from Candace. They refuse to call me anything but that."

She leaned back against the cushion. "I hate to tell you this, Jack, but what we need to work on most is your behavior. Those boys are crying out for positive attention and boundaries."

"I'm game," he replied.

"Good." She stood. "I'm going to go unload some things from my car."

He jumped up. "Need help?"

"No, I can handle it." Her eyes twinkled with humor. "Besides, you'd better save your strength. You're going to need it."

He followed her to the front door and watched as she went down the stairs, her hips swaying invitingly beneath the navy slacks she wore.

The background check he'd done on her had told him a lot of things about her, but it hadn't told him what he wanted to know at this moment.

Did she have a boyfriend? Was she in some kind of a committed relationship? Would he be a total fool to get involved with the woman he'd hired as a nanny?

He scoffed at his own thoughts. He'd be a real fool to think that a woman like Marisa would have any interest in a man like him. He was nothing but a washed-up rocker who she'd already seen as useless and ineffectual.

She was bright and beautiful and he could want her, but it was a desire he didn't intend to follow through on. She was here for his boys and that was enough for him…it had to be enough.

Chapter 3

As the day wore on Marisa told herself again and again that she was here for David and Mick and nothing more.

She could not allow herself to get caught up in her overwhelming attraction to Jack. She refused to allow herself to admit that she liked him. Still, she could admire the man he was now despite the fact that she had a feeling she would have disrespected the man he had once been.

During the afternoon she met Kent Goodall, who was one of Jack's closest friends. He was a tall, blond man who told her he used to play bass in a band with Jack when they'd been teenagers. He was affable but didn't stay long.

She also met the two ranch hands who worked for Jack. Sam and Max Burrow were brothers who had the dark leathery skin of men who had spent their entire lives out in the elements. They appeared quiet and uncomfortable as they stepped into the kitchen through the back door.

Sam had been sent to town to pick up childproof locks for the windows and doors in the house. Once he gave them to Jack the two disappeared back outside.

As Jack put them on, Marisa sat with the boys on the sofa and read them a story. David snuggled next to her on one side and Mick on the other. She had already lost her heart to the boys, who were definitely rambunctious but also responding to her gentle guidance.

It was at bedtime that things got wild as Marisa instructed Jack to put the boys to bed in their room. Every few minutes the boys came out of the bedroom and Jack carried them back in and tucked them in once again.

The boys screamed and cried, and Jack shot Marisa frustrated looks as he carried them back to their beds. It was after one in the morning when he returned from their bedroom and flopped on the sofa. Silence reigned.

"It will be easier tomorrow night," she said.

He scowled at her. "I hope that's a promise."

She smiled. "I forgot to mention that there are

going to be moments in this process when you'll probably hate me."

His scowl lifted, and he offered her a sexy half grin that ripped at her heart. "I'm not mad at you. I'm mad at myself for not doing this when I first got them here." His smile fell, and he gazed at her curiously. "Why aren't you married with a dozen kids of your own? It's obvious you love children."

The question pierced through her, bringing forth a longing that she knew would never really be satisfied. "I'm young. I have plenty of time for all that in the future," she replied airily.

"Are you seeing somebody?"

She nodded. "Yes, I have somebody I'm seeing." She needed to let him know that, but she also needed to remind herself. Patrick. Patrick was the man in her life at the moment and she definitely needed to remember that.

She stood, suddenly needing to escape from Jack. "Time to call it a night," she said. "Tomorrow is a brand-new day."

He got up as well, and together they walked down the hallway toward the bedrooms. "You'll let me know if you need anything?" he asked as they stopped in front of the room where she'd be staying.

"I'm sure I'll be fine," she replied. She released a soft gasp as he reached out and grabbed one of her hands.

"I just want to tell you how glad I am that you're

here," he murmured huskily. "You have no idea how grateful I am."

Those crazy butterflies winged through her stomach, and she pulled her hand from his, uncomfortable by the way his touch made her feel.

"Good night, Jack." She escaped into the bedroom and closed the door behind her.

What on earth was wrong with her? She had to get hold of herself and stop thinking about Jack as a man rather than a client.

She moved into the bathroom to get ready for bed. Her attraction to him wasn't just a physical one. There had been moments in the day when she'd sensed a deep loneliness inside him—one that had called to something deep inside her.

She was intrigued as well. There was a desperation about him that went far beyond a father concerned with his sons' behavior.

The light of dawn awoke her the next morning, but she remained in bed for several long minutes, going over the things she intended to accomplish that day.

She wondered why Jack hadn't already hired a nanny or a babysitter for the kids. Surely he needed to be outside doing things to keep the ranch running smoothly.

For the past four months, since the boys first came here, his life had been on hold, and it showed in the stress lines on his face when he dealt with the boys. He was muddling through parenthood, but he wasn't having any fun.

It was forty-five minutes later when she left her bedroom, freshly showered and dressed in a pair of jeans and a coral-colored tank top.

The house was quiet, but the scent of fresh brewed coffee led her through the house and to the kitchen. Jack was there, seated at the kitchen table as he stared out the window.

He didn't see her, and for a moment she simply stood in the doorway and looked at him. Once again she was struck by the sense of loneliness that clung to him. This man had once had thousands of adoring fans, but at the moment he simply looked like a man in over his head and so achingly alone.

"Good morning," she said as she walked into the room. She waved him down as he started to stand. "Just point me to the coffee cups and I can help myself."

He pointed to a nearby cabinet. "Did you sleep well?"

"Like a baby," she said as she poured herself a cup of coffee. She joined him at the table and tried to ignore the kick of pleasure she felt at the sight of him.

He was dressed in a pair of jeans and a gray T-shirt that enhanced the gunmetal hue of his eyes. His jaw was smooth-shaven, and his hair was still damp from a shower.

"What time does Betty usually get here?" she asked.

"She doesn't work on the weekends, so we're on our own for today and tomorrow. Meals are usually as easy as possible on Saturdays and Sundays."

"This morning I'd like to have breakfast alone with the boys," she said. "You can take an hour or two and go outside to chase a cow or ride the range or whatever you need to do."

"Really?" He sat back in his chair and looked at her in surprise.

She smiled. "Really." She took a sip of coffee and then continued. "Jack, you need to relax a bit. You're so tense when you're around the boys, and I think they're picking up on that. What you need to do is enjoy the process of raising them. You need to have fun with them."

He looked at her as if she were speaking a foreign language. "Fun?"

She laughed. "Remember fun, Jack?"

He smiled ruefully. "Actually, I don't remember it."

"That's what I'm going to bring back to your life, but I have to warn you things are going to get a little tough around here for the next couple days. You'd better enjoy your morning because there are going to be times you won't know who you want to strangle more—me or the kids."

He laughed. "I can't imagine that."

It was the first time she'd heard him really laugh, and the sound of his deep, rich laughter reached inside her and touched her heart. She mentally steeled herself against it, against him.

"You'd better go on before I change my mind about giving you some time off," she said with a businesslike briskness.

"You sure you don't want me to hang around and help you with breakfast for the boys?"

"I'm quite capable of taking care of it." She suddenly wanted him gone. She wanted him to take his deep, sexy voice, his clean male scent and his gorgeous robbing eyes and leave her be.

"Okay, if you insist." He got up from the table, carried his cup to the sink, then grabbed a cowboy hat from a hook near the back door. "I'll be back in a couple hours."

She nodded, and it was only when he left the house that she felt as if she could draw a deep, full breath.

There was no question that something about Jack Cortland touched her. She had never considered herself a rescuer, except when it came to the lives of children.

She had to maintain some emotional distance. She needed to focus only on her reason for being here, and that reason had nothing do with making Jack smile, bringing laughter to his lips and chasing away that cloak of loneliness that clung to him.

* * *

Jack lifted his face to the sun as he sat on the back of his horse, Domino. This was the third morning Marisa had chased him out of the house for a couple hours.

He'd been more than eager to get away this morning. He was irritated. The beautiful nanny who stirred him on a number of levels in the past two days had transformed into a mini drill sergeant barking orders.

Over the past two days she'd introduced so many new techniques his head was spinning. There was a little red chair that was a time-out place where the boys each had spent an abundance of time, and there had been times when he suspected Marisa would have liked to put *him* in that time-out chair.

She'd promised him fun, and she'd given him a rigid structure that had both he and the boys feeling downright cranky.

As he headed across the pasture, he focused his attention on the fencing, noticing several places where repair was needed.

The ranch hadn't been in great shape when Jack had returned here after his parents' deaths. He'd been back for two years, but the first year he'd done nothing but anesthetize himself with alcohol and drugs, and the ranch had fallen into more disrepair.

He waved to Sam, who was on a tractor cutting back weeds from around the barn. Then with a glance at his watch Jack realized it was time to get back to the house.

Even though he was irritated with Marisa, he couldn't help being eager to get back to the house with her and the boys. No doubt, the cute little nanny was definitely making him more than a little crazy.

He quickly brushed down Domino then put him back in his stall. Eventually he wanted to teach the boys to ride. Maybe it was time to buy a couple ponies.

He entered the house through the kitchen where Betty was working on lunch preparations. "Best thing you ever did was hire that woman," she said.

"I agree," he replied, although he'd liked Marisa better when she hadn't been riding him so hard.

"You can love them, but you also need to demand decent behavior from them. That's real love," she said.

He had just walked into the living room when the phone rang. He answered on the second ring, vaguely aware of the sound of laughter coming from the boys' bedroom.

"Jack, it's Harold."

A knot twisted in Jack's gut as he heard the sound of his ex-father-in-law's voice. "Hello, Harold."

"How are the boys?"

"Fine. They're getting along just fine," Jack replied.

"Really, that's not what I've heard."

Jack's stomach dropped to the floor. "What exactly have you heard?"

"That they have the table manners of hyenas."

Heidi. Damn, how had Harold found out about that dreadful meal? Had Heidi gone to the wealthy casino mogul man and told her tale for a price? Jack gripped the receiver more tightly against his ear.

"You don't have to worry about it, Harold," he said, pleased that his voice sounded cool and calm. "I've got a professional nanny working with them on their manners, along with some other things."

"Is she one of your bimbos from your past?"

A tide of anger swelled up inside Jack, but he stuffed it down, refusing to be baited into a screaming match with the man. Harold had never believed that Jack was faithful to Candace during their marriage. It didn't matter to Harold that his daughter probably hadn't been faithful to Jack.

"Her name is Marisa Perez. Check her out, Harold. I'm sure you'll find her credentials impeccable." At that moment Marisa and the boys came into the living room. They were all laughing and looked so happy he wanted to be a part of it. "Look, Harold, I've got to go. I'll talk to you later." He disconnected the call.

"Problems?" Marisa asked with a frown.

"I hope not," he replied, then forced a bright smile on his face. "And what has my two favorite boys laughing so hard?"

As Mick went into a long story about a bug on the floor in the bedroom, love swelled Jack's heart. He would do anything within his power to keep these boys with him.

That night he found himself alone in the living room with Marisa. The boys had gone to sleep in their beds at eight-thirty without a fuss.

"This is amazing," he said to her as he listened to the silence of the house.

She smiled. "And you were probably getting ready to fire me."

He grinned. "There have been moments in the past couple days that I thought you'd ridden me hard," he admitted. "It's taken me a while to realize that giving kids consequences for bad behavior isn't abusive."

"On the contrary, it's the most loving thing you can do for them," she replied.

All day long Jack had felt a simmering tension where she was concerned. He felt it now as he smelled the scent of her perfume, noticed how her T-shirt tugged across her full breasts.

She has a boyfriend, he reminded himself. *She's unavailable.* Still, thinking those words didn't ease the desire for her that seemed to grow stronger every day.

His irritation with her that morning seemed like an alien emotion as this afternoon he'd begun to see the results of her firm hand both with the boys and with him. By no means were things perfect yet, but they were definitely better than they had been before she'd arrived.

"I guess I should go to bed," she said.

"Don't go yet," he protested. "It's still early, and I enjoy your company."

Her cheeks turned a charming pink as she settled back into the sofa cushion. "It is early. I guess I could stay up for a little while longer." She looked at him curiously. "I might be overstepping my boundaries, but I couldn't help but hear you mention my name on the phone earlier."

A new tension twisted in Jack's stomach. "That was Harold Rothchild on the phone. Apparently he heard about a dinner that went bad just before I hired you." He quickly told her about the dinner with Heidi and the flying broccoli. When he was finished a small smile curved her lips.

"I'm sorry. I know it isn't funny," she exclaimed with her laughter barely suppressed. "But I'm just imagining that cheesy broccoli sliding down the front of her chest."

Suddenly they were both laughing with an abandon that felt wonderful. The stress of the past four months seemed to melt out of Jack.

"That felt good," he said when the laughter finally stopped.

"You need to do more of that," she replied, her brown eyes brimming with warmth.

"I haven't had anything to laugh about for a very long time," he confessed. "First there was the divorce from Candace, then my band fell apart and all the other members were ticked off at me. But the worst part was after the divorce when I wasn't getting to see the boys and I knew if I fought for custody I'd lose." He sighed heavily. "Then Candace was murdered. Now I'm struggling to pick up the pieces of my boys' lives. I still worry about losing custody."

She looked at him in surprise. "Why?"

"There's nothing Harold Rothchild would like more than to take the boys away from me—and the only way he can do that is to prove I'm an unfit father."

"Surely he couldn't do that," she replied.

Jack grimaced. "I'm not so sure. I have two strikes against me already. I'm a single man, and I don't exactly have a sterling past—and it will only take one screwup and he'll come swooping in."

"Then we can't have a screwup, right?" she replied.

She smiled, and at that moment Jack wanted nothing more than to move from his chair to the sofa and pull her into his arms. He wanted to explore exactly where that sexy scent emanated from on her body, what those lush lips tasted like in the heat of a kiss.

"Tell me about Harold Rothchild," she said, and

the question tamped down any wild desire that might have possessed Jack. "I heard he's some big casino tycoon and his family made their fortune in the diamond business."

"They owned some diamond mines in Mexico. There was a Mayan legend that one of the big diamonds that was found there held some sort of special powers. Its magic caused people to fall in love. It was made into a ring that Candace was wearing on the night of her murder."

"I read something about the ring. It was stolen that night, right? Isn't the diamond called The Tears of the Quetzal?"

Jack nodded and frowned as he thought of the man who at the moment was the bane of his existence. "Harold is working on his third wife. His first wife, June, died giving birth to Candace's youngest sister, Jenna. He and his second wife divorced, and from what I've heard the third wife is on her way out as well. Harold is powerful, and I think he hates me."

"Why would he hate you?"

"Because of my divorce from Candace. I think he believes that we split because I was sleeping around on his daughter. It doesn't seem to bother him that in all probability she was cheating on me. Maybe he thinks that if Candace and I had stayed together she wouldn't have been murdered."

"Were you in love with her?" Marisa asked.

Jack considered the question a long time before

answering. "Initially I was in lust with her. She was wild and beautiful, and we partied together for months in L.A. before we impulsively hopped a plane to Vegas and got married. Almost immediately she got pregnant with Mick. and I was ready for the partying to stop."

"But she wasn't ready to stop," Marisa said.

He nodded. "And then David came along. At the same time a couple of record producers contacted me. They told me they wanted to make me a star in my own right, turn me into a solo performer. I thought I had it all—two little boys, a gorgeous wife and a shot at becoming an artist of real standing."

His laughter held a touch of bitterness. "It wasn't until Candace and I split that I realized the record producers were more interested in her than in me. The deal fell apart, and the members of Creation were angry with me for even thinking about going out on my own. The band broke up and my marriage did the same. But I haven't answered your question, have I?"

He turned his head and stared out the window as he thought of the woman he'd married. He finally looked back at Marisa. "Did I love Candace? I loved the woman I hoped she'd become as the mother of my children, but that woman didn't exist."

"I'm sorry," Marisa said softly. "I'm sorry for you, but I'm also sorry for your boys. And now, I really should call it a night," she said and rose from the sofa.

Jack got up from his chair. "Me, too. Mornings come early with two little ones in the house."

Together they walked down the hallway, and when she got to the door of her room she turned to look at him, her gaze soft and warm. "Everything is going to be all right, Jack. You're a great father, and nobody is going to take those boys away from you."

He wasn't sure if it was her words or the fact that she looked so achingly feminine, so soft and touchable, but the desire that had simmered inside him for the past couple days returned with full force.

Almost without his volition he reached up and touched a strand of her long hair. He half expected her to jump back from him, but other than a slight flare of her eyes, she remained in place as if anticipating his next move.

He placed his hand on the back of her head and pulled her toward him until they stood breast-to-chest, hip-to-hip.

"I'm going to kiss you now," he said, unsure if it was a threat or a promise.

"I know," she replied breathlessly just before he lowered his mouth to hers.

Chapter 4

As Jack's lips claimed hers Marisa welcomed the kiss. She'd wanted this since the moment she'd met him. She'd needed to know just what his mouth would taste like pressed against hers.

Hot. It tasted hot, and as his tongue touched the tip of hers, she opened her mouth to him, allowing him to take the kiss deeper and more intimate.

In the back of her mind she knew this was wrong—that they were crossing a line that shouldn't be crossed, but she found herself helpless to stop it.

Instead she leaned into him as he wrapped his arms around her and pulled her more tightly against him. Here were the fireworks she'd missed on the

Fourth of July a week earlier, she realized as he kissed her with a mastery that weakened her knees.

It was only when he pulled her close enough and she could tell that he was aroused that her senses returned. She pushed against his chest and stepped back from him.

"That probably wasn't a good idea," she said as her heart banged rapidly in her chest.

He dropped his arms to his side. "You're right, but it was something I've wanted to do since the first moment I met you."

"Bad Jack," she said teasingly, even though she wanted nothing more than to be back in his arms. "And now it's really time for me to say good night."

She escaped into her room, her heart still beating an unsteady rhythm.

Patrick's kisses had never stirred her like this. He'd never made her feel the breathless excitement that now coursed through her veins.

For the next three days that kiss haunted her. Neither she nor Jack mentioned it again, but the memory of it was there in the air between them, snapping with energy and making things just a little bit uncomfortable.

It was mid-afternoon, and the boys were down for their naps when Jack and Marisa sat at the table in the dining room to discuss her further employment. The week of probation was over, and she had to decide if she was going to stay in his employ for the next two months.

From the kitchen the sound of a portable television played a soap opera, entertaining Betty as she began the preparations for the evening meal.

Even though Marisa's attraction to Jack made her more than a little bit nervous about continuing on here, her real concern was that she was losing all her objectivity where the boys were concerned.

She had fallen in love with Mick, who had a wonderful sense of humor and was surprisingly protective of his younger brother. And David had stolen her heart as well despite his attraction to getting through locked doors and windows.

Although they still hadn't bonded with Jack in the way she'd like to see them do, they had bonded to her, desperate for her attention and love.

She now faced Jack across the width of the dining-room table. "Our probationary week is over," she began.

"And I want you to stay until the boys are teenagers," he replied half-seriously.

She laughed and shook her head. "I can give you two months, Jack. By the end of that time the boys should be socialized enough to enter a preschool program. They need that. They need to learn to play with other children before they start school, and we need to get David out of diapers as soon as possible."

"I'll start working on that with him," Jack replied.

"You also need to understand that if I make the commitment for the two months, then I'll need my weekends off. I'd also like to take tomorrow evening off. Patrick has invited me to dinner." She needed to see the man she was supposed to be dating and was hoping that being with Patrick could banish the power of Jack's kiss from her brain.

"Why don't you invite him here for dinner?" Jack asked.

Marisa's first impulse was to say no, that she preferred to keep her work and her private life separate. But she knew that Patrick had mentioned he'd been a big fan of Jack's band, and maybe it would clear her head to see the two men together.

"That's very nice. I think he would enjoy meeting you. He told me he was once a big fan of yours," she replied.

"Good, then I'll tell Betty to make sure and set an extra plate at the table for tomorrow evening," Jack replied.

At that moment noise from the bedroom let them know the boys were awake from their naps, and with the next two months of employment arranged, Marisa got up from the table to tend to the boys.

Throughout the afternoon she reminded herself that whatever Jack felt for her was tied up in who she was professionally. She was the woman who had brought order to his chaotic existence. It was no wonder he'd kissed her. She was positive what had

prompted him to do so was a healthy dose of gratitude and nothing more.

She had to remember that. She had to remember
that Jack Cortland might make her heart race, but
she'd be a fool to fall into thinking Jack had any real
feelings for her. And Marisa had been a fool only
once in her life for a man. She wasn't about to repeat
the same mistake.

Rita Perez was frantic. She'd been frantic ever
since she'd realized the ring, Harold Rothchild's
million-dollar diamond ring, was missing.

It wasn't just a piece of expensive jewelry. It was
the ring Candace Rothchild had been wearing the
night she'd been murdered. The ring they called The
Tears of the Quetzal.

The ring not only had a Mayan legend attached
to it but it had also had a crazy past since it had come
into evidence, having been stolen from police
custody and then recovered.

And now it was gone once again.

For the hundredth time in the past week, she knelt
on the floor under her desk and searched the carpet,
even though she knew it wasn't there. The ring
hadn't accidentally fallen on the floor; it hadn't
dropped into a desk drawer. It had disappeared from
a small box that she kept locked in her gun safe.

She should never have checked it out from the
evidence room and brought it home, but she'd been

fascinated with it and had wanted to research more thoroughly how it had come to belong to the Rothchilds.

A wave of despair washed over her and made the wound on the side of her head bang with nauseating intensity. She'd probably be fired. Worse than that, if Harold found out the precious ring was missing again, he'd sue not only her but also the entire department for her negligence.

How had that ring disappeared from her gun safe? Whoever had stolen it had been a professional. They'd known just where to look and how to get in and out without her even knowing they were there.

What was she going to do? Sooner or later she was going to have to tell her superiors what had happened, and then all hell was going to break loose.

With a new burst of energy she began to pull out the desk drawers, hoping, praying that it would be found.

Once again Jack and Marisa were in the living room. It was just after nine, and David and Mick had been in bed asleep for half an hour.

"I still can't believe how easy bedtime has become," he said. "It's like a miracle."

Marisa smiled at him. "All it takes is a firm hand and consistency. That's the secret of good parenting."

"What about your mom and dad? Were they good parents?" he asked curiously.

"Absolutely." She leaned back against the corner of the sofa and drew her legs up beneath her. "Like Candace and the Rothchilds, money was never a problem in my family. My parents are quite wealthy, but they taught me values that had nothing to do with money. I started babysitting when I was about fourteen and even through college worked a variety of jobs. What about your parents?"

"They were terrific people, hardworking and possessed good old-fashioned values." A flash of pain darkened his eyes. "They taught me right, but when I got to Los Angeles and had more money than sense, all their lessons went right out the window. I think I broke their hearts."

There was nothing more appealing than a man who recognized his own frailties and regretted them, Marisa thought. "I'm sure they'd be proud of the man you've become," she said softly.

"Yeah, I'm just sorry they passed before they saw me pulling my life back together again."

"I'm sure they were confident that eventually you'd come back to the values they'd taught you as a young man," she replied.

He nodded. "You think the boys will ever call me Daddy?"

She heard the wistfulness in his voice and knew how important that was to him. "Maybe when they feel safe with you. I don't know much about their lives when they were with Candace, but from what little you've told me I would guess that most of the people who entered their lives were there only on a temporary basis. When they know you're not going anywhere and they can trust you, then maybe you won't be Jack anymore. You'll be Daddy."

He smiled at her. "What made you so smart?"

"Trust me, I'm not always smart. We all have things in our pasts that we'd prefer to forget about."

Jack raised a dark eyebrow. "Now you have me intrigued."

For just a moment she thought about sharing with him the heartache that would always be a part of her, one that had forever changed what she would expect from life.

She knew Jack would understand how foolish she'd been, that he of all people wouldn't judge her. But it felt far too intimate to share that piece of herself with him.

Once again she realized the lines were getting blurred between them. She had to remember that he was her employer and nothing more. She had to remember that she was one of those temporary people not only in the boys' lives but in Jack's as well.

She got up from the sofa. As always when it was just the two of them, she felt the need to get away, to escape from him. It was too appealing, too intimate to sit in his living room with him while night fell outside.

This whole assignment would have been easier if Jack had a wife, but of course if he had a wife Marisa probably wouldn't be here.

"Good night, Jack," she said, hoping he didn't follow her down the hallway to her room, yet in a small little place in her mind wishing he would. She wouldn't mind sharing another kiss with him, and that realization worried her.

Thankfully, he seemed to be caught up in thoughts of his own, for he murmured a good-night and remained in his chair.

Over the past couple nights they had fallen into the habit of staying up talking until around midnight or so. During those hours she'd heard a lot about the Rothchild family, and she'd told him how close she was to her aunt Rita.

Even though the conversations during those hours of the night were light and not overly personal, the end result had been a growing friendship between them. Still, it wasn't that friendship that made the most simple touch from him sizzle inside her.

She now paused in the doorway of the boys' room before going to her own. How could she not fall in love with these boys? They were children who desperately needed a mother, and she was a woman who was meant to be a mom.

With a soft smile, she went first to Mick's bedside and pulled the sheet up closer around his neck. She smoothed a strand of his blond hair off his face and pressed a kiss on his forehead. He said something incomprehensible but didn't awaken.

She moved to David's bed and tucked in one of his legs and an arm. He mumbled and smiled, as if enjoying the pleasant dreams of innocence. She kissed him, too, then moved back to the doorway.

Two months. That's all she was giving herself with them. By that time she'd have taught Jack what he needed to learn to be a good father, and the boys would have a new respect and love for him.

This was her job, to make things right for parent and child, then to walk away. But somehow she thought it was going to be more difficult than it had ever been to walk away from the boys.

And from Jack.

With a tired sigh she left the boys' bedroom and went across the hall to her own. She stepped inside, flipped on the overhead light and froze as she saw a masked man sliding open her window.

She has a boyfriend. Jack had to keep reminding himself that Marisa wasn't available to him, that she was a temporary fix in his life.

The worst mistake he had made since she'd arrived was kissing her. The memory of that single kiss had haunted him each night since. *She* haunted him, stirring inside him a want that he hadn't felt for a very long time—perhaps never before.

He was a fool. She was intelligent and had big plans for her future. She was eager to start her own agency, and the last thing she needed was to be involved with a man with his kind of past.

A scream shot him out of his chair.

Marisa! His heart leaped into his throat as he raced down the hall toward her room. She stood just inside, a hand over her mouth. When he entered she pointed to the window where the screen had been removed and the window was partially opened.

"A man. He was trying to get in," she exclaimed.

"Go check on the boys," Jack said.

"Should I call the police?" she asked.

"No." Jack barked the single word as he raced down the hallway to his bedroom. Once inside the room he pulled a lockbox from his bedroom drawer, unlocked it and withdrew his gun.

As he ran back down the hallway he glanced into the boys' room, grateful to see them both still sleeping and Marisa standing between the beds.

The hot July air wrapped around him oppressively as he left the house. He moved with stealth, keeping to the shadows of the house and trees. He was grateful for the moonlight that made his search that much easier.

When he reached the window of Marisa's bedroom he tightened his grip on the gun. The window screen was propped up against the house, but there was no sign of the intruder.

As he extended the perimeter of his search outward, a thousand questions flew through his head. Was this about Marisa? Had somebody been trying to get inside to harm her? Or was it about him?

Whoever it had been, he was apparently gone now. Jack put the screen back up in the window, then went inside.

Marisa met him in the hallway, her eyes large and still holding an edge of fear. "Nothing?" she asked.

"Nothing." He motioned her to follow him into the living room. "Whoever was out there isn't there anymore."

She curled up on the sofa, as if her fear had made her unusually cold. He set the gun on the coffee table then began to pace in front of her.

"Did you get a good look at him?" he asked.

"He had on a ski mask. Are you sure you don't want to call the police?"

"Right, I can see the headlines now. Intruder looking for drugs at Cortland Ranch. Harold Rothchild steps in to save Candace's kids." A ball of tension expanded in his chest, and for a moment he had trouble drawing a full breath.

"You think that's what it was? Somebody looking for drugs?"

He stopped pacing and looked at her. "I don't know what to think. Unless you know somebody who might want to break into your bedroom to harm you."

"I can't imagine anyone wanting to hurt me," she replied. "Surely Harold can't use it against you that there was an attempted break-in."

"You'd be surprised what he could use against me," Jack replied with an old touch of bitterness.

"Okay, if you don't want to call the police, why don't you let me call my aunt Rita? She's FBI. She can take a look around, maybe check the window for fingerprints and we can trust her not to say anything to anyone about this."

We. We can trust her. The use of the plural wasn't lost on him, and there was a certain sense of relief knowing that he wasn't in this alone.

"Would she mind coming over?" he asked.

In reply she uncurled herself and reached for the phone. Minutes later as they waited for Rita to arrive, they sat together on the sofa, and it was then that Jack decided to tell her what scared him more than anything.

"When Candace died and I was granted custody of Mick and David, Harold made a lot of threats. But the one he told me that upset me most was that it was possible that one or both of the boys might not be mine." A new surge of emotion filled his chest.

"I don't care about biology," he continued. "As far as I'm concerned both of them are mine, and I don't give a damn what a blood test would show. But one little mistake and I'm afraid Harold will order DNA tests. Then I risk losing the only thing that has given me any real meaning in my life."

She placed a hand on his arm. "Then we won't let that happen."

At that moment Rita arrived.

Jack immediately liked the no-nonsense woman who held an important role in Marisa's life. She briskly went about her work of checking for fingerprints in and around the window frame, but unfortunately there were none.

After looking around the area, she returned inside, where she sat with Jack and Marisa at the kitchen table. "If he was smart enough to wear a ski mask, then he was surely smart enough to wear gloves, hence no fingerprints," she said. She reached up and touched the bandage on the side of her head, then dropped her hand to her side.

"Maybe it was just somebody trying to get in to rob Jack," Marisa said.

"Maybe," Rita agreed. "Or I suppose it's possible it was an old fan wanting a piece of the famous Jack Cortland." She smiled at Jack, but the smile didn't last but a moment.

"What would concern me if I were you is that those two little boys of yours would be hot targets for kidnapping," she said.

Marisa gasped, and Jack sat up straighter in his chair, his blood chilling. "Everyone around these parts knows I spent most of my fortune years ago," he said.

"But not the Rothchild fortune," Rita replied. "Those boys are Harold's heirs, and everyone knows that he's probably worth more than the national debt. My recommendation would be that you beef up security around here."

An overwhelming sense of discouragement settled on Jack's shoulders as Rita stood to leave. He started to rise as well, but she waved him down. "Marisa will see me out," she said.

Jack nodded wearily as the two women left the kitchen. In the four months since he'd had the boys here with him at the ranch he'd never thought about the fact that they could be potential kidnap victims.

The idea of somebody taking his boys and using them for ransom was absolutely chilling. How did you keep children safe against an unknown threat? When there was no way to identify the face of a kidnapper? Somehow, some way he'd have to figure it out.

He forced a smile as Marisa came back into the kitchen. "Thanks for calling her."

She nodded, a worried frown creasing her forehead as she sat in the chair next to his. "She wasn't herself tonight. Something is wrong. I could feel it."

"Did you ask her about it?"

"Yes, but she assured me it was nothing, just something work related. I just hope it doesn't have anything to do with the wound on her head." She quickly told Jack about how Rita had gotten shot during the kidnapping of Jenna Rothchild.

"Yeah, I read about that in the paper," he said.

Marisa's gaze held his intently. "So what happens now?"

"I wish I knew. I guess the first order of business is to get a security system installed here. Maybe it was just somebody trying to get in to rob me," he said thoughtfully, "But it's definitely put me on notice, and I'm going to take whatever precautions I can to see that we're all safe here."

She reached across the table and gave his hand a quick squeeze, then got up. As she moved a strand of her shiny hair behind her ear, he noticed that her hand shook slightly.

Even though he knew it wasn't a good idea to try to comfort her, he got up and wrapped her in his arms.

She stood rigid for only a moment and then melted against him. He held her tight and felt the slight tremor of her body against his.

"I'm sorry you were frightened," he whispered against her ear, where he could smell that dizzying scent of her.

"It's not your fault," she replied as she buried her face into his shoulder.

"I should have had an alarm system put in here when I first moved the boys in, but nobody had ever bothered me out here and it just never entered my mind." He was rambling, wanting to keep talking, needing to continue holding her.

He'd felt alone for a very long time, but with her in his arms the loneliness no longer existed inside him.

When she finally raised her head to look at him there was no question that he was going to kiss her again. As he took her mouth with his, desire slammed through him. What he'd intended as a gentle kiss instead was hot and demanding.

She responded with a hunger that stunned him. She raised her arms and tangled her fingers in his hair as they stumbled backward and her back hit the refrigerator.

Their lips remained locked in a kiss that drove all other thoughts from his head. He slid his hands up the back of her T-shirt, wanting to feel the warmth of her bare skin against his palms.

She didn't protest but instead broke the kiss and leaned her head back, allowing him to trail his lips down the length of her neck and across her delicate collarbone.

"Marisa." He breathed her name on a sigh against her ear. "I want you. I've wanted you every day since you arrived here."

When she looked up at him he saw the flame of desire in her eyes, and that nearly shoved him over the edge. She didn't say anything but instead pulled his head back down so their lips could meet once again.

As he kissed her once again he leaned into her and slowly moved his hands from her bare back to her breasts. Her nipples pushed against the thin material of her bra, and he wanted her naked in his arms. He wanted her panting beneath him as he took her over and over again.

She moaned, a soft throaty sound that shot through him like a bolt of electricity.

He stepped back from her and took her by the hand. Neither of them said a word as he led her out of the kitchen, through the living room and down the hallway to his bedroom door.

They were just about to go into the room when Mick cried out from his bedroom. Both Jack and Marisa froze.

"Marisa," Mick cried. "I had a bad dream."

Jack dropped her hand. Whatever fire he had seen in her eyes moments ago was gone. "He needs me," she said.

Jack nodded. "Go on. I'll see you in the morning."

As she hurried back down the hallway to the boys' room two thoughts flittered through Jack's mind. Would he and Marisa ever be able to reclaim the moment that had just been lost? And would there ever come a time when his boys would cry out for him?

Chapter 5

By ten-thirty the next morning the new alarm system had been installed and Marisa prayed that these extra precautions would prevent another terrifying break-in from ever happening again.

After lunch and naps Marisa was on the floor in the living room playing with building blocks with the boys when Kent Goodall stopped by. She was grateful when the two men went outside on the front porch to visit.

Facing Jack this morning had been more difficult than she'd expected after the near intimacy of the night before.

She was grateful they hadn't followed through on

the desire that had momentarily flared out of control between them. She couldn't let herself get caught up in the heat of a moment that wouldn't last. That's what she'd done before, and she'd sworn she'd never allow it to happen again.

She was equally glad that Patrick was coming to dinner tonight. Patrick was safe. He didn't stir a craziness inside her.

She needed to see him. For the past week she and Jack had been living in a tiny bubble where it was just the two of them and the boys. She needed Patrick to bring the world in, to set her feet more firmly on the ground of reality.

"Marisa, watch!" Mick said as he built a tower of blocks higher and higher. He shoved his blond hair off his forehead with the back of his hand, a gesture Marisa had seen Jack do before.

"M'ssa, watch," David echoed and began slamming blocks one on top of the other. David's tower only got four high when the blocks tumbled to the floor. He laughed as if it were the funniest thing he'd ever seen.

As always, playing with the boys brought a wave of love into her heart. She knew from those late-evening talks with Jack that most of their early life had been spent in hotel rooms with hotel staff acting as babysitters. Then, after the divorce, Candace had shoved the boys off on nannies so they wouldn't hamper her wild lifestyle. There had been no sense of permanence and security for them from the moment they'd been born until they had come here to Jack's ranch.

They wouldn't even remember her. Within months of her leaving, the boys would forget the positive influence she'd had on their lives. It was the way it was supposed to be with professional nannies.

Still, she was surprised to realize this knowledge pained her more than a little bit. These boys had laughed and misbehaved their way right into the core of her heart like no other children had done before.

Maybe it was because on every other job she'd had in the past there had been a mother present. This was the first time Marisa had worked with a single parent.

The front door opened, and Jack stuck his head inside. "Kent and I are going to the barn. You and the boys want to come?"

Both of the boys headed for the door as Marisa pulled herself up off the floor. "Guess so," she said with a smile as the two boys barreled out the door and onto the porch.

Jack took Mick's hand and Marisa took David's. Together with Kent they all began to walk across the expanse of lawn toward the barn in the distance.

The July sun bore down on them with an oppressive heat that was searing. Marisa made a mental note to check with Jack about sunscreen for his fair little boys.

"I can already see a big change in the kids," Kent said to her. "They seem a little more calm than they were a week ago."

"That's because Jack is a little more calm," she replied with a teasing smile to Jack. "We still have a ways to go," she added.

"Still, it's nice to see them behaving better," Kent replied.

They hadn't gone far when she felt a prickly sensation in the center of her back. It was a whisper of intuition, the feeling that somebody was watching her.

She turned her head from side to side, seeking the source of the discomfort. She spied Max Burrow standing near the stables. The tall burly man leaned on a shovel, and it appeared that he was watching them…watching her.

The uneasiness increased as he met her gaze and didn't look away but rather stayed focused on them as they walked. She looked at Jack, then back toward Max, surprised to see that he had disappeared.

She mentally shook herself. Apparently the episode of the attempted break-in the night before had her more on edge than she'd thought. Surely Max hadn't been staring at her but was just resting for a moment before getting back to work.

Jack pushed open the barn door, and they all entered. Marisa caught her breath as she saw the wealth of memorabilia housed inside.

Life-size posters of the Creation band lined the walls and Jack's sparkling drum set was on a small raised platform in one corner. David released Marisa's hand and beelined to the drums.

"Welcome to Jack's past," Kent said to her. "And what a glorious past it was."

There were T-shirts and caps and CDs in glass frames. There was also a glassed-in room that Marisa assumed was the recording studio. "This stuff must be worth a fortune," she exclaimed.

"Yeah, Jack had it all after he left us poor folks behind for the big-time," Kent replied. He clapped a hand on Jack's back. "But we're glad to have him back here where he belongs."

David hit the cymbals and laughed with glee.

"David, I don't think you're supposed to touch that," Marisa exclaimed.

"He's all right," Jack replied with an easy smile. "He can't hurt anything."

"Maybe he's the next generation of drumming talent," Kent said.

"God, I hope not," Jack replied fervently. "I'd much rather see the boys go to college than join a band."

Mick had found a set of dolls fashioned after the band members and sat on the floor with them. "No wonder the boys like to come out here," Marisa said. "It's like a big wonderland." She winced as David banged on the snare drum.

Jack smiled and then touched Kent on the arm. "Come on, I'll get you that music you wanted."

As Jack and Kent went into the recording studio area, Marisa looked more closely at the posters on the walls.

Although his hair had been much longer and there had been a wildness in his eyes that was no longer present, Jack had still been one hot hunk when he'd been in his band.

She stopped in front of one particular photo and stared at him. He was standing at his drums, his sweaty T-shirt plastered against his broad chest and oh my…what a chest it was.

The memory of the kiss, the caresses they'd shared jumped unbidden into her head, and her body temperature rose at least ten degrees.

She whirled around as the two men came back out of the recording studio, Kent clutching several sheets of music in his hand.

"Thanks," he said to Jack. "I really appreciate it."

Jack shrugged. "I'm never going to do anything with it. Your band might as well use it." He smiled at Marisa. "We're done in here. Mick, David, come on. We're going back to the house."

David banged the cymbal once again as Mick put the dolls back on the stands where they belonged. David eyed his father with more than a hint of mutiny.

Marisa moved closer to Jack. "Give him a reason to do as you asked," she said softly.

"The time-out chair?" he asked below his breath.

Marisa smiled. "Why don't you try something positive?"

Jack frowned, and she tried not to notice that wonderfully clean male scent of him, desperately tried to forget how his hands had felt so hot and needy on her bare skin.

"Hey, buddy, let's go back to the house and we'll get out the trucks and make a road through the living room," Jack said.

David looked at him thoughtfully, then with a happy grin left the drums and approached Jack. Jack picked him up in his arms, and Marisa's heart expanded. Jack was learning and proving to be quite an amazing daddy.

"And we can make bumps in the road with pillows," Mick said eagerly as they all headed back to the house.

"Yeah, bumps!" David echoed.

Kent headed for his car and waved goodbye.

"You gave him music?" she asked Jack.

"A couple of songs I wrote a long time ago. I wasn't going to do anything with them, and Kent had some interest in using them with his band," he replied.

"That was a nice thing for you to do," she said.

He shrugged. "Kent's been a good friend over the years. It's really no big deal."

They entered the house, and for the next hour Jack sat on the living-room floor playing with his sons.

He's good with them, Marisa thought as she watched their play. He was patient and had a sense of make-believe that they responded to with glee.

As far as Marisa was concerned there was nothing more appealing than a man who could get in touch with the boy inside of him for the sake of his small sons. It didn't take long for the truck game to evolve into a wrestling match.

Marisa laughed as the two boys piled on top of Jack, screaming and giggling with abandon. It was the first time she'd seen the three of them just having fun together.

"Get M'ssa," David yelled, his bright blue eyes sparkling with excitement.

Suddenly it wasn't just the three of them on the floor in a pile but it was her as well. Jack had her on her back and tickled her ribs as the boys squealed with delight and danced around them.

"Stop, please," she cried amid bursts of laughter. He stopped, and for just a minute he remained on top of her, staring down at her.

There was no laughter in his eyes; rather there was a hot flash of fire that left her breathless in a way the tickling had not.

Instantly he stood and held out a hand to help her up off the floor. "Thanks," she murmured as she got to her feet. She didn't look at him as a blush warmed her cheeks. "Okay, boys, it's time to pick up the toys," she said.

"I'll see to the cleanup," Jack said, his voice deeper than usual. "I'm sure you'd like some time to shower and get ready for dinner."

Dinner with Patrick. She looked at her watch and realized dinner was less than an hour away. "Thanks, I appreciate it."

As she walked down the hallway to her bedroom, she tried to ignore the ball of heat that still burned in her stomach, a flame that had been ignited by the desire in Jack's eyes.

He'd confessed to her one night when the boys had been in bed that he hadn't been with any woman since his divorce from Candace. That was a long time for a man to go without a woman.

Surely it was nothing more than close proximity that had him looking at her as if she were his favorite dessert.

The worst thing she could do was allow herself to get caught up in the family atmosphere, in the intimacy of this particular assignment.

Jack was dangerous to her. She felt it in her heart, in her soul. The look in his eyes, the heat of his touch reminded her of that time in her life when she'd risked everything—and lost.

Jack didn't like him. It took him about fifteen minutes for him to make the judgment call that Patrick Moore was arrogant, abrasive and far too smooth.

He especially didn't like the way the man looked at Marisa—with a possessiveness that rankled Jack.

"It's a shame your band broke up," Patrick said as he helped himself to more of Betty's mashed potatoes. "But I guess that wild lifestyle really took a toll on you."

It was as if he wanted to remind Marisa that Jack was an old has-been with a questionable past. "It was time for me to move on to a new phase in my life," Jack replied easily. "I had more important things to do than make music." He looked pointedly at his sons, who so far had behaved admirably through the meal.

"Yeah, but I heard the transition from rock star to family man has been pretty tough for you. Didn't you have a stint in rehab?"

"Patrick!" Marisa let out a short uncomfortable laugh, and then gave him a look of disapproval.

"I'm just asking," he said with a look of innocence.

"It's all right," Jack said to Marisa, then turned his attention back to Patrick. "Actually, no. I never spent any time in rehab, and I'm too busy raising kids now to even think about drugs or alcohol."

"I didn't mean to offend you in any way," Patrick said hurriedly.

"No offense taken," Jack replied smoothly, although he found everything about Patrick offensive. His hair was too dark, too neat. His dress shirt didn't have a single wrinkle and he possessed a cool facade that annoyed Jack.

Marisa deserved a man with more passion, one who had a lust for life burning inside him. She deserved somebody like Jack. He mentally shook himself at this silly thought.

He conceded that his feelings for Patrick were colored by his growing desire for Marisa. He told himself he had no right to judge the kind of man Marisa dated.

Marisa was his employee, and in two months' time she'd be gone from his life. He needed to gain some distance from his lovely nanny.

Perhaps someday there would be a woman who would fit neatly into his life, but it wasn't going to be Marisa and it wasn't going to happen for a long time. David and Mick were all that were important to him, and what he wanted more than anything else on this earth was for them to trust him enough to call him Daddy.

The rest of the meal passed with pleasant, easy conversation, and when they were finished eating Jack took the boys into their bedroom to give Marisa and her boyfriend some time alone.

At seven-thirty he gave the boys their baths and got them into their pajamas. Once they had fallen asleep he remained in the room, seated between their two beds.

His mind raced back to the night before and what Rita Perez had told him. He'd never thought about his sons being likely candidates for kidnapping.

He'd been so busy just trying to get through each day with them he hadn't thought of the bigger ramifications of them living here with him.

There was no question that as Harold's grandkids, the boys would be worth a fortune to a potential kidnapper.

Was the man who had tried to break in simply a robber looking for a quick score of cash or drugs? Why break into a house where people were not only home but were still awake?

He frowned thoughtfully. If the intruder had watched the house for any length of time he might have known that it was habit for Marisa and Jack to stay up late talking in the living room. Perhaps he meant to use that time to get in, maybe steal whatever he could find in Jack's room, then get out before he and Marisa headed off to bed.

Or had he attempted to get in to somehow grab the boys? Had there been an accomplice standing outside the boys' bedroom window, waiting for sleeping kids to be handed to him? A rush of cold air blew through Jack at the very thought.

It was all assumption, but it was the kind of speculation that could keep a man awake at night.

He didn't know how long he'd been sitting there when the phone rang. He left the boys' room and went down the hallway to his bedroom, where he grabbed the receiver next to the bed.

"Jack, it's Harold."

Jack barely stifled his groan. "Hello, Harold. What's up?"

"Why didn't you tell me? I heard somebody tried to break into your house last night."

Jack stiffened. "How did you hear about that?"

"That isn't important. What's important is the safety of those boys. If you can't keep your home safe, then maybe it's time I step in."

"That isn't necessary," Jack exclaimed, his blood rushing to his brain in a burst of anger. "I've got it covered. In fact, I had a state-of-the-art security system installed this morning. I have it all under control, Harold. There's nothing for you to worry about."

"You're on notice, Jack. Keep in mind that it's very possible you have no real legal claim to the boys. If I hear any more news about potential threats to them, then I'll have them yanked out of your custody so fast your head will spin. And you know I have the power to do that."

"I'm well aware of what you're capable of," Jack replied dryly. "Like I said, everything is under control here. There's no reason for you to worry."

Jack slammed down the receiver, his stomach burning with frustrated rage. He hated the fact that Harold had managed to remind him that one or both of the boys might not be his.

"It's very possible you have no real legal claim to those boys." Harold's words whirled in Jack's head, making him feel ill. He'd like to think that

Harold wouldn't go there to get the boys, that he would be reluctant to paint Candace as a woman who didn't know who the father of her children had been.

But he knew that Harold was ruthless enough to do such a thing to get what he wanted. Candace's reputation wasn't exactly stellar to begin with, and if Harold decided he wanted custody of the boys then he'd do whatever necessary to get it.

He leaned his head back and listened to the sound of the boys' breathing. He felt like he'd already missed so many moments of their lives. He couldn't imagine them being ripped away from him now.

Who was feeding Harold this information? Did he have somebody watching the house? Or was somebody in his house sharing private info with the man?

He left the bedroom, and as he walked back into the living room Marisa came in the front door, apparently having walked Patrick out to his car to tell him goodbye.

"Thank you for this evening," she said and then frowned. "What's wrong?"

"Harold just called. He'd heard about the attempted break-in last night."

She sucked in a breath. "How?"

"I don't know, but I intend to find out." He motioned her to follow him into the kitchen, where he noticed she'd cleaned up all remnants of the evening meal.

They sat at the table, and he stared at her, his mind whirling at a frantic pace. "Somebody is feeding Harold information. When he heard about the dinner date gone bad I just assumed Heidi had somehow made contact with him. But this puts a whole new spin on things."

"Rita didn't know about your dinner date, and in any case she would never betray my trust," Marisa said quickly.

Jack nodded. "Then that leaves Kent, Sam, Max or Betty. And of course you," he added.

A stain of color crept into her cheeks, letting him know he'd made her angry. "If you really think I'm capable of such duplicity then you need to fire me right now," she exclaimed.

"I'm not saying you're responsible," he protested. "Marisa, think about it, I'd be a fool not to consider everyone right now." He sighed in frustration. "It appears that somebody I trust, somebody who is in my confidence, is betraying me."

Some of the color in her cheeks faded. "I know you have no reason to trust me, but it isn't me, Jack. I don't know Harold Rothchild. I've never spoken to the man in my life. I certainly want what's in the best interest of Mick and David, and I've told you that as far as I'm concerned that's having them here with you."

"I trust you, Marisa," he said, and as the words left his mouth he recognized the truth in them. Even though he'd only known her a little over a week, he trusted her without a doubt. "What I have to figure out is who is betraying me." He rubbed a hand wearily across his forehead. "Somebody is playing with my life, Marisa."

It had been a long time since Jack's anger had been directed outward instead of inward. But now a wave of anger bigger than any he'd ever known filled him. "More important, somebody is playing with my boys' lives, and when I find out who it is, I'll make them damned sorry they ever did."

Chapter 6

"I've invited Kent to have breakfast with us," Jack said first thing the next morning.

Marisa took a sip of her coffee and eyed him over the rim of her cup. He didn't look particularly friendly. A knot of tension throbbed in his jaw, and his eyes were stormy.

"You don't look too happy at the prospect of a guest for breakfast," she observed.

"I lay awake half the night thinking about who might be selling me out to Harold," he replied. He shoved his empty coffee cup aside and stared out the dining-room window, where despite the early hour the Nevada sun already looked blazing hot.

"What about Betty?" she asked softly, hoping the woman working in the kitchen wouldn't hear her. "Or maybe Sam or Max?"

Jack turned back to look at her. "I just can't imagine it. She's more interested in soap operas and talk shows than in what's going on in this house. As far as Sam and Max are concerned, I'm not even sure they knew what happened during my dinner with Heidi. That leaves Kent."

It was obvious by the expression on his face that the idea that his friend was capable of such a thing hurt him. "Maybe there's another answer. Maybe Harold has somebody watching the house," she offered.

She thought of those moments outside the day before when she'd thought somebody was watching her. Maybe it hadn't been Max's gaze that she'd felt on her. Maybe somebody else had been hiding nearby, watching her, watching them all.

"Maybe," Jack replied, but he didn't sound convinced. "I'll know by the time breakfast is over if Kent is really my friend or not." He shoved back from the table and stood. "He's always been a terrible liar. I'm going to head outside for a little while. I'll be back soon."

She watched him go and once again had the impression of a lonely man who wasn't sure who he could trust in his life.

What must it be like to have two precious

children and be afraid all the time that some powerful entity might steal them away?

She frowned thoughtfully and stared at his coffee mug. Did she dare? She knew what she was contemplating would far exceed the boundaries of her position, but nevertheless she grabbed Jack's coffee cup and carried it to her bedroom. A few moments later she then returned to the kitchen and asked Betty for a small paper bag.

Betty gave her the bag, then looked pointedly at the door, as if inviting Marisa to leave. But instead Marisa sat at the table and eyed the woman who had been working for Jack since the boys had come to stay.

"You enjoy cooking?" she asked, even though she knew it was a foolish question.

"It's what I know how to do," Betty replied.

"What made you decide to come and work for Jack?"

Betty stirred a simmering skillet full of hash browns then wiped her hands on a towel and turned back to face Marisa. "I was a good friend of Jack's mother. A fine woman, she was. When Jack put out the word that he needed some household help there weren't many people lining up for the jobs." She shrugged. "You know his reputation wasn't the best. But I knew Jack's mother would want those boys to eat well so I decided to come to work for him."

"And you like working for him?"

"The pay is good, between meals I get to watch my television shows and I'm in my own house by six every night. What's not to like?"

"Your husband doesn't mind you being here every day?" Marisa asked.

"My Joe left me a year ago. Dropped dead of a heart attack at a slot machine in downtown Vegas. We never had any kids." She sighed. "I knew early on that I wasn't one of those maternal types. This job fills in the long hours of the days."

"I know Jack appreciates you being here for him," Marisa said as she got up from the table. She wasn't sure what she'd hoped to accomplish, but like Jack she couldn't imagine this woman being the pipeline of information to Harold Rothchild.

She was about to walk out of the kitchen when Betty called her name. She turned back to face the old woman.

"That woman Jack married broke his heart. I hope you don't plan on doing the same thing."

Marisa stared at the older woman in stunned surprise. "I'm an employee, just like you," she replied.

Betty snorted and turned back to the stove.

Marisa hurried to her bedroom, where she tucked Jack's coffee cup into the paper bag. Then noise from the boys' bedroom let her know they were awake, and she hurried into their room to help them dress for the day.

It was eight o'clock when Kent arrived and they all sat down for breakfast. The conversation remained pleasant throughout the meal although Marisa could feel tension wafting off Jack. Kent seemed oblivious to the stress that tightened Jack's jaw and filled the air as the meal came to an end.

"I'll just take the boys to their room to play," Marisa said as she rose from the table.

"Why don't you let them play on their own? I'd like you to stay here," Jack replied.

She really didn't want to be a part of the confrontation she knew was coming, but she also didn't want to leave if Jack needed her to stay. She got the boys out of their booster seats, told them to play in their room and then returned to her chair at the table.

"What's up?" Kent asked as if for the first time feeling the tension that rode thick in the air. He looked at Marisa and then back at Jack.

"We've been good friends for a long time, haven't we, Kent?" Jack asked, his voice deceptively calm.

"Except for your Los Angeles years, sure. Best friends," Kent replied. Once again he shot a quick glance at Marisa, then looked back at Jack and shifted uncomfortably in his chair. "What's going on?"

"You've been a great friend to me, but I know you and your band have been struggling. I imagine money is tight," Jack said.

"Money's always tight," Kent said with a small humorless laugh. "There's nothing new about that, but I always get by."

"I've got a problem, Kent."

"What's that?" Kent gazed at him warily.

"Somebody close to me is feeding Harold Roth-child information about the boys." It was obvious from Jack's tone that this was difficult for him.

Kent sat back in his chair and stared at Jack. "Are you accusing me? You really think I'd do something like that?" His face reddened. "You invite me here for breakfast and then accuse me of something like that? You're crazy, man."

"Kent, I'm not accusing," Jack protested. "I'm just asking."

Kent scooted his chair back from the table and stood. "I can't believe you'd think I'd do something like that to you. You're my closest friend."

He slammed his hands down on the table and glared at Jack. "If I were you, I'd look a little closer to home." He looked pointedly at Marisa and then at Jack. "Remember Ramona? The showgirl who is friends with Marisa? Guess where she works, Jack. At Rothchild's casino. You want to find a snake? Beat the grass in your house, Jack."

Marisa gasped as Kent stalked out of the kitchen and a moment later the front door slammed shut with a resounding bang.

Jack reached for his glass of water and Marisa

couldn't help but notice that his hand trembled slightly. "That went well," he said dryly.

"Did you believe him?" she asked softly.

"I don't know what to believe." His eyes looked hollow and dark. "I just know I feel like I'm on borrowed time with the boys, and I don't know how to change that."

Mick came into the dining room. "David went out the window," he said. "He wanted to play the drums again."

Both Marisa and Jack jumped up from the table and raced for the front door.

"I thought these locks on the windows were child-proof," Marisa exclaimed.

"Apparently they aren't David-proof," Jack replied.

As Jack raced after the little boy who was halfway to the barn, Marisa stood on the porch and wondered how on earth this father was going to fight somebody as wealthy and as powerful as Harold Rothchild?

Jack wandered the living room long after the boys had gone to bed. Marisa had helped him get them settled in for the night then she had left to go visit her aunt Rita.

He was surprised by how much he felt her absence. It was as if she'd taken some of the energy in the house with her when she'd gone.

The fight with Kent that morning had left a bad taste in his mouth that had lingered throughout the day. Jack had never been the kind of man who looked for a confrontation. Nothing had ever been important enough for him to fight over until now. For Mick and David he'd confront a five-headed monster.

He went into the kitchen and decided to put on a short pot of coffee. He was reluctant to call it a night and go to bed until Marisa got home safe and sound.

It was funny how quickly she'd become a part of his routine. He liked the time they spent visiting after the boys had gone to bed. He enjoyed the sound of her laughter, a rich, joyous sound that never failed to make him smile.

It wasn't just the loving way she interacted with the boys that drew him to her. She seemed to know instinctively when to give him space and when to ride him hard.

He liked the way her hair sparkled in the light, how the scent of her flooded his senses.

In fact, there was nothing about Marisa Perez he didn't like.

After the coffee had brewed he poured himself a cup and sat at the table. He rarely sat in the kitchen, had come to consider the room strictly Betty's territory.

It was a nice, warm room, and he had many memories of meals at this very table with his mother and father. Many nights Kent had joined them, and Jack's mom had often joked that she must have been asleep when they'd adopted Kent.

He wrapped his hands around the warm coffee mug as he thought of Kent. Betrayal was always tough to take but particularly so when it came at the hands of a friend.

He was still sitting at the table at ten-thirty when he heard the front door open and the beep of the security alarm preparing to ring. The beeping lasted only a minute then stopped as the code was entered.

He smelled her before she entered the room, that slightly spicy floral that heated his blood and left him wanting more.

"Hi," she said. "I wasn't sure you'd still be up."

"I decided to make some coffee. There's a cup still there if you want it."

"No, thanks. Too late for caffeine for me." She sat in the chair across from him at the table. "Everything all right here?"

"Fine. I managed to fix the lock on the window where David escaped earlier today. If I ever have trouble opening a bottle of aspirin I'm giving the bottle to him."

Marisa laughed. "We're just going to have to be vigilant about keeping the alarm on not just at night but also during the day. That way we'll know when he manages to get a window or a door open."

"I don't understand why he keeps trying to get

out. Today he wasn't even running toward the barn. He was just running."

"Curiosity," she replied. "David is curious about everything. When he starts school he's probably going to challenge his teachers."

"I have a feeling he's going to challenge me. How was your visit with your aunt? Everything okay?"

She frowned. "I still get the feeling that something's wrong, that she's worried about something, but I can't get her to confide in me. She says it's work related and that's all she would tell me. You know she's been working on Candace's murder case."

"Maybe they finally have some leads to the killer," he replied. "It would be nice to see justice done and the guilty behind bars. I think maybe that would give Harold some peace."

"Have you heard any more from him? Any more phone calls tonight?"

Jack shook his head. "No, but I realize it's just a matter of time." A new wave of discouragement filled him. His heart felt as if it weighed about a hundred pounds.

"What made you decide to get clean and sober, Jack?" she asked.

He leaned back in his chair, surprised by the question. But he realized that in all the conversations they'd shared, they'd never talk about this particular part of his past.

"Candace and I were big on the party scene." He frowned thoughtfully. "It was what brought us together, and for a long time I think it was what kept us together. The only time we stopped was when she was pregnant with the boys."

He stared out the nearby window, thinking about those days with Candace. Many of the early days of their marriage were nothing more than a blur. They had rarely been sober back then.

He turned his attention back to Marisa. "It was after David was born that I tried to change our life. I wanted to be the kind of father the boys needed, and that meant no more booze and no more drugs." He sighed. "Ultimately I think that's why Candace divorced me—because I wasn't fun anymore."

"She wasn't ready to give up the fun?"

A dry laugh escaped him. "I'm not sure what it would have taken for Candace to turn her life around, but it wasn't me or the boys. So we divorced and she took the boys. She made it almost impossible for me to have any interaction with them. She took them to Europe for several months, then back to Los Angeles. She was rarely in one place for long."

"And so you came back here," Marisa said.

He nodded. "And proceeded to drink myself into a stupor. For the next six months I pretty much stayed drunk. It was Kent who came over to see that I ate, to check on me to make sure I was still alive." He grimaced. "It's a time in my life I'm not proud of."

"So what turned things around for you?"

"One morning I stumbled into the bathroom and stared at myself in the mirror. I looked dead. I looked like all I was waiting for was somebody to shovel dirt over me." He met her gaze. "On the sink in my master bath is a small photo of my parents. I stared at that picture and was ashamed of who I was, of what I'd become."

He thought of that single defining moment. It was as if his parents had reached out to him from their graves.

"I also realized at that moment that it was possible at some point in the future the boys might need me. I knew eventually I'd have to justify the choices I'd made in my life to them." His voice deepened. "I didn't know if it would be five years or fifteen, but some day those boys would want to get to know me and that got me clean and sober. Being a drunk wasn't something I wanted to have to explain."

Marisa stared at him for a long moment, then turned her head to look out the window, her brow furrowed in thought.

Jack tried not to notice the soft curve of her jaw line, how the yellow tank top she wore clung to her full breasts. His head filled with the memory of how those breasts had felt in his hands, how her mouth had clung to his as if they were both drowning.

He felt himself getting aroused at the very thought and chastised himself for letting his mind wander.

Needing to do something—anything—to cleanse the erotic images from his head, he got up from the table, poured himself another cup of coffee and stood with his hips against the counter. At least with this distance between them he couldn't smell her fragrance.

She finally looked at him, her gaze as somber as he'd ever seen it. "You told me that you have two strikes against you if push comes to shove over custody of the boys. The first was your past."

He nodded slowly, unsure where she was going with this.

"But you've never been arrested, and most of the stories of your legendary partying were in the tabloids, right?"

"Right," he agreed.

"Which are not always true."

"Definitely," he said dryly. "The tabloid reports were always full of untruths and exaggerations."

"You've kept a very low profile since moving back here to the ranch, and nobody can make a case that you aren't an upstanding citizen now."

He moved back to the table and sat, still unable to guess where she was going with all this. "I suppose that's right."

"So really the only issue is the fact that you're a

single man trying to raise two children alone. We could fix that. We could make sure that Harold couldn't use that fact against you."

"And how would we do that?" he asked.

She held his gaze intently. "You could marry me."

Chapter 7

Marisa saw shock take possession of his features. His eyes widened and his mouth fell open, and she took advantage of his momentary speechlessness.

"Think about it, Jack. It would be a strictly business relationship," she continued. "Everything would stay just as it is now, including our sleeping arrangements." She hoped the blush she felt inside didn't show on her cheeks. "The only difference would be the picture we present outside this house—as a happily married couple raising the boys in a two-parent home."

"That's a crazy idea," he said, but she couldn't help but see the hope that leaped into his eyes. "Isn't it?" he added.

"There's absolutely nothing questionable in my past, and raising children has been my job. No judge could look at me and the way I have lived my life so far and deem me unacceptable as a stepmother to the boys."

"But why would you want to do that?" He narrowed his eyes slightly. "What's in it for you, Marisa?"

"I'll get to raise Mick and David. Jack, I've fallen in love with your boys. I care about them. After all they've been through, they need a stable life, and I can help provide that for them. I wouldn't just be doing this for you but I'd be doing it for myself as well."

"But what about Patrick?"

"I told you that we were just casually dating. It's nothing serious," she replied.

"He didn't look like it was just casual for him." Jack took a sip of his coffee, his gaze not leaving hers over the rim of his mug.

"That doesn't matter. This is my choice, Jack." She'd thought about it all night and throughout the day. There was a part of her that knew it was an insane idea, but there was a bigger part of her that somehow felt it was right.

He lowered his cup to the table. "Marisa, you're bright and you're beautiful. Why would you want to get yourself involved in this kind of a relationship? Why not marry some man and raise kids of your own?"

Her heart squeezed painfully at the question. She looked down at the top of the table, unable to look at him as she revisited the most painful time in her past.

"I was a junior in college when I met a guy named Tom, and we started a wild, passionate relationship." Her throat grew dry as she thought of those nights with Tom—not because of any residual desire but rather because she'd been such a fool.

"I was crazy about him, and I thought he was crazy about me. I didn't realize I was nothing more than a booty call for him." This time she felt the heat that filled her cheeks. "I found out just how little I meant to him when I discovered I was pregnant and he told me I was on my own."

Jack's only response was a tightening of his jaw. "It was okay," she hurriedly added. "Even though the pregnancy was unplanned and Tom had disappeared, I was thrilled to be pregnant, and I wanted the baby desperately."

The knot of pain in her chest expanded, squeezing out the breath in her lungs. "I didn't tell my parents. I didn't tell anyone about my condition except Aunt Rita. I was going to tell my parents once I had it figured out how to continue college and be a single parent." A lump rose to her throat. "To be honest, I was afraid they'd try to talk me into getting an abortion, and that was something I'd never consider."

She halted, unable to go on for a moment as her

heart shattered all over again. Tears burned in her eyes, but she refused to allow them to fall. She'd cried enough tears to fill the ocean when she'd been going through the trauma.

Jack reached across the table and took one of her hands in his. He said nothing but waited for her to gain her composure.

The warmth of his hand, big and strong around hers, helped and she drew a deep, tremulous breath. "I was just beginning my sixth month when I started to bleed and then miscarried. I was devastated, but even more devastating than that was when the doctor told me in order to save my life they had to do a complete hysterectomy."

"God, Marisa, I'm sorry. I'm so sorry for you," he said. His features were filled with compassion.

She pulled her hand from his and instead wrapped her arms around herself. "Thanks, but now surely you understand why I'm willing to do this. I'm never going to have my own babies, Jack. I'm never going to have a family of my own." She swallowed hard. "So if you agree to this business arrangement we erase one of the strikes against you and I get to be a mommy to Mick and David."

She knew what she was proposing sounded impulsive, especially given the short time she'd known Jack and the boys. But she couldn't help but follow her heart, and her heart was telling her that this was where she belonged…at least for now.

He shoved a strand of his dark hair off his forehead with the back of his hand. "I need to think about this," he finally said. "I mean, this is all happening so fast."

"Of course," she agreed. She immediately got up from the table. "I'm going to bed. I'll see you in the morning."

She left him seated at the table, staring out the window into the dark of night. She had no idea if he'd agree to her plan or not. It was out of her hands.

As she got ready for bed she thought of the offer she'd just made to Jack. She wasn't sure when it had first blossomed in her head, but the moment it had she'd embraced it.

It made a crazy kind of sense. She could live in a loveless, passionless marriage if the payoff was being able to raise Mick and David. What she didn't know was if Jack was willing to make the same kind of sacrifice.

There was no question that there was a smoldering desire between her and Jack, but she wouldn't complicate matters by diving headfirst into something wild and hot and dangerous.

She fell asleep almost immediately and dreamed of Jack. In her dreams they were making love, and she awakened the next morning feeling restless and edgy.

After showering and dressing for the day, she remained in her room until it was late enough for her to call Patrick. Whether Jack agreed to her plan or not, she'd decided to call it quits with the handsome accountant.

She'd been comfortable dating Patrick because he didn't inspire great passion in her. Jack inspired passion, but she didn't intend to follow through on it. She was putting her heart far more at risk by offering to be Jack's wife, but as she thought of the two precious boys, she thought the risk was worth it.

Besides, it wasn't really fair to continue seeing Patrick knowing that they had no future together. Eventually Patrick would want to get married and have children, and that was something she would never be able to give him. It was time to cut him loose so he could find the woman who would be his future.

He answered his phone on the second ring, obviously identifying her cell phone number from caller ID.

"What a pleasant surprise," he exclaimed. "I was just getting ready for work and thinking about you."

"I've been thinking about you, too," she replied. She hated the fact that she was going to hurt him. But better to hurt him now in the early stages of their relationship than later.

"Patrick, you're a wonderful man and someday you're going to make some woman very happy," she began.

"Why do I get the feeling this call is a kiss-off?"

Marisa sighed. "Because I guess it is. Patrick, I've enjoyed the time I've spent with you, but I'm not in a place in my life right now to want a relationship. I'm focused on my work here and two little boys who need me."

"Have I done something to offend you?" he asked quietly.

"No, not at all," she hurriedly replied. "This is about me, Patrick, not about you. I just think it would be better if we stopped seeing one another."

"You know that's not what I want," he replied in a husky voice. "But I can't do anything but respect your decision. You know where to find me if you ever need anything."

"I do—and thanks." She was grateful it hadn't gotten messy and was rather surprised that it had been so easy. She hung up and went into the dining room, where Jack was already seated at the table.

"Good morning," she said and tried not to notice how handsome he looked in a short-sleeved blue shirt and his worn jeans.

The aroma of frying bacon came from the kitchen along with the faint noise of the small television.

Marisa sat next to him and a wave of heat shot through her as she caught the scent of shaving cream and minty soap that wafted from him. Yes, she felt desire for Jack, but she reminded herself that it was an emotion that caused more grief than pleasure.

"Did you sleep well?" he asked.

"Like a baby."

"Change your mind about what you proposed to me?"

She studied his features, trying to discern what he was thinking, but his face was schooled into an enigmatic mask that made it impossible to see into his mind. "No, I still think it's a viable plan."

At that moment she heard the sound of childish laughter and knew the boys were awake. "I'll be right back," she said.

It took her only minutes to wash and dress Mick and David and then get them buckled into their booster seats at the table.

By that time Betty had served breakfast and they all began to eat. Jack ate for a few minutes in silence, then put his fork down and looked at her once again.

"What happens if we go through with it and Harold manages to get custody of the boys anyway?" he asked.

"Then we divorce," she replied. "Quick and easy—no harm, no foul." She'd once held the idea that when she married it would be forever, that she would be with the man she chose to exchange vows with for the rest of her natural life. But fate had changed her expectations.

"You know we're both more than a little bit crazy to even be contemplating this." His gray eyes studied her thoughtfully. "I'm still not sure why you'd be willing to do this for me."

"I'm not doing it for you. I'm doing it for Mick and David, and I'm doing it for me," she replied. The last thing she wanted was for Jack to know that there was a small piece of her heart that belonged just a little bit to him. She didn't even want to access that place herself.

Strictly business, she told herself even as the thought of Jack's lips against hers created a small ball of warmth in the pit of her stomach.

"You have anything special planned for this afternoon?" he asked.

Her heart seemed to skip a beat. "Nothing out of the ordinary."

"Then why don't we get dressed up and head down to the license office, then visit one of the tacky wedding chapels Las Vegas has to offer?"

Now was the time for her to change her mind, she thought. Maybe it was crazy; perhaps she hadn't considered all the ramifications.

"M'ssa, look!" David said. He grinned at her as he balanced a piece of round oat cereal on the end of his nose.

"Marisa, look, I can do it, too," Mick said and dug into his cereal bowl.

As always, her heart filled her chest at their antics. Yes, this whole scheme was probably crazy, and she was positive she hadn't completely thought it all through. But she turned to Jack and smiled.

"Just tell me what time to be ready," she said,

knowing that she had just made a decision that would forever change her life. It could be a wonderfully positive change or it could leave her utterly desolate for the second time in her life.

Harold Rothchild had many things that he regretted about his life. At the moment there was only one regret on his mind as he gazed at the gorgeous blond trophy wife seated opposite him at the long mahogany dining room table.

He'd found her incredibly sexy when he'd initially met her and truth be told she'd stroked his ego by appearing to be crazy about him. They hadn't been seeing each other for long when she'd told him she thought she was pregnant. Impulsively he'd married her and regretted it ever since.

The pregnancy had yielded a son who was now five years old. Unfortunately the bloom had definitely worn off the marriage.

It hadn't taken Harold long to be bored—bored to tears with his young wife who could only have meaningful discussions about who had worn what to which charity function and what designer was having a tremendous sale.

It was enough to make a man think fondly of the wife he'd divorced. Anna had been a good wife and had tried to be a good mother to the three girls he'd brought into the marriage. And he'd come to love Anna's daughter, Silver, as if she were his own.

Lately he'd been thinking more and more about his second wife.

He focused his attention back on the financial section of the morning newspaper.

No matter how bad the economy got, people still loved to gamble. Business had never been better at the casino as people blew their money on the chance of hitting it big.

Still, he found his concentration wandering from finances to family matters. He wondered if things would have been different for Candace if his first wife, June, hadn't died.

Candace had been a handful from the moment of her birth. Wild and impetuous, beautiful and troubled, but Harold would always believe that the reason for her murder had been that damned diamond ring.

The Tears of the Quetzal, so named for the resplendent Quetzal bird of Mexico. Like the bird, the diamond had possessed magnificent colors of golds and greens and deeper hues of blue and violet. His stomach muscles clenched with tension as he thought of the diamond.

It had been found in one of his father's diamond mines, and Harold would never forget that day—it was burned into his head and occasionally gave him nightmares that awakened him in the middle of the night.

He knew the legend attached to the ring, that it

had special powers and would bring love to anyone who came into contact with it.

It was a charming little legend, but Harold knew the truth. He knew that until the ring was back in his possession, it had the potential to wreak havoc on his family. Candace's murder had only been the first of a string of tragedies waiting to happen.

Only Harold knew the true story, that from the moment the diamond had been found it had been bathed in blood. And he got up every morning and went to bed every night terrified by what might happen next.

Chapter 8

The chapel was gaudy, like so much of what Las Vegas had to offer. Jack suddenly wished he had picked another place to exchange vows with Marisa. She deserved better than this.

Marisa looked positively stunning in a pale-pink sundress that was cinched at her slender waist and emphasized the lush fullness of her breasts and hips.

She stood just inside the door with the boys on either side of her while Jack made the necessary arrangements for the ceremony.

There were a dozen wedding packages to pick from when it came to the actual ceremony. Aware that this was nothing but a business deal, he picked one that would let her carry a nosegay of roses but had fewer of the romantic accoutrements.

The minister had the scent of booze clinging to him, and the witness would be a paid stranger. It all felt slightly seedy.

Jack would have walked out but it was already after five and the boys had forgone their nap and were now getting cranky.

He also didn't want to give himself too much time to think, too much opportunity to let reason take over. He had no idea if this was a mistake or not, but he told himself that if it gave him an edge in a custody battle, then it couldn't be a mistake.

Still, he realized that Marisa should be wearing a white gown of ribbons and lace, and she should be exchanging vows with a man she loved beyond reason.

He wore a suit and tie for the occasion, but he had a feeling he also wore the expression of a deer caught in the headlights.

With the arrangements made and the ceremony paid for, he walked back to where she stood. "Last chance to bail," he said.

She smiled, but the gesture looked slightly forced. "I'm not going anywhere until this is done." She picked up David in her arms, and the toddler wrapped his arms around her neck and laid his head on her shoulder. "Let's just get it finished. The boys are getting hungry and tired."

It took fifteen minutes for Marisa to become Mrs. Jack Cortland. She held David during the brief ceremony, and Jack held Mick.

She only seemed to get emotional once and that was when Jack slipped his mother's wedding ring onto her finger. He'd never given it to Candace, who he'd known would have laughed at the small size of the diamond.

At the end of the ceremony the minister clapped Jack on the back as he walked them out of the chapel and told him he'd always been a big fan of Creation.

Thankfully there were no paparazzi hanging around outside so he didn't have to worry about their wedding becoming a tabloid story.

"I told Betty before we left that we'd be dining out tonight," Jack said as the four of them stepped outside the small chapel. "I thought we could grab a bite at one of the casino buffets or restaurants." He would have never attempted a meal out with the kids before Marisa had arrived and worked her magic with them.

"That's fine, although a restaurant would probably be easier than a buffet with the boys," she replied. David was no longer in her arms but at her side. She held his hand in hers, and in her other hand she clutched the bouquet of pink roses that had come with the wedding ceremony.

It was over a quiet dinner that Jack explained to the boys that Marisa was going to be their new mommy. David seemed to take it all in stride, but Mick looked at her worriedly.

"If you're our new mommy, does that mean you're going to go away?" he asked. His big blue eyes held far too much worry for a little boy.

"No, honey. I don't plan on going away," she replied. "Hopefully we're all going to be together for a very long time."

That seemed to satisfy Mick, who turned his concentration on dipping his French fries into the ocean of ketchup that pooled on his plate.

Marisa was unusually quiet during the meal. Jack watched her easy, loving interaction with David and Mick, and that eased the faint uncertainty that somehow they had made a mistake.

He wasn't worried about the mistake affecting him in a negative way. He'd made enough mistakes in his life to fill a book and had managed to survive them all.

But, he worried about Marisa. She might believe she was in this scheme wholeheartedly now, but how long could a woman exist happily in a loveless situation with just the comfort of two little boys?

There would come a day when she might regret not having a man in her life that she loved, when the love of two little boys just wasn't enough.

He tried to tamp down the simmer of desire that he always felt when he was around her. He had to put the memory of the kisses they had shared out of his mind.

She'd made it clear that this was strictly a platonic union and that the sleeping arrangements would remain the same.

She'd also emphasized that she was agreeing to this because of her own needs and the needs of his sons. She hadn't mentioned his needs at all when she'd made the offer.

Dinner was pleasant, and when they were finished eating they walked back to where they had parked his car. David was once again in Marisa's arms, and Mick rode on Jack's back.

Within the first five minutes of being buckled into their car seats, the boys were both sound asleep. As Jack headed back to the ranch, he cast a quick glance at Marisa, wondering what she was thinking, if perhaps she was already regretting the decision she had made.

"You okay?" he asked.

She turned and smiled at him. She looked relaxed, not stressed. "I'm fine. What about you?"

"I'm good. I think I'm just having a hard time processing what we just did."

He felt her gaze lingering on him. "This is going to be far more difficult on you than it is on me, Jack."

"And why is that?"

"Sex." The word hung in the air.

He shot her a quick glance, fast enough to catch the charming blush that colored her cheeks. "What about it?"

"I know how important it is to most men, but it can't be an issue between us. Getting involved in a physical relationship will only complicate things if this all falls apart." She frowned thoughtfully. "If this condition really bothers you, I suppose it would be okay for you to have an affair if you could do it as discreetly as possible."

He was stunned by her words and by the fact that she would think so little of herself as to agree to such a thing. "I was married to Candace for a long time and never cheated on her. During all my years of partying, I might have done a lot of morally questionable things but I never knowingly slept with a married woman.

"I won't have an affair, Marisa, and I'll respect your wishes about not having a physical relationship with you." He offered her a smile. "Contrary to popular myth, going without sex does not kill a man."

Turning onto the road that would lead them home, he offered her another smile. "However, if you ever change your mind about the no-sex part of this relationship, I hope I'll be the first to know."

"Trust me, you'll be the very first person I tell." Once again deep color filled her cheeks, and he wanted nothing more than to take her in his arms and show her what she'd be missing.

He was definitely going to have to take up splitting wood or something equally physical to ease the burn of the desire she stirred inside him.

He could do it. He would do whatever it took to

keep Marisa in his life. He would do whatever it took to make sure that his boys stayed in his custody, and if that meant living in a sexless marriage, he would do that.

Once they were home Marisa went into her bedroom to change her clothes, and Jack took the boys into the bathroom for a bath and to get them into their pajamas.

The tub was filled with bubbles, and the two boys splashed like fish. They wore the bubbles on their head and on their chins like little white beards.

"Look, Jack." Mick giggled as he built a tower of bubbles on his head. "It's a hat."

"Watch me, Jack," David exclaimed, vying for attention with his brother. He put his face into the water and blew, then raised his head and grinned with obvious pride.

"That's great, David, and Mick, I love your hat," he replied.

Love buoyed up inside him. He couldn't lose them. He needed them in his life and he liked to believe that they needed him.

By the time he got them out of the tub and dried and dressed, he was as wet as they had been. He handed them off to Marisa at the doorway so she could tuck them in and he could change his drenched shirt.

In his bedroom he pulled on a clean white T-shirt, then stood in the boys' bedroom door as Marisa got them into their beds.

"If you're our new mommy, then can we call you Mommy?" Mick asked her as she leaned over to give him a kiss on the forehead.

Marisa stood in obvious surprise and glanced at Jack. He shrugged to indicate that it was her call. She bent down next to Mick and smoothed a strand of his hair away from his face. "I think you should call me whatever you feel comfortable with," she said.

"And you'll be here in the morning when I wake up?" he asked.

Jack's heart squeezed. They had never asked about Candace in the months that he'd had them, and Mick's question indicated to Jack that there had been many mornings when the boys had awakened and not had their mother there.

"I'll be here," Marisa answered simply.

"You promise?" he asked.

"I promise," she replied.

"Okay, then good night, Mommy," he said with a sleepy sigh.

"Now me!" David exclaimed. "Kiss me good-night."

Marisa laughed and quickly kissed Mick on the forehead then moved to David's bedside. "'Night, Mommy," he said and Jack's heart squeezed even tighter.

"Now my turn," he said as Marisa moved toward the door. "Good night, son," he said to Mick as he bent down to kiss him.

"Good night, Daddy," Mick replied.

For a moment Jack remained frozen as a joy he'd never known coursed through him. Daddy. Finally, he'd heard that word from his son's mouth. Never had a single word sounded so sweet.

When David said the same thing, he left the room with a sense of wonderment. As he and Marisa walked out in the hallway he caught her by the shoulders and stared at her for a long moment.

"You did this," he whispered. "I don't know how you did it, but you accomplished a miracle."

She smiled, her eyes shining brightly. "It's no miracle, Jack. They love you, and finally they're willing to trust you. I didn't do this, you did."

He couldn't control himself. His joy was so great he had to kiss her. He grabbed her into his arms and commandeered her lips with his.

For a moment he could think of nothing but the happiness in his soul and the pleasure of her warm lips beneath his.

It was only when he felt her stiffen against him that he dropped his hands and stepped back from her. Jeez, they hadn't even been married five hours and already he had stepped over the line.

"I'm sorry," he said awkwardly. "I just got carried away with the moment. I won't let it happen again." He didn't wait for her reply but instead walked down the hallway to his bedroom.

Chapter 9

Marisa stood on the porch and watched the car pulling away from the house. She sighed in exhaustion. She'd arranged for a playdate for the boys and had spent the morning entertaining not two but four rambunctious, energetic little boys.

She was about to turn and go back into the house when she saw Sam and Max Burrow standing near the barn, their gazes directed at her. A small chill worked its way up her back.

During the course of the past week since the marriage, she'd felt them staring at her far too often. It gave her a creepy, unsettled feeling, and she couldn't help but wonder if Jack had vented his rage about who was feeding Harold information on the wrong person.

She closed the front door and set the alarm, then collapsed on the sofa in the living room, where Mick and David were playing with their truck collection.

The visitors had been previous charges of Marisa, the two sons of Margaret and John Covewell, who worked at one of the casinos. She'd worked for them for four months, until they had gotten themselves into a financial position where Margaret could be a stay-at-home mom.

Although the first hour had been a little rough as David and Mick weren't used to sharing either toys or attention with any other children, the last hour had gone remarkably smoothly.

Jack was outside somewhere. In the past week they had fallen into a routine that allowed him to work on the ranch during the day, then spend his late afternoon and evenings with the boys.

There had been no more interaction between Jack and Kent, and Marisa knew the rift weighed heavy on Jack's mind. They still had no idea what the man had wanted who had tried to break into the house, but thankfully nothing alarming had happened since then.

That wasn't exactly true, she thought. The most alarming thing happening in her life at the moment was the growing intensity of her desire for Jack.

It was hotter than anything she'd ever felt for her

boyfriend in college. They were all living like a happy family, but at night when she climbed into her lonely bed she ached for something more. And when she finally fell asleep it was to erotic dreams of making love with Jack.

In those dreams it wasn't just the sex that overwhelmed her. It was the fact that Jack whispered his love for her—a love that had nothing to do with his sons but rather that indefinable emotion between a man and a woman.

What she had to remember was that she was just a means to an end to better his chances if a custody battle should ensue. Their relationship was only about the boys, not about love.

Seeing that the boys were playing well together, she went into the kitchen, where Betty was finishing up the preparation of the evening meal.

"Is there anything I can do to help?" she asked.

Betty looked at her as if she'd just suggested murder. The old woman had been particularly cantankerous over the past week. "Do I look like I need help?" she asked. "Have you noticed the food not tasting right lately? Am I getting the meals ready on time?"

"No, I mean yes." Marisa frowned. "Betty, I didn't ask because I think you needed my help. I just wondered if you'd like any help."

Betty set down the knife she'd been using to cut up vegetables. "Just tell me now. Am I going to lose my job?"

Marisa looked at her in surprise. "Why would you ask?"

Betty shrugged her skinny shoulders. "With you and Jack married now, I've been wondering when you'd decide to take over everything in the house."

"I have no intention of taking over your job," Marisa assured her. "To be perfectly honest with you, there are some things I do very well, but I never really got the hang of cooking."

The taut line of Betty's mouth relaxed, and she picked up the paring knife once again. "It's not that hard if you put your mind to it."

Marisa leaned a hip against the counter. "How well do you know Sam and Max?" she asked suddenly.

"I've known those two since they were teenagers. Why?"

"I was just curious about what kind of men they were." Marisa didn't want to say that she had questions about their loyalty to Jack, and she definitely didn't want to mention that the two occasionally gave her the creeps.

"They're good men, not too bright but hard workers. Jack could do a lot worse."

At that moment there was a cry from the living room, and Marisa rushed from the kitchen to tend to a fight between the two brothers.

That night after the boys had been tucked into bed, Marisa and Jack sat in the living room as was their custom.

"Are you okay?" she asked. He'd been unusually quiet the entire evening.

"I'm fine. Why?"

"You just seem like you have a lot on your mind." She wondered if he was regretting the marriage. He'd reached a place with the boys where they would have been fine without her. Jack had learned to be consistent with discipline, and the boys had begun to trust him to be there for them.

He leaned back in his chair and released an audible sigh. "Things have been quiet for the past week. I haven't received even one phone call from Harold. I somehow feel like it's the calm before the storm."

"Have you heard from Kent?" she asked.

He shook his head, his eyes deepening in hue. There was no question that the topic of Kent hurt him. "But I didn't expect to."

"Maybe you should talk to him again, Jack. It would be a shame to throw away all those years of friendship that the two of you shared, especially given the fact that we don't even know for sure if he is the one who is feeding Harold information."

He rubbed two fingers across his forehead, as if fighting a headache. "I've lost all objectivity about all of this. Maybe you're right. Maybe I need to sit down with Kent and talk. I'll go over to his place tomorrow." He dropped his hand from his forehead and smiled at her.

That smile of his warmed a place inside her that no other smile had done. "You know, just because we got married doesn't mean you can't still pursue your dream of owning your own nanny agency," he said.

"To be honest, I haven't even thought about it for the past couple of weeks," she admitted. "But it is something I'd like to do. I'd need to create a Web site and do some advertising, and I'd also need to interview prospective employees but it's all something I could do from the house. I'd never have to leave the boys."

"I want you to do what makes you happy, Marisa." His deep voice was as soft as a caress. "You've already sacrificed so much for me. I'll support whatever it is you want to do as far as an agency is concerned."

It was far more difficult than she'd expected to maintain an emotional distance from him. She'd tried desperately since the moment she'd met him to keep herself detached, to ignore the simmering burn he evoked in her. But it was getting more arduous with each day that passed.

"I think I'll go to bed," she said, releasing a tired sigh. "The playdate today exhausted me." At that moment Mick cried out, obviously suffering from one of his nightmares.

"I'll take care of him," Jack said and got up from his chair. As Marisa went into her bedroom Jack disappeared into the boys' room.

She went into her bathroom and got undressed and into her silky nightgown, then pulled her robe around her and crept out into the hallway just outside the boys' bedroom.

Her breath caught in her chest as she heard Jack singing, his deep, melodious voice whispering of circus clowns and treasures found, of big balloons and smiling moons.

Marisa leaned with her back against the hallway wall and closed her eyes as warmth rushed through her. It was a warmth coupled with a horrible sense of dread as she realized she'd fallen hopelessly in love with her husband.

Jack sang until Mick fell back asleep. He remained in the chair next to the bed for a long moment, breathing in the scent of his boys, then quietly got up and left the room.

He nearly collided with Marisa, who was standing in the hallway just outside. She looked up at him with her liquid brown eyes, and the smile that curved her lips made his heart pound just a bit.

"That was beautiful," she said, her voice a husky whisper.

"I might not be good at a lot of things, but I always could sing," he replied. Every muscle in his body tensed as she didn't move away. He feared he might lose his mind if she didn't stop looking at him like that.

He shifted from one foot to the other. "Well, I guess I'll just say good-night," he finally said. He started to walk by her to return to the living room, but she stopped him by placing her delicate hand on his forearm.

"Jack?" Her eyes were luminous as she gazed up at him.

"Yeah?" The air between them seemed to shimmer with an energy that made it difficult for him to breathe.

She moistened her lips with the tip of her tongue, and Jack felt his blood pressure shoot through the ceiling. "I told you that you'd be the first to know if I changed my mind," she said.

Jack shoved his hands in his jean pockets, afraid of where they might roam, afraid that he might misunderstand what she was talking about. "Changed your mind about what?" He fought the urge to cough to clear away the huskiness of his throat.

A wild desire had crashed through him the moment she'd touched her lips with her tongue. The thin cotton robe she wore did nothing to hide her curves, and the tiny peek of red silk he saw only further heated the blood rushing through his veins.

"About not having anything physical between us." Her cheeks flamed, but she held his gaze with an uplifted chin. "I mean, if you were interested in having something physical between us, I wouldn't be upset."

"If I'm interested?" He pulled his hands from his pockets. "Marisa, I've been interested in a physical relationship with you since the moment you walked through my front door."

He felt frozen in place, afraid to move too fast, afraid to move too slow, scared somehow that he'd do something to shatter the moment and that gorgeous light in her eyes.

She took a step closer to him, engulfing him in that delicious scent of hers. "So do you intend to do something about it or are you just going to stand there and stare at me?"

Her upper lip trembled slightly, letting him know that she was nervous, that she was putting herself on the line and wasn't sure what reaction she might get from him.

He pulled her into his arms and placed his lips against hers. Softly, tenderly he kissed her as he cradled her against him. But the kiss didn't remain soft or tender. As she wrapped her arms around his neck and opened her mouth against his, his need roared through him like a loosened beast.

He wanted to devour her. He felt as if he'd been on a slow burn since the moment they'd met, and her sudden acquiescence was the fuel that exploded that simmer into a raging inferno.

He broke the kiss, wanting to get her into his bedroom, into his bed before she changed her mind.

As he stepped back from her he reached for her

hand and led her down the hallway toward his bedroom. She followed him without hesitation, but her hand trembled slightly in his.

The bedside lamp was on in his room, casting a faint golden light on the king-size bed he hadn't made that morning.

He dropped her hand and looked at her. As much as he needed to take what he wanted from her, he gave her one last chance to halt what they were about to do.

"Marisa, this wasn't what you offered to me when you agreed to marry me. I don't want to take advantage of you," he rasped out. "I want you, but I don't want you to feel pressured in any way to do this."

She didn't reply. She untied the belt at her waist and allowed the robe to fall to the floor behind her. The red silk nightgown hit her mid-thigh, and the deep V-neck exposed the swell of her upper breasts.

Jack bit back the moan that tried to escape him as he saw that her nipples were already hard and pressed tauntingly against the silk material.

"Trust me, Jack. I never do anything I don't want to do." She took a step closer to him, her eyes a pool of darkness that he could easily submerge himself in.

He felt as if he were in a fog as he grabbed her to him once again, his hands sliding down the silky gown to grab her buttocks and pull her as close to him as possible.

Once again their lips met in a hot, wild kiss that

had him hungering for more. He slid his mouth from hers and instead rained kisses across her jaw and down the length of her neck. She gasped in pleasure as he found a sensitive place just behind her ear.

The sound of her gasp ignited the flames inside him even more, and he stumbled back from her and yanked his T-shirt over his head.

At one time he might have been smooth, but it had been so long and he felt like a teenager preparing for his very first time. His fingers fumbled with his button fly as she pulled the nightgown over her head and slid in under the sheets.

He kicked off his shoes and finally got out of his pants, and then he tore off his socks and joined her in the bed. She was clad only in a little pair of red panties and he in a pair of briefs, but as they came together their naked skin warmed with the intimate contact.

He tangled his hands in her luxurious hair as he kissed her hungrily. She returned his kiss with a fever of her own, her tongue swirling with his as she pressed her naked breasts against his chest.

It didn't take long for Jack to want more than kissing. He rolled her over on her back and captured the tip of one of her breasts in his mouth. Gasping with pleasure, she writhed beneath him.

He laved first one nipple, then the other, fired up by the sounds she made as he cupped her breasts and made love to them.

She didn't remain a passive partner. Her hands roamed his body. She clutched his shoulders, then smoothed her palms down the length of his back.

Jack had forgotten the wonder of human touch, of body heat shared. But that wonder all came rushing back as their foreplay grew more intimate.

Smoothing his hand down the flat of her stomach, his heart pumped fast and furious. As he reached the waist of her panties, he felt her catch her breath.

He glanced at her, and her eyes glowed almost feral in the splash of illumination from the lamp. He held her gaze as he pressed his hand against her panties, her heat radiating out from the wispy material.

Even though he knew she was turned on, he sensed that she was holding back. He wanted her mindless. He wanted that control to shatter, wanted her to go to the place where there was nothing in the world but him and what they were sharing.

He caressed her through the panties, and a low moan escaped her lips as she thrust her hips upward to meet his touch.

Jack was quickly reaching the end of his own control. He grabbed hold of the sides of her panties and pulled them down. She aided him by rising up, her eyes filled with urgency.

He pulled off his own briefs and tossed them to the floor, then gathered her back in his arms for another soul-searing kiss.

As he kissed her, she reached down and closed her fingers around his arousal. The intimate touch nearly undid him. He grabbed her wrist. "Don't," he said in a raw whisper. "If you touch me for another second it will all be over."

Her eyes flared slightly, and she pulled her hand away from him as he once again began to caress her intimately. He moved his fingers against her moist heat, wanting her to tumble off the edge of reason, fall into the place where thought wasn't possible.

"Let go," he said softly. "Marisa, just let go."

She gasped and closed her eyes, and he felt her relaxing, welcoming his touch without reservation.

It didn't take long before her body began to tense and her breathing grew ragged. She arched her hips, and he felt the wave of release that shuddered through her.

Before she had a chance to recover he moved between her thighs. Her eyes opened and she looked up at him, but by the wild glaze there he knew she wasn't seeing him. She was lost in the sensual pleasure, and as he entered her, he let go of the last of his own control.

Chapter 10

Marisa awoke first. The faint glow of dawn crept into the window as she lay spooned against Jack. One of his arms was flung across her waist, and for just one sleepy moment she felt at peace and she felt loved.

Illusion, she told herself. Still, she didn't move, unwilling to break this magical spell until it was absolutely necessary.

Making love with Jack had been beyond anything she'd imagined. She'd expected passion. She'd anticipated fast and hot and wild. What she hadn't expected was his tenderness.

And there had been a wealth of tenderness. She

closed her eyes, her head still filled with thoughts of Jack.

She recognized that the hard-rocking, headbanging drummer that he'd once been had been a facade. The real Jack Cortland was a sensitive man who cared deeply about family and friends and perhaps maybe a little bit about her.

But she had no illusions about what had occurred between them the night before. It had been sex. Nothing more, nothing less. It had been an explosion of the sexual tension that had existed between them from the moment they'd met.

Jack wasn't in love with her. He might love her for what she was doing for him—and for the boys. But there was a difference between loving somebody and being in love with somebody.

She was in love with Jack, in a way she'd never been with Tom in college, but she had a terrible feeling that ultimately this all would eventually end in her heartbreak.

One day at a time, she told herself. Her days would be filled with taking care of Mick and David and building the business she'd dreamed of owning. And her nights—she wasn't sure where she'd be spending them, although she knew where she wanted to be…right here beside Jack.

His hands smoothed down the outside of her thigh, letting her know he was awake. "Good morning," he whispered against the back of her neck, his warm breath sending a shiver of pleasure through her.

She told herself she should get up and get out of his arms, but she remained where she was as she murmured a good-morning back to him.

She'd never had a morning with Tom. She'd never awakened in his arms after a night of lovemaking. She'd been nothing more to him than a quick convenience, and she had a feeling that's what she had become with Jack.

This thought drove her out of his arms and out of the bed. She grabbed her robe from the floor and pulled it around her nakedness.

"Gee, I was kind of looking forward to an encore," he said as he sat up.

He looked roguishly appealing with his hair tousled from sleep and a lazy, sexy smile curving his lips. His smile fell as he studied her features in the semidarkness of the room. "Please don't tell me you have morning-after regrets."

"No, no regrets," she replied. It was true; there was no way she could regret making love with him. "I just have a lot of things I want to get done today, and I thought I'd get a head start before the boys got up."

"You going to work on your business venture?" he asked curiously. She nodded and belted her robe more firmly around her waist. His smile fell. "We haven't talked about what you intend to do with your house. Are you planning on selling it?"

She thought of the little bungalow her parents had bought her as a college graduation present. She loved the little house, but if this had been a real marriage she would have sold it in a minute and completely melded her life with that of her husband's.

But this *wasn't* a real marriage, and she wasn't comfortable giving up everything without a crystal ball to see into the future.

"I don't plan on doing anything with it for a while," she replied. "I'm going to go shower. I'll see you in the kitchen in a few minutes." She left the room and went down the hallway to her own bedroom.

Eventually if she remained here with Jack and the boys she'd want some of the things from her house. But even though she'd made a commitment to remain here, in the back of her mind she couldn't help but feel that this whole arrangement was temporary. Keeping her house was a safety net in case everything fell apart.

The morning passed as always with Jack out on the ranch with his men and Marisa entertaining the boys and taking care of some of the housework. It was Saturday so they were on their own for meals. Breakfast was cereal, lunch was sandwiches and Marisa had ambitious plans to make spaghetti sauce for dinner.

It was when the boys went down for a nap that Jack told her he was going over to Kent's to have a talk.

"Good, I'm glad," she replied as she sank down onto the sofa.

He frowned thoughtfully. "I keep thinking about how it was when I moved back here after the divorce. I was in bad shape, and if it wasn't for Kent I'm not sure I would have survived." He leaned against the chair, and his gray eyes gazed at her thoughtfully. "What about your friends, Marisa? I don't ever hear you talking on the phone with anyone except your aunt and occasionally your parents."

"After I lost the baby, I pretty much withdrew from everyone." Emotion swelled in her chest as she remembered those dark days after the miscarriage. "I went through a period of mourning followed by a depression."

She pulled her legs up beneath her and leaned her head back against the cushion. "My friends didn't seem to understand that this wasn't something I could just put behind me, and they weren't comfortable with my grief. By the time I graduated from college I'd pretty well isolated myself, then I immediately began to work as a nanny. That kept me too busy to miss any of my friends."

She smiled at him, wanting to take away the frown that tugged his eyebrows low. "Don't look so worried, Jack. I'm relatively well-adjusted, and I'm open to the possibility of making new friends. Go on, get out of here and make peace with your friend."

"I shouldn't be too long," he said as he headed for the front door.

"Take whatever time you need. I'm going to do a little work on the computer, then see about making a pot of the best spaghetti you've ever eaten."

He grinned at her. "Sounds great. I'll see you later. Don't forget to set the alarm after I leave."

The minute he went out the door she pulled herself off the sofa and reset the alarm, then returned to her bedroom, where her laptop was plugged in.

She'd just started working on a Web site for her nanny agency when Jack had first hired her, and she eagerly dove back into it now. She tinkered with it for a half hour before the boys awakened from their naps.

As they played in the living room she made a call to the newspaper to place an ad for young women interested in becoming nannies, then joined the boys in the middle of the floor for playtime.

They were in the process of building a fort from several empty cardboard boxes when there was a knock on the door.

She looked out to see Patrick standing on the porch. What was he doing here? As she reached for the doorknob the ring that Jack had placed on her finger sparkled in the sunlight.

"Patrick." She greeted him with a cautious smile. "What a surprise."

"Hi, Marisa. I just thought I'd stop by and see

how you were getting along." He hesitated a moment, then offered her a smile. "Can I come in?"

She opened the door wider to allow him inside. "Come on into the living room. We were just in the process of building a fort."

Mick and David barely paid attention to Patrick as they colored the boxes in shades of brown and black.

"I miss you, Marisa," Patrick said. "I've given you a little time, and I was hoping that maybe you changed your mind about me…about us."

Marisa drew a deep breath. She had to tell him about marrying Jack, but she had to make a fast decision about what, exactly, she intended to tell him.

For some reason her pride wouldn't allow her to tell him the truth, that she and Jack had made a business arrangement for the sake of the two little boys who were now coloring their fort with purple and red crayons.

"Patrick, I'm sorry. I haven't changed my mind. In fact, as crazy as it sounds, I've fallen in love with Jack, and he's fallen in love with me. Last week we got married."

For a moment he looked stunned. "Wow, that was really fast. Are you sure you haven't made a mistake?"

"Positive," she replied without hesitation. "I've never been happier." The minute the words left her mouth she knew they were true. She had no idea how long this happiness would last, but she intended to embrace it for as long as it existed.

"Then I guess I'm happy for you," he said with a tight smile.

She relaxed. "Thanks."

"Well, then I guess I should get out of here." He headed for the door then paused and turned back to her. "I've heard Jack has a whole bunch of Creation memorabilia in the barn. Do you think I could take a peek at it?"

Marisa remembered him telling her that he'd once been a fan. "I guess it would be all right. I don't think Jack would mind. Boys, you want to go to the barn for a few minutes?" Just as she expected, the two raced to her side.

"Mick and David, you remember Patrick," Marisa said.

The boys murmured hellos, and Patrick raised a dark eyebrow. "Mick and David, as in Jagger and Bowie?"

She smiled. "That's right. Apparently Candace was a big fan of the legendary rock idols. Come on, let's take a walk."

The four of them left the house, the boys jumping and skipping with boyish energy. "I don't know how you keep up with them," Patrick exclaimed. There was a suppressed impatience to his tone that made her think perhaps Patrick wasn't so fond of children.

They would have never had a chance for a future together, she thought. One way or another children would have always been a big part of her life.

Neither Sam nor Max were in sight as they reached the barn. She figured the two were out someplace on the acreage. Jack had told her they were mending a section of fence almost two miles from the house.

The barn door creaked open, and the four of them entered. Patrick gasped in amazement. "My God, I'd heard rumors that he had a bunch of stuff in here, but this is amazing."

Marisa smiled as she watched him move around the room. David headed directly to the drums, and Mick found the dolls that he'd played with the last time they had been inside the building.

As he began to bang on the cymbal, Patrick winced. "Can you make him stop that?" he said, a touch of irritation in his voice.

Marisa looked at Patrick in surprise. She was definitely seeing a side of him she didn't find attractive. "David, come here, honey," she said, but he ignored her.

"Hey, I've got an idea," Patrick said. He pulled a chair in front of him and smiled at Marisa. "Why don't we play a game of cops and robbers?" He reached into his pocket and pulled out a small revolver. "Sit down, Marisa," he said, all attempt at levity gone.

She stared at him in incomprehension. "What are you doing? Patrick, what's going on?" Her heart thumped painfully hard in her chest.

"I said sit down," he replied. "You don't want me to get angry and upset the kids."

She sank down on the chair, almost hypnotized by the weapon in his hand. "Is this about me breaking up with you?" she asked.

"Don't be stupid," he exclaimed as he pulled a length of rope from his pocket. "Hey, boys, let's play a game and tie up Marisa." He leaned closer to her ear. "If you don't cooperate I'll kill them both,"

The low menace in his voice coupled with the hard glaze of his eyes made her believe him and her blood ran cold. "Patrick, please. Jack is going to be home at any moment. I don't understand. Why are you doing this?"

As he began to bind her hands behind her, the boys came to stand nearby, watching as Patrick tied her to the chair.

"Jack won't be home anytime soon," he said. "My partner will make sure he doesn't arrive here until it's too late."

He didn't speak again until both her hands and feet were bound to the chair. As he stepped back from her she tried to pull her hands free, but there was no give in the rope.

"Patrick, why are you doing this?" She tried to keep her voice as calm as possible, not wanting to frighten Mick and David, who were watching the two of them with widened eyes.

He drew himself up straight and proud. "My name isn't Patrick. Over the years I've had lots of names and lots of identities, but my real name is Paz Marquez. It was my father who found the diamond, The Tears of the Quetzal. It should have belonged to him, but Joseph Rothchild, Harold's father, found out about it."

Paz's handsome face twisted into a mask of hatred so intense it nearly stole Marisa's breath away. "Joseph killed my father. He buried him alive in a cave and walked away with the diamond. I got it back from Candace the night I murdered her, but it slipped through my fingers once again…and I've been targeting the Rothchilds ever since."

Marisa gasped. He'd killed before. He'd killed Candace. And clearly he was responsible for those other mysterious acts against the family that had been splashed all over the tabloids. Her sense of danger rose dramatically as fear lodged in her throat.

"I finally got it back." He smiled, and it was a cruel, hard gesture. "It's back where it belongs in my possession."

"Patrick, I had nothing to do with any of this. The boys had nothing to do with it. Let us go." Her voice trembled with terror.

"The boys have *everything* to do with this," he replied, seething anger still rife in his voice. "Right,

Mick? Right, David?" He cast the boys a friendly smile. "I figure they're worth at least a million a piece. Their grandfather is easily capable of paying that, and it's the least of what he owes me."

The blood that had been cold inside her turned even icier. "Patrick, you have the Rothchild ring. Isn't that enough? You have the diamond you said belonged to your father."

"No, it's not enough." His hands tightened into fists at his sides. "I want the Rothchilds' blood. I want their tears. I want them to know the kind of pain I've known because of them."

She struggled against the ropes as a deep sob wrenched from her. She had to do something. She had to save the boys.

The only thing she could do was scream and hope that either Sam or Max might hear her cry. The shriek that ripped out of her came from her soul. She never saw it coming, but she felt the crashing blow that landed on the side of her head...then nothing.

Pain brought her back to consciousness, an excruciating pain in her skull that made her feel nauseous.

As she opened her eyes she realized two things had changed. There was now duct tape plastered across her mouth, and the boys were nowhere in sight.

Dear God, where was Mick and David? What had he done with them? With a new fervor she pulled against the ropes that held her tight in the chair.

"Ah, I see you're back." Patrick stood in front of her, a large red can held in his hand.

Frantically she struggled to get free, screaming into the tape with a growing sense of horror. She cried out as the chair toppled to its side with her still bound to it. She lay with the side of her face pressed against the ground, and tears began to burn in her eyes.

"It's been nice knowing you, Marisa," Patrick said from someplace behind her. "Those two little boys are my ticket to wealth. Unfortunately you're worth nothing. Still, I'm hoping your death will make both Jack and Harold shed a tear or two."

She realized at that moment that it wasn't money that drove Paz, it was a rage-driven need for revenge. She heard the splash of liquid and instantly smelled the odor of gasoline. Fire! He intended to set her on fire.

The scent of the gasoline grew stronger as he continued to splash the liquid around the perimeter of the barn.

Marisa tried desperately to get herself untied, but it was a futile effort. Her wrists and ankles burned, and the fumes from the fuel were almost overwhelming.

Mick! David! Her heart cried out. She felt little fear for herself as her concentration was on the two little boys she'd grown to love with all her heart.

Jack, where are you? Come save your babies! Come save me!

"I guess this is goodbye, Marisa," Patrick said from behind her. She heard the strike of a match, then the loud whoosh of flames. The barn door slammed shut, leaving her alone with the fire that within seconds burned with a crackling heat.

Smoke billowed around her, making it difficult for her to see, almost impossible for her to breathe. She coughed and choked against the gag, and her lungs felt as if they were about to explode.

Dark shadows closed in, obscuring her vision altogether as unconsciousness reached out to her. Her last conscious thought was the bitter regret that somehow she'd brought a monster to Jack's door.

Chapter 11

It had taken a week for Rita to learn that Patrick Moore, the man Marisa had been dating, didn't exist.

She'd begun to get suspicious about him when she'd realized the last time she'd seen the ring had been just before he and Marisa had come over for dinner.

Rita knew her niece would never enter her office, and certainly would never take something that didn't belong to her. But she couldn't help but recall that Patrick had left the two women while they'd been clearing the dishes, supposedly to go to the bathroom, and gut instinct warned her that Patrick might have stolen the ring. However, she was still trying to wrap her brain around how he could have discovered where the ring was stashed and how he'd managed to seize it from a locked gun safe. This was clearly the work of a professional…

Yesterday she'd called the accounting agency where she knew Patrick worked, only to discover that he had quit his job there two weeks before. She'd gotten an address from them and had gone to the location late last night, only to discover that it was an empty lot on the outskirts of town.

While she stood on that vacant lot, a new fear had gripped her. Who was Patrick Moore, and why would he have a false address? It was something a criminal would do.

Rita had tried to call Marisa a few minutes ago to see if she could give her any information that might lead Rita to the young man's real identity or home address, but there had been no answer at Cortland's house.

Rita needed to recover that ring. Her career depended on it. But, more than that, she needed to alert Marisa that Patrick Moore wasn't the wonderful man they'd thought he was.

She had a sick feeling in her heart, one that usually portended something bad about to happen. She picked up the phone and dialed the Cortland ranch again. This time she just needed to check to make sure that Marisa was all right.

She sighed in frustration when there was still no

answer. She grabbed her keys and headed for her apartment door, unable to just sit still and do nothing.

She'd start with the accounting agency and see what Patrick's associates could tell her about the man that might lead to his whereabouts and the truth of his real identity.

"I really need to get back home," Jack said for the third time in the past fifteen minutes. He'd already been at Kent's for over an hour and a half. What had begun as a healing of the rift between the two men had transformed into a walk down memory lane.

"Hey, remember that time we played that gig in Riverside and the owner of the place paid us in beer?" Kent asked, obviously not ready to call a halt to the conversation.

Jack stood from the chair where he'd been sitting in Kent's tiny living room. "Yeah, I remember. We were all underage, and we ended up drunk for the next two days. Kent, I really gotta go. I need to get home to the kids."

Kent glanced at his watch and then stood as well. "Okay, I guess if you have to take off…"

"I really do," Jack replied.

"Hey, man, thanks for coming by," Kent said as the two of them stepped out on the front porch. "I really felt bad about our argument. I wish I knew who was feeding Harold information, but you should know I'd never do anything to hurt you." He held out a hand, and Jack gripped it in a firm hand-shake.

Minutes later as Jack headed back home, he still wasn't sure that he trusted Kent. Certainly Kent had mouthed all the right words, proclaiming his inno-cence with a resounding fervor, but Jack wasn't sure if it was just an act.

He realized that until he knew the truth of who Harold was talking to, the only thing he and Marisa could do was make certain nothing bad happened. If a mole had nothing to talk about, then he'd have to remain silent.

His thoughts turned to Marisa and what they had shared the night before. It had been amazing. They had fit together as naturally as if they'd been made for one another. Even now, just thinking about it, he felt himself getting aroused.

She had transformed his life and he would forever be grateful to her for all that she had done.

But the feeling that filled his heart when he thought about her had little to do with gratitude. He cared about her. He loved to see the light of a smile dance on her lips and shine from her eyes. The sound of her laughter filled him with a warmth he hadn't felt for a very long time.

Still, he wasn't convinced she was in his life for the long-term. If he needed any evidence of that it was the fact that she wasn't willing to give up her house. She was hedging her bets, making certain she had a fast and easy escape route if things went bad.

Funny how the thought of her not being in his home, in his life, filled him with regret.

He loved what she had done with his boys, but more than that he loved what she had done for him. She'd made him believe he could be the kind of man he wanted to be. She'd given him the confidence to not only embrace parenthood but also to hold close to who he was at his very core.

He saw the smoke as he turned onto the long gravel road that led to his ranch. It billowed upward, a dark gray snake slithering up in the sky.

His heart seemed to stop in his chest as he realized it was his barn that was on fire. He tromped on the accelerator and squealed to a halt in front of the burning building.

Sam and Max were already there with garden hoses spewing ineffectual sprays of water.

"Call the fire department," Jack yelled as he leaped out of his car.

"Already did," Sam replied above the roar of the flames.

Jack didn't give a damn about anything that was in the barn. It was just stuff from his past, things that no longer really mattered to him. But as he thought about how much Mick loved those stupid dolls and David adored the cymbals, he decided to try to get inside and at least retrieve those items.

He grabbed the garden hose from Sam's hand and sprayed himself down. Once he was soaking wet, he burst through the barn doors.

Visibility was next to nothing, and smoke seared his lungs as he raced toward the box where the dolls were kept. It was then that he saw her. Marisa—tied to an overturned chair and still as death.

He cried out in horror and raced to her. A million thoughts raced through his head. What was she doing out here? Who had tied her to the chair?

Overhead the fire raged, and the ominous sound of cracking wood made him realize the roof was about to collapse at any minute.

Instead of taking the time to try to untie her, he made the split-second decision to grab the chair with both hands and dragged it and her toward the door.

Don't be dead. Please don't be dead. The mantra went around and around in his brain as he struggled to get her out of the barn.

He nearly sobbed in relief as he pulled her out into the fresh air and her eyes opened. She began to cough, choking against the duct tape that rode across her lips.

He yanked off the tape, then straightened and looked back at the barn. *The boys. Oh, God, were the boys inside?* Once again his heart felt as if it stopped beating altogether.

"Marisa, are the boys in the barn?" he asked, his heart pounding so loudly he was afraid he might not hear her reply.

A breath whooshed out of him as she shook her head violently. But the relief was short-lived as she clutched him by the arm. "They're gone, Jack. He took them." Once again she was overcome by a spasm of coughing.

In the distance came the sound of sirens drawing closer. Jack leaned down to Marisa, the knot in his chest so tight he could scarcely draw a breath. "Who? Who has the boys, Marisa?"

Tears washed down her smoke-blackened face. "Patrick. Oh, God, Jack. I'm sorry. I'm so sorry." She began to sob as the fire engines pulled up in front of the barn and Jack's cell phone vibrated from his shirt pocket.

He straightened and walked back to his car as he pulled the phone out. The caller ID displayed the caller as anonymous.

"Cortland," he said as he got into his car and shut the door, grateful that the fire trucks had cut their sirens.

"I have your boys. If you go to the police I will kill them. If you talk to anyone in law enforcement, I will kill them. Do you understand?" Patrick's voice was deep and chilling.

Jack wanted to reach through the phone and kill him. He tamped down the rage, knowing that his sons' lives hung in the balance. "I understand. What do you want?"

"Two million dollars."

Jack barked a humorless laugh. "I don't have that kind of money. Don't you remember, I'm an old has-been who blew his cash on drugs and alcohol."

"You might not have it, but you can get it," Patrick replied.

"And how am I supposed to do that?"

"Harold Rothchild will be happy to pay that for the return of his grandchildren. I'll give you until nine o'clock this evening to get it together. I'll be in touch."

The line went dead.

Jack dropped the phone back into his pocket and gripped the steering wheel with both hands. Outside his car, chaos reigned. The firemen were losing the battle with the blazing barn, and Marisa was seated with an oxygen mask over her mouth and nose.

But the scene happening before his eyes had nothing on the drama that unfolded in his head. Mick and David were in danger, and tears stung his eyes as he thought of his precious sons.

His first impulse was to call the police, but as he replayed Patrick's menacing voice in his head he feared the consequences of that particular action. There had been an edge in Patrick's tone that had let Jack know he was capable of harming the boys.

Jack got out of the car and hurried over to Marisa, who pulled the mask off her face and burst into tears as he approached.

He pulled her up off the ground and into his arms,

knowing the particular kind of torture she must be going through.

"I'm sorry. I'm so sorry," she sobbed against his chest. "I couldn't stop him. He said he wanted to see some of your things from your band days. I never thought... I never imagined. He pulled a gun, and there was nothing I could do."

"Shh, it's all right," Jack said as he rubbed her back. "You need to pull yourself together, Marisa, and tell me everything that happened. You need to tell me everything he said."

Maybe he'd said something to her that would provide a clue as to where he had the boys.

She raised her head and looked at him, her brown eyes filled with torment. "He killed Candace, Jack. He told me that he killed her."

Ice rolled through Jack's veins. "Go get in my car," he said to her. "I'll be right there." As she headed for the vehicle he walked over to the fire chief. The fire was still burning, but it was obvious the barn was a complete loss.

Jack told the man in charge that he had to leave but would be in touch in the next day or two. Then he hurried back to his car where Marisa awaited him.

As he started the car Marisa began to tell him everything that had happened from the moment Patrick had appeared on the doorstep.

Jack's blood was cold as ice by the time she

finished telling him everything that lunatic had said. "Where does Patrick live?" he asked her.

"I don't know. He always came to my place." She wrapped her arms around her stomach, as if she were physically ill. "Are you going to call the police?"

"Patrick called me a few minutes ago. He told me he has the boys and if I contact the police he'll kill them." He gripped the steering wheel so tightly he feared he might snap it in half. "I believe him. I'm going to have to take my chances without any police reinforcement."

"He said he had a partner, Jack, and that partner would make sure you didn't get home too quickly. It has to be Kent," she said.

The flames that lit inside Jack's stomach were hotter than the ones that had consumed his barn as he thought of how Kent had stalled him again and again from leaving his place.

If he was going to find his boys, then it was possible the answer was with Kent. He tore down the highway toward Kent's place, the rage inside him building to mammoth proportions.

If anything happened to his boys and Kent had anything to do with it, then Jack would kill him. It was as simple as that.

He pulled up in front of Kent's small farmhouse, and as he got out of the car he was aware of Marisa shadowing just behind him.

The burn in his gut flamed hotter and when Kent opened the door, Jack swung his fist and punched him in the nose. Kent fell backward as blood blossomed and trickled from his nostrils.

"What the hell?" He scrambled to his feet and backed away as Jack came at him again.

"Where are my sons?" Jack roared. He would have hit the man again if Marisa hadn't grabbed on to his arm and held tight.

"I don't know what you're talking about," Kent yelled as he fumbled in his back pocket for a handkerchief. He pressed it against his nose and tried to look belligerent but Jack smelled fear.

"Patrick told me you were his partner just before he tried to burn me alive," Marisa said as her fingers bit into Jack's arm. "He killed Candace, Kent. Your partner is a murderer."

Kent's eyes widened and a gasp exploded out of him. "Nobody was supposed to get hurt," he said. "He promised me that nobody would get hurt."

"What have you done, Kent?" The words came from Jack in a tortured whisper.

"It was supposed to be easy. Just grab the kids, get the ransom then finally live on easy street for the rest of my life," Kent said.

"Why would you do something like this to me?" Jack asked as he stared at the man who was supposed to be his best friend.

Kent took a step backward from him, and his

eyes darkened with a hint of anger. "Because you left me behind. The whole time we were kids we talked about going to L.A. and building a band. Then you took off by yourself and never thought about me again. You had it all, and you left me here with nothing." His voice rose on the last few words. "Damn you, Jack. You just left me behind."

Jack stared at him in stunned surprise. This was about jealousy? "I don't have time for this. Where did he take my boys?"

"I don't know. He was supposed to call me when he had them, but I haven't heard from him." Kent pulled the bloodied handkerchief from his nose.

Jack wanted to smash him in the face again, but instead he whirled on his heels, grabbed Marisa's hand and raced back to his car.

"What do we do now?" Marisa asked as he pulled his cell phone out of his pocket.

"I've got to call Harold. I need two million dollars from him."

"When this is all over, he'll try to take the boys from you." Marisa's voice was a tortured whisper.

"Probably," he agreed and fought a wave of fear so intense it brought a mist of tears to his eyes. "But it's a risk I have to take."

He punched in the number for his ex-father-in-law, and when Harold answered his phone Jack explained to him what had happened and what he needed from him.

When he hung up he turned to Marisa and stared
at her with a hollowness he'd never felt before. It
was as if he were already grieving a loss too enormous to comprehend.

Marisa must have seen something in his eyes that
spoke of the depth of his despair. She placed a hand
on his forearm. "Don't give up, Jack. Mick and
David need you to stay strong. Patrick wants money.
Once he has what he wants he'll let them go."

"I hope you're right," he said. He started the car
and pulled away from Kent's. Once he had his boys
back safe and sound he would see to it that Kent
spent the rest of his life behind bars. Right now all
he cared about were his babies.

If anything happened to his boys, then there was
no place on earth that Kent or Patrick could hide.
Jack would make it his mission in life to find them
and destroy them.

Harold Rothchild was a handsome man. His
snow-white hair was in stark contrast to the black
suit he wore with a casual elegance.

He'd arrived at Jack's moments ago with two
large suitcases. He'd shown no emotion when Jack
had introduced Marisa as his wife.

During the time that they'd waited for him to
arrive Marisa had taken a quick shower, washing
off the soot and ash that had covered her. As she'd
stood beneath the spray of water she'd wept with

fear for Mick and David. She'd cried uncontrollably for Jack.

Jack spent the first few minutes after Harold's arrival telling the tall, lean man what had happened in the past couple hours. Harold said nothing but his piercing blue gaze never left Jack's face.

They were all seated at the dining-room table, Jack's cell phone in front of him as he waited for another call from Patrick.

"Patrick Moore." Harold frowned as he said the name. "He's a dead man and doesn't even know it yet."

With everything that had happened since Jack had pulled her from the fire, Marisa suddenly remembered what Patrick had told her about his real identity.

"His name isn't really Patrick Moore," she said. Both men turned to look at her. "I just remembered, he told me his name was Paz…Paz Martin or Martinez."

"Paz Marquez." Harold's voice was flat as he stared at Marisa.

"Yes, that's it," she replied. "He said something about a diamond and his father being murdered."

Harold leaned back in the chair, his face turning the shade of ash. "This isn't about money. It's about revenge. It's about that damned diamond." He reached a hand up and rubbed his forehead, as if a headache had suddenly made itself known.

"What are you talking about? Who is Paz Marquez?" Jack asked.

"Antonio Marquez, Paz's father, found the diamond that we now know as The Tears of the Quetzal." Some of the natural color began to return to Harold's face. "He didn't turn it over to my father like he was supposed to but rather pocketed it and quit his job. My father found out about it, and one night he met Antonio in the mine, retrieved the diamond from him, then buried him alive." He bowed his head, looking as if he carried the weight of the world on his shoulders. "I was just a kid, but I was there and saw it happen. I never told anyone, and now it appears I'm paying for my silence."

He reached up and straightened his black and silver tie, as if finding comfort in the small gesture. Marisa noticed that his hands shook slightly.

"I tried to make it right," he continued. "As soon as I was old enough I began sending money to Paz's mother, Juanita. Because of my father she was left a widow with three small children. I arranged for her to move to Arizona and start a new life. I thought it would be enough."

"Apparently it wasn't," Jack replied.

Harold offered him a tight smile. "I always thought it would be you who did something stupid and put those boys at risk. I never dreamed it would be me who brought danger to them."

"It doesn't matter now," Jack replied. "It's just

important that you and I work together to bring the boys home."

Marisa turned her head to stare out the window. The emergency equipment had been carted away, and the barn was nothing but a pile of rubble. Dusk was falling and the coming of night terrified her.

Where was David? Where was Mick? Were they afraid? Were they crying out for her?

Her heart ached with the need to have David and Mick back in her arms. In the short span of time that she'd been in their lives they had crawled so deeply into her heart that she felt as if she'd given birth to both of them.

It wasn't just thoughts of the boys that shattered her heart. As she looked across the table at Jack she wanted to weep with his pain.

He looked as if he'd been shot in the gut and couldn't staunch the bleeding. His face was an unhealthy shade of pale, and his eyes were feverish shards of pain.

The evening passed in a torturous tick of the clock. Each minute felt like an eternity as they waited for Patrick to make contact.

Marisa made sandwiches that nobody ate and coffee that they all consumed with alacrity as they waited for the call that would hopefully bring the boys home.

Home. That's what Marisa had begun to think of this place with Jack and the boys. Since their whirlwind marriage she'd been happier than she'd ever been in her life.

Even though she'd known better she'd begun to have dreams about their future. She'd fantasized about school carnivals and baseball games, about family outings and laughter. Always in those fantasies she and Jack were proud parents who not only loved the boys but also each other.

But they were just fantasies, and she knew without question that no matter what happened tonight the fantasy was coming to an end.

Even if the boys were returned safe and sound, she had a feeling that Harold would fight Jack for them, and in Jack's current frame of mind, she wasn't sure he would fight back.

The knot that filled her chest at telling them all goodbye was as painful as her gasps for breath when she'd been inside the burning barn.

It wasn't just the boys that she would miss. It was Jack. She'd known in the first five minutes of meeting him that he was the kind of man who could own her heart. She'd tried to keep herself distant from him but to no avail. He'd ingrained himself so deeply into her heart then when she finally would have to leave, she would leave a piece of herself behind with him forever.

She'd just gotten up for the coffeepot to refill their cups when Jack's cell phone rang. For a moment it was as if everyone in the room froze.

Marisa's heart beat so loudly in her head she wondered if she'd only imagined the ring of the phone. It was only when Jack leaped forward and grabbed the cell phone that she realized it really had rung.

"Cortland," he snapped.

The tension in the room was so intense it made Marisa's stomach churn. She'd grieved long and hard for a baby she'd never held, a baby who had never drawn a breath of air. She couldn't imagine grieving for Mick and David. The pain was simply too unbearable.

"I've got the money," Jack said. "I want to talk to my boys." He rose from the table with such force his chair crashed to the floor behind him. "Damn it, you put Mick on so I can talk to him."

His angry features instantly transformed to something softer. "Hey, Mick. Are you okay, buddy? Don't worry—Daddy is going to come for you, okay?"

Marisa could tell the moment Patrick got back on the phone as a hard mask of rage replaced the tenderness on Jack's face.

"Just tell me where to meet you and I'll be there with the money," Jack said. "Yeah…yeah, all right. I got it." His eyes narrowed to dangerous slits. "And, Patrick, if either of those boys has so much as a scratch then I'll kill you." He hung up the phone.

"Where?" Harold asked, his features as ferocious as Jack's.

"Eleven o'clock tonight behind the old King's Inn casino downtown," Jack replied.

"Shouldn't we go to the police?" Marisa asked, afraid that something was going to go terribly wrong. She knew the location of King's Inn. It had been a dive where some of the locals had gone to gamble, but three months ago it had been closed down.

"No, no cops," Harold said, and Jack quickly echoed the sentiment.

"But what about Kent? Shouldn't he be arrested as an accomplice?" she asked. "For all we know he's already left town."

"We'll get him," Harold replied. "He's a stupid man who would sell out a friend for the price of a six-pack of beer." He looked at Jack. "I imagine you know that it was Kent who was keeping me apprised of what was going on here with you and the boys."

"Yeah, it's amazing when you realize who you can't trust in your life," Jack said. His gaze sought Marisa's and he smiled. "And it's equally amazing when you realize who you can trust."

Rather than make her feel better, the smile shot an icy chill through Marisa. If anything happened to Mick and David she would be devastated, but she knew in her heart, in her very soul, that the man she loved would be completely destroyed.

Chapter 12

Jack drove slowly down the street toward the old King's Inn casino. The downtown area that most people visited was the Fremont Street Experience, five blocks of casinos and restaurants beneath a large barrel canopy with light shows to enthrall the crowd.

There was a seedier Las Vegas downtown, where small casinos served a desperate crowd and drug addicts lingered in the shadows. Pimps and prostitutes yelled to passing cars, and pickpockets and muggers lay in wait for an unwary out-of-towner.

It was to that area that Jack drove.

He was alone in his car with two million dollars

in cash and was hoping—praying—that Patrick had enough morality left not to harm his boys.

More than a touch of fear rode with him in the car. The terror burned in his heart that beat with enough adrenaline to fuel a football team in a championship game.

Harold had insisted that he was coming along, but Jack had refused to allow him to ride with him. Patrick had demanded that Jack come alone, and he wasn't about to break the rules of a game where Mick and David were the trophies.

It was agreed that Harold and Marisa would follow him and park a block away from the rendez-vous and wait for Jack to get the kids.

Jack knew the boys would want Marisa. They would need her loving arms wrapped around them and assuring them that everything was all right. Truth be told there had been moments in the long night of waiting where Jack had needed her arms around him.

As he pulled into the deserted parking lot behind the abandoned building that had once been a casino he glanced at his watch. He was fifteen minutes early.

He parked the car and turned out his headlights, then took a quick survey of his surroundings. An old trash Dumpster sat against the back of the building, barely discernible in the darkness. Other than that there was nothing in the area.

The streetlights from in front of the building barely pierced the darkness back here. Tension screamed inside him as he glanced at his watch once again.

He rolled down his window to allow in the stifling July night air, but the heat couldn't begin to melt the icy center inside him.

He touched the butt of the revolver on the seat next to him. There was no way he'd put himself in this kind of position without bringing a weapon. He had no intention of using it unless it was to save his own life. The last thing he wanted was to try to be a hero and wind up turning a volatile situation into something worse.

As far as he was concerned Patrick could have Harold's money as long as he returned Mick and David unharmed.

Money could be replaced.

Little boys could not.

He looked at his watch once again, apprehension roiling inside him. He had no idea from which direction Patrick would come so he swiveled his head in all directions as he waited.

"Don't take them away from me," he whispered. "I've only just learned to do it all right. Don't let it all be for nothing." Jack had never been an overly religious man, but he prayed now, hoping that God heard his prayers.

He was well aware of the fact that Harold would

probably push for custody when this was all over. Jack would fight him with every breath in his body. In his heart, Jack truly believed that those boys belonged with him.

And for the first time he recognized that he'd become the man he'd finally wanted to be—the man his parents would be proud of, the man Marisa had known was inside him.

He straightened in his seat as a car without its head-lights on slid around the building and parked facing his. For several agonizing moments nothing happened.

A throb of tension beat at the base of Jack's skull, and his hands grew slick with sweat on the steering wheel.

Suddenly the car's high beams came on, half blinding Jack.

The driver door opened and Patrick stepped out. The headlights gleamed on the metal of the gun in his hand. Jack grabbed the revolver from the passenger seat and opened his door as well.

As he got out of his car he smoothly shoved the revolver into his waistband in the small of his back. "Where are my boys?" Jack asked harshly.

"First things first," Patrick replied. "Throw your weapon on the ground," he demanded. Jack hesitated. "Come on, Cortland, I know you wouldn't be stupid enough to show up here unarmed. Now toss it and we can get this over with. Slow and easy. Don't make me get nervous. Trust me, you don't want me nervous."

There was no way Jack intended to take a chance. He didn't want to piss off Patrick. He just wanted to get his sons and walk away.

With a slow movement he reached behind him and grabbed the revolver, then bent down and placed it on the oily pavement and scooted it away with his foot. It clattered and came to rest several feet from where Jack stood.

"Where are my boys?" he asked again.

"I told you, first things first. Where's the money?"

"Two suitcases in the backseat of my car," Jack replied.

"Get them out."

Jack did as he was instructed and pulled the two heavy cases from the backseat of his car. The fact that he didn't see the boys in Patrick's car worried him. He hoped they were there, perhaps asleep in the back.

"Now, bring them halfway to me."

"First tell me where Mick and David are," Jack countered.

"They're in a safe place, and I'll tell you exactly where they are once I have the money."

"How do I know I can trust you?" Jack asked.

Patrick's teeth gleamed white as he smiled. "Well, now, I guess you really don't know."

The red wash of rage threatened to take over Jack, but he tamped it down. He'd never wanted to hurt a man so much, but he realized in this drama he was powerless to do anything but what Patrick asked of him. The stakes were too high for him to gamble in any way.

As he carried the cases forward, his heart beat so frantically he thought he might be on the verge of a heart attack. A thousand thoughts raced through his head. His heart didn't just beat frantically for himself but also for Marisa.

She'd already suffered an enormous loss in her life, and she'd loved the boys enough to give up her personal freedom, to bind her life to his in the best interest of the children. If this all went horribly wrong he recognized that he wouldn't be the only one devastated.

He dropped the suitcases where Patrick indicated. "Now step back," Patrick said. The gun remained pointed directly at Jack's chest.

As Jack backed away Patrick moved forward, his dark brown eyes gleaming with triumph, with greed. He knelt to open the first case but kept the gun focused on Jack.

"It's all there," Jack said. "Two million dollars in unmarked bills. Now give me my kids. We had nothing to do with your father's murder."

Patrick's smile fell, and raw emotion shone from his eyes. "So you know who I am."

"Marisa told me. I managed to get her out of the barn. She told me that you're Paz Marquez. Harold's father murdered yours in a mine when you were a boy. This isn't my fight, Paz, and it certainly isn't Mick and David's battle."

Paz's features twisted with rage. "He ruined my life."

"And you killed his daughter. I'd say the score is even."

"It will never be even," Paz exclaimed, the cords of his neck standing out. "Yeah, I killed Candace because I wanted the ring, the ring with the diamond that should have been mine. But Candace's murder was just the beginning. I took it upon myself to make the Rothchilds' life hell ever since I rid the world of Harold's precious little girl."

"How did you manage to evade the cops for so long?" Jack demanded.

"I was a master of disguise…and highly motivated. He smirked. "It wasn't hard to camouflage my identity when I kidnapped Jenna Rothchild and Marisa's aunt. I would have gladly killed them both if that's what it would have taken to get back the ring—but it wasn't necessary." He shrugged. "I knew Rita Perez had the ring, and I knew the easiest way to get close to her was to get close to Marisa. They made it easy for me to take the ring from Rita's apartment."

He was wired, babbling with pride but the gun never wavered in his grip.

"Harold tried to make it right," Jack said, trying to appeal to any reason Paz might possess. "He sent your mother money. He moved you to Arizona so you could have a good life."

"A good life?" Paz spat on the ground. "My mother went through money almost as quickly as she went through men. Harold even had a brief affair with her, which is how I knew that he was the one behind our sudden good fortune." He sneered. "He'd throw us a few dollars and then go back to his multimillion-dollar lifestyle. The score isn't even. It will *never* be even."

"Just give me my kids," Jack said, his voice cracking with his emotion. "You have the diamond ring, and you have the money. What else do you want from me? You want me to beg? I'll beg. For God's sake, just give my kids back to me."

Paz drew a deep breath, as if to calm the rage inside him. "I've been thinking that maybe this is just the down payment," he said.

Down payment? The implication of those words created a red fog inside Jack's brain. "Where are my boys?" he raged as he took a step toward Patrick.

"Get back or I'll shoot you," Patrick yelled as Jack took another step toward him.

Jack heard the sound of the gun, a sharp crack that echoed in his head.

There was a split second when his heart cried out. Not because he believed he was about to die, but rather because he would die without seeing Mick and David's first day of school, he'd miss seeing them become teenagers—become men.

His heart cried not just for his children but for Marisa, whom he now recognized he loved not just as the mother figure to his boys but as the woman he wanted in his life forever.

He tensed, waiting for the killing bullet, but instead he watched in stunned surprise as Patrick crumpled to the ground.

Harold stepped out from around the side of the building, a gun in his hand. "I couldn't let him kill you," he said.

Jack stared at the unmoving Paz with a growing sense of alarm. "Oh, God, what have you done?" Jack raced to the fallen man, vaguely aware that Marisa had joined Harold.

It took only one look to see that Paz was dead. Jack stared down at him with a growing sense of horror. He finally looked at Harold and Marisa. "He didn't tell me where the boys were. I don't know where Mick and David are." His voice cracked once again.

A cry escaped Marisa, and she ran to Paz's car and tore open the back door. "They aren't in here." She began to cry.

"I had to shoot him. Otherwise he would have killed you," Harold said, his voice a mix of anger and fear.

The trunk. Jack stared at the car with a new sense of horror. Was it possible that Paz had put his sons into the trunk of his car?

He leaned down and fumbled in Paz's pockets until he found the car keys. As he approached the trunk the only sound was that of Marisa's sobs.

A roar resounded in his head. Would he open the trunk lid and find them curled up together, not breathing? His hand shook so violently that it took him three stabs before he managed to get the key into the lock.

He opened the trunk and wasn't sure whether to be relieved or devastated. The trunk was empty. "Call the police," he said, his voice sounding as if it came from very far away. Where were his sons? Where in the hell had Paz stashed them?

They were all seated around a large interrogation table in the Las Vegas Metropolitan Police Department. Kent had been picked up and now sat in shackles next to Officer Jeff Cookson, who was trying to make sense of a dead body behind a deserted casino and one of the wealthiest men in the country seated next to him.

Marisa and Jack sat side by side, their hands clasped in a tight grip as they listened to Cookson grill Kent for any clues that might help them locate Mick and David.

An Amber Alert had been issued but so far had

yielded nothing. Officers were out searching the area around the King's Inn casino. It was the middle of the night and David and Mick were out there someplace, alone and hopefully still alive.

Marisa felt Jack's desperation radiating through his hand. It was a desperation she shared.

"I met Patrick in a bar," Kent now said. "We got to drinking and talking, and it wasn't long before he told me how much he hated the Rothchilds and I told him how much I hated Jack."

Kent looked at Jack with narrowed eyes. "We were best friends. You could have changed my life, but you left here and never looked back."

"You could have changed your own life, Kent," Jack replied with a rough edge to his voice. "I was never responsible for you."

They had already learned that it had been Kent who had tried to break in to the ranch. He'd watched the house and had known that Marisa and Jack often stayed up late in the living room talking.

The plan had been for Kent to break in to Marisa's bedroom and steal silently across the hallway to the boys' room. If they'd awakened they wouldn't have been afraid to see Kent. Patrick had been waiting just outside the window of that room to get the boys from Kent.

When that particular plan hadn't worked, Patrick had decided to take care of getting the boys on his own. When Jack had called Kent to make arrangements to meet at Kent's house and talk about their fight, Kent had called Patrick to let him know Marisa and the boys would be alone at the ranch.

As Marisa had listened to him talking about the plot her blood had chilled, something she hadn't thought possible, as her blood was already cold enough to freeze her solid.

What had Patrick done with the boys? Where could he have put them while he went to retrieve his ransom? Were they warm enough? Were they thirsty or hungry? Were they still alive?

Her heart lurched, and she shoved that particular thought away. She had to believe that they were all right. Any thought to the contrary was too difficult to fathom.

"I've told you a million times, I don't know what he did with the boys," Kent exclaimed. "I don't know where he was living or what his exact plan was. We only met in bars or at my place. This isn't my fault. I didn't know he was dangerous."

Marisa stared at Kent in incomprehension. How could he have done this? Even if he'd hated Jack how could he have placed those two little boys in harm's way?

Jack leaned across the table, his stormy gray eyes swirling with fury. "You didn't do anything to change your life in the past, but you've definitely done something to change your future. I'll make sure you stay locked up for the rest of your miserable life."

Jack unclasped Marisa's hand, stood and stalked out of the room. Marisa went after him, and she found him leaning against the wall outside the interrogation room.

Deep sobs wrenched his body, and Marisa wrapped her arms around him and held tight. Together they wept for the lost boys, their fear palpable in the air around them.

Marisa had no idea how much time had passed before he finally straightened, leaned back against the wall and raised a hand to shield his eyes as if embarrassed by his show of emotion.

"I'm trying to be strong," he finally said, his voice weary.

"You are strong, Jack." She reached up and grabbed his hand and looked into his eyes. "It's a courageous man who walks into a deserted back lot with two suitcases full of money. It's a selfless man who goes to the person he fears most to get the money to save his boys, and it's a strong man who faces up to his fear for his children."

"Where are they, Marisa? What could he have done with them?" The torment in his eyes reflected the emotion inside her heart.

"I wish I knew." Once again he reached for her and they stood in an embrace until Officer Cookson and Harold came out of the interrogation room.

"I don't think he has any information that can help us find your kids," he said. "He's been taken back to the jail, and he'll be charged first thing Monday morning. In the meantime I need to see what we're going to do with Mr. Rothchild."

Harold said nothing. In the past hour he'd looked as if he'd aged ten years. His skin held an unhealthy pallor, and his posture was that of a defeated man.

"He saved my life," Jack said. "If he hadn't shot Paz, then I wouldn't be here right now. You can't arrest him—he killed a dangerous man."

"We're going now to meet with the district attorney and explain the whole situation to him. It's doubtful that Mr. Rothchild will face any charges," Cookson said.

Before any of them could move from their position another officer appeared. "Hey, thought you might be interested that we just got a call from the Timberline Motel. The manager called to tell us he'd found a toddler wandering around in the parking lot. He's got the kid in the office and is waiting for somebody to respond."

Jack grabbed Marisa's hand so tight she winced beneath the pressure. "The Timberline Motel? Where is it?" he asked.

"Let's go," Cookson said. "You can follow me."

Within minutes Marisa was in the passenger seat of Jack's car and Harold was in the back as they barreled down the street just behind Cookson's patrol car.

Marisa's heart beat frantically, although she was

afraid to acknowledge the tiny ray of hope that tried to emerge. It could be the child of somebody staying at the motel. It might have nothing to do with David or Mick.

Jack's knuckles were white on the steering wheel and a muscle knotted in his jaw. She wanted to tell him not to hope too much, but she saw it shining from his eyes—the need to believe that the child in the parking lot of the motel was one of his own. And even though she was afraid for him, she didn't want to be the one to take that hope away.

The Timberline Motel was located in the downtown area about ten minutes from the abandoned casino behind which Paz had been killed.

In the land of flashing, gaudy lights the one-story building was woefully inadequate, as the vacancy sign sported more than a dozen burned-out bulbs. It was obviously a low-rent operation, the kind of motel that probably rented out more by the hour than by the night.

Jack's car squealed to a halt in front of the office, and all three of them jumped out of the car and raced toward the office door.

Marisa was just behind Jack as he burst through the door. She cried out in sweet relief as she saw both David and Mick sitting on chairs in the small lobby.

"Daddy!" Mick cried, and met Jack halfway. Jack released a deep sob as he grabbed Mick to him, then rushed to David and picked him up in his arms, as well.

"Daddy, David needs time-out. He went out the window again," Mick exclaimed with a hint of indignity.

"Time-out," David said and nodded his head with a happy smile.

"We'll worry about time-out later," Jack replied through his tears.

Little David had pulled his Houdini act, climbing out the window of whatever room they had been in. Marisa gave Jack a moment to hug and kiss them, then she moved forward, needing those little-boy hugs and kisses for herself.

As the four of them had a group hug, Officer Cookson and Harold questioned the manager of the motel. "Room 121. He checked in as Martin Bale," Cookson said to Jack. "He didn't show identification and paid cash for one night. I've called in the crime-scene unit to check it all out."

"I'm taking my boys home," Jack said. He held Mick in his arms, and Marisa hugged tight to David, reveling in the warmth of his little arms around her.

"I'm sure we'll have more questions for you," Officer Cookson protested.

"Not tonight," Jack said firmly. "It's way past my boys' bedtime. I'm taking them home now so they can sleep in their own beds." He looked unflinching at the officer. "If you have any questions for me you can come to the ranch either tonight or in the morning, but right now we're going home."

"I'll stay here," Harold said. "I can tell them whatever they need to know, and then Officer Cookson can take me back to my car."

As they walked out of the motel office, a euphoric joy flowed through Marisa's heart. It was over. The danger, the drama, the terror, it was all over now and her family was safe and sound.

Her family. A fierce protectiveness surged through her. Mick and David and Jack. In a shockingly short period of time they had become her heart, her very soul. They were a unit of love she couldn't imagine not having in her life.

They had just buckled the boys into their car seats when Harold walked toward them. Instantly Marisa tensed.

In the minutes that they had driven together and followed Jack to the back lot of the King's Inn casino, Harold had talked a lot, and in that conversation Marisa had recognized him as a man who admitted the mistakes he'd made in his life, a man who had sounded as if he wanted to make amends, turn things around.

But as he approached their car every protective urge she had inside her rose to the surface. She couldn't forget that Harold was the one person on earth who could possibly take the boys from Jack.

"Jack," he called. "We need to talk."

She stepped between Jack and Harold. "Mr. Rothchild, it's late and we need to get the boys home where they belong." She emphasized the last words. "Surely whatever you have to say can wait for another day."

To her surprise Harold's mouth turned upward in a half smile. "You're a pushy little thing, aren't you? I can see what Jack sees in you. I think Jack will want to hear what I have to say."

Jack placed a hand on Marisa's shoulder and faced his father-in-law. "What is it, Harold?"

"I've made a lot of mistakes in my life, Jack. I haven't always been a good man, a righteous man."

"You came all the way out here to tell me that?" Jack asked dryly.

Harold shook his head. "I came all the way out here to tell you that I see now that taking those boys from you would be just another mistake for me. I won't fight you for custody," he said. "I see how those boys love you...how you love them. I just wanted you to know that I have no intention of causing you problems." He looked him straight in the eye. "I promise you that you don't have to worry about me anymore. I might be a lot of things, but you know that I'm a man of my word."

He held out his hand to Jack. Marisa released a tremulous sigh. She believed Harold and apparently so did Jack, for he grasped Harold's hand and they shook.

Marisa felt it in the air, the healing between the two men who both only wanted what was best for the precious little boys who were already sound asleep in their car seats.

"If you need anything for them or for yourself, you call me and I'll see that you get it," Harold said as the handshake ended.

It was only when they were in the car and headed home that the full significance of Harold's words hit Marisa and all the joy she'd felt minutes before whooshed out of her.

Jack now understood what the boys needed from him, both as a disciplinarian and as a loving parent. Harold had promised he had no intention of fighting Jack for custody.

That meant her role in Jack's life was now unnecessary. The very reason for their marriage no longer existed. She was no longer needed. She glanced over at Jack and wondered just how long it would take before he came to the same conclusion.

Chapter 13

Jack sat in the boys' room for hours after they'd come home from the police station. He'd needed to be close enough to them to hear them breathing, to smell the familiar scent of them.

When he thought of how close he'd come to losing them, his heart ached and the memory of his terror nearly froze him in place. So close—so frighteningly close.

They were safe and home where they belonged, and Harold had promised that he wouldn't try to take them away.

Jack believed him. As Harold had said, he might be many things but as he'd reminded Jack he was also a man of his word. He would cause no more anxiety as far as the boys were concerned. Jack could sleep nights knowing that Harold was no longer a threat.

It had to have been the love that Harold saw that existed among the four of them, the family unity that they'd shown must have been what had made him come to his decision to leave them alone.

Sure, there would probably be times in the future where Jack and Harold would butt heads, and certainly Jack expected Harold to be a part of the boys' lives. But the fear of losing them had eased out of Jack's heart, leaving nothing but his intense love behind.

It was near dawn when Marisa appeared in the doorway. She was clad in her little red nightgown and her long hair was tousled around her head—the very sight of her chased any memory of the terror away and he finally rose from the chair and left the boys' room.

"You need to get some sleep," she said softly.

He raked a hand through his hair and released a weary sigh. "Yeah." He smiled and reached out and traced his finger down the side of her cheek, the warmth of her skin stirring him. "Come to bed with me?"

There was a moment of hesitation as she gazed up at him. "All right," she said.

Together they walked down the hallway to his

bedroom. He stripped off his clothes as she crawled in under the sheets.

He was exhausted, both physically and emotionally, but the minute he got into bed next to her and drew her warm body against his, he wanted her.

He didn't want to talk. He didn't want to hash over what the night had held. He just wanted to make love to his wife.

She seemed to sense what he needed. She pulled off her gown and tossed it over the side of the bed, and they came together with a tenderness that was healing.

The horror of the night fell away, replaced by the heat of her lips and the comfort of her naked body against his.

There was a sense of desperation in her kiss, in the way her hands clutched his shoulders, and he guessed that she was chasing away the demons that had plagued them through the long night.

He held her tight and kissed her with all the passion, all the love that burned in his heart. This was the woman he'd been meant to marry, the woman who completed him like no other.

The winds of fate had blown her into his life. She'd needed his boys and they had needed her. The fact that Jack had fallen so deeply in love with her was just icing on the cake.

As he caressed her she cried out softly in pleasure. He loved the feel of her silky flesh, the taste of her skin as he ran his lips from one breast to the other.

He'd never felt this way with Candace. He'd never felt this need, this connection that went far beyond the physical. When he knew she was ready he moved to take her completely.

He entered her and looked down at her, her face bathed in the dawn light. Tears oozed from the corners of her eyes, tears he assumed were of relief, of pleasure.

He closed his eyes as the sweet sensations of being joined with her swept over him. He was lost in her, and being with her chased the last of the horror away, leaving him sated and at peace.

The sound of the boys awoke them just after eight. Jack released a small groan and tried to pull Marisa closer against him, but she quickly slid out of bed and pulled her nightgown over her head.

"Get some more sleep," she said. "I'll take care of them."

Jack closed his eyes as she left the room. Minutes later he heard the sound of Mick's and David's laughter, and there was no way he could stay in bed.

He wanted to be a part of that merriment. He needed to be surrounded by Mick and David and Marisa. His family, he thought with a proud, protective surge.

He got out of bed and pulled on a pair of jeans, then left the room to join the love and laughter.

* * *

"Harold won't face any charges," Rita told Jack and Marisa as they sat in the living room. She had arrived at the ranch just after lunch to check in on her niece and see how everyone was doing.

"I didn't figure he would," Jack replied. "Sure you don't want some coffee or anything?"

"Thanks, but no, I'm fine. Besides, I can only stay a few minutes. We're still sorting through this whole mess." She looked over to where Mick and David sat on the floor with their trucks. "We found some child liquid pain medication in the room. We believe Paz tried to drug the boys before he left them alone last night, but apparently he didn't give them enough to keep them asleep."

"Thank God," Jack said.

"Mick told me they had hamburgers and a drink, then he and David fell asleep on the bed," Marisa said. "They woke up sometime later and they were alone. That's when David decided it would be more fun outside the room. He couldn't manage to twist the door lock, but he could climb up on the dresser just below the window."

"This is one time I'm glad he has a fascination with going out windows," Jack exclaimed.

He gazed at his sons, his heart filling with joy. His gaze shifted to look at Marisa. She'd been quiet this morning, distant and withdrawn since the moment she'd gotten out of bed.

"If Harold hadn't killed Paz, then Paz would have spent the rest of his life behind bars. We know he killed Candace, and we have DNA evidence from Jenna Rothchild's kidnapping that will probably tie him to that, as well." Rita raised a hand to the bandage on the side of her head. "He came way too close to killing me, and it still scares me to think that Marisa might have died in that fire."

Marisa reached out and grabbed her aunt's hand. "Thank God that didn't happen."

"The good news is we located a deposit box in a bank where Paz had placed The Tears of the Quetzal. The ring is now back in police custody where it belongs," Rita said.

"And you still have your job," Marisa said teasingly. Rita had explained to them about the missing ring and how desperate she'd been to find it.

Rita grinned. "Thank goodness my supervisor has a heart. And I've promised that I'll never check out any evidence and bring it home again."

"So all's well that ends well," Jack said.

"We still don't know the extent of Paz's crimes. It might take us some time to unravel it all," Rita said.

"His hatred had years to fester," Marisa said.

"Like Kent's did." Jack frowned as he thought of the man who had once been his friend. "He was too afraid to leave here and take off on his own, too afraid to risk Los Angeles, but he hated me for having the courage to do it without him."

"He'll have a lot of time to think about it in prison," Rita said.

The three talked for a few more minutes, then Rita stood to leave. "Marisa, will you walk me out?"

Jack said goodbye to the FBI agent, then watched as Rita and Marisa left the house together. He got down on the floor between Mick and David and began to play with them.

Now perhaps they could all go back to the life they'd been living before the kidnapping. He wanted that. He wanted the comfortable routine. He wanted the boys and laughter in the daytime and Marisa and passion at night.

For the first time in forever, Jack saw his future before him and he liked what he saw, was eager to live his life—a life filled with love.

Marisa came back inside and went directly to her bedroom. Jack frowned. Her mood was making him uneasy. What was going on in her head? Today should be a day of joy, but a sense of sadness clung to Marisa, a sadness Jack didn't understand and one that worried him more than a little bit.

He thought of the tears he'd seen in her eyes when they'd made love. He'd believed at the time that they had been tears of joy, of relief after the trauma they had suffered. Had he been wrong?

His worry increased when she poked her head out

of her room and called to him. "Jack, could I speak to you for a minute?" she asked.

"I'll be right back, boys," he said as he pulled himself off the floor.

"Hurry up, Daddy. We're going to have a truck race," Mick exclaimed.

As always the word *daddy* shot sweet warmth through him. Bad Jack was gone. Even when he reprimanded them now, they still called him Daddy. Marisa had given him back his fatherhood.

Jack stepped into the guest room, which smelled like her perfume. "What's up?" he asked.

"Aunt Rita brought me something that I thought you'd want to have." She held out a white envelope toward him.

He frowned. "What's that?"

"It's the results of a paternity test for you and the boys."

He looked at her in confusion. "I didn't take a paternity test."

A flash of guilt sparked in her dark brown eyes. "I took swabs from inside the boys' mouths and a coffee cup that you had used and took them to Rita. I know it wasn't my place to do it, but I also knew that paternity was a threat that Harold was holding over your head. Anyway, Rita called in a couple of favors and got it done immediately at the FBI lab."

Jack stared at the envelope as if it were a poisonous snake. He thought of all the times Candace had hinted that she'd been unfaithful, all the times Harold had told him that there was a strong possibility that at least one of the boys wasn't his.

"It doesn't matter," he finally said. He shoved his hands into his pockets. "It doesn't matter what's written on that paper. Both those boys are mine. They're my heart, and a stupid test isn't going to change that."

"Open it, Jack. Go on. It will put an end to the question." She held the envelope closer to him.

Reluctantly he pulled his hands from his pockets and reached out for the envelope. The paper felt hot between his fingers. His mouth went dry as his heart began to beat a quickened rhythm.

He'd told her the truth. It didn't matter to him what the test revealed. Both David and Mick were his sons in every way that counted. Whether or not his blood ran through their veins wouldn't change his love for them.

Still, in knowledge was power. Even though Harold had promised not to try to take the boys, there might come a time when paternity became an issue. Wasn't it better he be armed with the truth now?

His fingers felt big and clumsy as he fumbled to open the envelope. He pulled out the paper inside and allowed the envelope to flutter to the floor at his feet.

"Go on, Jack. Look at it," Marisa said softly. Her

eyes shone overly bright and what he wanted to do was throw the paper on the floor and take her to bed. Instead he opened it and looked.

He released a small cry as he read that in the case of both boys he was their father. There was absolutely no question about it. He looked up to see Marisa's smile. "You knew," he said softly.

She nodded. "I read it before I gave it to you."

"What would you have done if the results had been different? Would you have still given it to me?"

She frowned thoughtfully. "I'm not sure. Thank goodness I didn't have to face that particular dilemma."

It was only then that Jack glanced over her shoulder and saw her suitcase open on the bed. "What are you doing?" he asked.

The smile that had lifted the corners of her luscious mouth fell and her eyes darkened. "I'm packing."

"Packing?" He looked at her in bewilderment. "Where are we going?"

"Not we—me." She averted her gaze from his and took a step backward. "You don't need me here anymore, Jack. You're doing fine with the boys, and Harold has promised he won't fight you for custody. There's really no reason for me to stay here."

A million thoughts flew through Jack's head, a million reasons that he wanted her to stay. "The boys need you," he said.

"They have all they need in you," she replied, her gaze still not meeting his.

She walked over to the closet, pulled several blouses from their hangers and laid them on the bed next to her suitcase.

A crazy sense of panic filled him. It wasn't alarm over the fact that when she left he'd have nobody to help him with Mick and David. He knew she was right. He'd be fine alone with the boys—he just didn't want to be.

The panic came from the fact that he needed her, that he loved her, but it wasn't fair for him to put that on her. She'd made it clear from the very beginning that she was here for his boys, not for him.

"I wish you'd reconsider." His words were woefully inadequate for the pain that filled his heart.

She shook her head. "It's for the best." She walked back to stand in front of him and pulled off the ring he'd given her when they'd exchanged their vows. "This is yours. I just had it out on loan."

He shoved his hands back into his pockets, unwilling to take the ring that had once belonged to his mother and now in his mind belonged to Marisa.

She shrugged and placed the ring on the top of the dresser, where the sunlight sparkled on the little diamond. "I would prefer you not tell the boys I'm leaving for good. I'll tell them I'm taking a little trip. They're young. In a couple of weeks they will forget all about me." Her voice cracked slightly.

As she began to fold the blouses and place them in her suitcase Mick yelled and Jack left her bedroom to tend to the boys.

He knew how to make music. He knew now what to do when one of the boys misbehaved. But he didn't know how to stop the woman he loved from walking away from him.

Hot tears pressed at Marisa's eyes as she sat on the edge of the bed. She tried to staunch them, but they came without volition, fast and furiously running down her cheeks.

She'd awakened that morning with the warmth of Jack's arms around her, with the scent of him lingering on her skin, and she'd known she had to leave.

It would be less painful now than it would be later. At least she was leaving of her own volition rather than being asked to leave by Jack.

Still, that didn't ease the pain that crashed through her. She'd thought she could do this. She'd believed she could marry Jack for the best interest of the boys and keep herself emotionally distant from Jack.

She'd been wrong. Jack had stirred a love and passion in her far greater than she'd ever felt before and it terrified her.

Eventually he wouldn't be satisfied being married to a woman he'd wed only in an attempt to assure his continued custody of his sons. It was better she leave now than wait until Jack's unhappiness forced her out.

She couldn't stay here knowing she had Jack's respect, his gratitude and occasionally his desire without his love. It was just too difficult.

It would have been easier to sneak out like a thief in the night without telling any of them goodbye, but she hadn't been able to stand the thought of not getting goodbye kisses and hugs.

She pulled herself up from the bed and continued her packing. She tried to ignore the noise of the boys playing in the living room, the deep melodious sound of Jack's voice as he spoke to them.

As she finished her packing she realized there had been a small part of her that had expected this moment to come. It was why she hadn't done anything about selling her house.

All too quickly she had her bags packed and was ready to leave. Once again tears pressed hot against her eyes. She didn't want to leave and yet the depth of her emotions for Jack made her want to run, to hide, before the pain got any greater.

With a weariness that weighed heavy she stood and grabbed the suitcase that she'd initially arrived with. It felt heavier than it had when she'd carried it into the house, and she knew the additional weight was the emotion she'd packed inside as she prepared to leave.

When she went into the living room Jack and the boys were in the middle of the floor, a toy truck rally taking place before them.

"M'ssa, watch!" David said as he ran a truck over a pillow and up Jack's arm. Those familiar words nearly broke her. But she refused to weep in front of the boys.

"David, Mick, come sit here with me for a minute." She sat on the sofa and patted either side of her. The boys clambered up beside her, and she put her arms around them.

The pain that cascaded through her was unbearable. For a moment she couldn't breathe. These were the children she was supposed to have, and the man seated on the floor in front of them was the man who would forever own her heart.

"I have to go away for a little while," she finally said. "I want you to be good boys for your daddy while I'm gone."

Mick stared at her. "You promised," he said, his little features screwed up in outrage. "You promised you wouldn't go anywhere."

"Yeah, you promised," David echoed. "Bad M'ssa."

She didn't know whether to laugh or to cry. She looked at Jack, but he offered her no support. He remained on the floor, his gray eyes slightly accusing.

"I know," she said. "But you don't need me

anymore. You have your daddy, who is going to take care of you forever."

"But we want you, too," Mick said.

David leaned into Marisa with his sturdy little body and eyed her angrily. "Bad M'ssa," he repeated.

They were breaking her heart. She couldn't stop the tears that escaped, and she looked at Jack for support. "Bad M'ssa," he said.

She got up from the sofa, knowing if she didn't go now she never would. The two little boys were bad enough, but the pained look in Jack's eyes was killing her.

"I'll see you soon," she said to Mick and David. She grabbed her suitcase and started for the door, which had blurred with a new mist of tears.

"Marisa, wait."

Jack got up from the floor and walked over to her. "Boys, see if you can use those blocks and build a road."

As the two went back to their play, Jack took her by the shoulders. His mesmerizing gray eyes held hers, and again her heartbreak shuddered through her.

"I can't let you leave here without telling you something," he said.

She closed her eyes for a moment, unable to look into his eyes as he told her once again how much she appreciated what she'd done here for him and his sons.

"Marisa, I love you."

Her eyes flew open, and she stared at him in stunned surprise. "I wasn't going to say anything," he continued, "because I know that loving me had nothing to do with what you've been doing here."

"You're just grateful to me," she said as thick emotion pressed hard against her chest.

"You're right, I am grateful. But that's just the beginning of what I feel for you. I love you." He reached up and placed his palm on her cheek. "You excite me, Marisa. You inspire me. I want you to be the woman who is standing beside me as the boys grow from rambunctious little boys into fine young men…and I want us to spend the rest of our lives together."

He dropped his hand from her cheek, and his eyes darkened as if in anticipation of pain. "But I don't want you to stay here because of the boys. I want it to be because you love me, and I'll understand if you have to walk away."

"Oh, Jack, I was leaving because I'm in love with you, because I couldn't stand the idea of staying here with just your gratitude." She smiled through her tears. "I love you, Jack Cortland, and I would be honored to be the woman standing next to you for the rest of our lives."

She barely got the words out of her mouth before he took possession of her lips in a kiss that broke through any fear that might have lingered in her heart, one that electrified her with passion and with the promise of a love to last a lifetime.

"Get Mommy and Daddy," Mick yelled, and grabbed Jack around the knees. Jack toppled to the floor, and pulled Marisa along with him and there was laughter and tickles and love and Marisa knew that this was where she belonged forever…with the family of her heart.

Epilogue

People milled around the front yard, where tables heavy with food stood next to a three-piece band that filled the air with good old country music.

It had been two weeks since the kidnapping, and Jack and Marisa had decided a party was in order to celebrate their life together. They had invited all the Rothchilds as well as Marisa's family.

The party had begun an hour before and was in full swing as Marisa stood on the front porch and surveyed the scene.

Her parents stood next to Harold and his second wife, Anna. The four of them chatted with animation. Probably discussing Las Vegas real estate and the current depressed situation in the market.

Harold had gone home from the police station the morning after the kidnapping and had told his trophy wife he wanted a divorce. She'd moved out with their son, and she and Harold were now hammering out the details of the breakup. In the meantime Harold had been seeing a lot of his previous wife, Anna.

Conner Rothchild, Harold's nephew, had arrived with his new wife, Vera LaRue, a sweet, sassy woman who had worked as a dancer, and standing near the food table was Natalie, Candace's twin sister, and Natalie's new husband, Matt.

"I've got more beans ready to go out," Betty said from the doorway behind Marisa. "You know the rules, I cook—but I don't serve."

Marisa smiled at Betty. "Thanks, I'll be right in to get them." Betty had worked for the past two days fixing food for this event without a complaint. She'd even begun to allow Marisa to have her morning coffee in the kitchen, and the two women had become friends.

Jenna Rothchild and her fiancé, FBI agent Lex Duncan, stood with Rita, and Marisa could only guess that they were hashing over the subject of Paz Marquez and his numerous crimes.

She went into the kitchen and grabbed the large pan of baked beans that Betty had ready to go out on the food table.

As she carried it out she saw Sam and Max standing

awkwardly together a small distance from the crowd. They no longer made her nervous. She'd come to realize that they were painfully shy. She motioned them closer as she placed the bean pan on the table.

"I hope you two plan on getting something to eat," she said. "And maybe later you'll show me how to two-step to this music."

Sam's cheeks turned a hot pink. "I don't dance, but I definitely eat."

"I might do a little two-stepping later," Max said, his gaze going to a cute blonde named Suzie who had come as a guest of one of the others.

A hand fell on Marisa's shoulder, and she turned to see Rita. "Nice party," Rita said.

"Thanks. It's nice to see all the Rothchilds playing nice together," Marisa replied.

"Did Harold tell you he got the ring back? It's now in a warehouse waiting to be catalogued. He's donated it to his touring collection of art."

"I say good riddance. That ring caused far more heartache than good," Marisa replied.

"Oh, I don't know about that. If you believe the Mayan legend, then anyone who comes into contact with the ring finds their true love."

Marisa laughed. "I think I proved the legend wrong. I was close to the ring when Patrick and I were together, but it definitely didn't work on me where he was concerned."

Rita smiled. "You must have had some of the

ring magic on you when you met Jack. From what you've told me it was love at first sight for the both of you." Rita pulled Marisa into a hug. "I've never seen you look so happy."

"I've never been so happy," Marisa said as Rita released her.

"And I hear you've started interviewing for nannies for your agency."

Marisa nodded. "I had my first interview yesterday. Within two months I hope to have the business up and running."

"Good for you," Rita exclaimed. "And now I'm going to get a plate of this delicious food."

As Marisa headed back to the front porch she noticed Anna's daughter, Silver Rothchild, in one of the lawn chairs, her handsome husband, Captain Austin Dearing, at her side.

As Marisa watched the two, Austin smiled and reached out and touched Silver's protruding stomach. It was an intimate touch between a man and the pregnant woman he loved, and it sent just a tiny wave of pain through Marisa.

She would never know the touch of a man on her pregnant tummy. She'd never experience morning sickness or the flutter of life inside her.

The pain quickly vanished as she heard David's laughter riding the hot breeze. She looked beyond the scorched ground where the barn once had stood, out to the stables in the distance.

Jack had surprised the boys with ponies, and he was now leading them on their first pony ride. Her heart filled her chest as she gazed at the man who hadn't rocked her feet with the rhythm of his drums but had definitely rocked her world with his love.

"He's become quite a man." Harold's deep voice spoke from just behind her.

Marisa smiled at the dapper older man. "Yes, he has. He's always been a good man. He just needed someone to believe in him."

"And you do."

"With all my heart," Marisa replied.

Harold's gaze swept the area and came to rest on Anna. "It's important to have somebody in your life who believes in you, somebody who loves you. I'm hoping this time I'll get it right. Anna is a good woman."

He frowned as a cell phone rang from his pocket. He pulled it out and answered. His face turned ashen, and he held the phone away from his ear and stared at Marisa. "It's June," he said, his voice a stunned whisper.

"June?" Marisa knew that was Harold's first wife. "But I thought she was dead."

"So did I," Harold ground out. He placed the phone back to his ear and wandered away.

Marisa watched him go, wondering what new drama was about to hit the lives of the Rothchilds. She returned her gaze toward the stables and saw Jack motion to her.

Her heart filled her chest as even with the distance she could feel his love reaching out to her. It would probably be rude for her to abandon their guests and run down to the stables.

She hesitated only a moment and then took off at a quick pace toward Jack and the boys. Surely everyone would recognize that she was hurrying toward the little boys who were the sons of her heart. Surely her guests would forgive her for leaving them to run toward the man she adored and the future that shone bright with the promise of laughter and love.

* * * * *

Welcome to your new-look
By Request series!

RELIVE THE ROMANCE WITH
THE BEST OF THE BEST

This series features stories from your favourite
authors that are back by popular demand—
and, now with brand new covers, they
look even better than before!

See the new covers now at:
www.millsandboon.co.uk/byrequest

A sneaky peek at next month...

By Request

RELIVE THE ROMANCE WITH THE BEST OF THE BEST

My wish list for next month's titles...

In stores from 16th May 2014:

❏ Misbehaving with the Millionaire –
Kimberly Lang, Margaret Mayo & Lee Wilkinson

❏ Hot Summer Nights! –
Kelly Hunter, Cara Summers & Emily McKay

In stores from 6th June 2014:

❏ Royal Seductions: Diamonds –
Michelle Celmer

❏ Wedding Wishes – Liz Fielding,
Christie Ridgway & Myrna Mackenzie

3 stories in each book - only £5.99!

Available at WHSmith, Tesco, Asda, Eason, Amazon and Apple

Just can't wait?

0514/05

Special Offers

Every month we put together collections and longer reads written by your favourite authors.

Here are some of next month's highlights— and don't miss our fabulous discount online!

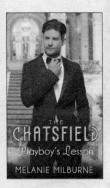

On sale 6th June

On sale 6th June

On sale 6th June

Save 20%
on all Special Releases

THE CHATSFIELD®

LUCY MONROE   MELANIE MILBURNE   MICHELLE CONDER   CHANTELLE SHAW

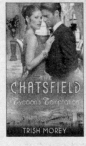

TRISH MOREY   ABBY GREEN   ANNIE WEST   LYNN RAYE HARRIS

Collect all 8!

Buy now at
www.millsandboon.co.uk/thechatsfield